Encounters on Contested Lands

performance works

SERIES EDITORS
Patrick Anderson and Nicholas Ridout

This series publishes books in theater and performance studies, focused in particular on the material conditions in which performance acts are staged, and to which performance itself might contribute. We define "performance" in the broadest sense, including traditional theatrical productions and performance art, but also cultural ritual, political demonstration, social practice, and other forms of interpersonal, social, and political interaction which may fruitfully be understood in terms of performance.

Encounters on Contested Lands

Indigenous Performances of Sovereignty and Nationhood in Québec

✦

Julie Burelle

NORTHWESTERN UNIVERSITY PRESS
EVANSTON, ILLINOIS

Northwestern University Press
www.nupress.northwestern.edu

Printed in the United States of America

10 9 8 7 6 5 4 3 2 1

Library of Congress Cataloging-in-Publication Data

Names: Burelle, Julie, author.
Title: Encounters on contested lands : indigenous performances of sovereignty and nationhood in Quebec / Julie Burelle.
Description: Evanston, Illinois : Northwestern University Press, 2019. | Series: Performance works | Revised and expanded version of the author's thesis (doctoral)—University of California, San Diego, 2014. | Includes bibliographical references and index.
Identifiers: LCCN 2018035290 | ISBN 9780810138971 (cloth : alk. paper) | ISBN 9780810138964 (pbk. : alk. paper) | ISBN 9780810138988 (ebook)
Subjects: LCSH: Indians of North America—Québec (Province)—Ethnic identity—Drama. | Indians of North America—Rites and ceremonies—Political aspects—Québec (Province)—Drama. | Indians of North America—Land tenure—Québec (Province) | Indians of North America—Québec (Province)—Government relations. | Indians of North America—Québec (Province)—Politics and government. | Self-determination, National—Québec (Province)—History. | Decolonization—Québec (Province)—History.
Classification: LCC PN2051.B87 2019 | DDC 792.089970714—dc23
LC record available at https://lccn.loc.gov/2018035290

Niminunakuitishun
nuash nishkana tshetshi uapatakaniti
tshetshi pishkapatakaniti
nin eka nita
tshe tipatshimikauian.

Je me suis faite belle
pour qu'on remarque
la moelle de mes os,
survivante d'un récit
qu'on ne raconte pas.

I made myself look pretty
So that they will notice
The marrow of my bones,
Survivor of a story
That no one tells.

—Joséphine Bacon, *Bâtons à message Tshissinuatshitakana*

The very notion of *indigenous* nationhood which demarcates identity and seizes tradition in ways that may be antagonistic to the encompassing frame of the state, may be simply unintelligible to the western and/or imperial ear.

—Audra Simpson, *Paths toward a Mohawk Nation: Narratives of Citizenship and Nationhood in Kahnawake*

CONTENTS

ACKNOWLEDGMENTS

I would like to thank the scholars, artists, mentors, and friends I have met on this journey that started in Montréal and led me to San Diego via Vancouver, Boston, and Toronto. I owe to Christine Heitzmann and to our students in Boston my rekindled love for theater's power to speak. In Toronto, Antje Budde ignited my interest in theory, and Lee Maracle pushed me to think critically about settler colonialism.

This book expands and deepens the research I conducted for my Ph.D. dissertation. I had the privilege of working with an outstanding committee: Emily Roxworthy (an inspiring mentor), Patrick Anderson, Ross Frank, Ketu Katrak, and Frank Wilderson. Thank you for taking me under your respective wings, for teaching life-altering seminars, and for braving the wildfires of May 2014 to attend my dissertation defense. I would not have finished this project without the nurturing environment that my fellow Ph.D. students provided. I want to thank in particular Matt Chapman, Jason Dorwart, Sonia Fernandez, Raimondo Genna, Janet Hayatshahi, Lily Kelting, Melissa Minnifee, Naysan Mojgani, Heather Ramey, Rana Salimi, Jade Power Sotomayor, and Jaye Austin Williams.

I want to thank my colleagues in the Department of Theatre and Dance at the University of California at San Diego and the Department of Drama at UC Irvine for welcoming me into their ranks. The staff at UC San Diego is truly amazing, and I am grateful for their labor and support. I want to thank the graduate students with whom I have taken some of this book's ideas for a test drive: Michael Moshe Dahan, Laura Dorwart, Sam Mitchell, Kara Raphaeli, Jon Reimer, and Kristen Tregar. I have been blessed to encounter generous readers, colleagues, and writing partners in this process: I want to thank in particular Teddy Chao, Bruno Cornellier, Jean-François Côté, Claudine Cyr, Mique'l Dangeli, Megan Finn, Hadley Friedland, Helen Gilbert, Melva Grant, Nawel Hamidi, Erin Hurley, Holly Jones, Darryl Leroux, Val Napoleon, Yumi Pak, Karyn Recollet, Dylan Robinson, Pierrot Ross-Tremblay, Jacqueline Shea-Murphy, and Tria Blu Wakpa. They have all helped me find my way out of what seemed like insurmountable impasses, and I have learned so much from their precious guidance.

Selamawit Terrefe, my writing partner for whom I have great love and admiration, has seen me at my most disheveled and has championed my work at all times. I am profoundly indebted to her. For conversations, creative partnerships, and well-timed inspiring encounters, I want to thank Ami

Admire and the Rincon Youth Storytellers, Preston Arrow-weed and Helena Quintana Arrow-weed, Mélanie Carrier and Olivier Higgins, Xavier Huard, Gordon Johnson, Ric Knowles, James Luna, Eddy Malenfant, Alexi Marchel, Rhonda Meier, Philippe McKenzie, Nadia Myre, Justin Neal, Ghislain Picard, Yves Sioui Durand, Catherine Joncas, Amélie Girard, and the St-Onge sisters (Anne-Marie, Évelyne, and Fernande) for the hospitality and conversations in Mani-Utenam; Jean Bruce Scott and Randy Reinholz and all the wonderful playwrights and artists of Native Voices at the Autry; and Amrah Salomon, Burgundy Fletcher, Yelena Gluzman, Sarah Klein, Christina Aushana, and Louise Hickman.

For their encouragement, I am grateful to Jim Carmody, Gloria Chacon, Ross Frank, Nadine George-Graves, Joseph Hankins, Cassandra Hartblay, Roshanak Keshti, Marianne McDonald, Janet Smarr, and K. Wayne Yang. Thank you to Denis Farley, Paul Litherland, Martine Doyon, Michel Ostaszewski, *Le Nouvelliste*, and all who helped me secure the rights for this book's images. An earlier iteration of chapter 4 appears in *In the Balance: Indigeneity, Performance, Globalization*, edited by Helen Gilbert, J. D. Philipson, and Michelle Raheja, and published in 2018 by Liverpool University Press. *TDR: The Drama Review* published a version of chapter 5 in spring 2015. Revised versions of these chapters are included here with permission.

A deeply heartfelt thank you to Nicholas Ridout, Gianna Mosser, Michael Levine, the people at Northwestern University Press, and Ideas on Fire. Patrick Anderson, you have believed in this project for a long time, and your witty humor and deep sense of community continue to provoke and nourish me in beautiful ways. Two anonymous reviewers generously commented on my manuscript and I want to thank them, wherever they are. The introduction and second chapter are indebted to reviewer two's excellent suggestions, while chapter 5 benefited from reviewer one's insightful critique. I gratefully acknowledge that a UC San Diego Faculty Career Development Award and a Hellman Fellowship helped me finish this book.

My family in Montréal is an undying source of love and encouragement. I am so thankful for my father André, my two brothers Yan and Mathieu and their respective families, my sister Pascale Boyer and her family, and my aunt Marie-Thérèse, and the entire Proulx clan. Thank you also to Lorraine Barner and the Barner family, Lysanne Lacouture, the Bordeaux-Labarre, Ivano Caponigro, Daniel Kane, Nancy Baird, and David Baillot, my San Diego family.

I am truly blessed to have David Barner in my life, and I am grateful for the supportive and loving space we give each other to pursue our dreams. The incessant questions and avid curiosity of our daughter Anouk, who was born as I began this project, have been a source of inspiration for me, and I owe her the courage to question what is uncomfortable.

My mother Nicole Proulx passed away as I was starting my Ph.D. She was a luminous soul, a wonderful parent and friend, and a profoundly just being.

I have not yet fully mapped all that we lost when she passed. She will never know me as a scholar, but she is present in this work.

Lastly, I gratefully acknowledge that the bulk of my research was conducted on Kumeyaay, Luiseño, Haudenosaunee, and Innu territories. It is not lost on me that so much of the privilege of writing this book stems from my belonging to the very settler-colonial structures that I critique in my work. This is my attempt to participate in a conversation about change, justice, redress, and Indigenous sovereignty.

Encounters on Contested Lands

Figure I.1. Patrick Cloutier and Brad Larocque, alias "Freddy Krueger," come face to face in Oka, Québec, on September 1, 1990. (Photo by Shaney Komulainen, The Canadian Press)

Introduction

✦

Nation, Spectacle, and Colliding Narratives

Among the numerous photos of the infamous standoff at Oka[1] in 1990 (also known as the "Oka Crisis"), one iconic image exemplifies the central questions of this book. Shaney Komulainen, a freelance photographer for the Canadian Press, took the photo on September 1, 1990, on the fifty-third day of the seventy-eight-day conflict between the Mohawks of Kanehsatà:ke and various forces deployed by the Québécois and Canadian governments (figure I.1). The image immortalizes a tense confrontation between a "Vandoo"[2] and an Ojibwa Warrior who joined forces with the Mohawks to protect their land (and in particular a pine forest and burial site) against further encroachment by the nearby predominantly white and francophone town of Oka. In Komulainen's photo, the two men stand on either sides of the perimeter established by the army to seal off Mohawk territory, and their eyes are locked in an intense stare-down. While their bodies are almost touching, the structural, cultural, and historical divide between these two men is immense and, in this instant, the men's bodies are saturated with evocative, performative powers. On one side, the Vandoo represents a settler state that deputized him to maintain "law and order" and protect its borders. On the other, the Warrior, standing as a national "of a precontact Indigenous polity that simply refuses to stop being,"[3] calls this settler state into question and challenges its discourse of lawfulness and legitimacy. He is, as Kiera Ladner (Cree) and Leanne Simpson (Anishinaabe) argue, boldly "living up to [his] responsibilities to take care of [the] lands,"[4] and to continue a two-hundred-seventy-year battle to have the pine forest and burial site recognized for what they are: Mohawk land.

As Komulainen later reflected in an interview commemorating the twenty-fifth anniversary of the events in Oka, Private Patrick Cloutier looks painfully young[5] in this photo, and his expression betrays fear, despite his best efforts to appear imperturbable. Cloutier's face is as bare and open to scrutiny as the face and identity of his opponent are concealed, hidden by a pair of dark sunglasses and a bandana and thus, illegible—so much so that during the events in Oka, the press mistakenly identified the Warrior in the photo as Ronald "Lasagna" Cross, a Mohawk steelworker and member of the Warrior society. The press made Cross a villain by falsely arguing that he was a foreigner (an Italian from New York rather than a Mohawk) and a small-time criminal. Cross was neither, and would in fact acquire a criminal record only as a result of the events in Oka. To be clear, Cross did participate in the resistance, but he is not the Warrior in Komulainen's photo and, after enduring a particularly violent arrest by members of the provincial police force, he was sentenced to prison for charges related to the events of 1990. However, through Komulainen's photo, the press misread and miscast Cross as part of its favored narrative of lawlessness. This reductive narrative not only undermined the complex identities and motivations of those who chose to oppose settler-colonial forces in Oka, it also served to criminalize and delegitimize Indigenous resistance.

In reality, the man facing Private Patrick Cloutier was Brad "Freddy Krueger" Larocque, a soft-spoken student of economics at the University of Saskatchewan. Larocque was not much older than Cloutier during the standoff, but his youth is invisible to the viewer in Komulainen's photo. Taller than Cloutier by only a few centimeters, Larocque nevertheless possesses a towering presence, and he dominates the soldier. Larocque's attire echoes Cloutier's military gear, but here the Warrior's camouflage hat and combat fatigues reappropriate the very visual markers that give his adversary authority and legitimacy. Larocque's army gear unequivocally positions the Mohawks as a sovereign nation at war with the invading forces of Québec and Canada. This is in no way a new conflict—a "crisis" as it was presented in the press and perceived by many Canadians—but the continuation of a 400-year-old battle against "a white civil and legal order that is from its inception in Mohawk and Iroquois territory, intent upon eliminating them."[6] Audra Simpson's reflection, articulated from her perspective as a Mohawk scholar years after the events in Oka, describes what I would call the same *colonial present tense* and *tense colonial present* that Larocque occupies in Komulainen's photo. Though years apart, Simpson and Larocque remind us that settler colonialism is not an event of the past but an ongoing and resilient "structure."[7]

The smooth functioning of this tense colonial present, this structure, depends on what Slavoj Žižek describes as a triumvirate that includes "subjective violence" ("the most visible portion") and two forms of "objective violence" that act as its less visible counterparts.[8] Žižek describes these two forms as "symbolic" and "systemic" violence. Subjective violence, he contends, is the most apparent and spectacular. It is the violence of so-called crisis, violent attacks, or terrorism. "Objective violence," on the other hand, "is invisible since it sustains the very zero-level standard against which we perceive something as subjectively violent."[9] Subjective violence, then, is perceived as "a perturbation of the normal," which Žižek describes as an illusory "non-violent zero level"[10] guaranteed by forms of objective violence that are constant, rendered invisible, and normalized. Symbolic violence, for instance, is "embodied in language and its forms, what Heidegger would call 'our house of being,' " and is manifested in the imposition of certain ways of understanding the world. Systemic violence, for its part, comprises the "often catastrophic consequences of the smooth functioning of our economic and political systems."[11]

The events in Oka rendered visible these three levels of violence, even if they were not equally legible to all who encountered them. I see Komulainen's photo as a distillation of the *colonial present tense* and *tense colonial present*, a performance of the various levels of violence that coexist(ed) in Oka. The encounter between Larocque and Cloutier could be read solely as a moment of subjective violence, a moment of crisis, a clashing encounter. In reality, it performs in the open the very objective violence (the everyday encounters with systemic inequalities, sanctioned land appropriation, and symbolic violence) that underlies Canada and Québec and maintains their coherence. The press and the authorities' criminalizing vocabulary and erasure of the Mohawks' legitimate claims are examples of symbolic violence. Similarly, the encounter between the Vandoo and the Warrior stems from the "normal" functioning of settler colonialism; that is, from the insatiable hunger for Indigenous territories and resources that defines its structure.

A number of seemingly irreconcilable narratives are at play in this photo. For many Indigenous people across the country who watched the media coverage of the events in Oka, Brad Larocque embodied the "othering" of Indigenous peoples in Canada, their violent and ongoing marginalization by an ever-expanding settler-colonial state fueled by what the late Patrick Wolfe called a "logic of elimination."[12] "Settler colonialism," Wolfe tells us, "erects a new colonial society on the expropriated land base" of Indigenous populations.[13] This new society, which is based on the accumulation of Indigenous territory, is then stratified following an "organizing grammar of race"[14] that devalues Indigenous lives while being wholly dependent on their lands. Here, Žižek's concept of objective violence echoes Wolfe's explanation of the logic of elimination. The town of Oka's plan to carve out yet another piece of Mohawk territory clearly exemplified this logic of elimination. In this context, the dissent of the people of Kanehsatà:ke, their refusal to be expropriated and erased—a refusal embodied and performed by Larocque in the iconic photo—powerfully interrupted the settler-colonial project's seemingly unstoppable consumption of Indigenous land and bodies. If the press and the Canadian and Québécois public read this refusal as a crisis, it is because so much is at stake in keeping alive the idea of the settler state as the nonviolent zero-level normal state of things. Many non-Indigenous people were angered and confused by the events in Oka, but for a lot of Indigenous people, that summer ushered in a new era of decolonization activism. The Mohawks' refusal catalyzed widespread Indigenous support across North America, in addition to a sense of common purpose that the 2012 Idle No More[15] Indigenous grassroots movement re-harnessed.

For their part, the federal and provincial governments found a poster-perfect soldier in Private Patrick Cloutier, a *French Québécois de souche* (of old stock). Here, I employ the term *French Québécois de souche* to refer to the white descendants of early settlers from France, who still speak French and understand themselves (through various contradictory narratives that this book explores) as settlers no more, colonized by the British first and, later, by the Anglo-Canadians, and rightfully belonging to the territory of Québec. The press fashioned Cloutier's identity, his pale eyes, whiteness, and youthful innocence, and, above all else, his palpable fear during the encounter with Larocque into a narrative of close and imminent danger. The narrative that surrounded Cloutier was so powerful that it succeeded in obfuscating, for many Canadians and Québécois, the basic facts behind the Mohawks' resistance, namely the town of Oka's unilateral decision to appropriate a sacred Mohawk pine forest and burial site and transform them into a luxury golf course and condominium project. The Mohawks called into question what the Koenpul/Quandamooka scholar Aileen Moreton-Robinson describes as the "patriarchal white possessive logic" that underlies settler colonialism. This possessive logic, she claims, ensures the protection of "white supremacy as hegemony, ideology, epistemology, and ontology," which requires "the possession of Indigenous lands as its proprietary anchor within capitalistic economies."[16] White proprietary rights are embedded in the law, recognized, and protected in ways that continuously disavow Indigenous sovereignties. In that sense, the events in Oka are not a refusal of a specific expropriation; rather, the Mohawks' organized resistance performs an indictment of white possessive logic writ large.

In this context, Cloutier and the narrative of endangered white possession he came to embody succeeded in obscuring yet again the settler-colonial history of these contested parcels of land. This history, which goes back to Nouvelle-France, is one of continual encroachments and broken promises first made to the Mohawks by the Jesuits, and then successively by Britain, Canada, and Québec. As it happens, the Mohawks, as a territorially anchored polity, have always stood in the way of settler development. That the Mohawks of Kanehsatà:ke had been expropriated of their ancestral land and cheated of their rights became secondary or largely illegible in the minds of large segments of the Québec public who watched the so-called crisis unfold in the nightly news. In the media warfare that surrounded the events in Oka, the voice of the otherwise widely unpopular prime minister Brian Mulroney resonated powerfully with Québec and Canada's settler communities when he stated, "The Mohawks are terrorists and Canada does not negotiate with terrorists."[17] Mulroney's criminalizing statement framed the events of Oka as an aggression against Canada, an attack on lawful white possession, while obfuscating the historical context that led to this confrontation. Mulroney swiftly recast the Mohawks—a sovereign nation protecting itself against further settler-colonial encroachments—as criminals, terrorists, and foreigners and framed the settler societies of Québec and Canada, and their possessions, protected and naturalized by capitalistic laws, as the injured and invaded parties.

In 1990, the question of Québec's place within Canada was unresolved and tense following a close-call referendum in 1980 and a series of failed attempts at constitutional changes. The question remains unresolved today, but the rawness and urgency that framed it in 1990 have arguably diminished in intensity. Québec's nationalism still exists, and a large proportion of white francophone Québécois, separatist or not, perceive themselves as fundamentally distinct from the rest of Canada and would like to see this difference officially recognized. This identity formation, its emancipation discourse, and what Wendy Brown would call its "wounded attachments" to a narrative of colonization and alienation,[18] attachments that affect and shape all discursive spheres in Québec, are at the heart of this book's exploration, which takes the events in Oka as a historical starting point. As Jocelyn Létourneau argues, Québec's public sphere currently remembers the past as one of sorrow and grievances. "It seems there is one thing that is impossible for Quebecers to forget, and that is their having been victims of the other."[19] This book meditates on how these wounded attachments shape contemporary encounters between Indigenous and what I call the French Québécois de souche in Québec.

When the Mohawks came under scrutiny in 1990, it had been a decade since the Parti Québécois, led by the charismatic and beloved premier René Lévesque, held its referendum on Québec's sovereignty-association; and despite the Canadian prime minister Pierre Trudeau's promises of change, Canada's new constitution, the Constitution Act of 1982, was ratified without Québec's assent.[20] If Québec was left out, the Constitution Act began to change Canada's relationship with Indigenous peoples. Section 35 indeed recognizes and affirms "the existing aboriginal and treaty rights of the aboriginal peoples of Canada" (which include "Indian, Inuit, and Métis peoples of Canada").[21] In 1987 the Canadian government negotiated the Meech Lake Accord, a series of constitutional amendments that had been proposed in order to rally Québec and gain its acceptance of the constitution. If some of the proposed changes[22] met Québec's demands, they left others in Canada profoundly dissatisfied, and rightly so. Indigenous people in particular felt that the proposed amendments, devised without their leaders' input, relegated Indigenous issues to a future and indeterminate round of negotiations. When each province had to vote on the accord before the June 23, 1990 deadline, Elijah Harper (Oji-Cree), the only Indigenous elected representative in Manitoba's Legislative Assembly at the time, raised a feather in dissent and filibustered Manitoba's vote. Along with Harper's dissent, the province of Newfoundland's refusal to vote on the accord and the negative public campaign led by Trudeau succeeded in derailing the Meech Lake Accord. Thus, when the crisis erupted in Oka in the summer of 1990, many Québécois felt deep resentment toward Canada and attributed some of the blame for the Meech Lake Accord's failure to Elijah Harper, the Oji-Cree man who had dared to dissent.

For Indigenous peoples, the events in Oka followed a "barrage of Indigenous practices of disruptive counter-sovereignty that emerged with increased frequency in the 1980s."[23] There had been the Innu occupation of a military base in Goose Bay in Labrador, the Lubicon Cree struggle against gas and oil development in Alberta, Indigenous blockades against the British Columbian and federal governments' stalling of the comprehensive land-claim process, the anti-logging campaign led by the Algonquins of Barrière Lake in Québec,[24] and the Temagami Indigenous blockades in Ontario. Most of these protests took place in relatively rural areas, which may explain why they did not register as clearly on the settler majority's radar, but Oka was right in the heart of the most densely populated region of Québec. For many it read as "an embarrassing demonstration that Canada no longer had its shit together with respect to managing the so-called 'Indian Problem.' "[25] Oka rendered visible the accumulated frustration of a new generation of Indigenous leaders who were no longer willing to sit patiently; it also afforded the settler state an opportunity to stage a spectacularly muscled military operation (the largest since the Korean War) that would reinscribe Canada as a nation in control.

The resistance in Oka was not easily quashed, and it rendered visible structures of settler domination that attracted international condemnation. In the aftermath of Oka, Canada established the Royal Commission on Aboriginal Peoples (RCAP) in 1991 as an appeasing gesture, appointing an Indigenous leader, Georges Erasmus, and René Dussault, a French Québécois de souche jurist, as cochairs. The commission was charged with investigating the evolution of the relationship between Indigenous peoples and the Canadian government as well as Canada's culture at large. Its lengthy final report (more than 4,000 pages), published in 1996, illuminated the gross violations of Indigenous sovereignty and rights and unfolded a twenty-year plan to implement changes in Canada. It called, for instance, for the creation of an Indigenous order of government and parliament. This pathway to a more equal form of nation-to-nation partnership with Indigenous people, much like the report as a whole, was quickly shelved and largely ignored.

Despite the constitutional debacles of 1990, the French Québécois de souche, particularly those with nationalist aspirations, should have been uniquely positioned to empathize with the Mohawks given their self-fashioned and predominant narrative as a "colonized" minority in Canada whose cultural and linguistic survival is threatened by the anglophone majority. This was not the case. While it would be easy to attribute this lack of solidarity to the recent constitutional failures, this interpretation, I argue, is too simplistic and misses the deeper structural and ontological questions the Mohawks illuminated in refusing to let the town of Oka proceed with its development plan. To be clear, some French Québécois de souche did voice their outrage over the government's lack of good faith in negotiating with the Mohawks, but a significant segment of the population around Oka resorted to violence and rioting, stoning a caravan of cars evacuating Mohawk elders, women, and children from Kanehsatà:ke and burning the effigy of a Mohawk Warrior at a busy intersection in Châteauguay.[26] These public spectacles betrayed a large segment of Québec as profoundly threatened by Mohawk dissent and struggling to maintain its narrative as a colonized minority in the face of a Mohawk discourse that clearly aligned the French Québécois de souche with the perpetrators rather than the victims of settler colonialism. The Mohawk resistance called into question Québec's "wounded attachments," its investment in its own "history of suffering," and the ways its attachment to a colonized/minoritized narrative came into conflict "with the need to give up these investments in the pursuit of an emancipatory democratic project."[27] For the Mohawks, this emancipatory project is nothing less than decolonization, a dismantling of current structures of power and relationships to land that would reposition Indigenous sovereignties as central and as coexisting as equals with the sovereignties of Québec and Canada.

Public spectacles, as Diana Taylor argues in her study of Argentina's "dirty war," are both a "locus and mechanism of communal identity through collective imaginings that constitute 'nation' as 'an imagined political community.'"[28] Spectacle, she writes, "builds and dismantles a sense of community and nation-ness," "forges and erases," and "stirs and manipulates," drawing a population in while obfuscating the elements that threaten the nation's narrative and sense of coherence.[29] As discussed earlier, Patrick Wolfe describes settler colonialism as "inherently eliminatory," depending on the erasure (real and symbolic) of native populations for the creation of a new colonial society. However, Wolfe notes that the "process of replacement" that structures settler colonialism always maintains "the refractory imprint of the native counter-claim."[30] In other words, this replaced but not vanished Native "other" serves as the ultimate marker of difference that secures the borders of settler societies. The Chickasaw scholar Jodi A. Byrd defines this perpetual deferral of Indigenous people, their role as "figures of transit"[31] through and against which the settler state can imagine itself, can articulate the notion of personhood, intimacy, and freedom, as a condition of settler colonialism. Spectacles of nation-ness in settler colonial societies thus always replay, in one form or another, this organizational scenario of elimination, appropriation, and deferral.

Benedict Anderson famously described nations as "imagined communities," constructed through a collective will to simultaneously celebrate commonalities and actively "forget" dissonant elements that might threaten the community's integrity.[32] Building on Anderson's work, Joseph Roach argues in *Cities of the Dead* that circum-Atlantic societies like the United States and Canada have invented themselves through performances of "incomplete forgetting."[33] In the case of Canada, this performance simultaneously forgets the genocide of Indigenous peoples and invokes its trace as a symbol of settler-state identity. This trace or refractory imprint of "Nativeness," then, functions as the condition of possibility for the settler-state project: the erasure of real Indigenous bodies legitimates settler states' so-called rightful occupation of a *terra nullius* (a land belonging to no one), and the strategic deployment of objectivized "Nativeness" signals the emergence of a New World identity that differentiates the settler from its Old World relative.

In Komulainen's photo, Cloutier occupies a multilayered position. He represents Canada though his military role, but he also embodies and performs Québec's sense of self as a colonized people within Canada. While it might be tempting to see these two positions as irreconcilable, they are not. In fact, the conflict between Québec and Canada takes place, as I argue in this book, within the confine of white settler colonialism and opposes two settler-colonial forces. If one of these forces, Québec, has the distinction of having been subjugated by the other, its aspirations as a nation are not, despite its discourse of liberation, predicated on decolonization. On the contrary, Québec's nationhood depends on the continued dispossession of Indigenous peoples. Québec and Canada articulate themselves as imagined communities within the same settler-colonial framework, the same logic of white possession. Cloutier's bare face and legible identity attest to this imagined community's sense of legitimacy and of rightful occupation of the land of Oka and of the territory called Québec. Cloutier is there to defend the integrity of these imagined communities.

For his part, Larocque exceeds the mere refractory imprint of the Indigenous counterclaim described by Wolfe. Indeed, Larocque is the Native (following Wolfe's expression) who refuses to disappear and whose obstinate presence, insistent gaze, and mirroring military gear challenge the hegemonic discourses that stabilize settler societies. Larocque renders visible Canada's and Québec's attempts to eliminate Mohawk sovereignty and that of Indigenous peoples at large, but his presence also hints at a deeper structural genocidal violence. The disproportionate repression that meets Larocque's defense of the Mohawk community illuminates the Indigenous reserve (or reservation)[34] as a genocidal space imagined with the end of Indigenous peoples in mind, a space open to gratuitous violence and military deployment.

To read the Oka Crisis though the framework of settler colonialism uncomfortably brings to the fore Canada and Québec's role as settler societies whose sense of self is not only predicated upon the structural elimination of Indigenous peoples as sovereign peoples, polities, and cultures, but also on what Lorenzo Veracini calls a historical trajectory culminating in settler colonialism's own "self-suppression."[35] In other words, as Bruno Cornellier argues:

> The decisive triumph of settler colonialism corresponds to such a moment of deferral when settler societies manage to represent or

> declare themselves as *not colonial anymore*—a moment that is often coterminous with a celebratory and ostentatious repudiation of race, understood as the principal visible marker of the colonial "past."[36]

In criminalizing Mohawk dissent and qualifying it as an act of terrorism, both Canada and Québec attempted to obfuscate their ongoing settler-colonial relationship with Indigenous peoples. To recognize the Mohawks' right to defend their land would amount to admitting that Québec and Canada are indeed ongoing settler-colonial states. Casting Mohawk dissent as criminal, repositioning Oka as the injured community, and portraying the military as peacekeepers are all discursive and performative strategies that betray a form of willful forgetting. Here, Québec and Canada actively suppress the memory of their past, yet retain the power and privileges that come from that which they deny: the usurpation of Indigenous lands and bodies.

In 1990, Canada and Québec had largely embraced a narrative that framed colonialism (and Indigenous peoples) as an event of the distant past. The failure of the Meech Lake Accord and the Mohawk resistance threw a wrench into this celebratory refashioning. Since then, while Canada has employed the falsely egalitarian language of multiculturalism as its new strategy to erase its colonial past, Québec has followed the opposite path and adopted a discourse that both downplays its colonial past, recasting it as almost benevolent, and brandishes the province's status as a colonized minority in order to advance Québec's national project. As I will discuss throughout this book, it remains difficult to critique Québec's narrative of itself without being accused of performing "Québec-bashing," especially if one is from what is commonly referred to as the "ROC" (rest of Canada). While English Canada's intelligentsia is guilty of numerous reductive statements made in bad faith that portray the province as pathologically insular,[37] Québec's public sphere is often incredibly thin-skinned and quick to deploy its wounded narrative in order to deflect criticism. A quick online search yields numerous articles devoted to decrying Québec-bashing (the term has its own Wikipedia page), and major Québécois newspapers have printed countless editorials and special dossiers on the question.

These sensitivities have their roots in history. Indeed, the relationship between Canada and Québec is complex, thorny, asymmetrical, and informed by the marginalization and ambivalent racialization of French Canadians in the nineteenth century. In the period following the British conquest of 1760, French settlers and their descendants were increasingly portrayed as "non-white" in ways that echoed the othering of Irish, Jewish, and Italian communities in the United States in the late nineteenth century.[38] The Durham Report of 1839, for instance, described Canada as dealing with a struggle between the French and the English "races." Corrie Scott traces how, following Durham, the press and politicians depicted French Canadians as backward, indolent, and as a "not so money-making race."[39] French

Canadians were often portrayed as apes and monstrous others in the press, and these visual and narrative tropes were used to justify the subordination of French Canadians and the assimilation policies the Canadian government deployed during the nineteenth century.

Far from stable, the concept of race and the discourses around it are highly relational and are deployed to stabilize hegemony. Of race, Scott writes that it is a "relational, privileged and performative phenomenon rather than a fixed, self-evident, corporeal, biological category or characteristic."[40] She contends that in the relationship between English and French Canada, race "is a tool, a kind of shorthand, used to cite normative and regulatory imperatives of Anglosaxon white patriarchy" and to legitimize and normalize "the cultural, economic, linguistic, and religious domination of French Canadians."[41] Simply put, in the nineteenth century, French Canadians were not quite white because they were no longer in power and because they needed to be assimilated for Canada's project to succeed. "Ironically," Scott notes, "French Canadians were mostly French European descendants, and the French were also busy colonizing both Africa and the Americas, often using a very similar racist logic."[42]

In tracing how French Canadians went from being "not quite white" to an unquestionable incorporation into the expansive category of whiteness, Scott asks an important question about the role of race in Québec's identity discourses. Building on her reflection, I argue that race, with whiteness as its ultimate arbiter, is the unstable terrain on which settler-colonial anxieties are performed through a pas de deux between abjection and incorporation. If the French Canadians eventually became white, the same cannot be said for all inhabitants of the province of Québec. What makes this capacity for racial mobility accrue to French Canadians? I contend that the French Canadians or, as I call them in this book, the French Québécois de souche's relationship to Anglo power was always articulated along the lines of a common structural positioning predicated in part on racial mobility. If the French Canadians could be demoted from their alpha status through the humiliation of defeat, they nevertheless retained a capacity for mobility that others, namely Indigenous peoples and black individuals, did not possess in relation to whiteness. In other words, the French and the British were both capable of being settlers because they belonged, to various degrees perhaps, to the same category of so-called civilized Europeans, even if one party had defeated the other. They occupied the same structural positioning, which came with access to whiteness.

Despite having the capacity for racial mobility, the Québécois, particularly the emerging intelligentsia of the 1960s and 1970s, remained attached to this past racialization; the parasitic trope of the Québécois as "not quite white" persists in Québec's mythscape even today.[43] For instance, Pierre Vallières, a political activist, wrote a famous manifesto in 1968 entitled *Nè***s blancs d'Amérique*[44] in which he analogizes the marginalization of the Québécois to that of the African Americans living under slavery and Jim Crow. Strikingly, as Scott argues, Vallières exploits the figure of the nè***, opening it here to all oppressed workers (relating "négritude" to alienated labor rather than race and the position of social death attached to blackness). The nè*** of Vallières is without a body; it is a convenient idea that Vallières claims in a parasitic way to render the marginalization of the French Québécois de souche legible. Ultimately, Vallières is not interested in solidarity with black folks; and the liberatory trajectory he imagines makes little space for the very real black communities that existed and continue to exist and face discrimination in Québec.[45]

Québec's discourse betrays a form of strategic ambivalence toward settler colonialism. In fact, Québec's settler population have effectively recast themselves as natives to the land they occupy, using terms like *Québécois de souche* or *Québécois pure-laine* to differentiate the francophones with real or supposed ties to Nouvelle-France from newcomers. While *pure-laine* literally means "pure-wool" and evokes untainted ancestry, *souche* means "root" or "stem"; when attached to the word *Québécois*, these qualifiers connote lineage or Nativeness. In other words, the Québécois de souche or *pure-laine*, that is, the white descendants of French settlers, now imagine and position themselves as equally "native"[46] to Québec as the province's Indigenous people.[47] In this performance of competing Nativeness, Québec resorts to a discourse of shared oppression, aligning with Indigenous communities against Anglo Canada.

As I argue throughout this book, Québec's self-proclaimed narrative as a colonized minority is a relatively recent concept. It was only in the 1960s, as Sean Mills argues in *The Empire Within: Postcolonial Thought and Political Activism in Sixties Montreal*, that "the vast majority of oppositional groups in the city had come to accept that Quebec was a colonized society,"[48] but this understanding was not without tensions and ideological conflicts, as I will discuss more specifically in chapters 1 and 2. Mills writes:

> Montreal has a complicated and layered history of colonization and conquest and, by the 1960s, this history had scarred the city's landscape with distinct geographies of power. Nearly two thirds of the city's population spoke French, yet in the city's wealthiest neighbourhoods, the commercial establishments of the downtown core, and the halls of the most prestigious financial, cultural, and educational institutions, English prevailed. Montreal's francophone majority, along with its racial and ethnic minorities, were far removed from the centres of power, often living in the poorest parts of town. Their language and culture were devalued in the workplace and in the encounters of everyday urban life.[49]

While this geography of power prevailed in Montréal, it did not organize the rest of the province with the same strength and, more importantly, it did not erase the French Québécois de souche's colonial role vis-à-vis Indigenous peoples. The regions that were more homogeneously the space of the French Québécois de souche in particular saw other forms of mappings that principally relegated Indigenous peoples and racialized others to the margins.

Interestingly, despite its relative prosperity and booming industrialization, Montréal was "profoundly affected by Third World theory" in the 1950s and '60s. There, "dissident writers adapted the ideas of Frantz Fanon, Aimé Césaire, Jacques Berque, Albert Memmi, and others, to develop a movement proposing that Quebec join with the nations of the Third World."[50] These authors, Memmi and Césaire in particular, often expressed dismay at how white descendants of French settlers appropriated and deployed their theoretical interventions. Black Caribbean and Indigenous activists were also quick to point out the contradictions inherent to this positioning. From their perspective, the French Québécois de souche were not a colonized but a colonizing group. However, the narrative took hold among the French Québécois de souche's intelligentsia and became a central element of its self-concept.

The cultural and political performances (plays, films, marches, etc.) that I examine in this book engage with Québec's analogizing discourse of shared dispossession and thus destabilize the province's narrative as an oppressed minority. The events in Oka in 1990 provide the historical starting point of this book, which focuses on Indigenous performances of cultural identity, sovereignty, and nationhood in Québec and examines how these instances of self-representation challenge Québec's minority discourse and its own narrative as a nation. Reading these performances as diagnostic tools, this book meditates on the seemingly irreconcilable divide between the Indigenous people of Québec and the province's French Québécois de souche settler majority and takes as a starting point Lyle Longclaws's words: "Before the healing can take place the poison must first be exposed."[51] While imagining healing may be currently impossible, and even undesirable, if it means finding spaces of accommodation within the unethical project of settler colonialism rather than fundamentally altering it, I believe that exposing Québec and Canada's violent relations to Indigenous people is both possible and necessary.

During the Truth and Reconciliation Commission of Canada on Indian Residential Schools (TRC) in Montréal in April 2013, a panel of Indigenous leaders and intellectuals reflected on the role Québec could play in reconciliation and in decolonizing its relationship with the Abénaki, Anishinaabe, Atikamekw, Cree, Huron-Wendat, Innu, Inuit, Maliseet, Mi'kmaq, Mohawk, and Naskapi nations, with whom it currently coexists. Exhorting Québec to own up to its complicity (past and ongoing) in settler colonialism and referring to Québec's historical trajectory from Nouvelle-France to a province of Canada, the Mohawk activist Clifton Nicholas states that reconciliation "has to start in Québec. That's where it all started. They were colonized but they are also colonizers."[52] What follows is an attempt to respond to Nicholas's challenging invitation.

A Note on Nomenclature and Positionality

Nomenclature is important: to name oneself is an undeniably potent political gesture. Accordingly, there are variations in and shifting opinions about the terms used by Indigenous people to self-identify to non-Indigenous people or to discuss and represent themselves in intra-community settings. These variations align with the incredible diversity of Indigenous peoples and their wide range of opinions about the meaning and the merit of certain terms. I make choices in this book, while acutely aware that names are both loaded and imperfect.

Broadly, the legal term *First Nations* applies to the group of people officially known as Indians under Canada's Indian Act, a body of laws that regulate the federal government's relationship with the Indigenous people it recognizes. The Indian Act does not include or apply to Métis and Inuit peoples. While the province of Québec includes the Inuit in its definition of First Nations people, this is not the case in the rest of Canada, where Inuit and Métis populations, along with individuals and communities who do not meet the definition of *Indian* set forth by the federal government, are not legally considered as First Nations, but rather fall under the category of *Aboriginal people* whose status is not regulated by the Indian Act. The term *Aboriginal* was officially adopted in 1982 in the Constitution Act and is not as narrowly defined as *First Nations*. For its part, the term *Indigenous* is inclusive and tends to have international connotations: it exceeds the confines of specific countries and attends to a structural relationship with settler-colonial forces writ large. The term *Métis* (capitalized) defines the Indigenous nation born out in the Prairies of the early intermarriages of French men and Indigenous women (mostly Cree), and that quickly developed a sense of self as a "New Nation" with its own customs, languages (Cree, Michif, Bungi, and others) and ways of life. It does not include all persons of mixed white and Indigenous ancestry.

The eleven Indigenous nations that live in the province of Québec are neither homogenous in terms of culture or language, nor in their respective historical relationship with the governments of Québec and Canada. For instance, the Innu, Huron-Wendat, Anishinaabe, and Mohawk nations have been in sustained contact with settlers since the sixteenth century, while the Inuit, for their part, were relatively isolated from the encroaching force of settler communities until the twentieth century. In this book, I refer to the eleven nations whose ancestral territories are now located in Québec as *Indigenous peoples* (with a capital I). I do so for the sake of clarity and succinctness, but also as a way to challenge arbitrary settler regulations of First Nations identities. However, if the context requires it, I use the terms *First Nations*, *Métis*, or *Inuit*. To the best of my abilities, I also attend to the cultural and historical differences of each nation when discussing specific performances. Furthermore, I avoid the commonly used expression "Québec's First Nations," since it reproduces a hierarchy of sovereignty that I specifically want to trouble and take to task. Finally, following Wolfe, I use the term *Native* to describe both a relation to a place of origin and a contested structural position within the settler colonial project that settlers themselves attempt to appropriate.

I am not Indigenous and make no claim to speak in the names of the artists and activists I discuss in this book. I conducted my investigation as a scholar occupying the structural position of a French Québécoise de souche (with all its related privileges); that is, as a white person with ancestors from France (as well as other colonial forces), who is both attached to Québec as an imagined community and extremely critical of its vast areas of incomprehension and dissonance along racial and structural lines. I want to situate myself precisely because it matters immensely to my work. My critique is oriented toward the community that I call the *French Québécois de souche*: my critique engages with that community's narratives and aims to unsettle them. I refrain from using the term *francophone majority/community* because it seeks to solely explain the relationship between Indigenous and non-Indigenous peoples as one of cultural and linguistic differences rather than one structured by settler colonialism. Furthermore, such a category runs the risk of erasing the very real experiences of the many francophone "arrivants"[53] of color who have immigrated to Québec from Haiti, Lebanon, Vietnam, and other parts of the world in recent history, and who face forms of erasure and discrimination that I do not want to ignore. The narratives that give coherence to the French Québécois de souche and establish their zero-level of normalcy depend on violence toward these communities, and while my book does not adequately engage with this symbolic and structural violence, I nevertheless want to refrain from reinforcing it. I am aware that the term *French Québécois de souche* remains imperfect and slightly inelegant. However, it has the advantage of zooming in on the bases of the imagined community I seek to encounter and challenge in this book.

My research and this book are fueled by a desire to illuminate the ethical fissures in Québec's national project, to reveal how and why the French Québécois de souche's imagined community cannot currently accommodate (let alone comprehend) the concept of Indigenous sovereignty. More broadly, the province has now struggled to define itself as a community for more than sixty years and still wrestles with its wounded attachments. It has gone through two close-call referendums on separation and a string of separatist governments. Unlike English-speaking Canada, where discussions about the nation are less of a political imperative, Québec's political and cultural spheres are dominated by questions surrounding the province's nation-ness that have yet to be fully answered. As this book argues, Québec's imagining of nation-ness is currently taking place within parameters that take the extinction and/or subjection of Indigenous peoples' lands, modes of governance, and sovereignty as a given or a starting point. The Indigenous performances that form my case studies argue otherwise. They obstinately remind the province and more specifically, the French Québécois de souche that there are alternative ways to imagine the future and remember the past of this contested territory. Importantly, these performances insist on the contested nature of the territory that is Québec: they reframe this land not as a white possession, but as a territory animated by competing sovereignties. In that sense, the performances I discuss do not merely reveal the current state of settler-state violence, but also labor to imagine an alternate future that is predicated on decolonization.

I am aware of the legacy of academia in objectifying and silencing Indigenous voices, intellectual traditions, and epistemologies. As the Stö:lò scholar Dylan Robinson remarks, performance studies run the risk of performing yet another kind of extractive work in mining Indigenous cultural practices for their "performance resources" without attending to what he calls their "functional ontologies," namely, what they do "*as* politics, acts of history, and law-making."[54] To examine Indigenous performances thus requires a methodology that receives them not merely as aesthetic practices but also, and more importantly, as situated speech acts performing diplomacy and legal and historical ties to the land and to other nations, and so on. Attentive to Robinson's critique, my analysis of the various performances included in this book thus aims to be as polyphonic as possible, privileging interventions from Indigenous scholars, artists, and activists in conversation with other non-Western and Western traditions.

Structure: The Encounter

The chapters of this book are organized around a central motif—the scenario of encounter. This scenario holds particular power in organizing the multiple and competing stories adopted by this continent's current inhabitants to explain their particular trajectories. Encounters between Indigenous nations before the arrival of Europeans led to complex networks of kinship, alliances, and confederations as well as to conflicts of all sorts. There were also encounters between Indigenous peoples and Viking and Icelandic voyagers before there were sustained encounters with the French, the Dutch, and the British, among other settler-colonial forces. Europeans, however, framed these encounters as "discoveries" in ways that emphasized "the white man's adventurous spirit and tenacity, which is central to the construction of white supremacy and colonialism."[55] If we strip the false notion of "discovery" from the colonial enterprise in the Americas, we are left with a series of sensate encounters—some failed, others less so, many with profoundly altering or catastrophic consequences. Misunderstandings, or a mutual incapacity or unwillingness to understand the other's worldviews, shape most of these encounters. And, because these encounters were and are overwhelmingly archived in the voice of the conquerors, these misunderstandings (ill-intentioned or not) hold tremendous and enduring power. The Americas, in a sense, are a series of colliding encounters.

The notion of a benevolent (or at least less violently colonial) encounter between Indigenous peoples and French settlers plays a central role in the French Québécois de souche's mythscape. For instance, when Québec City commemorated its 400th anniversary in 2008, the city chose to recast the "encounter" between explorer French colonizers and Indigenous peoples as "peaceful" and as the symbolic genesis of the Québécois as a people. Darryl Leroux traces in his work how Québec's official commemorative event, incidentally entitled Rencontres (Encounters), "imaginatively reconstitutes [Samuel de Champlain] as the founder of the liberal ethic of cultural pluralism common in Québec,"[56] positioning the province as inherently benevolent while suggesting that these encounters have somehow produced a deep *métissage* that indigenizes (and thus legitimizes) the Québécois. Daniel Salée critiques "the at-times quick and reckless use of the language of encounter, of métissage and of interculturalism" to narrate the beginning of what is now Québec, arguing that these encounters were marked from their origins by "brute force" and by "fundamentally unequal power relations that, despite several successful indigenous movements of resistance, always turned in favor of Europeans."[57] Salée and Leroux, as well as the Métis scholar Adam Gaudry and others, question this trope of benevolent encounter between French settlers and Indigenous people.

As a performance-studies scholar, I am interested in encounters because of their sensate nature: one encounters the world, the other, through one's senses, one's body, and encounters are framed by what Diana Taylor calls "scenarios." She writes that the "*scenario* includes features well theorized in literary analysis, such as narrative and plot, but demands that we also pay attention to milieux and corporeal behaviors such as gestures, attitudes, tones not reducible to language. Simultaneously *setup* and *action*, scenarios frame and activate social dramas."[58] Embedded in the scenario is the seed of its opposite, what performance scholars mine as resistant embodied practices and counter-narratives. This book examines such performances that dramatize, subvert, romanticize, or critique the scenarios that frame encounters between the eleven Indigenous nations of Québec and the province's French Québécois de souche community.

I use the term *performance* to harness a broad ensemble of embodied practices and events that actively shape and/or defy how nations as imagined communities perceive and define themselves. These performances take place on stage, on the big screen, during road protests, in urban settings, and on reserves and other contested territory. Drawing from such a heterogeneous pool of performances demonstrates that settler colonialism permeates all spheres of identity and national discourses. It also renders visible the multiple sites of resistance that animate Indigenous peoples' ongoing decolonizing struggle, sites that Dylan Robinson describes as spaces of "sensate sovereignty."[59] Robinson echoes here the work of a number of Indigenous scholars whose research troubles and expands the notion of sovereignty. The Tuscarora scholar Jolene Rickard and the Seneca scholar Michelle Raheja theorize "visual sovereignty," while the Tsimshian scholar Mique'l Dangeli's work reflects on sovereignty in the embodied work of Indigenous dance groups from the Pacific Northwest and Alaska. Kevin Bruyneel, drawing from Homi Bhabha's concept of a third space of enunciation, reflects on spaces of sovereignty that exist on the boundaries of settler colonialism, arguing that they are "inassimilable" and "expose both the practices and the contingencies of settler-colonial rule."[60] In other words, performances that articulate these spaces of Indigenous sovereignty render visible the very structures of power and elimination that the settler state attempts to erase.

Chapter 1, entitled "*Neptune* Redux: The (First) Nation(s) Enacted in Alexis Martin's *Invention du chauffage central en Nouvelle-France*," begins with a missed encounter between the French Québécois de souche playwright Alexis Martin and the Indigenous "other" that his play claims to render visible. Martin's 2012 *Invention du chauffage central en Nouvelle France* is the first of an ambitious trio of plays retracing the history of the francophone community in Québec from Nouvelle-France until 1998. *Invention* thus participates in the solidification of the French Québécois de souche identity through the creation of a national mythscape, a concept defined by Duncan Bell as the symbolic "page upon which the multiple and often conflicting nationalist narratives are (re)written" and a "perpetually mutating repository for the representation of the past for the purpose of the present."[61] While Martin seemingly reimagines the Québec mythscape as *métissé*—the play finds its central motif in an Algonquian legend and includes Indigenous characters (problematically played by non-Indigenous actors when the play premiered)—*Invention* nevertheless falls short of its inclusive mission. In fact, *Invention* echoes in disturbing ways Marc Lescarbot's 1606 *Théâtre de Neptune en la Nouvelle-France* (*Theater of Neptune in New France*), an early colonial performance in which French men dressed as "Savages" willfully offered their land to the King of France. Drawing from Alan Filewod's analysis of *Neptune* as a foundational spectacle of Indigenous people's erasure in Canada, I trace echoes of *Neptune*'s settler-colonial gesture in the ventriloquizing of Indigenous voices performed by Alexis Martin's *Invention*. The play indeed imagines Québec's becoming as a nation through a parasitic relation with Indigenous presence, bodies, and absolution that echos the willful surrender of their land imagined and performed by the redface "Savages" in Lescarbot's 1606 play.

I further explore this parasitic relation in chapter 2, "Les Racines Imaginaries/Mythical *Métissages*: Québec and the Ruse of the Métis Turn," which focuses on two recent award-winning documentary films that address Québec's eternal settler anxiety. The two films are trying to understand who "we," the French Québécois de souche, might be by turning to Indigenous peoples. *L'Empreinte* (2014) by Carole Poliquin and Yvan Dubuc yearns for a simple explanation for our identity malaise and comes to the following thesis: "We," the French Québécois de souche, have forgotten the prelapsarian moment of harmonious intermixing with Indigenous peoples that defined "us" in Nouvelle-France, and "we" need to remember it in order to become whole again. In other words, the film suggests, "we" were born as a nation from the close encounters of early French settlers and Indigenous women, and "we" now need to recognize and reclaim ourselves as a métis people. For its part, *Québékoisie* (2014), by Mélanie Carrier and Olivier Higgins, builds on the notion of creating encounters between Indigenous peoples and French Québécois de souche. Their film provides a more nuanced reflection on questions of identity but problematically returns to what the scholars Pierrot Ross-Tremblay (Innu) and Nawel Hamidi call the "fiction of blood" to articulate the Québécois' claim to Nativeness.[62]

Chapter 3, titled "Cinematic Encounters on the Reserve," meditates on four cinematic encounters with the Native reserve and puts in conversation the Abénaki filmmaker Alanis Obomsawin's *Kanehsatake: 270 Years of Resistance* (1993); *Mesnak* (2011), the first film directed by the Huron-Wendat director Yves Sioui Durand; and two films produced by the Wapikoni Mobile project. Utilizing Žižek's meditation on subjective and objective violence, I examine these four films, which offer complementary vantage points on the reserves—now euphemistically referred to as "communities" by settler governments—as spaces of continuous settler-colonial violence. *Reserve* is the term in use in Canada as opposed to the term *reservation,* which is prevalent in the United States. Obomsawin's documentary film focuses on the 1990 events in Oka and present the reserve as a space that seals and secures the borders of settler-colonial communities. Her film offers a powerful examination of the violence that erupts when these borders are called into question by the Indigenous peoples who exist at their margins. For his part, Sioui Durand explores the intramural conflicts of the reserve and meditates on its inhabitants' internalized violence and colonization. Shaped by the legacy of the Residential Schools and the Indian Act's other tentacles, the reserve is a space of abject filiation and interrupted lineage in Sioui Durand's film, which transposes Shakespeare's *Hamlet*—its protagonist's struggle against a rotten state and within a damaged family structure—to a fictive reserve in Québec. Sioux Durand unflinchingly examines the forces that shape the reserve as a space of containment, but also as a space where Indigenous cultures survive against the odds. I conclude the chapter with an examination of the two Innu films produced by the Wapikoni Mobile project—*Tour de Char* (2009) by Jean-Baptiste Bacon-Riverin and Malcolm Riverin, and *L'Enfance déracinée* (2013) by Réal Junior Leblanc—which present portraits of Innu reserves as spaces where healing is taking place.

Two close and sustained performative encounters with the Indian Act lie at the center of chapter 4, entitled "Endurance/Enduring Performance: Nadia

Myre, La Marche Amun, and the Indian Act's Tumultuous Geographies." The first, Nadia Myre's monumental visual-art piece *Indian Act* (1999–2002), uses a traditionally feminine beading technique to bead over the entire text of Canada's Indian Act, a law that intimately rules and organizes Indigenous peoples in Canada. In what amounts to a veritable feat of endurance, Myre (Anishinaabe) and a group of volunteers encountered and rewrote the Indian Act, denaturalizing it with more than 80,000 red and white beads over the course of three years. The result is a striking visual piece—part illegible document, part topographical map of all that was hidden by the law's potent words. Myre's piece finds a parallel in the 2010 Marche Amun, a protest march led by a group of Innu women to demand an end to the gendered discrimination contained in the Indian Act. Collectively, and over the course of walking the 300 miles (500 kilometers) that separate the Huron-Wendat reserve of Wendake from Ottawa, the women encountered and challenged the current lines of exclusion created and naturalized by the Indian Act and remapped spaces in which discussions about decolonization could emerge. Reading these two interventions as endurance performances, chapter 4 proposes a reflection on Indigenous endurance as ontology and as a resistance tactic. The performance scholar Patrick Anderson's work on endurance performance, as well as the reflections of Bonita Lawrence (Mi'kmaq), Sarah Deer (Muscogee), and Mishuana Goeman (Seneca) on settler colonialism's gendered violence, underlie this exploration.

The last chapter, "Theater in Contested Lands: Repatriating Ancestors amid Violence," adopts Chadwick Allen's "trans-Indigenous methodology"[63] to connect the repatriation work performed onstage by Ondinnok, a Montréal-based Indigenous theater company, with the Native American Grave Protection and Repatriation Act (NAGPRA) repatriation struggle that pitted the Kumeyaay nation against a group of researchers from the University of California, San Diego, until 2016. NAGPRA is a federal law designed to correct the United States' long history of insensitive and unethical handling of Indigenous bones and funerary objects, particularly by museums and other federal institutions. Leveraging Ann Kakaliouras's anthropological concept of the "repatriatable"[64] to discuss theater and performance, this chapter argues that, as a nexus of competing narratives and worldviews, the repatriatable remains found at UC San Diego gain a wider performative quality and become what I call "performative repatriatables." These performative repatriatables include remains but also living bodies, such as those of the performers in Ondinnok's play, that do not fall under NAGPRA and can be repatriated in a more symbolic realm. These "performative repatriatables" embody what Joseph Roach calls memory and "counter-memories";[65] that is, they render visible Indigenous presence and epistemologies where they have been and continue to be violently erased. This chapter's intervention departs from Québec and extends to a larger American context. In drawing transnational connections, I do not want to flatten or deny the specificity of each Indigenous nation's history, resistance practices, and articulations of sovereignty. I draw instead from Allen's invitation toward the *trans*, attentive to the transnational, transformative, and translating work performed by these very different performances of repatriation. This chapter examines how Indigenous groups' performances of mourning and the groups' repatriation of ancestral remains encounter resistance from settler-colonial institutions. This resistance exists across time and place: it is one of the mechanisms that normalize Žižek's objective violence. This resistance, I argue, betrays the same deep-seated colonial anxiety that fueled the reactions in Oka when the violence against Indigenous peoples that underwrites civil society in the Americas and infiltrates even its reparative laws was exposed.

Chapter 1

✦

Neptune Redux

The (First) Nation(s) Enacted in Alexis Martin's *Invention du chauffage central en Nouvelle-France*

Invention du chauffage central en Nouvelle-France (*Invention of Central Heating in New France*) is the first of a trio of plays penned by Alexis Martin as part of his project entitled *Histoire révélée du Canada français 1608–1998* (*A Revealed History of French Canada 1608–1998*).[1] A prolific and beloved actor, director, and playwright, Alexis Martin has been a central figure of Québec's theater scene since the early 1990s. While he works regularly in film and television, he is closely associated with Montréal's Nouveau Théâtre Expérimental (NTE) and with its founders Jean-Pierre Ronfard and Robert Gravel. Martin has been the artistic codirector of the company since 1999, a role he now shares with his close collaborator Daniel Brière (the two were at the helm of the *Histoire révélée* trilogy produced by the NTE between 2012 and 2014). As a playwright, Martin often investigates the centrality of language in Québec, creating existential encounters between colorful characters from various socioeconomic, linguistic, and even temporal strata. His eclectic theatrical world is thus composed of past productions in which Mafiosi and intellectuals, Hitler and God, priests and waitresses uncomfortably and often hilariously rub elbows. Unsurprisingly, *Invention du chauffage central en Nouvelle-France* features encounters between Samuel de Champlain, Jesuits, an Innu spiritual leader, and a group of aficionados of historical "cosplay" (costume play as a hobby).

In a 2012 interview, Martin mused on what he perceived as the relative absence of historical dramas in Québec's theatrical canon. Noting the scarcity of texts dramatizing the early days of Nouvelle-France, the defeat of the French forces on the Abraham Plains, or the lives of historical figures such as Marc Lescarbot or the Comte de Frontenac, for example, Martin asked whether this silence, this form of cultural forgetting, was "the lot of the defeated."[2] The title of Martin's ambitious trilogy—*A Revealed History of French Canada 1608–1998*—clearly positions the plays as a corrective gesture to Québec's so-called cultural and historical forgetting and announces the author's desire to illuminate what he sees as Québec's obscured past. If Martin is quick to point out that he is not a historian and that his plays do not pretend to show the truth about the past, the trilogy's website[3] and *Invention du chauffage central en Nouvelle-France*'s program nevertheless feature an exhaustive bibliography of the scholarly and historical texts Martin consulted to pen his plays, giving the whole project the seal of legitimacy that comes with archival research.

As its title suggests, *Invention du chauffage central en Nouvelle-France* (hereafter *Invention*) explores history through the theme of cold and positions frigid temperatures and harsh weather conditions as central driving forces in the formation of Québécitude (which I use here to denote the French Québécois de souche identity). Explaining this dramaturgical choice, Martin notes in an interview published in the major newspaper *Le Devoir*: "Cold has really forged our identity. And it still does. From the beginning, cold, for example, has made us create alliances with Aboriginal people, if only so that we could survive the first winters."[4] In each of *Invention*'s interwoven storylines Québécitude thus emerges from the thermal shock of winter, from unlikely alliances devised in times of need, and from the ingenuity required to survive the long winters' extreme cold. The action of the play jumps from the winter of 1606, which led to the formation of L'Ordre de Bon Temps (the Order of Good Cheer) in the colonial outpost of Port Royal, to the "Storm of the Century" in 1971 during which more than eighteen inches of snow fell on Montréal in less than twenty-four hours, burying the city under a thick white blanket. Bookending the play is the ice storm that paralyzed the southern part of the province (including Montréal) in 1998, leaving thousands without heat for weeks in the dead of winter.

According to Martin, the structure of the play and of the trilogy as a whole emulates the geometrical structure of a snowflake:

> The play comports 6 branches that each constitutes a condensed scenario, the temporality of which is reversible. This dramatic structure is diachronic-hexagonal and evokes the shape of a snowflake. Thus, 6 sequences of events (or scenes) converge to a center, which is the temporal space that structures the trilogy as a whole. This center, always the year 1998, is the neutral space that allows the transit from one era to the next, from one theme to the next.[5]

The notion of reversible temporality is important here, since it allows Martin to jump back and forth in time and to revisit and establish resonance between disparate historical and fictive events. Through these episodes of extreme winter weather, Martin imagines, often with poetic humor, a genealogy for the French Québécois de souche in which survival and adaptation, colonial alienation and a desire for liberation, and ultimately nationhood produce a narrative of resilient presence on a harsh landscape.

In conversation with Martin's *Invention* and its articulation of Québécitude, this chapter first meditates on theater's intimate role in shaping national memory and a community's sense of self. As Alan Filewod argues, "theatre models the society in the process of enactment . . . transform[ing] experience into a community narrative and . . . materially construct[ing] in the audience the community it addresses in its texts."[6] The nation and theater produce and legitimize each other in "the elation of spectacle."[7] Through the process of bringing people together to witness storytelling, theater (the space and the performance) solidifies a community's sense of self in a process that simultaneously erases that (bodies, events, etc.) which threatens its narrative's coherence. In this sense, theater participates in what Ernest Renan qualified as a form of necessary forgetting in this oft-cited passage of *Qu'est-ce qu'une nation?*

> Yet the essence of a nation is that all individuals have many things in common, and also that they have forgotten many things. . . . All French citizens must forget the Saint-Barthélemy, the massacres in the South of France during the XIIIth century.[8]

Renan, who wrote a century before Filewod, illuminates here how nations obtain and maintain their cohesion in the tense balance between shared remembrance and collective forgetting.

What is this past that Alexis Martin wants us, "the defeated," to remember? *Invention* makes it clear it is the memory of the French Québécois de souche that Martin wants to jolt back to life. It is Québécitude that is at stake. The defeated here are not the Indigenous people whose expropriation and erasure constituted the conditions of possibility of Nouvelle-France and, later on, of Québec. As for remembering, Martin is selective. A thick description of his play reveals that the playwright certainly "remembers" the crucial role played by Indigenous people in the creation of Québécitude in North America. This is laudable in a context where Indigenous characters and stories are all but absent from mainstream media in Québec (save for the occasional images of devastation or conflicts on reserves). To its credit, the play features a large cast of Indigenous characters. But, as I argue in this chapter, their presence is always in service of a stable Québécitude. If, as Martin argues, *Invention*'s hexagonal dramaturgical structure allows temporality to be reversed, echoed in the present, and revisited, then his Indigenous and French Québécois de souche characters are not afforded the same temporal mobility. Indigenous characters, though celebrated in the past, are portrayed as vanishing and are only imagined as "providing the conditions of possibility" for Nouvelle-France/Québec "to manifest its intent."[9] After having disappeared Indigenous characters from Québec's trajectory after the era of Nouvelle-France, *Invention* ends with a group of Indigenous workers from Mexico vanishing in a fire in a sewing plant in Montréal. Martin, it seems, can only imagine Indigenous people as spectral figures.

In imagining Indigenous people as mere conditions of possibility, Alexis Martin reproduces the well-worn scenario that organized the very first Western play written and performed in what is now Canada: Marc Lescarbot's 1606 *Théâtre de Neptune en la Nouvelle-France*, a redface performance that features a group of French men dressed as "Sauvages" who willingly surrender their land to the King of France in a choreographed nautical masque that was performed on the waters of the Annapolis Basin (in what is now Nova Scotia). Provoking an encounter between these two plays, I examine in this chapter how French settler, French-Canadian, and later on French Québécois de souche identities have always been performed in what I call a parasitic relationship with Indigeneity. This relationship, in which the parasite draws from its host in a nonreciprocal relationship, extends of course from the stage to everyday life. My analysis of *Neptune* is indebted to Alan Filewod and Jerry Wasserman. Both have written at length on *Neptune* as a colonial spectacle, and they locate in its 1606 performance the genesis of Canadian theater, the initial moment in which Canada as a nation is articulated on stage through the simultaneous presence and erasure of Indigenous bodies. A close examination of Martin's play (which incidentally features the characters of Marc Lescarbot and of the historical figures that performed *Théâtre de Neptune en la Nouvelle-France* in 1606) demonstrates that Lescarbot's gesture of erasure still permeates French Québécois de souche's identity narrative.

Finally, in tracing Martin's ambivalent intervention, this chapter explores how *Invention* struggles with the notion of reconciliation with Indigenous people in the wake of Canada's Truth and Reconciliation Commission (TRC) mandated by the Indian Residential Schools Settlement Agreement. Reconciliation begins with an encounter of the other's pain, with a seeing and a hearing of their story. Martin seems well aware of this necessity for encounters, but he falls short of creating them in any meaningful way. Indeed, Martin's play was written in 2011 and performed in 2012: this was a period that coincided with the public audiences conducted by the TRC, which began in 2010. *Invention* labors to imagine and stage reconciliation, but does so while sidestepping an admission of the province's complicity in the oppression of Indigenous peoples. The play both renders Indigenous peoples visible *and* reconsolidates their erasure. Focusing on a scene between Takraliq, an Inuk Residential School survivor, and a young French Québécoise de souche who witnesses her disheveled testimonial in a bar in Montréal, I reflect on this missed encounter as reflective of the as-of-now impossible path to reconciliation between the French Québécois de souche community and Indigenous people. As I argue, Québec's narrative of itself currently forecloses the very first step in the process of reconciliation, which is to recognize the province's own role in the violent oppression of Indigenous peoples. *Invention*'s struggle to name Québec's complicity in the administration of the Residential School system (one arm of Canada's genocidal project) marks a moment of overture in Martin's play. However, given that the play was mostly performed by non-Indigenous actors[10] in theaters led by French Québécois de souche and far removed from Indigenous populations, the reconciliation and absolution imagined and performed in absentia of Indigenous peoples in *Invention* falls short of its reconciliatory endeavor and echoes in disturbing ways the willful offering of the land performed by the "Savages" of Lescarbot's 1606 *Théâtre de Neptune en la Nouvelle-France*.

Je Me Souviens? Exploring Québec's Will to Forget

Martin's diagnosis of Québec's cultural amnesia[11] may come as a surprise to many. After all, remembrance is Québec's official motto, replicated on every automobile license plate in the province with the phrase *Je me souviens* (I remember). Québec's cultural industry has been, and still is, heavily invested in affirming Québec's distinct culture through a celebration of a certain version of its past. If Alexis Martin posits that theater is exempt from this memorializing trend, Québécois cinema, on the contrary, has consistently mined and dramatized Québec's *terroir* (agrarian past) in films like *Séraphin: Un homme et son péché* (2002) and *Le Survenant* (2005), among others.[12] Television series like *Les Belles Histoires des pays d'en haut* (1956–70), which is currently being given a remake on the Radio-Canada television channel; *Le Temps d'une paix* (1980–86); *Les Filles de Caleb* (1990–91); and countless others have celebrated Québec's Everyman and -woman, those folks *nés pour un petit pain* (born to be poor, of inconsequential birth) under the dominion of the Catholic Church and the rich Anglais (British and, later on, American). The province's friction with Canada also constitutes a rich source of inspiration for films such as *Octobre* (1994), *15 Février 1839* (2001), and *Le Déserteur* (2008) that dramatize important conflicts between Québec and Canada.[13] The film scholar Bruno Cornellier relates these commemorating gestures to Québec's "will to remember as a political imperative."[14] Indeed, Québec's cultural institutions and governments (separatist or not) have wielded and continue to deploy the concept of collective memory, an investment in commemorating the province's wounded attachments and its history of suffering, as a weapon against assimilation into the Anglo-American sea that surrounds the province.

To be fair, Québec's recent cultural productions have also explored the province's turn toward cosmopolitanism and dramatized its contemporary urban reality. Movies like Ricardo Trogi's *Québec-Montréal* (2002) and Anaïs Barbeau-Lavalette's *Le Ring* (2007), as well as Xavier Dolan's entire filmography, mark a sharp turn from the theme of the *terroir*. They remain however, resolutely white, and the films or television shows that center on non-French Québécois de souche are few and far between. According to recent statistics provided by the Union des Artistes (the francophone actors' union in Canada), the most popular shows on Québécois television in 2014–15 counted less than 5 percent of their casts as actors of color.[15] Theater boasts the same pitiful numbers, and the province's cultural industry has been remarkably tone-deaf when it comes to racist practices surrounding the representation of racialized bodies.[16] When a non-Québécois de souche does appear on screen, he or she often occupies the periphery or "serves to participate in and reflect the stabilization of an identity and a memory from which he or she is nonetheless excluded, like an external witness."[17] Importantly for this project, these two historicizing currents in Québécois cinema—*terroir* and cosmopolitanism—have in common the near-complete erasure of Indigenous characters who are, if rendered visible, reduced to the roles of one-dimensional artifacts of the past.

Martin claims that Québécois theater is uninterested in history, and he is both right and wrong. I would contend instead that history is remembered selectively in Québec's public sphere. This can be explained by Québec's aforementioned complex and contradictory status as a colonized/colonizer minority. Only certain parts of Québec's history—those that stabilize Québécitude as an oppressed and colonized minority identity—are remembered and mythologized. The Québécois de souche cultivate a certain cognitive dissonance when it comes to their genesis as settlers and their subsequent complicity in Canada's settler-colonial project. This is what Mark Rifkin calls "settler common sense," which he describes as "the ways the legal and political structures that enable non-Native access to Indigenous territories come to be lived as given, as simply unmarked, generic conditions of possibility for occupancy, association, history, and personhood."[18] In other words, Québec's remembered narrative never questions the very foundation and questionable legitimacy of the de souche's national project.

Indeed, settler common sense presents Québec's sovereignty as an unquestionable premise and obscures the dispossession and erasure of Indigenous peoples that form its condition of possibility. I borrow the notion of mythscape from Duncan Bell, who describes it as the symbolic "page upon which the multiple and often conflicting nationalist narratives are (re)written." A mythscape, he adds, "is the perpetually mutating repository for the representation of the past for the purpose of the present."[19] Bell echoes the work of Benedict Anderson, who famously described the nation as an "imagined community"[20] whose sense of self, articulated on a perceived shared culture and history, is propagated and reified through mass communication. As many have argued since Anderson, the nation as a constructed entity finds its emotional and political legitimacy in an ensemble of foundational myths—a "mythscape"—that often simultaneously naturalizes its members' authenticity and sense of belonging, and often justifies the exclusion of those who lie at the nation's margins.

Québec's mythscape rests on a "standard historical teleology of Québec's colonial struggle under British domination and Anglo-American capital"[21] that is reproduced, stabilized, and naturalized in quotidian and staged performances to accommodate the French Québécois de souche's modern, national self. This narrative bypasses Québec's settler-colonial role entirely. In the 1960s, it presented the province as an oppressed minority on an equal footing with colonized Algerians, with African Americans, and other dispossessed communities. Cornellier writes that

> 1960s Québec intellectuals . . . labored to translate the struggle of others, as theorized in the influential work of Frantz Fanon, Aimé Césaire, Albert Memmi, or Édouard Glissant, in a language that allowed Québecers to makes sense of their own peculiar location as white colonial/colonized subjects in the margins of the Anglo-American sphere of dominance.[22]

As a result of this discursive realignment with the colonized and oppressed of the world, Québec became "the new Native population, fighting against the British (and the American capitalists) as foreign invaders."[23] In Québec, this discourse of competing Nativeness often takes the form, as I discuss in chapter 2, of a "Métis Turn." Through this narrative of *métissage*, the French Québécois de souche or "pure laine" are able to reimagine themselves as métis, that is, both francophone and Indigenous to Québec. Their national narrative, which becomes that of the majority, thus discursively supplants that of the eleven First Nations for whom Québec is ancestral territory.[24]

Martin explores and dramatizes Québec's identity discourse in his play. I am particularly interested in how his rehistoricizing of the French Québécois de souche through the lens of cold naturalizes this identity as one with, or indigenous to, the province's land and climate. To be clear, Martin's play does give voice to Indigenous characters, but their preexisting sovereignty on and relationship to the land of Québec are presented as transient and, in Martin's narrative, they do not challenge Québec's cartographical integrity. *Invention* features historical figures like the Mi'kmaq chief Membertou[25] as well as fictional characters like Takraliq, among other Indigenous characters. In giving them a voice, Martin's play appears to disrupt the aforementioned historicizing trends in Québécois theater and cinema; and thus, at first glance, it offers a critique of Québec's collective forgetting with regard to Indigenous people and revisits history in a more inclusive way. However, the play often falls short of its inclusive mission, instead reinscribing in complex and at times ambivalent ways the erasure that defines Québec's relationship with Indigenous peoples and the reductive collapsing of indigeneity and natural elements that is so central in colonial imaginings.

If Martin explores Québec's forgetting as the collective psyche's response to the shame of British colonization ("Is this the lot of the defeated?"), I

Figure 1.1. *Invention du chauffage central en Nouvelle-France*: a fictive Port Royal in 1608. *Left to right*: Alexis Martin, Pierre-Antoine Lasnier, Émilie Bibeau, and Luc Guérin. (Photo by Michel Ostaszewski)

argue that Québec's forgetting is symptomatic of a far more complex psychic wound that constantly threatens the coherence of the province's sense of self. This sense of self rests on remembering and elevating Québec's history as a colonized cultural and linguistic minority within Canada as a way to justify Québec's nation-building project and shield the province from criticism surrounding the discourses and policies it puts in place in pursuit of this goal. In other words, Québec deploys its own history of dispossession/marginalization at the hands of the British in order to obscure its own past as a colonizer and justify its ongoing role as a settler community oppressing the Indigenous nations whose territories Québec identifies as its own national land base. These two positions—"colonized" and colonizer, oppressed and oppressor—seem irreconcilable and create the forgetting that Martin misattributes solely to the shame of being on the side of the defeated.

A Nation of Frozen Words

Directed by Daniel Brière, Alexis Martin's longtime collaborator and artistic codirector at the NTE, *Invention du chauffage central en Nouvelle-France* was presented from February 7 to March 8, 2012, at l'Espace Libre in Montréal.

(See figure 1.1.) The production then toured the province and was staged at the Théâtre Français of the National Arts Center in Ottawa in November of the same year. Brière and Martin presented the second part of the trilogy, entitled *Les chemins qui marchent*, in 2013, and the last installment, *Le pain et le vin*, premiered in 2014 at l'Espace Libre during Montréal's prestigious Festival Transamériques as part of a marathon, six-hour performance of the entire trilogy. In all productions, the cast[26] portrayed *Invention*'s dozens of characters on an inventive traverse stage covered with a rough pine floor and furnished with an old-fashioned woodstove, a rustic pine table, and stools—all evocative of the rudimentary log cabins that housed early settlers in Nouvelle-France.

In Michel Ostaszewski's versatile scenic design, large sliding glass panels enclose the stage on all sides, leaving an open corridor along its periphery on which the Narrator (Carl Poliquin) can circulate and address the audience. The scenic design ingeniously allows winter—snow, wind, and frost—to permeate the stage. When closed, the glass panels seal the playing area, protecting the audience from the multiple snowstorms or windstorms that rage within its perimeter over the course of the play. At times the actors themselves create the storms onstage with handheld leaf-blowers and artificial snowflakes, while at other times, Nicolas Descôteaux's lighting effects and Anthony Rozankovic's soundscape manufacture the meteorological incidents that structure the play's arc. The audience, removed from the stage's enclosure, witnesses the characters struggling against the elements as if viewing a page of history behind the glass of a museum display. Dates and locations projected on a large horizontal screen sitting on top of the glass enclosure onstage help situate the audience as scenes change, facilitating the navigation between the multiple temporal and geographical planes that coexist in Martin's play.

Dramaturgically, *Invention* draws its central motif from an Algonquian (most likely Innu) story about Pipmuacan, a land where words are frozen and await their liberation. The story is mentioned in passing in the *Jesuits Relations* of 1654 in relation to the Algonquians' migration from their winter hunting quarters to their spring camp on the shores of the Saguenay River near Tadoussac. In *Invention*, the Narrator, standing outside of the sliding panels during the prologue, tells the audience:

> Ancient Amerindian elders say that there is, North of Tadoussac, a land where the cold is so great, the air so thick, that WORDS lie frozen. All the WORDS pronounced in the middle of winter and that escape us despite us, despite all things: these frozen words join the mysterious land of Pipmuacan, hundreds of inches from our mouth and our conscience.[27]

This description echoes, albeit with some poetic license, the Jesuits' version of the story. However, it leaves out the following passage: "quand le Printemps approche, ces paroles viennent à se dégeler" and "on entend quasi en

Figure 1.2. *Invention du chauffage central en Nouvelle-France*: Pipmuacan, where the words are frozen (Marie-Ève Trudel and Carl Poliquin). (Photo by Michel Ostaszewski)

un moment tout ce qui s'est dit pendant l'hiver" ("when spring approaches, these words become unfrozen" and "we hear, almost in one moment, all that had been said during winter").[28] The Jesuits describe how, upon arriving on the shores of the Saguenay River, the Algonquians "say publicly without shame or punishment" that which has been said and done in the dead of winter. In oral cultures, stories like that of Pipmuacan are far more than poetic allegory; they contain moral and legal principles, they speak of a nation's mode of governance.[29] The Jesuits, in relaying this story, name, in essence, a process of community accountability, transparency, and atonement on which I will comment later.

The scenic design—the glass-box in which Martin's characters search for a sense of Québécitude—as well as the lighting and sound designs render visible and audible this land of frozen words that serves as the play's leitmotif. The frozen words themselves exist as a soundscape of muffled and intertwined sentences heard through scene changes throughout the play. They are also felt visually in the form of a luminous force that envelops the characters. Toward the end of the play, for example, the Narrator and Lucie (figure 1.2.), his old flame and research partner who now lives as a recluse, meet again in Pipmuacan where they admire its frozen surface under which words lie, seemingly lifeless. The words are invisible to the audience but are translated instead through a form of radiating heat that emanates from the ice. Lucie, her face bathed in that light, explains that the ice of Pipmuacan contains "une mémoire qui ne peut pas se déployer"[30] ("a memory that cannot unfold"), as well as a call for liberation. As the two characters observe almost hypnotically the luminous ice of Pipmuacan on the stage floor, the spectators find themselves gazing at the glass surface of the sliding doors, performing the same reflective gesture as the characters onstage. At other moments during the play, the closed glass doors muffle the words pronounced onstage, effectively holding them captive like the ice of Pipmuacan. The stage's glass panels thus actualize the story's narrative of a collective memory encased in ice and help inscribe Martin's multiple storylines in a larger narrative of a nation frozen in its trajectory, awaiting liberation.

A chorus of women dressed in old-fashioned long thermal underwear sings to mark the transitions between the play's multiple spatiotemporal planes. Over the course of the play, the women layer costumes over their long underwear when they embody different characters, but they always return to this timeless, skinlike apparel when they sing as a chorus, giving these interventions a sense of suspended temporality. The chorus's poetic songs appear at times to perform the premonitory work of oracles in Greek theater, while at other times their voices render audible the torrent of words frozen in Pipmuacan.

> Snow Snow in your blue-turning procession
> Children smiles that fall thick
> Among the deathly housewives
> Snow Snow the vaginal salts of dark births
> For Fuck's sake you will freeze with these wet boots
> Snow Snow hurling of primordial forgetting
> Sheet of absolute in the great shredder
> Ah how the snow has snowed! Ah how the snow has snowed!
> Ah how it has snowed the snow! [My translation][31]

The chorus's song contains many references to some of Québec's most recognizable poetic texts about winter as a marker of national belonging. Making their way into Martin's chorus are fragments of the tragic poet Emile Nelligan's 1903 poem "Soir d'hiver" (Ah, comme la neige a neigé!).[32] Nelligan, Québec's Verlaine, wrote his entire corpus as a young man before schizophrenia took hold of him and he was placed in a psychiatric hospital. Nelligan is a mythical figure in Québec and has inspired countless songs, plays, an opera, films, and paintings. The chorus also echoes Gilles Vigneault's 1964 song "Mon pays" ("My Country"), in which the singer-songwriter claims that "Mon pays, ce n'est pas un pays, c'est l'hiver" ("My country, it is not a country, it is winter").[33] Vigneault, who cites Nelligan as an influence, is a central character in Québec's de souche culture. He began his career in the 1960s, has composed "Gens du Pays," Québec's unofficial national anthem; and has produced new work as recently as 2014. The poet Gaston Miron, another staple of Québec's literary and nationalist scene, is also present in the chorus's song. This particular excerpt features poetic images that align closely with the linguistic and imagistic world of Miron's 1963 cycle "La Vie agonique."[34] Martin's "Ménagères de la mort," for example, echoes Miron's images of the "émancipés malingres" or the sickly emancipated from the poem "Compagnons des Amériques" and emulates Miron's investment of sites of hope and promises with anguish. Finally, the chorus's "grande déchiqueteuse" references Robert Charlebois's darkly humorous 1967 song "Demain l'hiver," in which the singer invokes children being swallowed by snowplows as one more reason to flee Québec's winter for warmer shores.[35]

These poetic fragments stem from authors whose investment in French Québécois de souche nationalism is well documented. Together these references and citations form a recognizable lexical field for most French Québécois de souche who came of age or grew up during or after the Révolution Tranquille of the 1960s in Québec. Tellingly, these fragments belong to Pipmuacan in Martin's play: they are the words that have not yet succeeded in defining a nation, in bringing it to life. Like the chorus that sings them, these poetic images exist in a moment of suspension in the land of frozen words just like Québec's repeatedly postponed national project. Interestingly, while all of the authors cited in these fragments are men, the chorus is a feminine entity and the images it harnesses—"sels vaginaux des naissances obscures" ("obscure births' vaginal salts"), "ménagères de la mort" ("deathly housewives")—problematically mark the unfinished nation of Québec as suspended in an immature or feminine state. National narratives, as Diana Taylor reminds us, are often gendered in particularly violent ways. Nationhood, she writes, can be "as much a physical territory as a longing for heroic transcendence, as much a virginal space to be penetrated . . . as an aspiration to male greatness."[36] Writing about this conflation of woman and nation in Québec's literature, Lori Saint-Martin posited in 1984 that the celebrated authors Hubert Aquin, Jacques Godbout, and Victor Lévy-Beaulieu, whose novels are often positioned as marking the passage of Québécois literature from infancy to maturation, were writing "des livres attentats"[37] (books that attack), in which narrators killed their female companions in the name of their personal and national liberation.

Like the chorus, the play itself contains layer upon layer of cultural and historical references, which appear pell-mell across temporal planes (what Martin calls "reversed temporality"). In some instances, this citationality takes the form of creative anachronisms and moments of poetic license that allow Martin, for example, to humorously attribute the creation of Québec's iconic Kanuk coat (a fixture of contemporary winter fashion in Québec, sold by a company founded in 1974) to the French writer and explorer Marc

Lescarbot (1570–1641). In Martin's imagined version, Lescarbot, upon facing another harsh winter in 1608, fashions a winter coat (a rough version of what the Kanuk looks like today) that allows his men "to keep their French appearance and follow Parisian fashion"[38] while borrowing from the clothing habits and survival expertise of their Mi'kmaq neighbors. From this moment of hybrid colonial haute couture in Port Royal, Martin traces an imagined genealogy of Lescarbot whose most recent incarnation in 1991 is Alain Lescarbot, the CEO of a business manufacturing Kanuk-like garments. This modern Lescarbot—who, contrary to his ancestor, does not exist outside of Martin's play—is a ruthless businessman who has relocated his business to Chihuahua, Mexico, and who lives in Québec City in an old Catholic monastery converted to high-end condos. Martin maps onto this fictive Lescarbot Québec's own trajectory from a deeply religious and mostly manufacturing province, in which an English minority held the lion's share of the economic power, to the radical shift to secularization and French Québécois de souche entrepreneurship that occurred during the province's Révolution Tranquille in the 1960s. Alain Lescarbot, unmoored without religion and community, is unhappy. He chooses to live in a place that exemplifies the dramatic decline of the Catholic Church's stronghold in Québec. Martin deploys citationality and his reversed temporality here to create a genealogy of Lescarbots imagined as part of the same project.

While this genealogical writing helps weave a national mythscape, it also serves to critique what Martin sees as Québec losing touch with its communal roots. In the last scene of the play, in which a group of Lescarbot's Indigenous Mexican workers occupy a company's sewing plant in Montréal to demand better working conditions, Martin draws (perhaps unintentionally) an interesting but underdeveloped parallel between the Mi'kmaqs and the Indigenous Mexicans. He alludes to how both groups have provided the raw material and know-how for the Lescarbots to produce the winter garments that secure the survival and flourishing of white settlers. Supported by historical sources such as Lescarbot and Champlain's correspondences, which have documented instances of collaboration between Mi'kmaqs and settlers in Port Royal, Martin portrays the creation of the initial Kanuk-like coat as a collective endeavor. What happened after this initial collaboration—the betrayal of these first instances of solidarity and early alliances—is well documented by scholars like Gilles Havard, Pierrot Ross-Tremblay, Daniel Salée, and others, yet is completely absent from *Invention*'s narrative. As I will argue in chapter 2, Québec's mythscape rests on a benevolent framing of Nouvelle-France. Mark Rifkin, borrowing from Raymond Williams, calls this framing the "modes of feeling" of settlement.[39] These modes of feeling guarantee the ethical and narrative coherence of Québec's de souche project. As Darryl Leroux argues, many scholars in Québec are deeply invested in this structure of feeling and reject scholarly critiques that take the province to task for its past and current settler-colonial role.[40]

When Québec celebrates these early alliances as a sign of a more benevolent form of encounter with Indigenous peoples, it fails to account for the long history of betrayal[41] that followed these alliances and that eventually left these so-called allies on the margins of their own territory. While Canada's role in betraying alliances since the creation of the country is undeniable, the province's investment in a narrative that portrays Nouvelle-France as somehow more benevolent, better intentioned, or more fraternal demonstrates here a form of selective memory that supports its own identity politics. *Invention* does little to disrupt this idealized narrative of the past. For instance, it is Philippe, Lescarbot's estranged brother, who brings the Indigenous Mexican workers to Montréal to force his brother to rethink the way he treats his employees. While Martin clearly argues that exploitation is currently taking place in Mexico, his critique of Alain Lescarbot centers on the latter's turn to a form of individualistic capitalism that betrays Québec's roots as a small nation built on communal solidarity. In attributing Lescarbot's exploitation of workers in Chihuahua to his loss of communal values and estrangement from Québec's roots, Martin fails to see how the current exploitation of Indigenous populations abroad is actually a continuation of Québec's colonialism and the expansion of its parasitic relationship to Indigenous peoples in the province. In Alain Lescarbot's lack of attachment to a past that his brother Philippe defends, Martin critiques Québec's propensity to forget and links this forgetting to a form of uprooted existence that is antithetical to a nation-building project—which, as Anderson and others argue, demands a stable sense of the collective. This critique, however, has little to do with Québec's relationship with Indigenous peoples of the province, even though it is partly the exploitation of Indigenous people in Mexico that serves as the symptom of Lescarbot's disarray. Martin employs these Indigenous workers as a mirror reflecting the Québécois malaise. It is through them (but not in relation to them) that we come to understand the erosion of Québec's community.

Martin deploys citationality in yet another way when he blurs the line between various levels of reenactment. To be clear, a great number of historical figures who are central to Québec's mythscape—like Champlain, Lescarbot, Radisson, and Papineau—appear in *Invention*. In some instances, these characters appear in scenes as themselves—that is, the actor portrays the historical figure—while in other scenes, Martin deploys them metatheatrically, by making them appear onstage as a persona played by one of *Invention*'s characters. In one scene set in 1608, for example, the historical Champlain designs a winter coat with Lescarbot, and the scene is presented as a revisiting of a stable past. As the scene ends and transitions to the next, the actor who plays Champlain becomes an actor, Guy Langlois, who, in 1971, joins his friends after portraying the historical figure of Champlain in a local play entitled *La Passion du Sieur de Champlain*. The 1608 Champlain who envisions a fruitful collaboration with the "savages" in Port Royal symbolizes in 1971 an identity that the French Québécois de souche must shed in order to gain access to modernity and success. Guy Langlois, along with his friends Steeve and Candy (who have English-sounding and, in the case of Steeve, incorrectly spelled names), are fascinated with all things American, seeing in the American dream the response to what they perceive as Québec's lack of ambition. Speaking to his mother who is a small-business owner, Steeve argues:

> United States of America! Christ, these people have put a man on the Moon! But here, we're stuck on old stuff; we're lost in our memories, fuck! We have to get over old stuff, France, spruce beer and eel fishing, for fuck's sake![42]

As Steeve speaks to his mother, Guy Langlois/Champlain arrives at Steeve's Montréal apartment riding a snowmobile through the 1971 snowstorm. He appears as one such *vieille affaire* (old thing or relic) that Steeve and his group would happily forget in their quest for the American dream.

Upon seeing Langlois in these anachronistic clothes, Steeve exclaims, "Que cé qui fait là en ski-doo pis en habit de français fif?"[43] ("What's he doing there on a skidoo dressed like a French fag?"). Champlain here is a figure of mockery who stands for Québec's old attachments to France, a motherland that, more so in 1971, sees Québec as no more than a provincial curiosity. Langlois (a tongue-in-cheek name since Anglois is the archaic spelling of Anglais, or English) openly ridicules the character he plays, adopting a French accent that impresses Steeve's mother, but is clearly meant as an object of ridicule for Langlois and his generation. The branding of Langlois as *fif* (a pejorative term for "gay" that has a definite effeminate connotation) once again serves as a metaphor for a national trajectory in which Québec must shed or reject the feminine/feminized to reach its full potential.

Throughout the play, Martin actively blurs the line between historical events and characters and the imagined genealogy that he draws from them, and between the dramatization of documented historical events and the impersonation of these historical figures as overt characters on stage. While this strategy links the past and the present and illuminates its traces and repercussions, it only does so for characters of the French Québécois de souche. Indeed, the Indigenous characters who appear in scenes taking place in Nouvelle-France do not traverse temporality in the same ways that their settler counterparts do; they are irrevocably presented as creatures of the past whose trajectory no longer intertwines with that of the French Québécois de souche after the arrival of the British. This suspension in time, Jodi A. Byrd argues, is what defines Indigenous bodies as "figures of transit" in the liberal states. Byrd argues that Indigenous bodies form the terrain on which "the liberal state and its supporters and critics struggle over the meaning of pluralism, habitation, inclusion, and enfranchisement." All the while, "indigenous peoples and nations, who provide the ontological and literal ground for such debates, are continually deferred into a past that never happened and a future that will never come."[44] Thus, from their status as early allies, *Invention* quickly relegates Indigenous characters to the position of figures of transit—or, as I argue, recasts them as operational sites for Québec's elaboration and cohesion of its sense of self. Membertou, Carinogan (the Innu spiritual leader), and the other Indigenous characters of the early scenes do not have a genealogical capacity that extends to the present. The Mexican workers who object to Lescarbot's work conditions in Chihuahua are the only exception to this phenomenon, but the genealogy they trace displaces Indigeneity to a foreign country rather than seeing its present incarnations in Québec. As the Mexican workers set the Lescarbot sewing plant ablaze, burning alive with Lescarbot and his coats, Martin also forecloses their future, making the workers' trajectories end with the fire that will finally liberate Lescarbot (and by extension, Québec) from forgetting, allowing frozen memories to flow again.

The play's citationality, its clever juxtaposition of recognizable signs of Québec's French de souche culture, imagines an ideal audience that is limited. Of course, all plays have a target audience, but Martin's play, in its gesture of historicizing a particular community, participates in, as Filewod contends, imagining and actualizing this community's constitutive elements. As Benedict Anderson argues, the inclusivity of nations is finite and cannot forever stretch its boundaries without losing its cohesion.[45] Martin's intended audience is clearly the French Québécois de souche for whom the play's signs are legible. Thus, the play misses one of its intended goals, that of including Indigenous audiences in an act of remembrance. If Martin decries the status of Indigenous peoples as "strangers from within," his play's hermetic citationality further illuminates their estrangement rather than performing a gesture of inclusion or a co-narration of the multiple histories that have shaped Québec's contested territory.

I argue that citationality functions in *Invention* as a way to embed Québec's mythscape in History with a capital H. Despite Martin's aforementioned disclaimers about history and the truth, his play's reiteration of certain signs that have supported the French Québécois de souche's mythscape—the so-called founding alliances between the French and the Mi'kmaqs, for example—fails to question the stability of the mythic sign itself. Martin plays with historical figures, pointing to the artifice of historicizing plays, but he goes only so far; and ultimately, the history he weaves in *Invention* reinscribes Québec's de souche narrative. That is, Martin may revisit the past, but he does not question its structural underpinnings and only contemplates decolonization as part of the French Québécois de souche community's trajectory. In other words, it is the French Québécois de souche who need to liberate themselves from their English Canadian shackles and colonized mentality. Martin's play, which so clearly writes Québec's mythscape as a gesture toward the future of the French Québécois de souche community, fails to ask a fundamental question: is Québec even capable of imagining itself as a nation outside of the settler-colonial frame in which Indigenous peoples are always already subjugated? Martin, it seems, fails to imagine Québec's decolonization—the complete rethinking of what equal cohabitation with Indigenous peoples might mean for this aspiring nation—as the way to liberate the words frozen in Pipmuacan. The imagined genealogy dramatized in *Invention* relies on Indigenous peoples as first interlocutors but fails to rethink Québec's relationship with them and thus perpetuates their status as strangers from within, alienated from the genealogical ability that Martin grants the French Québécois de souche.

Linguistic Alienation

Martin's historical exploration is by no means exhaustive: his play jumps from 1608 to 1635 and then to the Patriots' Rebellion of 1837 and, from there, leaves out two centuries of Bas-Canada and then Québec history before landing in the 1970s. The decades that preceded the 1970s are important. From 1945 to 1959, the province, led by Premier Maurice Duplessis, went through intense changes and witnessed the rise of the urban population and of a middle class, and the creation of a Québec intelligentsia and cultural elite—and all of these changes created a new ideological space in Québec. The traditional elites—the Catholic Church and Duplessis's conservative government—responded to these rapid societal changes by a tightening of the conservative policies in place. As a result, the province went through a period now referred to as "La Grande Noirceur" (the Great Darkness) characterized by censorship and isolationist policies and the positioning of Québec as an exporter of natural resources. The 1960s Revolution Tranquille, or Quiet Revolution, marked a dramatic change in Québec, as the new cultural and political elite that had emerged under Duplessis came of age and brought the Québécois, who had long been described as "nés pour un petit pain," to international prominence.[46] Under various leaderships, the province took control of and nationalized natural resources, implemented social reforms, and, with Expo '67 as a flagship event, forged a place for itself on the national and international scenes.

Invention does not engage with this period and jumps instead from Nouvelle-France to the decade that immediately followed the Quiet Revolution, dramatizing the emergence of nationalism in Québec's cultural and political arenas in the years from the mid-1960s through the 1970s. Martin pays particular attention to how the French Québécois de souche, inspired by critiques of colonialism like those of Fanon and Memmi, begin to define themselves as colonized subjects.[47] Martin dramatizes this emergent consciousness as a colonized people in a scene between Gaston Miron, the aforementioned poet whose work meditates at length on the colonized subject's linguistic alienation, and a young Pierre Lebeau, a well-known actor in Québec and a close friend of Martin's. Both are, of course, played by actors; the scene puts the two characters in conversation in 1972 at the National Theatre School, where Lebeau is studying to become an actor. As they unpack the poetic images in Miron's work, the two men engage in a philosophical conversation on the liberatory potential of language for colonized subjects. Speaking of Lebeau's experience of moving from *joual,* his stigmatized lower-middle-class Québécois patois, to the supposedly neutral French taught in theater schools and other elite-forming institutions, Miron echoes what Memmi calls the "bilingualism of colonized subjects." *Joual*, the dialect's name, is the representation of how its speakers pronounce the word "cheval" (horse). While Memmi refers to the specific situation of North African colonies in which the majority's language is supplanted by the language of the colonial minority (French, in this case), the situation of Québec differs in important ways. Indeed, linguistic alienation in Québec is felt, as Miron and Lebeau discuss, vis-à-vis two poles: European French and English. Referring to Lebeau's experience of being as foreign to Molière as he is to Shakespeare, Miron argues:

> MIRON: You have to go from colonial French, alienated, to French, and then you have to jump again to literary French? That's two jumps. Are you good at jumping Pierre?
>
> LEBEAU: I don't know.
>
> MIRON: We have lost the instinct for French, do you understand? We would have to reach the right riverbank again but our mouths are full of honey, non-assimilated English honey, and our guts are filled with bitterness; we have lost the instinct for sharp language, we are word-poor and metaphors no longer flow, I tell you.[48]

Echoing the legend of Pipmuacan, Miron argues that colonialism has frozen Québec and imprisoned its language in the shame of marginalization. He locates in language a liberatory site and claims that through poetry and a reappropriation of language, one can stage attacks against the *la marée dominante* (the dominant tidal wave).[49] He argues, "J'écris des poèmes comme on écrit des anticorps littéraires contre la Grande Dissolution" ("I write poetry like one writes literary antibodies against the Great Dissolution").[50] The "Great Dissolution" here is the end of the French Québécois de souche as a people, its dissolution into the dominant Anglo tidal wave. In a later scene, Serge, a member of the Comité Action-Chômage St-Roch (a support group for the unemployed in one of Québec City's historically working-class neighborhoods), attests to this state of alienation when he claims that he cannot translate the images that rise in him when he tries to participate in the exercise of self-historicizing: "The images don't want the words to speak! Ok! . . . Speak the people's sadness . . . the images don't want the words to speak Christ! Fuck! It seems pretty clear!"[51] Words fail him, Martin suggests,

Figure 1.3. *Invention du chauffage central en Nouvelle-France*: a meeting of the Comité Action-Chômage St-Roch (Pierre-Antoine Lasnier, Émilie Bibeau, Benoît Drouin-Germain, Marie-Ève Trudel, Alexis Martin, Luc Guérin, and Danielle Proulx). (Photo by Michel Ostaszewski)

because the pain and shame of colonization have suspended the capacity to name and speak a reality that hurts. It is this reality, repressed in a hidden part of his psyche, that Serge can no longer access and verbalize. (See figure 1.3.)

The character of Henri de Valence further embodies this notion of the alienated colonized subject in the second half of the play. De Valence, an actor who plays the French explorer Radisson[52] on a television series for the publicly funded television channel Radio-Canada, is kidnapped in the play by members of the Cartel de Libération du Québec, a separatist group that views the actor as a lackey of the federal propaganda machine. The scene echoes real events, namely two kidnappings of political figures by the Front de Libération du Québec (FLQ), a nationalist terrorist organization active in Québec in the 1960s and 1970s.[53] De Valence's real name in the play is Gratien Patenaude. He has changed his name and adopted an affected European French accent to hide his lower-class background and humble "colonized" identity. Again, multiple temporal layers and identity narratives are at play onstage. The Cartel refers to Radio-Canada as the "Empire's official organ" and equates de Valence's work, his affected accent, and his denial of his roots with a form of prostitution for the masters. That de Valence portrays Radisson on television is yet another sign of his complicity in advancing English

Canada's project of assimilating French Canadians in his abductors' eyes: Radisson was a Frenchman who became *coureur des bois*, only to switch allegiances from the French to the British in the fur-trading business of early colonization.

With this scene, Martin captures the very real anger that led to October 1970: English Canada did aggressively pursue assimilation policies toward francophone communities, especially the ones residing outside of Québec; and, as Mills and others have argued, the balance of power in Québec heavily favored the province's anglophone minority until the last three decades of the twentieth century. In jumping from the 1970s to the 1990s without touching on the real gains achieved by the French Québécois de souche politically, economically, and culturally, Martin suggests that Québec's liberation has yet to happen. He employs the legend of Pipmuacan as a metaphor for the identity crisis that plagues Québec and hampers the French Québécois de souche's becoming a liberated people. As Lucie argues vehemently in the aforementioned scene with the Narrator, Québec's sense of identity cannot emerge from the irreconcilable nature of its foundational and colonial descriptors—*Canadiens* and *Français*—two words that Martin's play attempts to exorcise.

Exorcising Colonial Descriptors?

Invention's exorcism of Québec's colonial descriptors aptly begins with a tense exchange that positions these irreconcilable poles (Canadien and Français) in the audience's minds. The scene takes place in 1998 in a restaurant in Old Québec City, where a tourist couple from France, Ségolène and Damien, are breaking up in the midst of Québec City's famous Winter Carnival. Damien and Ségolène are unemployed in France and, in a gesture that mimics the impulse of the first settlers of Nouvelle-France, they have left Dieppe and come to Québec on an "open ticket" in search of renewal, opportunities, and adventures. Damien is aggressively drunk (because, as he argues, *c'est ca qu'on fait dans les colonies* [that is what one does when visiting the colonies])[54] and he openly despises Québécois as hicks, imitating their accent with open disgust. Perhaps to mark the split between France and Québec, Martin wrote the dialogue between Ségolène and Damien in a form of French argot that exacerbates the differences rather than the commonalities between Québec and France. *Verlan*, which consists in transposing or inverting syllables (*verlan*: *l'envers*), is a form of French slang. Words like *ouf* (for *fou*), *keum* (*mec*), and *meuf* (*femme*) are not commonly used in Québec, where the argot grows out of more North American influences. Reflecting on this linguistic gap, Charles, an amateur historian from Québec City who witnesses the couple's altercation and helps Ségolène send Damien on his way, remarks humorously: "Quatre siècles nous séparent, mais une langue blessée nous réunit, si je puis dire, ah ah!" ("Four centuries set us apart, but a wounded language unites us if I may say so, ha ha!").[55] The two become friends, Charles helping the French newcomer survive her first winter nights on the continent like Indigenous people did in Nouvelle-France.

Ségolène, the lost soul from Dieppe, and Charles, the amateur historian leading history workshops for the unemployed and disenfranchised, embody two pillars of Québécitude in Martin's play. Ségolène stands in for the early colonizers who left a hostile environment in France to try their luck in Nouvelle-France, while Charles embodies Québec's collective memory, which is threatened by what Pierrot Ross-Tremblay and Nawel Hamidi call "Durham Syndrome,"[56] a form of forgetting specific to Québec's status as a colonized-colonizer. Ross-Tremblay and Hamidi borrow their appellation from the infamous 1839 *Report on the Affairs of British North America*, commonly known as the Durham Report. In this report, commissioned by Britain after the 1837 Patriots's Rebellion in Bas-Canada (Lower Canada), Lord Durham recommended that the freedoms granted to French Canadians under previous proclamations be rescinded and assimilation policies put in place to bring the French Canadians—who, according to Durham, had no history and no culture—into the British fold.[57]

The Durham Report is a wound in Québec's psyche and is frequently invoked to shape and solidify its imagined community. Durham, as Corrie Scott writes, employs the racial rhetoric of colonial regimes to describe French Canadians as inferior, "not so civilized, so energetic, or so money-making a race as that by which they are surrounded."[58] Ross-Tremblay and Hamidi locate the roots of Durham Syndrome in the string of assimilation policies that followed the Durham Report and positioned French Canadians as devalued within Canada. For the two authors, this marginalization led to the francophone majority defining itself through a discourse oscillating between abjection and desire vis-à-vis two poles—the colonizing English Canadians and the *sauvages* (savages). Ross-Tremblay and Hamidi identify in the French Canadians' fear of being *sauvages* the "collective interiorizing of a will to not mix with them (the savages), perhaps as a way to gain the approval of the new British masters." They continue:

> Added to this fear of being "savages" is the opposing gesture, an attempt to assuage one's sense of guilt by claiming "I too have Indian blood." This quest for "Indianness" linked to the fiction of blood quantum and genetics reveals a central element of Québec's identity crisis.[59]

While *métissage* may have played a part in the early experience in Nouvelle-France (see chapter 2), the structural positions occupied by the French settler and the Indigenous woman were never fundamentally challenged by this early period of cohabitation. Indeed, if French settlers could move in and out of *indianité*, the same could not be said for the women with whom they formed unions. Race, as many scholars argue, is profoundly relational. When British colonization occurred, most French Canadians became lesser citizens, indeed, but citizens nevertheless. Their assimilation was imagined by the British crown as taking place within the structural family of white citizenry. That is, the French Canadians were imagined as inferior but nevertheless possessing the racial mobility necessary to reintegrate whiteness. The "savage," however, became a ward of the state who could only, and much later, become a citizen through a process of total cultural assimilation. In other words, French settlers could play at being Indian, but it was understood, in the racializing discourse of colonialism, that they remained part of the larger family of those who, like the British, had the capacity to colonize and civilize—a capacity that the "savages" did not have.

Genealogical Performance: *Neptune* at the Comité Action-Chômage

As I will argue in chapter 2, Québec is currently taking a métis turn, revisiting its past to affirm that we are, in fact, a métis people, born of the encounter between benevolent French men and Indigenous women. I contend that this recuperative move allows the French Québécois de souche to reposition themselves as Indigenous, claiming a position that legitimizes their national project. A scene in the second half of the play exemplifies this recuperative gesture. Members of Charles's group, the Comité Action-Chômage St-Roch, reenact segments of Québec's history dressed in period costumes in honor of Québec's famous Winter Carnival taking place outside. This exercise is meant to encourage the participants "to become more than passive witnesses of their own narrative" and instead become "the authors of their history," as one of the members, Madame Circé-Côté, explains.[60] The real Éva Circé-Côté (1871–1949) was a free spirit: a writer and a feminist, she founded the first municipal library in Montréal. In the play, she leads the theatrical game in her living room near a woodstove that she fuels by feeding it "fresh copies of the Durham Report," positioning the report's impact on Québec as ongoing.[61] The game is intended to empower the disenfranchised members of the group and effectively constructs an imagined community by enacting its narrative onstage. Dressed as Papineau, Captain Perry, or a member of Port Royal's Order of Good Cheer, the members of Charles's group rewrite the past with the help of Madame Circé-Côté. While they vehemently decry anachronisms, they seem oblivious to how their exercise reinscribes the erasure of Indigenous peoples through a process of surrogation that replays a very early colonial gesture.

Indeed, it is Ségolène, the French woman, who is assigned the role of an Indigenous woman in the group's reenactment. Madame Circé-Côté gives her "un costume Etchemin . . . un costume de squaw en peau que ma mère avait mis au Bal du Gouverneur quand la reine était venue en '56" ("an Etchemin costume . . . a buckskin squaw costume that my mother wore to the Governor's Ball when the Queen visited in '56").[62] The layers of surrogation contained in this embodiment of an Etchemin (Maliseet) woman are numerous and echo Philip Deloria's famous work on America's habit of defining itself through and against symbols of "Indianness." Ségolène's "squaw costume" marks Québec's identity through difference. Originally worn by a French-Canadian woman (Circé-Côté's mother in the play) at a colonial ball in honor of the Queen of England's visit to her colony, the costume is saturated with many narratives of affiliation and contestation. Given that the original wearer was part of the marginalized French Québécois de souche community, this masquerade of Indigeneity may have been deployed to perform what Ross-Tremblay and Hamidi described as the fear of "being savages,"[63] exteriorized here through a turn to the carnivalesque. The costume may have also performed the political gesture of aligning its original wearer with a form of indigeneity to the continent, signifying a refusal of Britain's assimilation policies toward the French Canadians. Even in the latter gesture, French Canadians' claim to indigeneity on unceded Indigenous territories could only happen through the erasure of its original inhabitants. This instance of racial masquerade thus marks the erasure of Indigenous bodies, their marking as figures of transit, as a precondition for a French Québécois de souche identity to emerge.

This collapsing of Ségolène (herself a French character played by a Québécoise) with the Maliseet/Etchemin woman harks back to the first Western theatrical performance recorded in what is now Canada (the continent's Indigenous peoples had of course been performing before that date). On November 14, 1606, a group of French men from the outpost of Port Royal (now Nova Scotia's Annapolis Royal) staged *Théâtre de Neptune en la Nouvelle-France*, a nautical masque written by Port Royal's interim leader, Marc Lescarbot. Lescarbot wrote the short play to celebrate the return of Samuel de Champlain and the Sieur de Poutrincourt from a long exploration voyage that had left Port Royal vulnerable to mutinous discontent. Lescarbot and his men had faced a difficult and deadly winter and, on the eve of the new cold season, the men's morale was in dire need of an infusion of patriotism. Emulating the public masques and nautical extravaganzas in vogue in France since the Renaissance, *Théâtre de Neptune* was performed on the open waters of the Annapolis Basin for the French men from the outpost and the neighboring Mi'kmaq people assembled on the beach. Traveling on the ocean aboard "a small flotilla of boats decorated with classical motifs,"[64] Neptune, six tritons, and four "Indians" (Frenchmen in redface)—or *sauvages*, as they were called in French—welcomed the returning party, offering praise and sustenance to Poutrincourt as the representative of the King of France. Following the Tritons' welcoming speech to Poutrincourt, the four *sauvages* pledged submission to the King of France:

It is not only in France
That Cupid reigns,
But also in New France.
As with you he also lights
His firebrand here; and with his flames
He scorches our poor souls.
And plants there his flag.[65]

This nautical masque was more than a source of entertainment to rally French morale: it served to inscribe through enactment the imagined community of Nouvelle-France. As Jerry Wasserman writes in the introduction of the 400th-anniversary reprint of Lescarbot's playtext: "Through the symbolism of performance, the play dramatically reinforces the contract between ruler and ruled that promises the subjects' survival and prosperity in return for their fealty."[66] The colonizers ventriloquized Indigenous peoples as a way to reaffirm and legitimate their colonizing project at the eve of another winter that could undermine their resolve. Survival may have necessitated friendlier interactions with the Mi'kmaq, but colonization nevertheless necessitated their submission. The masque performs here an ideal scenario of desired conquest, the *sauvages* willfully offering their land. This scenario never happened, of course: Québec and the Maritime provinces still stand for the most part on unceded territories for which, aside from a few exceptions, no treaties were ever signed (see chapter 3).

This ventriloquizing of Indigenous peoples by settlers served then and still serves today to consolidate the settler community's coherent sense of self. Meditating on the possible reactions of the Mi'kmaq spectators upon seeing their identities reenacted by colonizers who pledged allegiance to a foreign king in perfectly phrased couplets, Filewod writes: "We don't know because of course, nobody asked them."[67] He observes that for the Mi'kmaq viewers, the spectacle of Lescarbot's *Neptune* was probably incomprehensible as text and as performance, and that "two sets of eyes" (those of the French and the Mi'kmaq) "saw two very different events"[68] that day in 1606. This perceptual and representational gap, as Filewod calls it, still organizes the ventriloquizing relationship between Indigenous peoples and settlers today.

Invention creates a similar ventriloquizing moment by imagining and staging what amounts to the idealized missing reaction shot in which an imaginary camera captures the Mi'kmaq's reception of the masque as they stood on the shore in 1606. The reaction shot, a basic element of film grammar, supplies the audience (here the French Québécois de souche community) with images of an interlocutor's response in a dialogue or after an event, thus guiding the audience's emotional response. To be clear, *Invention*'s reaction shot is a delayed one, since it takes place two years after the performance of Lescarbot's play, but the scene I will now discuss features the same historical figures who participated in or witnessed *Neptune* two years earlier. In

Figure 1.4. *Invention du chauffage central en Nouvelle-France*: a Jesuit meets an Innu shaman (Alexis Martin, Shaddy the dog, Pierre-Antoine Lasnier). (Photo by Michel Ostaszewski)

Invention, the scene takes place between Lescarbot, Champlain, Membertou, and other Port Royal settlers. Since the winter of 1606, the men of Port Royal have created L'Ordre de Bon Temps (the Order of Good Cheer) as a mutual aid society in which settlers and Mi'kmaq join forces to provide food for the settlement during winter.

The scene begins with a scenario that closely echoes *Neptune*'s encounter. Champlain addresses Membertou, thanking him for his exemplary hospitality, wisdom, and kindness. The French settler remarks that if not for their lack of religion, Membertou's peoples (who were Mi'kmaq, not Maliseet, as Martin's use of the word *Etchemins* might suggest) would be equal to Frenchmen on all points. Membertou replies "Visage pale parle avec sagesse et Membertou et les Etchemins l'en remercient. . . . La terre est assez grande pour accueillir ta tribu" ("Pale face speaks with wisdom and Membertou and the Etchemins thank him. . . . The land is big enough to welcome your tribe").[69] The rest of Membertou's speech is poetic, but in his attempt to convey Membertou as a newcomer to the French language, Martin nevertheless flirts with stereotypical renditions of "Hollywood" Indian speech; that is, of Indigenous characters reduced to speaking in primitive forms. Numerous accounts from Indigenous and non-Indigenous sources attest to the great oratory traditions of many Indigenous nations.[70] Martin's writing thus performs ambiguous work here. More importantly, Martin's reaction shot, the moment in which the audience turns to Membertou and hears his support of the settlers' enterprise, replays a scenario in which Indigenous peoples willfully surrender their land and offer their friendship to the Europeans. As Filewod and others argue, no historical documents surrounding the *Théâtre de Neptune* accounts for the Mi'kmaq's response to the performance: their reaction is of no consequence in the historical records of the French empire. Martin's imagined scene in Port Royal, two years after Lescarbot's masque, imaginatively closes this gap and, in the process, problematically re-legitimates French settler colonialism by staging yet another moment of Indigenous consent. Indeed, two years later, Membertou is still an ally.

That Martin chooses to imagine a reaction shot in early Nouvelle-France and then remove Indigenous characters from most of *Invention*'s scenes taking place after early colonization betrays a selective memory. A reaction shot in 1990, during the events in Oka, would disrupt Martin's benevolent narrative of alliances between the French and Indigenous peoples and surely circumscribe any prelapsarian moment of comradeship to a very short moment that should not be deployed as an extenuating factor in Québec's current relationship with Indigenous peoples.

Reconciliation in Absentia

Nowhere is the surrogation process that began with *Théâtre de Neptune* more palpable than in the scene in *Invention* between Mireille and Takraliq, the Inuk survivor of the Residential School system put in place by Canada and enacted in each province by various churches and provincial and federal governmental agencies. Residential Schools in Canada, with their mission of "killing the Indian within the child," lasted for over a century, and their effects were devastating on Indigenous communities. Besides their direct attacks on the fabric of Indigenous cultures and communities, the schools were deadly places: malnutrition and epidemics in unsanitary conditions accounted for their high death toll. Physical, sexual, and mental abuse left many more wounded, a pain that has trickled down to the following generations. The parents and communities left behind also suffered an immense trauma, as the federally mandated Truth and Reconciliation Commission has recently attempted to illuminate. The TRC, while flawed in many important ways, provided a public space for these harrowing testimonials of multigenerational trauma.

While the lack of transparency from institutions such as various levels of government and churches complicit in the Residential School system have been and should continue to be criticized as obstacles to reconciliation, the public audiences and various testimonial rooms allowed survivors to come forward and speak their truths. Many survivors spoke of their testimonials as a gesture of self-healing and questioned the settler communities' willingness to participate in a real dialogue, in real reparation and healing, given their governments' and institutions' lack of transparency. During the TRC, Indigenous witnesses and supporters asked critically how they could reconcile with a government that would not transparently come forward and which continued to oppress them on other fronts.

This is the pain that Takraliq nurses in a bar in Montréal in *Invention*. The scene, which takes place during the 1998 ice storm, begins as Mireille, a young *qallunaat*, or white person,[71] seeks refuge from the storm and enters a neighborhood bar on Ontario Street. There she meets Takraliq, whom the barman describes as "a paquet de troubles,"[72] a heap of troubles. The stage directions describe Takraliq as "a fifty-something Inuk woman standing in front of a strange disco light, in a state of tranquil stupor."[73] On stage, the disco lights' bluish hue envelops Takraliq and evokes the frozen surfaces of Pipmuacan. Takraliq is in the midst of an inner monologue in which Inuktitut, French, and English collide, with all language proving inadequate in naming her pain.

> *Qannipuq*
> *Aputiit angiyurlait, aputiit tingmiaq isaruriyuyaartangit*
> *Aputik atyigiituinnaq*
> *Aputik taannasainnausuni katagaqattatuq*
> *Uqumaittuusuni qasiutsunilu*
> *Taikuuna ullukut*
> *That day*
> *A white man*
> *The white man came the same day it was the same snow as today*
> L'homme blanc a dit que mes parents auraient plus les allocations familiales si leurs enfants allaient pas à l'école des blancs.
> À l'école des blancs
> Huit cent *miles* de chez nous! 800 *mailinik anarraniivanga*
> Au Sud!
> *At the beginning I was alone, for days alone*
> *Empty beds around me and the silence*
> *Heavy*
> *Falling snow.*[74]

Words pour out of Takraliq at the very moment when the *qallunaat* city that normally pays so little attention to her is imprisoned in ice and forced to a standstill. Martin seems to suggest that it takes this moment of suspension for Takraliq's words to be heard. Perhaps this is why Mireille decides to listen to Takraliq while all the other customers ignore her. Takraliq, sensing Mireille's interest, interrupts her monologue to say, "You want my photo, *qallunaat*? Pay me a drink!"[75] While drinking together, Takraliq tells Mireille about her Residential School experience, naming the shame she felt when she left school, and the sensation of cold she experienced for the very first time when she started wearing the *qallunaat* clothes the school provided. Cold also permeated her life when she was forbidden to speak Inuktitut (her words frozen inside her). Takraliq's story betrays how churches, including the Catholic Church (Québec was, before the Quiet Revolution, staunchly Catholic) and the provincial and federal governments are all complicit in the implementation of the Residential Schools that broke families and imposed a regime of shame and violence on generations of Indigenous children.

Takraliq alternates between the three languages that have shaped her life under the settler-colonial regime of Canada and Québec; her inclusion of French signals Québec's complicity in the Residential Schools system, which is too often simplistically described as a federal policy. While the federal government did create the schools, they functioned with the assistance of the provinces and the local churches, which generally chose to ignore the violence that took place within school walls. In having Takraliq speak in these three languages at this moment, Martin hints at the violence that underlies Canada and Québec's civil societies, a violence that was tolerated as a way to solidify the borders of civil society and settler identity. In other words, one was Canadian or Québécois because one was shielded from—could not be sent to, as "savages" were—these Residential Schools. Martin seems to suggest that this shameful past can only emerge in the fissure in time created by the ice storm, a moment that rendered Québec vulnerable.

If Martin seems to open a space of repentance here, he quickly closes it. When Takraliq's torrent of words comes to an end, Mireille shivers and responds, "J'ai froid" ("I am cold").[76] The world that Takraliq describes is threatening, a thermal shock for Mireille's conception of herself. Like that, the play quickly turns away from Takraliq's pain to attend to its impact on Mireille's white fragility. The scene becomes about Mireille's shivering and ways to warm her up. Takraliq offers Mireille a piece of seal blubber, "qu'on donne au chasseur quand y fait froid" ("that which we give to the hunter when it is cold"), and in the process of chewing the blubber together, the two women seem to reach a point of reconciliation.[77] The stage is then bathed in warmer shades of light, and fog appears on the panels of the glass enclosure, suggesting that Takraliq has offered a form of absolution to all *qallunaat*, a gesture translated visually by the warmth that permeates the stage. Mireille does not say much in the scene; she mostly listens to Takraliq's testimonial. This certainly embodies a first step in the right direction when it comes to the silence surrounding the horrors of the Residential Schools in Canada.

To be sure, Mireille's few words ("J'ai froid"), with the accompanying stage direction that specifies her affect as *émue* (touched), reflect a form of empathy and her sense of accessing and identifying with Takraliq's pain and cold loneliness. While this gesture of communion can be read as potentially liberating and healing, bringing the two parties to a sense of understanding, I would like to reflect for a moment on the gesture of consumption—the sharing and chewing of blubber—through which Martin imagines this closure. Saidiya Hartman has compared empathy to a form of "facile intimacy"[78] in which the empathizer, in the process of making the other's pain her own, "begins to feel for [her]self rather than for those whom this exercise in imagination presumably is designed to reach."[79] In other words, empathy is slippery and facile precisely because it brings the empathizer back to herself through the consumption of the other's pain. Mireille's consumption of Takraliq's pain leaves her feeling cold, a malaise that Takraliq then alleviates by sharing the blubber. This time, consumption signals Takraliq's forgiveness and closure.

Despite its good intention, there is something troubling in Martin's staging of this theatrical reconciliatory act in the absence of an Indigenous audience. In its first production *Invention* featured an all-white cast. Takraliq was thus played by a non-Indigenous actor. While this changed when Dominique Pétin (Huron-Wendat) joined the cast on tour and for the 2014 remount for the Festival Transamériques, she was not identified as Indigenous in any of the material about the play. And the fact remains that the play's intended audience is imagined as (and is) non-Indigenous. Indeed, the Nouveau Théâtre Expérimental audience is predominantly non-Indigenous (as is the case with most theater companies in the province). To reach a large number of Indigenous audience members, the NTE would have had to actively reach out to the regions of the province where Indigenous communities are situated.

This is not to say that reconciliation with Indigenous peoples should not enter Québec's definition of itself, but the reconciliation that Martin imagines here is a one-way street. Martin's play meditates at length on the Québécois de souche's resentment vis-à-vis the British colonizers and imagines Pipmuacan as the vehicle through which resentment and alienation can be purged. When it comes to the resentment that Indigenous people may feel, *Invention* quickly demands closure. This is because Indigenous resentment, as I will argue in chapter 4, threatens to expose the fissure, the ethical incoherence in Québec's discourse. The French Québécois de souche's sense of identity as a colonized minority is indeed irreconcilable with their role as a settler community in the past and with their ongoing participation in the oppression of Indigenous cultures, languages, and territories.

Where the resolution of the French Québécois de souche's identity crisis leaves the Indigenous peoples of Québec is unclear in Martin's narrative. What *Invention* makes abundantly clear, however, is that it is once again through Indigenous peoples that the settlers will weather that (identity) storm. Indeed, as stated in the play when the words of the land of Pipmuacan will finally be freed, it is not the identity crisis of the Algonquians or any of the Indigenous nations of Québec, or even the relationship between these nations and the French Québécois de souche, that will be resolved. The resolution that Martin envisions will liberate the French Québécois de souche from their colonial forbears: Canada and France. It will "give birth to a child liberated from resentment."[80]

The TRC was circulating when *Invention* premiered, and the commission held its public audiences in Montréal in April 2013. The Truth and Reconciliation Commission is based on the premise that listening and bearing witness are the first steps toward reconciliation. If the TRC, like any other reconciliation process, involves testimonials or "truth-sharing" (an appellation meant to appease those who might see it as a tribunal), it also demands that perpetrators recognize their own roles in the conflict. In moments of truth-sharing in Montréal, witnesses simply listened to a survivor's story, offering their support in the release of the survivors' personal narratives. As Catherine Cole argues in her book on South Africa's TRC, so much of the reconciliatory potential of these commissions has been located in the liveness of their hearings and in the fact that victims and perpetrators had to encounter one another, and face each other, when presenting their testimonials. The audience, she argues, is then called upon to bear witness to the victims' trauma and simultaneously act as judges of the offenders.[81] Philip Auslander argues that there is an assumption of truth in liveness, "an unexamined belief that live confrontation can somehow give rise to the truth in ways that recorded representations cannot."[82] Echoing Auslander, Cole argues that this assumption needs challenging and that testimonials and the act of witnessing do not necessarily give access to or open up the truth.

If live testimonials cannot grant access to the whole truth, a reconciliation performed by a settler voice in the absence of Indigenous voices reveals very little truth, if any at all. It presents the audience with the possibility of empathic identification without making any demands on them. There is no discomfort, there are no real face-to-face encounters with the survivors of the Residential Schools that existed close to one's settler community, and there is no responsibility as a witness. If Martin comes close to a moment of discomfort for his intended audience, he quickly finds a way to restore the relationship between Mireille and Takraliq to where it has always been in Québec's imaginary: Takraliq reaches out and provides the blubber that will warm Mireille, that will appease the part of her that might have been unsettled for a moment upon hearing Takraliq's story. Takraliq's offering strangely resembles that of the three "savages" in Lescarbot's play. In all cases, the figure of the "savage" voluntarily offers up land, knowledge, and sustenance in a gesture that gives coherence and legitimacy to the settler's sense of self. In sharing the blubber with Takraliq, Mireille is somehow absolved.

Alexis Martin's cycle of plays belongs to a moment in Québec in which Indigenous art in particular is garnering unprecedented attention. Short films by the young First Nations filmmakers of the Wapikoni Mobile project receive consistent praise in festivals in Québec and abroad, and musicians like Samian (Anishinaabe), Shauit (Innu), Florent Vollant (Innu), and Elisapie Isaac (Inuk) all have a growing fan base among the French Québécois de souche community. While this climate of relative openness is undoubtedly positive, it is important, as this chapter argues, to remain vigilant about the narrative and the status of Indigenous peoples as figures of transit that these gestures of inclusion perniciously reinscribe. As *Invention* demonstrates, the narrative that holds Québec together as an aspiring nation demands the affirmation of Québec's status as a colonized minority vis-à-vis English Canada, the racialization of its Franco-European population, and the erasure of Indigenous nations to elevate the French Québécois de souche community to the status of rightful owners of the land. Even given its inclusive mission, *Invention* cannot accommodate the competing narrative of presence, sovereignty, and cultural survival of the Indigenous nations whose preexisting narratives and presence compete with Québec's narrative of belonging. Instead, the play reinscribes their willful surrender, relegates their presence to a distant past, and, when Indigenous presence erupts in the present, quickly ventriloquizes a form of absolution of the French Québécois de souche and a reconciliation that solidifies the latter's identity as, if not an oppressed minority, then at least a lesser evil than English Canada has been toward Indigenous peoples.

Chapter 2

✦

Les Racines Imaginaires/Mythical *Métissages*

Québec and the Ruse of the Métis Turn

> Aboriginality [*l'autochtonie*], it is the community of people born or who arrived in a country, on a territory, in a geographical space in order to inhabit it but above all else, to love inhabiting it.
>
> —Jean Désy, *Amériquoisie*

> As I put it, settler-colonizers come to stay.
>
> —Patrick Wolfe, "Settler Colonialism and the Elimination of the Native"

While promoting the documentary film *L'Empreinte* (2014; *The Imprint*), the actor and environmental activist Roy Dupuis appeared on Québec's hugely popular talk show *Tout le monde en parle* (*Everybody Is Talking about It*) hosted by Guy A. Lepage, a well-known comedian and provocateur. The show airs on Radio-Canada television on Sunday nights and, like the original French talk show it emulates, *Tout le monde en parle* consists of lively interviews and round-table discussions of recent news and important events. Its guests are public personalities from various spheres of interest, and it is not rare to see intellectuals rub elbows with actors or sports celebrities.

Roy Dupuis was on *Tout le monde en parle* on February 22, 2015, as the narrator and main protagonist of *L'Empreinte*, a film that purports to be a "journey at the heart of our identity."[1] There, Dupuis quickly made clear whose identity the film is exploring: "our" identity here points to that of the French Québécois de souche or the *né-natif*, to borrow an expression often used in Québec to indicate French Québécois' multigenerational (and thus seemingly rightful) belonging to a particular place. The Québécois de souche is usually understood as white and counts French ancestors who came to North America to populate Nouvelle-France. Thus "our" identity, as the film imagines it, does not include new immigrants to the province, non-white francophones, or those who cannot claim a connection to France.[2]

According to *L'Empreinte* and its narrator, the ever-debated identity of the French Québécois de souche is in a state of crisis. Echoing Alexis Martin's diagnostic of amnesia, the film suggests that "we" have forgotten who "we" are and what makes "us" distinct. Roy Dupuis, meditating on his own identity quest, told Lepage on *Tout le monde en parle*:

> I was shooting a film in France. To me, France was the motherland. Somehow, I thought it should have resembled me . . . I realized that, in the end, I was not French at all. France is a society with a strong hierarchy, for instance, and that is not part of my values as a Québécois. I came back and asked myself: If I am not like them, who am I? Where am I from?[3]

Dupuis's sense of alienation from France, a country that he, like many in the province, had long claimed to explicate his identity as a French Québécois de souche, shook the actor and left him with pressing questions that *L'Empreinte* now explores. Dupuis and the film ask: if "we," as French Québécois de souche, cannot trace the roots of our collective cultural identity back to France (and our national narrative certainly still forbids affinities with the British or Americans), then who are we? To be clear, Dupuis's estrangement cannot be generalized, but it represents a growing trend in the province, as Darryl Leroux and Adam Gaudry note in their recent work.[4]

In a cinematic gesture marked by romantic longing and colonial appropriation, Dupuis and *L'Empreinte*'s writers and directors, Carole Poliquin and Yvan Dubuc, turned to Indigenous peoples (as have many before them) for a solution to their case of settler anxiety. Indeed, the film traces the answer to Dupuis's identity conundrum back to Nouvelle-France and its oft-mythologized *société métissée* (mixed/métis society). I touched on this idyllic trope in my discussion of Alexis Martin's play *Invention du chauffage central en Nouvelle-France* in chapter 1. However, contrary to *Invention*, which gives the *société métissée* trope a finite temporal (that is to say, past) frame, *L'Empreinte* invests this narrative of *métissage* with unprecedented explanatory power when it comes to Québec's contemporary identity and futurity as a distinct nation. According to *L'Empreinte*'s creators, many of Québec's current policies, social institutions, and ways of being can be explained by "our" connection with Indigenous cultures, which Dupuis describes, paraphrasing the Huron-Wendat scholar Georges Sioui, as "circular, women-centered, and egalitarian."[5] Dupuis and the film contend that this imprint—this *empreinte*—made centuries ago by the early *métissages* in Nouvelle-France is at the core of who "we" now are. The film yearns for a simple explanation for "our" identity malaise and comes to the following thesis: "we" have forgotten the prelapsarian moment of harmonious intermixing with Indigenous peoples that defined "us" in Nouvelle-France, and "we" need to remember it to become whole again. In other words, "we," the

French Québécois de souche, need to recognize and reclaim ourselves as a métis people.

What explains this "métis turn," as I will call it in this chapter, as the remedy to the French Québécois de souche's unresolved identity crisis? The relationship between the French Québécois de souche and Indigenous peoples is ambivalent at best. While institutions are slowly changing, racism and intolerance against Indigenous peoples remain alive and well in the province. Take, for instance, the Sûreté du Québec's predatory behavior toward Indigenous women in the city of Val d'Or, a police brutality scandal that only recently made the headlines,[6] despite the fact that this form of institutional violence is neither new nor isolated. Indeed, police brutality toward Indigenous peoples is not an aberration, but a continuation of the same violence that excludes them from real decisional power and often coerces their consent in negotiation processes in which so-called better living conditions are conditional on the extinction of Indigenous territorial rights. This violence is quotidian and exemplified in how Indigenous peoples' health, education, environmental safety, and sovereignty are always positioned as secondary to those of the majority. In 2016, the Innu poet and slam artist Natasha Kanapé Fontaine and the novelist Deni Ellis Béchard published *Kuei, je te salue: Conversation sur le racisme* (*Kuei, I Salute You: Conversations on Racism*) as an urgent call for a frank discussion on the widespread racism toward Indigenous peoples in Québec.[7] How, then, does a film like *L'Empreinte* manage to coherently claim as kin this other who is otherwise widely positioned as abject?

I contend, drawing from Bruno Cornellier, that it is with the idea of Nativeness as a thing, which is irrevocably located in the past and dislocated from the lived reality of, and tremendous violence faced by, Indigenous peoples that the film and those whose position it represents claim affiliation. Cornellier calls it *la chose indienne*, that "Indian thing," and describes it as "an index designating a conveniently imprecise truth about 'them.' "[8] The film is enamored with that *chose indienne*, that "convenient Indian," to play on Thomas King's expression,[9] because it gives French Québécois de souche identity, or Québécitude, a convenient and absolving frame in which to redefine itself. And while the film happily claims an Indigenous imprint, it certainly does not link this newfound métis-hood to a concrete form of reparation or restitution for Indigenous peoples in the present. On the contrary, the film indirectly suggests that all French Québécois de souche have a claim to Nativeness (and, indeed, that Nativeness can be acquired), and that this shared Nativeness should serve as the basis of "our" renewed identity. One of the interviewees, the anthropologist Serge Bouchard, goes so far as to suggest that we should "remake our national history" to reflect this métis identity.[10] Where this exploration leaves Indigenous peoples, the very people whose identity is at play here, is left unsettled.

Indeed, as I argue in this chapter, the film is not a real sensate and possibly altering encounter "with our Indian brothers" as Dupuis asserts, but an exercise, like Alexis Martin's play, in reaffirming Québécitude in a parasitic relationship with Indigenous peoples. To do so, the film builds on affect to solidify its explanation of who "we" are. In a later part of his *Tout le monde en parle* interview, Roy Dupuis explains how working as an environmental activist in Québec allowed him to encounter the province's "Native civilizations" and that, through this contact, he began to feel that the cultural ties that unite Québécois and Indigenous peoples were stronger than those with France. I insist here on the word "feel" because so much of *L'Empreinte*'s affective charge hinges on what I call a discourse of "felt Nativeness." Time after time, the film reinforces this notion that to "feel" Native is somehow enough, never problematizing how this desire to possess Nativeness, to absorb it, is, as Aileen Moreton-Robinson argues, inherently settler-colonial. It betrays a desire to somehow dislocate oneself from the side of the oppressors, performing what Tuck and Yang aptly call a "settler's move to innocence." These settlers' moves to innocence "problematically attempt to reconcile settler guilt and complicity, and rescue settler futurity."[11] *L'Empreinte* attempts to do just that—that is, to coerce the past into legitimating the futurity of the French Québécois de souche as métis or, at the very least, as aligned with Indigenous peoples in their common status as "oppressed" peoples.

This chapter examines what is at stake in proposing a national creation story that positions the French Québécois de souche as métis from the start. This proposal has occurred in a context of heated debate over who can self-identify as Métis following the 2003 *R. v. Powley*[12] and the 2016 *Daniels v. Canada*[13] decisions by the Supreme Court of Canada, which have led to a rise in self-identifying métis nations.[14] If *L'Empreinte* never goes as far as claiming these rights for all French Québécois de souche, it certainly suggests, using poorly contextualized genealogical data in ways that conflate blood and culture with peoplehood, that most of "us" have "Indian blood." Drawing from Donna Haraway and Kim Tallbear, I examine in this chapter how *L'Empreinte* performs telling slippages employing genetic sciences to legitimize a creation story that effectively appropriates Nativeness.

Finally, this chapter also turns to the award-winning film *Québékoisie* (2014) by Mélanie Carrier and Olivier Higgins and traces how it too flirts with the métis turn. This film, though it provides a more reciprocal attempt at encountering Indigenous peoples, nevertheless turns to what Pierrot Ross-Tremblay calls "the fiction of blood" to reconcile Québec's settler project with a form of Native futurity. I am particularly interested in the narrative of an Innu man who embarks on a quest to discover a distant French ancestor in Normandy. The film follows him as he patiently seeks and finally finds distant relatives in France. Higgins and Carrier juxtapose this sequence with that of a number of French Québécois de souche who claim to have Indigenous ancestors. The film is attached to a redemptive narrative in which upon finding that we "all have a bit of each other's blood," Indigenous peoples and French Québécois de souche might come to a better understanding of one another and to a common societal project. Drawing from this example, I reflect on how genealogical data, when harnessed in service to specific agendas, can become tools to further erase the racial mobility of white settlers.

The "Mythology of *Métissage*"

Before I turn to an analysis of *L'Empreinte*'s affective labor, however, I find it important to provide some context around the notions of métis, Métis, and métishood. While this chapter does not engage directly with the political debates surrounding the articulation of métis identity in Canada, I acknowledge that the aforementioned terms are loaded. The words *métis*, *métissé*, and *métissage* are often used to signal mixed ancestry in French as well as in Canadian politics at large. For instance, in his recent national bestseller *A Fair Country*, John Ralston Saul declared Canada a "métis nation,"[15] a thesis that Dupuis, Poliquin, and Dubuc clearly endorse in *L'Empreinte*. If for Saul et al. to be métis gestures broadly to being mixed, the term *Métis* with a capital "M" means something different in the Canadian Prairies, most notably around the Red River Valley in Manitoba. There it signals an Indigenous people, the Métis, who possess "a sense of separate identity"[16] from settlers and, for that matter, other Indigenous nations. Historically, the Métis (and their diaspora) were born out of the early intermarriages of French men and Indigenous women (mostly Cree), but this community quickly developed a sense of self as a "New Nation" with its own customs, languages (Cree, Michif, Bungi, and others), ways of life, and so on. In other words, Métis identity is not "a waypoint" or a "transfer station between Whiteness and Indianness,"[17] remarks the Métis scholar Adam Gaudry; it is an Indigenous identity with its own living culture, geographical affiliation, and political history.

As Gaudry and others argue, the name *métis* has been rendered vulnerable to misappropriations by changes in institutional terminology effected by various Canadian governments. For instance, the replacement of the appellation *half-breed,* which was deemed pejorative, with the seemingly more neutral word *métis* shifted the definition of the term away from Métis peoplehood and toward a racialized categorization of métis-as-mixed. This métis-as-mixed understanding opens the appellation to all and de-historicizes the Métis nation. It also implies a hierarchy of authenticity, with métis identity being somehow diluted or less Indigenous (which is erroneously imagined as unmixed).

For Gaudry, Métis identity is profoundly historical and situated, and events like the Battle of the Seven Oaks (1816) and the Red River Resistance (1869) show that Métis people have fought time and time again to remain Métis, with their own forms of governance and legal principles. "They did not view their identity as a waypoint on a longer journey. This was who they were, and nobody was going to take that from them."[18] For the Métis scholar/

blogger Chelsea Vowel, Métis people are too often reduced to the status of hybrid people and portrayed as a "catchall" identity for anyone "who has a single Indigenous ancestor 300 years ago" or for "those who otherwise find themselves without a clear indigenous label."[19] Métis scholars differentiate between métis-as-mixed and Métis as a form of peoplehood and, for many, this peoplehood only applies to the Red River community and its diaspora. In line with these scholars, I use *Métis* (capitalized) for the nation and its diaspora, and *métis* (not capitalized) to describe identity claims that espouse the conception of métis-as-mixed.

Where does this leave *L'Empreinte*'s claim that the French Québécois de souche are essentially métis? On shaky grounds, to say the least. Intermarriages did take place in the Canadian Northeast but, as the Métis scholar Olive Dickason argues, these early unions between French and Indigenous women did not lead to the emergence of a "New Nation" like they did in the Prairies. Dickason explains that in the east, particularly in Acadia,

> a common enemy (the English) in dangerously close proximity did much to encourage good relations between allies and blood relatives. It also did much to discourage the emergence of the métis as a separate group. The tensions of protracted frontier warfare . . . encouraged good relations. In other words, the children of mixed unions tended to identify with either the French or the Amerindians rather than considering themselves as a separate entity.[20]

Dickason does not question whether or not intermarriages took place in what is now Québec and the Atlantic provinces. They did. Scholars may argue about the exact number of intermarriages and about the ways they were or were not recorded in parishes and other public documents, but most agree that this *métissage* did occur. But these unions, even if their numbers turned out to be significantly higher than records currently show, did not lead to the creation of a Métis nation with its own culture, language, and creation stories in the east as they did in the prairies. Furthermore, these early *métissages* were quickly disavowed by governmental forces under the French and British regimes and later on by influential historians such as Lionel Groulx, as well as by religious authorities. Until recently, these unions were, for all intents and purposes, equally disavowed by the majority of French Québécois de souche who struggled with the aforementioned "Durham Syndrome" theorized by Ross-Tremblay and Hamidi. Thus, a Métis identity did not exist alongside the French-Canadian or, later, French Québécois de souche identities in Québec. Indeed, as I will discuss later, Québec propelled itself into modernity with a national narrative that erased Indigenous peoples. One thing is for sure: the French Québécois de souche certainly did not see themselves as Métis during the events in Oka in 1990 when the Mohawks of Kaneshatà:ke fought to protect their territory against settler encroachment.

Neither do they understand themselves as Métis when violently encountering the Anishinaabe blockades at Lac Barrière, or the demands for better living conditions formulated urgently and consistently by the Assembly of First Nations of Québec and Labrador.

The Métis Turn

It is tempting, not to mention convenient, to perform a rhetorical pirouette and claim a posteriori that French Canadians were métis all along. It would prevent them from "being disturbed by their own settler status," from facing their complicity and the fact that they might have "harmed others just by being"[21] themselves. This claim, however, does not align with the data, as I will discuss later on, and reflects more who Poliquin et al. want the Québécois to be than who the French settlers might have been. It ignores the French "cultural arrogance" and the government's assimilative project. While it is true that the French favored intermarriages, they only did so as a means for the "francisation" of Indigenous peoples and for the purpose of trade. It was expected that the children of these early unions between French men and Indigenous women would assimilate and be French-speaking, Roman Catholic, and sedentary farmers.

The Québécois have long been fascinated with genealogy, as scholar Darryl Leroux's insightful research demonstrates, and tracing ancestors back to specific regions of France is a popular hobby in Québec, *La Belle Province*. If genealogical inquiries have mostly focused on illuminating one's European heritage, a shift has recently begun to take place in Québec, where genealogical and, to a lesser extent, genetic science are now deployed to support claims of métishood and cultural affiliation with Indigenous peoples. During the last decades, a number of self-proclaimed métis organizations have surfaced in Québec. For instance, the Mikinaks in the Montérégie region; La Nation Métis du Québec, which defines itself as distinct, francophone, and nationalist; and the Communauté Métisse Autochtone de la Gaspésie, Bas-Saint-Laurent et Îles-de-la-Madeleine,[22] which actively seeks to "reclaim Métis land, ancestral rights and culture."[23] The Mikinaks' "chief," Lise Brisebois, argues that anyone can be métis, even if it dates "eight generations back," as long as they "feel it"[24] inside them. As the Métis scholar Chris Andersen writes, "the so-called métis population ha[s] skyrocketed by 43 percent since the previous census (in 1996), a five-year increase that strained demographers' ability to make statistical sense of it."[25] Andersen adds that, by 2006, "these numbers roughly doubled again, producing an equally perplexing overall increase of nearly 100 percent in only a decade."[26] This phenomenon illuminates how the notions of métis-as-mixed and Métis-as-peoplehood uncomfortably coexist in Québec and Canada. *L'Empreinte*, with its thesis of métishood, is yet another sign of this shift.

The reasons behind this métis turn are numerous. At a symbolic level, white settlers have always "played Indian," as Philip Deloria convincingly argues, as a way to "tangle with their ideological dilemmas."[27] Race, as Corrie Scott contends, is relational and contextual; and playing Indian, from the Boston Tea Party "Mohawks" to Bill Clinton's and Elizabeth Warren's supposed Cherokee lineage, has served as a potent marker of mostly white national belonging. U.S. Americans have deployed "Indianness" or "Nativeness" as a way to differentiate their identity from that of their European ancestors and to anchor and legitimate their presence on the American continent. John Ralston Saul's claim that Canada is métis participates in the same logic by positioning the country as postcolonial and by naturalizing its settler population as native to the territory it occupies. Scholars (Métis and non-Métis) have criticized Saul for his recuperative and, I argue, parasitic rewriting of Canada's mixed genesis. With the development of genetic sciences, scientists and the larger public alike are no longer solely playing Indian. They are now "on the hunt for 'Native American DNA' " according to Kim Tallbear (Santee Dakota), who adds that "some have romantic visions of documenting that 'spiritual connection' they've always felt to Native Americans," while others want to articulate land claims, or tap into what they imagine as vast government "handouts" to Indigenous peoples.[28] For these seekers, the discovery of any amount of so-called Indian blood may lead to a profound rearticulation of their identities, a reframing that has political and cultural consequences.

These recuperative turns to Indigeneity are surely at play in the explosion of Métis self-identification in a province like Québec.[29] In arguing this, I am in no way minimizing the reality of those Indigenous peoples who have been left behind by the exclusionary clauses of the Indian Act. These are real claims, and I examine them in chapter 4, which focuses on Indigenous women's longstanding battle against the Indian Act, which led to the reforms enshrined in Bills C-31 and C-3. What interests me is how the terms *Métis* and *métishood* become entangled in settler discourses of legitimacy and innocence, and deployed as a way to co-opt and reshape Indigenous discourses, articulations of sovereignty, and political demands in Québec. Indeed, if all who have a distant Indigenous ancestor now claim to be métis (a category that the recent *Powley* decision has rendered blurrier), then this large group of newcomers could potentially shift the balance among those categorized as Indigenous in Québec. This would undoubtedly change the discourse of Indigenous people as a group vis-à-vis the Québécois government, the ways territorial claims are articulated, and so on. This is not a benign claim, despite *L'Empreinte*'s romantic tone. It is a disappearance through absorption. As Tuck and Yang argue, "the desire to reconcile is just as relentless as the desire to disappear the Native; it is a desire to not have to deal with this (Indian) problem anymore."[30] If we are all "a little bit Indian," then settlers don't have to face the hard work of repair and redress, and Indigenous claims run the risk of being subsumed under that of the majority.

Québec's Exceptionalism

L'Empreinte employs interviews with a cast of personalities to support its imprint (*empreinte*) argument. While a few interviewees are Indigenous—the Innu poet Joséphine Bacon and the Abénaki anthropologist Nicole O'Bomsawin, for instance—the majority, unsurprisingly, stems from the French Québécois de souche community. They are historians, anthropologists, workers in a forestry cooperative, a fiscal specialist, a community organizer, a judge, and a psychologist. Through them, the film makes a number of claims about contemporary Québec. For instance, it asserts that the French Québécois de souche react adversely to hierarchy and tend to favor the community over the individual. The film cites Québec's unique way of redistributing wealth, its generous social safety net, and its flourishing cooperatives and *tables de concertation* (issue tables). It focuses on Québec's unique hybrid justice system in which a traditional antagonistic legal model coexists with mediation, an approach based on dialogue and mutual agreement. All Québécois have access to a judge-mediator, who, in effect, shares decisional power with all parties involved, and this is unique in Canada. Finally, the film asserts that Québec has historically favored reparative over punitive justice, a fact that differentiates the province from the rest of Canada. All in all, *L'Empreinte* draws a portrait of Québec as having always been, from its origins as a "new" France to its current iteration, a benevolent, tolerant, and egalitarian society.

That Québec's societal model distinguishes it from the rest of North America is not at the heart of this chapter's investigation (though for the record, some of *L'Empreinte*'s claims about Québec exceptionalism are thinly supported at best). What interests me, instead, is how and why *L'Empreinte* and its interviewees come to draw a causal relation between the aforementioned cultural traits, practices, and institutions in contemporary Québec and the *métissage* that took place in Nouvelle-France four centuries ago. Why this particular connection rather than, say, exploring how Québec's institutions and values developed in relation to the Catholic Church whose influence was not only broad but also sustained over time, and why have these distinct values been articulated as a way to unify defiance to English Canada? To support its imprint claim, the film conveniently ignores all other sources of cultural influence and cross-pollination and rests on a narrow reading of French colonization as somehow benevolent, a thesis that many may find hard to reconcile with the hundreds of years of systemic erasure of Indigenous cultures in Canada and Québec. Some in Québec continue to blame the Catholic Church and the Québécois bourgeoisie who collaborated with the Anglos for this colonial violence, a violence that was also directed, they say, toward Québec's *petites gens* (poorer folks). This argument, I would argue, is yet another move to innocence, and one that is quickly debunked by the overwhelming evidence of racism toward Indigenous peoples that continues to permeate all strata of Québec society long after the *petites gens* amassed some political, economic, and social capital.

L'Empreinte, in focusing on two historical moments—the distant past of Nouvelle-France and Québec's present—refuses to engage with such variables as the period between 1763 and the present, during which Indigenous peoples were forcefully relocated to reserves, violent assimilation policies were put in place, and contacts with Euro-settlers were drastically altered. If the *coureurs des bois* and other French settlers married Indigenous women after the Grande Alliance of 1603,[31] these unions (which were not as widespread as the film suggests) and the harmonious coexistence that the film memorializes had already decreased before the arrival of the British in 1763.

In fact, Nouvelle-France was a slave-owning society, a reality that stands in stark contrast to the discourse of prelapsarian harmony favored by the film and many of its interviewees. The scholar Maureen G. Elgersman writes that "French Canadians enslaved Panis (Pawnee) Indians as well as Africans . . . Panis slaves were found in the houses of the bourgeoisie, while less numerous Blacks . . . generally served the rich."[32] Furthermore, there was, between Nouvelle-France and the 1960s' Révolution Tranquille (during which many of Québec's contemporary institutions were created), a long period marked by the segregation of Indigenous peoples in Québec. Let us not forget that between 1885 and 1945, the reserves were regulated by the pass system, which required that Status Indians obtain a pass in order to leave the reserve. Those who did not comply could be imprisoned. During that time, Québec and Québécitude were shaped by a number of forces (British colonialism, capitalism, nationalism, Third World decolonization theories, and the labor movement, to name a few) that the film barely acknowledges. The film also omits the fact that Indigenous peoples were barely acknowledged, let alone consulted, when the province wrote itself into modernity with the vast social programs the film claims as being imprinted by Indigeneity. Instead, the film privileges a narrative according to which who "we" are now is the result of our mixing, our *métissage* with Indigenous peoples for a short period of time nearly 400 years ago.

Shared History: Shared Culture?

The film's first interview begins, as Nouvelle-France did, on the windy shores of a great waterway. The camera captures Roy Dupuis and Denys Delâge, a respected historian and professor emeritus at the Université Laval, standing next to the Saguenay River, near Tadoussac.[33] Across the water, the two men can see the Pointe Saint-Mathieu (today the Pointe aux Alouettes) where the explorer Samuel de Champlain, representing the French king Henri IV, and Anadabijou, or "Sagamo," leader of the Montagnais (Innu), met in 1603. Delâge, recalling this important meeting, explains: "Nouvelle-France does not begin with the conquest of the territory or with wars against Indigenous people. It starts with alliances with Indigenous people" (my translation). Delâge refers here to the famous Grande Alliance of 1603 between Champlain and Anadabijou, in which the French promised to join forces with the Montagnais (Innu), Algonquians, and Etchemins (Maliseet) against their common enemy, the Iroquois. In exchange, the French were primarily interested in establishing a stronghold in the lucrative fur trade.

That the French, to carry out their strategic plan, performed according to the customs and ceremonial protocols of the Innu, Algonquians, and Maliseets they encountered is undeniable. It was in their best interest. And one does not have to speculate about their intentions, since numerous letters to the metropole outline how alliances were perceived as performances of goodwill in the most theatrical definition of the term. French leaders may have performed as if Anadabijou and other Indigenous emissaries were equal partners, but "these alliances nevertheless participate[d] in a colonial logic which will become more obvious during the nineteenth century when Aboriginal people lost some of their economic and military might."[34] Furthermore, the Frenchmen's lack of understanding of Indigenous cultures and customs soon jeopardized the 1603 alliance. In 1617, 1627, and again in 1633, violence exploded between the allies.[35] In other words, all was not well and harmonious between Indigenous peoples and French settlers. The historian Maxime Gohier reminds us that "to consolidate their stronghold over the fur trade, the French reneged on their promise in 1645 when they negotiated a secret alliance with the Iroquois, the terms of which stipulated that the Iroquois could attack all Amerindians allied to the French if they had not converted to Catholicism."[36] If the French posed as mediators in the first decades of their presence in Nouvelle-France, a growing number of historians, especially outside of Québec, remind us that rather than uncritically romanticizing this mediation, we should examine it as an interested performance made to appease the metropole and various Indigenous factions.

L'Empreinte relies heavily on non-Indigenous historians and anthropologists from Québec to draw a portrait of Nouvelle-France. The sources cited by these historians—letters sent by explorers or missionaries to the metropole, for instance—form the official archive of a settler-colonial project and are, as Diana Taylor suggests, instruments of power. These sources tell one side of these first encounters and have forged a lasting narrative around such events as the Grande Alliance of 1603. As Ross-Tremblay and Hamidi contend, this alliance has been "mythologized" in Québec as an "intercultural alliance" in which both parties found equal benefits and as "the foundation of a new civilization in North America."[37] They add that "another interpretation of this narrative, transmitted through oral tradition, affirms that the relationship with the French quickly deteriorated."[38] The French morphed from friends to feudal masters, appropriated territories through questionable transactions, and failed their allies, but this "transgression is largely evacuated from the cultural memory of the Francophones of North America."[39] In other words, the prelapsarian moment of harmonious relationships between French and Indigenous peoples that *L'Empreinte* glorifies was short-lived at best. This Eden ended well before the Proclamation Royale of 1763 which established a British regime in what was Nouvelle-France.

L'Empreinte unwittingly draws attention to a central issue when it comes to the narration of the history of Indigenous peoples in Québec: this narration remains the province of non-Indigenous people, especially in academia. All academic presses in Québec that boast collections dedicated to Indigenous history and current issues are still headed by white, male scholars.[40] Similarly, academic positions that pertain to Indigenous studies continue to be occupied by non-Indigenous scholars at a rate far higher in Québec than in the rest of Canada. This monopoly over the interpretation and circulation of an Indigenous historical narrative is yet another form of white possession. It is part and parcel of a colonial enterprise (in which I participate, albeit frustratedly).

"Our Sons Shall Marry Your Daughters"

I say nothing new when I state that, as a societal project, Nouvelle-France was irreconcilable with Indigenous sovereignty. After all, France's goal was to establish a colony in North America where absolute monarchy could be established and commerce and Catholicism could flourish. Dickason explains that, like other powers such as Portugal and Spain, "France also sought to assimilate Amerindians, but added a new dimension by trying to use racial intermixing as an instrument of empire."[41] Dickason points out that France's ultimate goal was certainly not for this mixing to result in the development of a sense of "separate identity, the spirit of the 'New Nation.' "[42] Again, Delâge proposes a different reading in *L'Empreinte*:

> The Aboriginals demand marriages between the French and themselves [as part of the alliance]. It is the Aboriginal way. Champlain will wish that "our French sons wed Indigenous women so that we become one people." This is unique in colonial history. This is a proximity that we don't see elsewhere. It is a distinct aspect of our colonial history, an aspect of which we should rightly be proud rather than trying to hide it.[43]

Delâge imagines here a level playing field that never existed. Darryl Leroux and many others argue that despite many French Québécois de souche scholars' desire to present France as a benevolent colonial force that favored miscegenation, the reality is that these unions were always understood as part of an asymmetrical relation of power. Miscegenation was meant to create new French citizens who would adopt the French culture, language, and ways of being. The French historian Gilles Havard summarizes these "unequal alliances" well: "the French authorities assigned a special place to Indians, outside the sphere of citizenship."[44] He adds that "Indians were in fact placed under a form of 'domination' called 'protection' . . . Far from being an affirmation of sovereignty, protection was understood as an unequal alliance, a greater power being able to take a secondary power under its wing upon request."[45] In other words, Indigenous cultures and sovereignties were never encountered as equal and were quickly imagined as subordinate to the French. The same could be argued for religious representatives such as the Jesuits who encountered Indigenous peoples as communities in need of enlightenment, childlike souls to be converted to Catholicism.

Furthermore, there was tremendous resistance to French assimilation on the part of Indigenous peoples. Despite incitative policies (generous dowries were offered to Indigenous women who would marry Frenchmen and adopt French ways), assimilation did not work. Indigenous women might have intermarried for the sake of creating alliances or in individual contexts, but as a whole they were not interested in becoming French. The number of intermarriages remained relatively small. In fact, Darryl Leroux's reflection on Québec's genealogy (which draws from Hubert Charbonneau's extensive research) shows that there are "only 13 Indigenous women in marriage registries before 1680, out of almost 1,900 women. In the first 150 years of colonization, 65 marriages were recorded."[46] Gérard Bouchard, Kim Tallbear, and Darryl Leroux warn against a "genealogical illusion": after eleven generations, they each explain, one has more than 2,000 ancestors. While most French Québécois de souche may count the offspring of one of these 65 marriages as part of their lineage, the métis turn relies on giving these distant ancestors a disproportionate influence over the fabric of one's identity. Darryl Leroux explains that despite many French Québécois de souche scholars' attempts to demonstrate the contrary, "most Québécois have more chances of having British stock than Native blood."[47] But such kinship with the British does not align with Québec's narrative as a minority colonized by the British or with the reality of its ongoing settler-colonial relationship with the Abénaki, Anishinaabe, Atikamekw, Cree, Huron-Wendat, Innu, Inuit, Maliseet, Mi'kmaq, Mohawk, and Naskapi.

L'Empreinte proposes a thesis that leaves many crucial questions unanswered. Can cultural *métissage* really take place if there is no profound understanding of one another's ways of seeing and being in the world? We know, for instance, that during a diplomatic trip to visit the Wendat in 1615, Champlain described them as "without religion, without divine, political or civic laws."[48] He failed to understand the Wendat's role in a well-organized confederacy of four nations, or the value of the four wampum belts he received from them as legal recordings. *L'Empreinte* maintains that "we" carry the imprint of the Wendat, Cree, Mohawk, Innu, and other Indigenous cultures that the French encountered in Nouvelle-France. If that is the case, do we even have the epistemological frame to make sense of this imprint? In other words, if we could not encounter Indigenous cultures and worldviews as equal then, what would make us capable of doing so now? It seems to me that we can debate ad nauseam about the numbers of recorded marriages between settlers and Indigenous peoples and the extent of the *métissage*, but this somehow misses the point. There was and still is an epistemic divide that subjugates this desired Native imprint and subsumes it within Western understandings of race, blood, self, identity, land, property, sovereignty, and jurisdiction.

How lasting is a cross-pollination based on necessity? That is, what happens when the necessity to coexist with Indigenous others, to benefit from their survival skills, territorial knowledge, and numerical advantage quickly disappears? This is what happened between the first failings of the French alliances and the early 1960s, when the Cree forced Québec into a modern treaty over its unilateral plan to develop hydroelectric dams on Cree and Naskapi territories. At the time, as Michel Brault and Claude Jutras's 1962 film *Québec-USA ou l'invasion pacifique* clearly exemplifies, many in Québec believed that there were no Indigenous people left in Québec. The oppressed "other" was the French Québécois de souche. This position was espoused by many left-leaning nationalists—the intellectuals of the Parti Pris movement, for instance, which analogized Québec's status within Canada with that of African Americans in the United States. This false analogy flourished with Pierre Vallières's 1968 manifesto *Nè**es blancs d'Amérique* and found a visual translation in Brault and Jutras's film. Indeed, the film features a long scene in which a French-Canadian guide takes an African American couple on a tour of Québec City, driving their new car through the narrow streets of the old city, where French Canadian children swarm around the car, asking for change, and singing songs in French for the couple's entertainment. These images echo visual tropes of poor Southern towns in the United States, or shantytowns in Third World countries. The film, a visual example of the predilection of Québec's intelligentsia for Fanon, Memmi, and Césaire, labors to align French Canadians with African Americans, and presents images of the Québécois as the blacks of Canada, all the while obliterating the Indigenous presence in Québec. Indeed, when asked, the guide tells the couple quite bluntly, "There are no Indians in Québec."

The relationship of Québécitude with blackness exceeds the mission of this book. Scholars such as Rachel Zellars, Délice Mugabo, Charmaine Nelson, Corrie Scott, Bruno Cornellier, and others have written at length about the specific erasure of black bodies in Québec and Canada and how anti-blackness is alive and well north of the United States border.[49] I nevertheless want to take a moment to meditate on how the parasitic relationship I trace in the French Québécois de souche's articulation of identity requires black bodies as well as Indigenous bodies to define itself. This parasitic relationship is not based on commensality. Where commensality involves cohabitation without harm to the host, the relationship I examine here is an opportunistic one based on utter consumption. It is yet another failed encounter. We can see this in the turn to black bodies performed by Vallières's manifesto and Brault and Jutras's film. This turn deploys blackness as a lens through which Québécitude becomes coherent and its national project ethical. It allows the French Québécois de souche to imagine their national project as liberatory rather than as a continuation of an exploitative relationship to black and Indigenous bodies. What Vallières, Brault, and Jutras demonstrate in their interventions is an opportunistic approach where the parasite capitalizes on the host's compromised defenses and vulnerable position (the result of settler colonialism *and* anti-blackness's objective violence) as a way to survive and grow.

The analogy that the French Québécois de souche are the blacks of Canada should have collapsed under the slightest of critical pressure, but it has endured specifically because it provides a reassuring narrative, proving how robust national mythologies can be. The métis turn currently espoused by many in Québec is yet another incarnation of this parasitic appropriation of Indigenous and black bodies as conditions of possibility for white settler society. *L'Empreinte* fails to acknowledge this appropriative and recurrent trope. This makes sense: the French Québécois de souche's narrative as a distinct colonized society demands and depends on a narrative in which the Québécois de souche are the "nè***res" of Canada (never mind the real black bodies who live in Québec and Canada, and the country's history of slavery), and on a romanticized Native affiliation. Otherwise, the francophone majority's narrative is revealed for what it is: another colonial mythscape that depends on the appropriation of Indianness/blackness and the erasure of Indigenous/black bodies themselves. As I will now discuss, *L'Empreinte* deploys Roy Dupuis as a surrogate for this romanticized past, positioning him as the Québécois de souche's Everyman, a timeless *coureur des bois* whose rugged persona aligns well with the idealized *sauvage*.

Roy Dupuis as Québec's Everyman

L'Empreinte begins with Jorane's fluid music. The cellist and singer is known for her use of invented language and haunting sounds, and the soundtrack she created for the film is melancholic and evocative. As the music plays, the camera follows huge pans of glassy ice as they drift along the vast expanse of the Saint Lawrence River. Dupuis speaks extra-diegetically:

> A part of myself escapes me. When I landed in the Americas, I was French and soon, I no longer lived nor thought as a Frenchman. I had become Canadian, from the Iroquoian word *Kanata*. My tribe gave

> itself many names since—French Canadians, Québécois—but in the idea that we have of ourselves, something has vanished, a thread was broken along the way. It might not be a coincidence if the question of identity constantly resurfaces in our history, as if no answer had completely satisfied us.[50]

This opening sequence sets the stage symbolically for *L'Empreinte*'s argument: it equates the drifting ice with Dupuis's sense of self and that of the French Québécois de souche for whom he stands. Like the pans of ice, "we," the French Québécois de souche, are represented as having been separated from a larger ice cap. "We" too are floating, unaware, it seems, of our point of origin. In fact, the film repeatedly employs stunning natural vistas to anchor its "journey at the heart of our identity." Dupuis often conducts interviews near or on waterways (he shares a canoe with the Abénaki anthropologist Nicole O'Bomsawin, for instance), in lush forest settings, or on wild shores battered by the wind. In staging the interviews in these natural spaces, the film casts Dupuis and his identity as belonging to this land, at ease with its elements, native.

Dupuis's narration starts at an intimate level—"A part of myself escapes me"—but soon evolves to the communal. The actor then positions himself as Québec's Everyman using expressions such as "my tribe" and "the idea that we have of ourselves." The possessive determiners he deploys are important and mark him as a surrogate for all the descendants of white Euro-settlers epitomized in Québec's mythscape by the figure of the *coureur des bois*. Dupuis is no stranger to this mythical figure. As an actor, he has lent his rugged masculinity to multiple versions of the *coureur des bois*, be they in television series or films celebrating Québec's *terroir*. For instance, he was the wild Ovila Pronovost in the historical saga *Les Filles de Caleb* (1990), a man who fled responsibilities to become a settler in the province's remote region of Abitibi. Later, Dupuis was the untamable Alexis Labranche in *Séraphin: Un homme et son péché* (2002), embodying yet again a man whose desire to *prendre le bois*, or live a nomadic life in the forest, is stronger than his desire to settle down. Dupuis has come to embody what Bruno Cornellier calls "an archetype of the wild Québécois masculinity and of its filial ties and métissage, its co-dependence even, with the natural world associated with *indianité* [Indianness]."[51] The series *Les Filles de Caleb*, which launched Dupuis's career, made television history in Québec for a particularly erotically charged scene between Ovila (Dupuis's character) and his future wife Émilie Bordeleau (played by Marina Orsini). In this much-discussed scene of obvious symbolism, the pair witness the mating of a stallion and a mare. The scene captured an important element of Québec's mythscape that the anthropologist Serge Bouchard calls *le fantasme d'ensauvagement,* or the fantasy of becoming savage. For Bouchard, Ovila Pronovost is a continuation of his ancestor, the *coureur des bois*, a character who stands in sharp opposition to the farmer of the semifeudal system of seigneuries in Nouvelle-France. "The farmer in 1685 worked hard, had the priest on his back at all times, had to pay taxes, had responsibilities and was a nobody." Young men, Bouchard continues, saw the forest as a space of liberation where they "could hunt, travel, discover," "find women and become a 'sauvage,' a métis."[52] Ovila Pronovost, whose fictionalized life takes place long after Nouvelle-France, epitomizes the lasting power of this fantasy. He is the young man described by Bouchard who chooses to live at the border of white settler society. Of course, this fantasy resembles the trope of Indianness in the American imaginary—and, like this trope, it merely requires the idea of Indianness, its role as an index for liberty to function.

Coincidentally (or not), in *L'Empreinte*, Roy Dupuis conducts all interviews dressed in what a cynic might describe as a modern, hipster version of a *coureur des bois*'s attire. Indeed, Dupuis sports a beard with longish hair, and wears a variety of fashionable plaid flannel shirts, worn jeans, and fur hats throughout the film. Through him, positioned here as the quintessential French Québécois de souche, the viewer is invited to embark, as the film's tagline suggests, on "a journey to the heart of our identity." The poster, which features the silhouette of the actor filled with an image of the boreal forest, establishes Dupuis as profoundly linked with the nature and territory of Québec.

This connection between Dupuis's body and Québec's territory and memory had already been explored in *Mémoires affectives* (*Looking for Alexander*, 2004) a fiction film directed by Francis Leclerc.[53] Leclerc, it should be noted, is the son of Félix Leclerc, who, as one of Québec's first and most beloved folk singers of the *terroir*, epitomized the ruggedness of the *coureur des bois* long before Dupuis took up the torch. In *Mémoires affectives*, which translates as "affective memories," Dupuis plays Alexandre Tourneur, a man suffering from aphasia and amnesia who has to relearn everything upon waking up from a long coma caused by an accident. He soon discovers that his traumatic injury has left him with strange abilities. Indeed, Tourneur is now capable of stealing other people's memories in order to reconstruct his own lost identity. Furthermore, this French Québécois de souche now thinks in Innu-Aimun (the language of the Innu people) and can speak it fluently under hypnosis. In other words, it is through others, be they his contemporaries or what Cornellier calls the figure of the "archaic Indian," that Alexandre Tourneur can rewrite himself into being. Where his contemporaries (who are mostly new immigrants) provide a recent anchor, the archaic Indian acts as a primordial vessel through which Alexandre can legitimize his belonging and claim to the territory he occupies. The film symbolically claims a native lineage that makes Alexandre *un fils de la terre* (a son of the earth) on equal footing with the continent's Indigenous peoples. In doing so, *Mémoires affectives* follows a long cinematic tradition in Québec on which Cornellier comments: "Thus, the Indian, when liberated, disembodied from his political and historical reality, and submitted to the discursive and pedagogical regime that places/inscribes him in the dominant nationalist mythology, becomes one of the main symbols of Québec's cultural difference and territorial belonging in America."[54]

It is tempting to read Dupuis's participation in *L'Empreinte* as a reprisal of his role as Alexandre Tourneur. In both cases, Dupuis is tasked with healing a form of amnesia resulting from trauma. If Tourneur's memory loss is the result of a car accident, *L'Empreinte* suggests that collectively, the French Québécois de souche cannot recall who they really are (that is, the Indian within) because of the trauma of British colonization, which the film presents as having forced the end of the harmonious filial relations that united French and Indigenous people in Nouvelle-France. But as the scholar Peter Cook writes, "the study of the first contacts between Aboriginals and Europeans in America is anchored in partiality."[55] As we have seen in Martin's play, discussed in chapter 1, it is not enough to stage an encounter with the archives of the past if one is not willing to do the hard work of decentering one's gaze and epistemological frame and of questioning one's recuperative intent.

Dupuis has come to embody the essence of the romanticized *coureur des bois*. Perhaps this identification helps explain his visceral reaction to the portrayal of French Canadians in the Oscar-winning film *The Revenant*, directed in 2015 by Alejandro González Iñàrritu. Dupuis was approached to play the *coureur des bois* Toussaint, a role that he refused despite its potential for international recognition. Fabrice Adde, a French actor from Normandy, was eventually chosen to play the role. When the film came out, Dupuis expressed anger at the movie's depiction of Toussaint as a violent rapist, killer, and slave-owner, calling the film "anti-French-Canadian" and "historically incorrect."[56] That Dupuis relies on a selective reading of history is clear, and his reaction betrays a deep anxiety about a past that refuses to adhere to Dupuis's métis desires.

Felt Nativeness

Halfway through *L'Empreinte*, Dupuis interviews the psychoanalyst Jacqueline Lanouette against a backdrop of lush greenery. It is not clear why Lanouette was chosen as an interviewee. She is a French Québécois de souche who has worked in international settings, with the Touareg population in particular, but she possesses no particular expertise on or relation to Indigenous peoples or colonial trauma that might explicate why her voice is privileged here. In fact, her intervention epitomizes the discourse of "felt Nativeness" that the film deploys to support its imprint thesis. Reminiscing on her own childhood, Lanouette explains: "I did not want to be métis, I wanted to be Native. I imagined so many stories. We would go to the woods and in my personal narrative, I was Native through and through." Lanouette marks a difference between métis and Native that buys into discourses of racial purity/authenticity. She wanted to possess full-bloodedness. Apparently, unable to support her fantasy, Lanouette settled for an imagined mixed identity: Québécoise, but with a pinch of Indianness.

Having related her fantasy, Lanouette then turns to Dupuis and asks: "As a child, you never thought that your father or your mother could be Native?" The actor responds, somewhat bashfully, that he too had "always felt a form of pride," that somehow he "would have liked to be Native." Both dwell on how they have always "felt Native," but neither mentions that, had they been Indigenous, both would have been forced to attend Residential Schools like most Indigenous children of their generation. Dupuis grew up in Amos in the Abitibi region, near the Lac Simon Anishinaabe reserve. This region, as I mentioned earlier, is still plagued by structural racism against Indigenous people. Lanouette and Dupuis claim an identity *métissée*, but seem oblivious to the white-settler privileges that grant them this form of racial mobility in the first place. It is these privileges that shield them from the gratuitous violence and systemic racism that continue to disproportionally accrue on Indigenous bodies.

In their desire to possess Nativeness, neither Lanouette nor Dupuis are particularly original; they embody Moreton-Robinson's "white possessive" and echo what Shari Huhndorf calls "going Native" and Philip Deloria defines as "playing Indian."[57] That is, they turn to Nativeness (real and imagined) to define their own identity. These settler strategies do not lead to an encounter with Indigenous peoples. Encounters are embodied and sensate, and would, in this case, involve an Indigenous interlocutor. Unfortunately, most of these examples of desired possession evacuate Indigenous bodies and foreclose the possibly productive nature of sensate encounters. In fact, Indigeneity is deployed in the service of the regeneration of settler identity. Lanouette and Dupuis both profess admiration for what they define as "Native" culture (and I should point out that their definition erases all differences among these very culturally distinct cultures), yet they invoke their Nativeness as a way to redefine a Québécois identity that is ultimately white. Dupuis later adds: "Will we one day be able to dream ourselves starting with our real roots? And then reattach the broken thread of our history?" This desire to reformulate an identity for the French Québécois de souche is what fuels *L'Empreinte*. Chelsea Vowel writes:

> Some people, merely by *feeling* more Indigenous than French, want to identify as Métis. Unique. Not French (European), but *something else*. Something that belongs here. Something that does not engender guilt. Something that washes away Québec's history of colonialism while reinforcing Québec's own experiences as a colonized people.[58]

Indeed, this claimed métishood never threatens the integrity and power of white settler society. In fact, it reaffirms its supposed superiority. The

Québécois are suddenly the Indigenous people who have successfully survived colonialism, carried their métis values into modernity, and formed a thriving cultural and political project. This narrative positions the French Québécois de souche as the better, more resilient version of their supposed Indigenous ancestors.

If claiming métishood serves to regenerate white settler identity, it also cleanses settlers from their responsibilities by repositioning their identity as wounded. If we follow the logic of the film, Québec's ongoing role in perpetuating racial inequalities and colonial policies stems from a psychic trauma that Lanouette couches in psychoanalytical terms. She focuses, for instance, on the expression *On n'est pas des sauvages* (We are not savages), reflects on its usages in Québec parlance, and surmises that this saying is symptomatic of "our unconscious speaking to our conscious selves, claiming that we are, in fact, *sauvages*." Lanouette frames this intervention by saying that this is what she "likes to tell herself." In other words, Lanouette is not drawing from clinical experience or a systematic study of the unconscious of the French Québécois de souche. For her, the Québécois are dealing with a psychic wound created by our forced betrayal of our true Indigenous origins. "We feel guilty. It is hard to live with this." It is this betrayal of who we are that explains why contemporary relations between Indigenous peoples and French Québécois de souche are so tense. "We have trouble encountering one another," Lanouette argues. This difficulty, according to her, is not due to Québec's settler-colonial role or its complicity with Canada in carrying on a genocidal agenda; it is the French Québécois de souche who are wounded (rather than Indigenous people), and it is their psychic wound (not the real violence faced by Indigenous people) that becomes the injury.

Denys Delâge agrees with Lanouette. He explains that the Canadiens or Canadians (the name that the inhabitants of Québec gave themselves), once they were defeated and conquered by the British, had no choice but to disavow their ties with the *sauvages*. After seeing the massive deportation of the Acadians—who, according to the British, had become *ensauvagés*—the Canadians feared for themselves: "If the Canadians wanted to be recognized by the new master, they had to be recognized according to the master's codes."[59] Thus, they rejoined the ranks of the so-called civilized and denied their past relations with Indigenous people. I see several unaddressed issues in Delâge and Lanouette's reading of this traumatic separation. It fails to note the privilege of racial mobility that allowed French settlers to reintegrate into white civil society (albeit with less institutional authority and autonomy) and left Indigenous people at the margins. It is this same privilege that allows a film like *L'Empreinte* to suddenly reclaim Indigeneity, or that motivates the anthropologist Serge Bouchard to "rewrite our national history" according to this narrative of traumatic separation. It seems lost on Bouchard and Lanouette that this one-sided remaking of Québec's history violently perpetuates settler-colonial privileges. Indeed, settler-colonial societies have long depended on a rewriting of history to legitimize their existence. *L'Empreinte* seeks to "remake history" in ways that fail to unsettle Québec's settler-colonial past and perpetuate instead settler-colonial domination in the present.

For Pierrot Ross-Tremblay and Nawel Hamidi, the métis turn is symptomatic of a profound malaise among the Québécois. They write: "Is it possible to explain the erosion of the Québécois identity, their sense of collective agony, by looking at the amnesia of this country which literally sits on another?"[60] In other words, colonial denial must end. Ross-Tremblay and Hamidi contend that Québec's identity crisis is due to its refusal to recognize its past, a past complicated by an internalized sense of shame that came with the British regime. They call this, as I mentioned in chapter 1, the Durham Syndrome. Both are quick to point out that the British assimilatory policies deployed against the francophones do not annul or exonerate this community from its past and ongoing settler-colonial role. They warn against the fiction of blood as a way to claim innocence for the French Québécois de souche.

This malaise that plagues the French Québécois de souche can be further explicated by turning to the figure of the Wiindigo or Wétiko from the Algonquian oral tradition. As the scholar Jessica Kolopenuk (Nehiyaw Cree) writes:

> According to Nehiyaw, Anishinaabe, and other Indigenous tribal beliefs, the wiindigo or wetiko is understood to be a figure that personifies cannibalistic greed and hunger and, when left unstopped, is perpetually driven by its emptiness caused by disconnection. There never seems to be a shortage of "lost" people trying to find out their TRUE ancestry.[61]

Kolopenuk reads the industry of genealogical ancestry through the lens of the Wétiko. She reflects on the ways the genealogy industry targets individuals who may feel lost and are hungry for a sense of community and belonging in an increasingly homogenizing world. The industry promises to uncover the connection, the gene that might provide an individual with a quick answer to a profound identity crisis. Indigenous DNA, she argues, is thus consumed as a quick fix to settlers' woes.

The legal scholar Val Napoleon (Cree) writes that the Wétiko is "an affliction well known to Indigenous peoples: a sickness often born of hunger, cold, and the long darkness."[62] Napoleon and her colleague Hadley Friedland study the oral tradition about the Wétiko, which details how communities dealt with this destructive force. Both contend that these stories are archives of a particular community's legal principles, tradition, and precedents. For her part, Leanne Simpson compares the Canadian bureaucracy, which ensures that Indigenous claims stagnate in court for decades, to the Wétiko.[63] The desire of many settlers to possess Indigenous blood similarly embodies the spirit of the Wétiko. Settlers, driven by a sense of disconnection, or by guilt or shame when it comes to their complicity with the oppression of Indigenous people, construct a narrative of self that renders them innocent. They do so by cannibalizing Indigenous cultures, territories, and filial connections. This hunger stems from something deeply unresolved in the French Québécois de souche psyche. While I agree in part with Ross-Tremblay and Hamidi's reading of the French Québécois de souche identity as disconnected, I contend that their analysis remains too generous. The French Québécois de souche are consuming mythical narratives of *métissages* because facing what lies at the core of their identity would be too painful. It would require coming to terms with their own settler-colonial violence, their own perpetuation of white possession. It would necessitate that they admit their complicity in a genocidal project and cease to invoke the innocence and benevolence of Nouvelle-France and instrumentalize it as a way to constantly defer Indigenous demands for redress and equality.

Nation *Métissée*

The camera in *L'Empreinte* moves in on a pensive Dupuis as he is seated on the porch of what looks like a rustic cabin. Dressed yet again in a plaid shirt, Dupuis is writing as his voice meditates off-camera:

> We have had Indian mothers. A few Indian fathers as well, but mostly mothers. Their voices soothed us. Like three-quarters of the Québécois of French Canadian origins, I too have Aboriginal ancestors. I discover in my genealogy a family that mixed many times with First Peoples. Thus, I have 92 family ties. I also recognize the surnames of interpreters and famous explorers that have lived among First Peoples, that were adopted by them. The Couture, Marcellet, Perreault, Pelletier, Lefebvre, and that is without taking into account all the settlers who, for the duration of a trading trip, succumbed to "the magic of the forest."[64]

"The magic of the forest" is a convenient euphemism to hide the fact that data do not support the film's thesis of widespread intermarriages. Indeed, as Leroux indicates, many Québécois scholars have tried to make genealogical data support their claim of métishood. They have claimed that not all marriages had been recorded, that marriages in remote regions may have gone unnoticed, that not all unions resulted in official marriages, and so on. When genealogical data failed to collaborate, they turned to genomics, arguing that blood could prove what the archives could not. Again, the data are uncooperative.[65] The historian and sociologist Gérard Bouchard notes: "in the 1950s, Jean-Jacques Rousseau [*sic*] argued that were we to shake the genealogical tree of the Québécois, feathers would fall from it. The image stuck."[66] But as Gérard Bouchard rightly remarks, Jacques Rousseau's predictions were grossly exaggerated, and rigorous archival and genealogical research conducted by several Québec universities and collated on the BALSAC database[67] demonstrate that "the proportion of First Nations genes in the Québécois gene pool is very low (less than 1%)."[68] *L'Empreinte* not only chooses to disregard this data but also adopts a discourse that problematically conflates genealogy culture, political citizenship, and ancestry.

Despite these uncooperative numbers, *L'Empreinte*'s narrative stubbornly emphasizes blood in both its symbolic and its biological richness. And as Melissa Meyer argues, "blood metaphors have a primal quality."[69] Blood has been understood as the site of the soul, a taboo substance denoting women's impurity, a marker of purity and community, or the vehicle of one's temperament. In the United States as well as in Canada, blood continues to shape the discourse surrounding Indigeneity at a legal level as well as in everyday parlance. Indian blood was once seen as a mere obstacle on the road to civilization: it was understood as having the property to be diluted and thus assimilated through miscegenation (a property not afforded to the black community). Kim Tallbear adds, "Paradoxically, Indian blood also became a desired object. Its complete loss would be lamented as the 'First American' is central to the country's nation-building project—to constructing moral legitimacy and a uniquely American identity. The Indians, at the moment of their subdual, become ancestors."[70] For many people, Indigenous and non-Indigenous alike, blood, "instead of serving merely as a potent metaphor, . . . was believed to convey essential attributes."[71] Following this logic, there is Cree blood, Québécois blood, French blood. Blood has come to stand in for, and act as a shorthand for, identity and belonging.

Therefore, when Dupuis asks his interlocutors if they "have Innu blood in their family," he is saturating blood with many layers of meaning. He conflates blood with culture or peoplehood. *L'Empreinte* fetishizes "Indian blood" and "Indian ancestry" and mobilizes the notion of a set of inherently Indigenous traits being passed on, and resulting in the French Québécois de souche's unique cultural character. This proposition is in conversation with the field of epigenetics. Epigenetics, the study of heritable changes in gene expression, demonstrates that many variables—such as class, levels of education, exposure to certain substances, geography, and traumatic experiences—can influence if and how certain inheritable traits express themselves. The presence of a gene does not guarantee its expression, nor does it reveal a fundamental truth about a person. Recent research on historical trauma does point, however, to how sustained trauma may alter how certain genes are expressed across generations. Recent research on historical trauma calls the Québécois narrative into question. While the notion of historical trauma was first studied in relation to the multigenerational effects of the Holocaust on Jewish communities, as early as 1998 Maria Yellow Horse Braveheart leveraged this concept to discuss the impact of settler colonialism on Indigenous communities. Historical trauma "highlights the idea that the accumulation of collective stressors and trauma that began in the past may continue to increase risk for negative health and social outcomes among contemporary Aboriginal peoples."[72] If a film like *L'Empreinte* wants to discuss blood and genealogy and address the inheritability of certain traits, it should perhaps question the devastating impact of Québec and Canada's political projects on the expression of certain inheritable traits among Indigenous communities.

Québékoisie

I now turn to *Québékoisie*, a 2013 multiple-award-winning documentary film by Mélanie Carrier and Olivier Higgins. If *L'Empreinte* is a meditation on who "we" are, *Québékoisie* is an exploration of who "they"—the Indigenous peoples whose territories now form Québec—might be. Like *L'Empreinte*, *Québékoisie* is deeply invested in questions of identity, but its journey stems from a slightly different set of questions. Contrary to *L'Empreinte*'s deployment of the métis turn as a way to reaffirm a distinct French Québécois de souche identity, *Québékoisie* seems genuinely invested in fostering encounters with members of the eleven Indigenous nations for whom Québec is traditional territory. Higgins and Carrier are clearly invested in finding common ground and ways to suture Québec's national project with Indigenous political and cultural discourses. While raising awareness of the situation of Indigenous people in Québec is a laudable goal, it can only work if the film is willing to ask some hard questions about Québec's societal project, structural racism, and unwillingness to see Indigenous sovereignty as anything else than secondary to its own. Carrier and Higgins tiptoe around these questions and veer at times toward a homogenizing discourse. As trained biologists, they turn at times to a slippery fetishizing of ancestry as a way to suture French Québécois de souche and Indigenous narratives.

The film begins with Higgins's narration over images of the filmmakers' previous film, *Asiemut* (2006), which documents their cycling journey across Asia. Higgins recalls a conversation he had in Tibet where a man described the effects of the Chinese occupation on his nation, community, and culture. In return, Higgins shared his own national narrative as a French Québécois de souche, the very same mythscape central to Alexis Martin's play or Roy Dupuis's exploration. Perhaps being so far from Québec's gravitational pull and from the investment it requires in its wounded attachments gave Higgins pause. In any case, in that moment, faced by an Indigenous Tibetan living under occupation, the young man questioned his own national narrative. Why did he need to come this far to encounter Indigenous people when Québec counts more than fifty Indigenous communities whose political status is analogous to that of his Tibetan interlocutor? Higgins's extra-diegetic voice ponders: "Why weren't we taught about First Peoples in school? . . . What else might have been obscured in Québec's narrative? What is omitted in the stories we tell ourselves?" A proud French Québécois de souche, he admits, "I have always celebrated Québec, but now, I wonder what it is I am defending." The starting point for *Québékoisie* is thus an outward movement, a desire to know more about the Indigenous people who call the territory of Québec their ancestral land. This is the impetus for the two filmmakers' exploratory journey.

The film thus follows Carrier and Higgins as they cycle the 600 miles (1,000 kilometers) that separate their home in Québec City from Natashquan in the Base Côte-Nord region, traveling on Provincial Route 138 and stopping along the way in Indigenous communities. The film features interviews with a cast of Indigenous interlocutors—the delightful sisters/educators/activists Anne-Marie André, Evelyne, and Fernande St-Onge from the adjacent Innu communities of Uashat and Mani-Utenam; the Innu sociologist Pierrot Ross-Tremblay; the Atikamekw painter Eruoma Awashish; and others. It also features non-Indigenous interviewees such as Francine Lemay, whose brother, Corporal Marcel Lemay, died during the events in Oka in 1990; the anthropologist Serge Bouchard, who also participated in *L'Empreinte*; bystanders encountered on Route 138; and a specialist in demographics affiliated with the aforementioned BALSAC project. Together these portraits attempt to reposition Indigenous people in the Québécois conscience as vibrant, diverse, and contemporary and to illuminate the journeys of some French Québécois de souche who have created deep and life-altering ties with them.

Route 138 is a richly symbolic choice for Higgins and Carrier. The pair has long been fascinated with what happens to individuals as they travel through a particular territory, on historical paths or waterways. In a previous film entitled *Rencontre* (2011; *Encounter*), the two filmmakers followed a group of teenagers from Innu and non-Indigenous communities from the Saguenay region and from the Huron-Wendat community of Wendake, on a 21-day expedition. Accompanied by a guide, the teenagers cycled and canoed along the ancestral Indigenous route that unites Lac St-Jean to Québec City. The 190-mile path, now known as the *sentiers des jésuites* (the Jesuits' trail), was once a vital artery for transportation and exchanges. The organizers of this project hoped that this physical encounter with the land and with each other might help dispel prejudice and distrust between Indigenous and French Québécois de souche youths. *Rencontre* marked the filmmakers' first attempt at encountering Québec's Indigenous communities.

Route 138 originated as Nouvelle-France's first roadway, Le Chemin du Roy, which was built between 1660 and 1737 to unite various seigneuries between what are now Montréal and Québec City. It is one of the oldest roads in North America and, for a while, its 170 miles made it one of the longest. In its current state, Route 138 starts at the U.S. border with the state of New York, crosses the Mohawk community of Kahnawà:ke, and traverses Montréal where it becomes Sherbrooke Street, before heading to Québec

City. Along the way, Route 138 crosses towns and villages where it often becomes Notre-Dame Street. To follow Route 138 is thus to visit some of the oldest cities in North America, which were built close to the Saint Lawrence River: Montréal, Trois-Rivières, Québec. The road passes by Baie-Comeau, where one can see Tadoussac, where the Grande Alliance of 1603 took place across the Saguenay River. Route 138 officially ends in Natashquan, more than 600 miles (1,000 kilometers) northeast of Québec City, but there are plans to extend the road toward Blanc-Sablon and Labrador. Innu, Huron-Wendat, Mohawk, Abénaki, Atikamekw, and Cree communities live in close proximity to Route 138, but to visit the Anishinaabe or the Inuit, for instance, one would need to travel roughly the same distance in other directions. The province of Québec, let us remember, occupies more than 560,000 square miles (1,500,000 square kilometers), and many Indigenous communities have always been located far from urban centers. Some, particularly in northern Québec, remain extremely hard to access.

Bouchard, whom we know from *L'Empreinte*, is one of the Québécois de souche scholars in *Québékoisie*. Bouchard, a charismatic man, has become the go-to expert on all things related to Québec's past and, most importantly, on expressing Québec's settler innocence. His Indigenous counterpart is Pierrot Ross-Tremblay, an equally engaging Innu sociologist and professor at Laurentian University in Sudbury, Ontario, whose discourse could ruffle some of Bouchard's feathers if only he was featured in the film as extensively as his counterpart. Bouchard, speaking to Carrier and Higgins, argues: "Every culture sacralizes the road and the notion of pilgrimage. Think of Compostelle, Highway 66, etc." Bouchard laments Québec's lack of stories about Route 138, which he views as holding the province's memory. Echoing Alexis Martin, Bouchard deplores a certain amnesia: "We, who are oral people, the descendants of great storytellers, have sacrificed stories to access modernity." He exhorts the two filmmakers to "travel the 138 and tell our story, the story of the Innu, the truckers, the métis . . . You don't owe anything to anyone. Invent the story!"

It would be too simple to read Bouchard's comments as flippant or revisionist. While they certainly are, they nevertheless should be contextualized: the anthropologist fervently argues that "the history of the American continent is comprised of myths and scandalous lies" that need to be debunked. He speaks here of the doctrine of discovery and *terra nullius*. While this is perhaps laudable, Bouchard's participation in *L'Empreinte* shows us that in lieu of this myth, the anthropologist proposes the equally problematic trope of benevolent *métissage*. In *Québékoisie*, Bouchard contends that "America is a vast new métis nation. But this memory has been euthanized. Métissage was everywhere. Why is the extent of this métissage unknown to First Peoples? And why is it unknown to the Québécois?" He continues: "Because we were separated, our memory was killed. When and where did we break up with our territorial roots, our historical roots?" He argues that the Catholic

Church silenced the métis memory and proposed instead this myth of "francité" (frenchedness) that was heavily influenced by the rise of scientific racism.

Contrary to *L'Empreinte*, which seemingly evacuates the influence of the Catholic Church, Bouchard recognizes the major role it played in shaping the French Québécois de souche's narrative (as well as that of Indigenous peoples). But more than anything here, Bouchard is performing his desire to be made innocent of his settler-colonial complicity. Indeed, "directly or indirectly benefitting from the erasure and assimilation of Indigenous peoples is a difficult reality for settlers to accept" and they often "hurry toward any reprieve."[73] Ross-Tremblay calls this *l'épreuve de la vérité*, or the "challenge of truth," which often transforms encounters with Indigeneity into a performance of settler fragility. These encounters force Indigenous people into the role of the torturer (the ones whose truth pains settlers), and grant settlers a way out. For Bouchard and for many French Québécois de souche, the myth of *métissage* and Nouvelle-France's prelapsarian harmony offers such reprieve. However, as I previously demonstrated, Bouchard's narrative of *métissage* does not hold when faced with genealogical data or when confronted with the assimilatory project that underlay Nouvelle-France.

The French Québécois de souche are particularly invested in what Mary Louise Fellows and Sherene Razack call "the race to innocence." To maintain their narrative as an oppressed, colonized minority in Canada, the French Québécois de souche have had to "believe [their] own claim of subordination is the most urgent, and that [they] are unimplicated in the subordination of other[s]."[74] This self-positioning conveniently affords them the possibility to both deny their complicity in the ongoing oppression of Indigenous people *and* to claim solidarity with them as another minority within Canada. As we have seen, the events of 1990 in Oka punctured Québec's claim to innocence. Indeed, the province, rather than joining forces as an equally oppressed minority, turned to the federal government for help in quashing the Mohawks' territorial and sovereignty claims.

To its credit, *Québékoisie* struggles with these questions and allows its Indigenous interviewees' experiences to challenge Bouchard's narrative of innocence and brotherly love. Take, for instance, Pierrot Ross-Tremblay's reaction to the notion of Québec as a somehow more benevolent force than the rest of Canada: "How much longer will we be able to endure such suffering? We live together but our relation is . . . [he mimes crushing]. You are sitting on me and you ask me what I think about our relation . . . Do you really want to know? It does not work at all." Another interviewee, Marco Bacon (Innu), reports a similar experience, citing "difficult relations with the Québécois." Interviewed in his office at the University of Québec in Chicoutimi and at his own home, Bacon recalls: "I heard racist things, but I needed to integrate, so I did not react to them. I played the hypocritical card often in those days." When faced with the refusal of white settler society to grant him any form of racial mobility, Bacon turned to a discourse of racial purity that is a direct consequence of settler-colonial policies of blood quantum. He remembers how important it was for him to proclaim that he was "100 percent Innu." "We rejected them [white people] because they rejected us."

Originally, "Bacon" was not an Innu surname. Eventually, Marco Bacon became interested in knowing how his family had acquired this patronym. After doing some genealogical research, he discovered that the name Bacon originates from France, specifically Normandy. Higgins and Carrier met Bacon as he was about to leave for a pilgrimage to Normandy in search of his ancestors, and the two filmmakers chose to accompany him on his journey. Bacon reflects: "[If] you would have told me fourteen years ago, 'You have non-Aboriginal blood in your veins,' I would have been angry. I felt pure Indian." In Normandy, Bacon and his wife consult local archives and establish that his ancestor, the one who gave his name to the entire Bacon line in the Innu community, was born in Québec City to parents from the city of Caen, Normandy, who came to Nouvelle-France in 1647. Armed with this piece of information, Marco Bacon searches for any distant relative in Normandy. With the help of the local post office clerks and various other locals who seem bewildered by his quest, Bacon finally locates a Bacon from a nearby town who seems both puzzled and happy to encounter his *cousin d'Amérique*.

Marco Bacon's reaction to all this is hard to interpret at times. He attempts to see himself or some family resemblance in the promptness and facial expression of his distant French relative. However, the two men, standing side by side, reveal how tenuous the connection is between who they are and this single ancestor who came to Nouvelle-France in the seventeenth century. If individuals who discover one distant Indigenous ancestor often begin to self-identify as métis, it is not clear how a similar discovery of French blood shapes Marco Bacon's sense of self. Bacon, whose physical appearance marks him as Innu, is clearly not afforded the same racial mobility that Dupuis, Lanouette, and the protagonists of *L'Empreinte* can so easily claim as white settlers.

The system of federal recognition is based on the notion of "Indian blood" as a barometer of identity and belonging. As Ross-Tremblay argues, "blood quantum is part of the colonial logic" based on the elimination of Indigenous cultures. Unfortunately, as he laments, this colonial tool of exclusion has now been adopted in many communities, where the notion of blood quantum can often trump all other forms of community belonging. Settler-colonial policies have penetrated the psyches of all involved, and decolonization is a long, arduous, and uncomfortable process that few are willing to tackle. Carrier and Higgins's film explores relationships as a step in that direction, but the subjects they encounter are complex and ambivalent. These subjects resist simple narratives and are full of contradictions. Bouchard's poetic license with history allows him to champion Indigenous people and simultaneously use them to affirm whites' innocence. Some Indigenous participants reject the French Québécois de souche outright, while others, like Marco Bacon, want to create bridges. There are no easy answers, and the interviewees oscillate between their desire to refute race and blood and their incapacity to divorce identity from these concepts. This is perhaps summed up best by a motorcyclist that Carrier interviews at a rest area. "Indians are not sociable," he claims. "It is in their blood. They eat wild meat and that makes them wild."

Québékoisie begins with a quote from Linus Pauling which argues that life does not reside in molecules but in the bonds that unite them. If Higgins and Carrier's film emphasizes the importance of relationships, it also turns at times to biology in perhaps a naive way. As Kim Tallbear argues, too many people believe the oft-repeated claim that science is neutral, "has disproven the existence of race," and thus "will end racism."[75] Yet, in the case of Indigenous peoples in particular, science has often been deployed in the service and support of racist agendas. Today, the industry of DNA testing is profoundly invested in the notions of biological markers of race. These notions are lucrative to that industry. Tallbear thus warns: "Understanding what Native American DNA portends for Native Americans requires, in large part, understanding how gene discourses and scientific practices are entangled in ongoing colonialisms. What 'they' think and do have always determined how much trouble 'we' have."[76] So, when Carrier and Higgins interview Hélène Vézina from the BALSAC database project about the genetic makeup of Québec, it is not a neutral move. Vézina argues that "50 to 85% of Québécois de souche have at least one Indigenous ancestor," but Higgins and Carrier fail to contextualize this information and report on how having a distant Indigenous ancestor (which is common, since the founding pool in Nouvelle-France was small) translates to one's genetic code. For instance, Vézina shows in other published works that the genetic code of the French Québécois de souche is made of less than 1 percent of so-called "Aboriginal genes."[77] Higgins and Carrier do not provide such information.

After sharing her genealogical data, Vézina remarks: "But when are we Aboriginal? The question remains and I will not be the one to answer it." Indeed, what makes one Indigenous? Is it certain genes? And what distinct traits are encoded in these genes? Tallbear explains: "Given the prevalence of genetic determinism in our popular culture, it seems important to clarify that most markers used to show ancestry and close biological relationships are not known to code for anything."[78] Bacon, upon returning home from Normandy, explains: "We can't fool ourselves. Ancestors can help us understand history, but it is the community that helps us build history in the now." Andersen, Tallbear, Vowel, and many others argue that to claim Indigenous ancestors does not give one access to Indigenous culture (which is nation-specific and never static), tribal citizenship, and political consciousness. Quite simply, the lived experience of being Indigenous is not transmitted genetically.

Espaces de Parole

Toward the end of *L'Empreinte*, Dupuis interviews Professor Merham Ebrahami, who studies the culture of the workplace and comments on the unusually high number of committees and commissions that exist in Québec's institutions. According to him, the Québécois create spaces where speech can take place, where people can be consulted to reach a consensus. For Dupuis, this cultural trait comes from Indigenous peoples, whose societies are organized around the notion of circle and sharing speech. Many Indigenous communities were traditionally organized around, and many still privilege, a circular approach. This is a truly admirable model. What struck me as I watched Dupuis's interview, however, is how absent Indigenous people are from the *espaces de parole* that helped define and continue to shape the French Québécois de souche identity. Indigenous people have been pushed out of the circle for a long time now, and they continue to be an afterthought when it comes to consultations on projects that affect their communities and lives.

What would happen were these *espaces de parole* truly opened to Indigenous people? What would we hear from them? *L'Empreinte* may claim Indigenous peoples as brothers and sisters, but do they claim us in return? As Chris Andersen, Chelsea Vowel, and others argue, it is not enough to declare oneself métis; one also has to be recognized by the community. And there lies the problem. *L'Empreinte* never really asks Indigenous people if they are willing to claim "us" as we want to claim "them." Joséphine Bacon tells Roy Dupuis: "It wasn't supposed to be that way, we shared everything for so long. We gave you an identity. You walk in the footsteps we left you." And what have we given in return? In the light of all we have taken, one is left with the following question: We may want to claim filiation to Indigenous people as a way to exonerate ourselves, but why would they want to claim us in return?

Chapter 3

✦

Cinematic Encounters on the Reserve

> These territories inhabited exclusively by Aboriginal peoples are Canada's shame. These ghettos financed with billions of dollars for decades are, for the most part, inhuman spaces. Isolated, removed from any civilization, they propagate misery from one generation to the next and their inhabitants are among the wretched of the Earth.
>
> —Denise Bombardier

> Above all, reserves are communities with histories, families, and aspirations. They experience challenging social and economic conditions. But it is vital to recognize they also create conditions for resilience.
>
> —Chelsea Vowel, *Indigenous Writes*

Denise Bombardier published these inflammatory comments about Indigenous reserves and their inhabitants in her column for the *Journal de Montréal*, a populist, right-leaning Québécois newspaper. Bombardier, Québec's Barbara Walters, holds a Ph.D. in sociology from the Sorbonne and is a journalist, a television host, and a novelist. Bombardier honed her skills as an interviewer with important political figures from all over the world, but she is equally at home with famous artists like Céline Dion, about whom she wrote a book in 2009. She is a member of the Order of Canada and an officer of the Légion d'Honneur in France, and her voice is valued and legitimized by mainstream media. Her characterization of Indigenous peoples as belonging to "a deadly, antiscientific, and victimizing" culture and her portrayal of the native reserves as spaces of misery are thus very damaging.[1] Her ill-informed statements masquerade as a balanced reflection about Indigenous people and can act as pedagogy for her readers.

A trailblazer in terms of (white) women's rights, Bombardier has otherwise proven to be an ardent defender of the French Québécois de souche status quo. Under the pretense of liberalism, the journalist regularly writes self-congratulatory columns that celebrate "good immigrants" (those who assimilate and do not ask for "special accommodations"), defend (Western) "universal values," and advocate for a certain kind of pluralism in Québec (read: selectively inclusive).[2] When it comes to Indigenous people, Bombardier's track record aligns with the 41 percent of Canadians who recently expressed their desire to see the "advantages" afforded to Indigenous people abolished.[3] Of course, these perceived "advantages" are a gross misnomer, as studies consistently show that Canada invests far less per capita for the education, health, and housing of Indigenous people than it does for the rest of the Canadian population.[4] The so-called advantages most often decried by white settlers, such as not paying taxes and electric bills, or benefiting from free housing or education, are either simply untrue or could easily be contextualized by columnists such as Bombardier, if those writers did not satisfy themselves with the empty platitudes that comfort settlers in their self-righteousness. Indeed, reframing the reserves as spaces where unearned advantages are squandered and transformed by their inhabitants into a "misery passed on from one generation to the next" strategically puts the blame on the shoulders of Indigenous individuals and communities. It conveniently avoids looking at the history of reserves and at the violent structure of setter colonialism that created those reserves and maintains them in place.

The reserve, this "shameful space" that Bombardier wants to see disappear, is at the heart of this chapter's exploration. The vast majority of the images of First Nations[5] reserves that circulate in mainstream media paint a sensationalized portrait of what Žižek calls "subjective violence": that is, of perpetual crisis, misery, rampant suicide and abuse, and what Jill Carter (Anishinaabe-Ashkenazi) calls "the mortification of Indigenous flesh" for settler consumption.[6] The reserve, for many Canadians, is a space of despair, unfit for modernity, afflicted with many ills, and imagined as a haven for criminals, especially cigarette smugglers.[7] It is a space presented and often read through a narrative of crisis that frames each wave of suicides, each new ecological disaster, and each new housing shortage as a discrete incident befalling the community as in some Greek tragedy.

At the root of these discrete events is the normalized genocidal violence that quietly structures the reserve and which the "reserve-as-crisis" effectively obscures. This objective violence, to borrow from Žižek, is less spectacular in nature and takes various forms, ranging from the constant erosion of territorial rights to restricted and imposed modes of self-governance, to severe chronic underfunding, environmental degradation of reserve land from nearby industries, and lack of economic opportunities. In other words, the reserve is shaped by a form of everyday objective violence that is punctuated by moments of spectacular trauma. This was perhaps best exemplified by a highly symbolic blunder that occurred at the height of the H1N1 flu epidemic in 2009, when the federal government sent body bags in lieu of much-needed vaccines to reserves in Manitoba.[8] It would be easy to dismiss this event as a purely clerical error—but I argue, as did the leaders of these communities, that in fact, sending body bags instead of vaccines aligns in a sinister way with Canada's policies toward Indigenous peoples at large and First Nations peoples in particular (through the machinations of the Indian Act), which are predicated on the expectation of their eventual disappearance. Indeed, the reserve circulates in the Canadian imaginary landscape as a space of erasure, a cul-de-sac where, had the Indian Act accomplished its stated goals, First Nations peoples would have ceased to be as a people.

This historical, relentless, and largely invisible violence, Žižek's objective violence, is mostly absent from or simplistically approached in public discourse. Furthermore, missing from this narrative of the reserve-as-crisis exemplified by Bombardier's editorials is how the reserve, though born of the settler-colonial genocidal project, is vitally shaped by a host of Indigenous forces that have and continue to devise ingenious tools of survivance and (re)-surgence.[9] Gerald Vizenor coined the term *survivance* and explains: "Native survivance is more than survival, more than endurance or mere response; the stories of survivance are an active presence . . . an active repudiation of dominance, tragedy, and victimry."[10] The images of the reserve that circulate document real pain, need, and trauma, but they fail to capture how the reserves have also served in a subversive way to protect Indigenous cultures, the very thing that settler-colonial policies were intended to destroy. Reserves, as Chelsea Vowel points out in this chapter's epigraph, have fostered practices of freedom, anticolonial actions that challenge "the white possessive,"[11] and forms of radical kinship. Despite being *in* Canada, the reserves are in many ways not *of* Canada. The reserves have been supported by changes made to the Indian Act that abolished the pass system and increased the mobility of Indigenous people; by the decriminalization of cultural and ceremonial practices; and by access to legal representation for Indigenous peoples. These reserves—as well as the urban spaces inhabited by Indigenous peoples—incubate various resurgence practices in Canada, and have triggered a return in force that became highly visible with the Idle No More movement in 2012.

Turning away from settler-colonial depictions of the reserve-as-crisis, this chapter examines cinematic explorations of the reserve by Indigenous film directors as a way to illuminate the complex and contradictory forces that shape the reserve both as a space of what Lisa Marie Cacho calls "living death"[12] and of what I dub "tortured filiation," and as a space of resilience where Indigenous futurity is articulated against tremendous odds. The four films I examine in this chapter labor to illuminate the baseline violence that underlies the reserve while rendering visible the multiple modes of survivance and opposition deployed by its inhabitants. I examine first the 1993 documentary *Kanehsatake: 270 Years of Resistance*, by the acclaimed Abénaki filmmaker Alanis Obomsawin. The film examines the 1990 Oka "Crisis" during which the Mohawk[13] (Kanien'kehà:ka) community of Kanehsatà:ke[14] became a highly visible and contested space in Québec's public sphere. While Oka certainly appeared as a crisis for many Québécois and Canadians for whom Indigenous presence was a thing of the past, it was an event long in the making that momentarily brought to the surface the settler-colonial forces against which the Mohawks had been fighting for centuries. Moreover, this so-called crisis did not follow what I would call the settlers' preferred tragic scenario, in which Indigenous people are framed as helpless victims of modernity whom settlers can then generously rescue. The events in Oka stemmed not from helplessness but from the obstinate refusal of Mohawks to see their land eroded once more and from their assertion of sovereignty, which forced settlers to perform violence openly.

I then turn to a 2012 fiction film entitled *Mesnak* by the Huron-Wendat director Yves Sioui Durand. The film transposes Shakespeare's *Hamlet* from Elsinore to a fictional reserve in Québec and meditates on the violent intramural dynamics of the reserve as a space shaped by settler-colonial forces, internalized racism, and the severe trauma inflicted on communities by state-sanctioned Residential Schools and the subsequent "sixties scoop." Rather than adopting the reserve-as-crisis narrative, *Mesnak* unflinchingly dramatizes long-standing conflicts that find their roots in the genocidal policies deployed by the settler state against Indigenous peoples and which have transformed the reserve into a space of what I call tortured filiation. The film gestures to a space outside of the reserve, "the ancestors' territory," where Indigenous people can heal. But as *Mesnak* ultimately asserts, echoing Lyle Longclaws's famous comments about Indigenous trauma, "before the healing can take place, the poison must first be exposed."[15] And so the reserve and the forces that shape it must be examined in the open.

Finally, I locate this impulse to name, expose, and heal in the work of a cinematic project entitled the Wapikoni Mobile. A mobile recording studio that visits Indigenous communities in the province of Québec, and across the Americas, this project, founded in 2003, assists individuals from Indigenous communities who want to create short films or music. I conclude this chapter with a brief engagement with two short films created through the Wapikoni Mobile project that explore the reserve through the eyes of its inhabitants. The first film is Innu filmmaker Réal Junior Leblanc's *L'Enfance déracinée* (2013), a visual homage to the survivors of the Mani-Utenam Residential School (near Sept-Îles) who reclaimed the land on which the institution once stood on the reserve. The second film is *Tour de Char* (2009) by Jean-Baptiste Bacon-Riverin and Malcolm Riverin, a short film in which two young Innu men take the viewers for a car ride around Pessamit (formerly Betsiamites), a reserve in the Côte-Nord region of Québec. In both cases, the reserve is portrayed as an anchoring space of tremendous resilience, which the new and fast-growing young generation of Indigenous people is busy radically reimagining.

An important note before I turn to the films: the reserve holds powerful signifying power in the public sphere as *the* space of Indigeneity, but in reality, 40 percent of Status Indians and an even larger percentage of Indigenous people who are not recognized in the eyes of the federal government live outside the reserves, in various urban settings. Exploring Indigenous urban spaces exceeds the scope of this chapter, but scholars such as Karyn Recollet, Bonita Lawrence, Angie Morrill, Eve Tuck, and the Super Futures Haunt Qollective, among others, offer powerful reflections on Indigenous bodies and presence in these landscapes.[16]

The Material Reserve/The Symbolic Reserve

As Audra Simpson notes, "Indians in Canada can never own land in a full sense, in a Lockean fashion."[17] In legal and material terms, a reserve is "a track of land, the legal title of which is vested in her Majesty, that has been set aside by Her Majesty for the use and benefit of a band."[18] While some reserves were created through treaty-making before the creation of the Dominion of Canada, it was the Constitution Act of 1867 that assigned legislative jurisdiction over "Indians and Lands reserved for the Indians"[19] to the Parliament of Canada. After 1867, Canada embarked on an era of intense treaty-making. Since the very beginning, treaties have been understood by the parties involved in vastly different and often irreconcilable ways. Treaties are constitutionally recognized "agreements that describe exchanges where Aboriginal groups agree to share some of their interests in their ancestral lands in return for various payments and promises."[20] It is important to reiterate that a treaty always involves two parties: discrete Aboriginal nations and the federal or provincial governments deputized by the citizens who elect them. In other words, all Canadians (and not just Aboriginal people) are treaty people, and we (the settlers and their elected governments) haven't been holding up our end of the bargain. The so-called advantages that the aforementioned 41 percent of polled Canadians vehemently decry are, in many cases, obligations agreed upon by two parties.

For many Indigenous people, treaties are understood as sacred moral and ethical covenants between nations.[21] They are binding, and the spirit of the treaty must be respected even as circumstances change. Furthermore, they are understood as confirming Aboriginal rights on certain territories (one could only share what one possessed in the first place, even if ownership was not necessarily understood in a capitalist, Lockean fashion) and as establishing a relationship between two independent, self-governing peoples. In contrast, non-Aboriginal treaty-makers have often envisioned treaties "as cheap and expedient ways to strip Aboriginal title from most of the lands in Canada so that resources could be exploited by other groups."[22] Federal and provincial governments have, as much as possible, maintained that Aboriginal peoples "ceded, surrendered, and yielded"[23] all their Aboriginal rights and titles through these treaties, which often comprised ridiculously small one-time payments or continuing payments (about five dollars per treaty Indian per year).

Québec, like British Columbia and other portions of Atlantic Canada, rests largely on unceded territories for which no treaties were signed by federal (Crown) or provincial powers until very recently (and even now, only for a small proportion of the territory). That is not the case in the Canadian Prairies and Ontario where the Crown signed treaties one to eleven between 1871 and 1922. These are known as historic or numbered treaties. Treaties signed after 1923 are therefore referred to as modern treaties. Their negotiation was triggered by Indigenous resurgence in the 1960s that led to a number of landmark court decisions beginning in the 1970s. These decisions (the 1973 Calder case about the Nisga'a nation of British Columbia and the 1973 Malouf decision about the James Bay Cree and Inuit, for instance) brought about a shift in the recognition of Aboriginal rights in Canada and ushered policy changes. The Convention de la Baie James et du Nord Québécois, signed in 1975 by the province and the Cree and Inuit nations of northern Québec, stands as Québec's first modern treaty. It still relied on the extinction of Indigenous rights on large parcels of their territory. This agreement was celebrated by many, but Québec, after signing the accord with great fanfare, ultimately perpetuated the federal model of reneging on promises made. The Cree nation took Québec to court and held the province accountable and in 2003, a new treaty, La Paix des Braves, was signed to ensure that the promises made in 1975 would finally be fulfilled.[24]

The Indian Act, which I explore in depth in the next chapter, was created in 1876, at the same time that Canada was aggressively pursuing land cession from Indigenous people. The Indian Act is a series of laws that regulate who is Indian in the eyes of the federal government and the nature of their relationship with the state. It has been amended numerous times since its creation in order to accommodate and accelerate Canada's racist settler-colonial project. The reserves, as one branch of this project, are thus profoundly racialized spaces. Lisa Marie Cacho writes: "Racism is a killing abstraction. It creates spaces of living death and populations 'dead-to-others.' It ensures that certain people will live an 'abstract experience' where 'living [is] something to be *achieved* and not *experienced*.' "[25] Patrick Wolfe has famously described settler colonialism as destroying to replace: this is a mechanism vastly different from the logic of accumulation that underlay chattel slavery in the Americas. "Indigenous people obstructed settlers' access to land, so their increase was counterproductive. In this way, the restrictive racial classification of Indians straightforwardly furthered the logic of elimination."[26] The reserve was thus meant to be a space of confined living death where Status Indians, given the arithmetic of exclusion that regulates the granting of status in the Indian Act, would eventually cease to exist. Reserves were not imagined as spaces of life but as spaces of erasure. They were monitored, gated, isolated; and for more than a hundred years (1876 to 1996), when children left them, it was to go the Residential Schools, which similarly acted as spaces of living death or, tragically in many cases, physical death. Today, many reserves continue to function in conditions where life is achieved rather than experienced due to housing crises, unemployment, and food and water shortages. By August 31, 2016, eighty-nine reserves had boil-water advisories on a semipermanent basis.[27] Some have lived under such advisories for decades. But, just like the Indian Act failed to assimilate Indigenous people, the reserves have ultimately failed in their intended assimilatory goals. Instead, I aim to illuminate how the reserve provided the grounds for the survivance and (re)surgence of Indigenous culture.

The reserves featured in this chapter are different in nature. The Mohawk reserve of Kanehsatà:ke, where Obomsawin shot her documentary, and the Innu reserves Mani-Utenam and Pessamit, in the Wapikoni Mobile films, all exist as real entities. In contrast, Kinogamish, *Mesnak*'s fictive reserve, is a metaphorical space; each of its attributes and inhabitants are thus saturated with heightened signifying powers.[28] By examining these films in relation to one another, I hope to illuminate how the reserve operates materially and symbolically against and under settler colonialism in Canada.

Oka, the So-Called Crisis, and the Criminalization of Indigenous Dissent

If *Mesnak* examines settler-state violence through a fictional lens, *Kanehsatake: 270 Years of Resistance* meditates on a historical moment in Québec's history, the 1990 "Oka Crisis," in which reality echoed Shakespearean drama in vivid ways. The events in Oka began, like *Hamlet*, with ancestors whose disturbed burials unleashed dramatic confrontations in the present (a scenario repeated in the events explored in chapter 5). While the ghost of his slain father visits Hamlet in Shakespeare's world, it was an entire Mohawk (Kanien'kehà:ka) burial site that was threatened in 1990 when the nearby town of Oka decided to expand its luxury private golf course and add a series of high-end condominiums to the project. This expansion project, unilaterally devised by the town of Oka and its mayor, Jean Ouellette, planned to utilize as its building site the disputed pine forest at the border of Oka that forms the Kanien'kehà:ka burial ground. Kanehsatà:ke's unusual fragmented cartography, the result of many previous expropriations, rendered it especially vulnerable to such settler encroachments.

Obomsawin's film documents the Kanien'kehà:ka response to this invasion. Her camera captures what began as a peaceful occupation of the contested burial site and surrounding dirt road, but quickly escalated to a violent 78-day standoff in which the Mohawks opposed the full array of governmental forces of repression, which were there to protect white possessions and uphold white possessive logic. The events of 1990 marked a turning point not because expropriation was new, but because of the Mohawks' visible refusal to be invaded. In stating this, I do not mean that refusal itself was new, since the Mohawks had and have been fighting for their land since the arrival of the French. The highly publicized nature of their refusal, however, created a different kind of encounter with the state apparatus, one more urgently visible and open to scrutiny. In 1990, the Mohawks of Kanehsatà:ke were joined by Warriors from the nearby reserve of Kahnawà:ke who showed their support by blocking the Mercier Bridge, one of the main arteries between Montréal and its suburbs (60,000 vehicles crossed the bridge each day in 1990). An overwhelmed Mayor Ouellette then asked the Sûreté du Québec (SQ)[29] to intervene, going against the council of Québec's minister of native affairs, John Ciaccia. Ciaccia, a well-meaning negotiator, was well aware of the SQ's long history of brutality toward Québec's Indigenous population and wanted to avoid an escalation of violence.[30] His worries proved prophetic. When the SQ agent Corporal Lemay died in a chaotic gunfire exchange[31] in the pine forest on July 11, 1990, the Kanien'kehà:ka sensed that retaliation would be brutal and built a barricade around their land, preparing for siege. Obomsawin was on site from the beginning and filmed the SQ raid as well as the subsequent siege, documenting how the military employed food deprivation and medicine rationing as well as the repression of journalistic freedom in order to force the Kanien'kehà:ka and the Warriors to surrender.

Many describe Obomsawin as the grande dame of documentary cinema in Canada.[32] Her work at the National Film Board (NFB) spans decades and is widely celebrated. Obomsawin is a tireless advocate, and her films are profoundly invested in telling stories from and to Indigenous peoples. Her cinematic engagement with the Oka Crisis includes four documentary films—*Kanehsatake: 270 Years of Resistance* (1993), *My Name Is Kahentiiosta* (1996), *Spudwrench: Kahnawake Man* (1997), and *Rocks at Whiskey Trench* (2000)—in which she captures the stories of some of the central figures of this historical event. In many of these films, and most particularly in *Kanehsatake: 270 Years of Resistance*, Obomsawin labors to suture the lives of the inhabitants of Kanehsatà:ke and their neighboring settler communities through a discourse of shared humanity. Obomsawin's work, aptly described by the scholar Randolph Lewis as operating "on the middle ground,"[33] has always aimed at bridging the gap between Indigenous people and the rest of Canada. An optimist, Obomsawin says about the power of documentary films: "It changes society. It brings knowledge about the others that you always call the 'others.' And all of a sudden you realize that they feel like you, and they have stories that are similar, and they need you, and you need them."[34]

Unsurprisingly, Obomsawin labors cinematically in *Kanehsatake* to heal the divide between settlers and Indigenous people created in Québec and in Canada by the events in Oka. While attentive to the undeniable force of her work, Bruno Cornellier is critical of how the NFB recuperated Obomsawin's suturing work in ways that solidify rather than question settler colonialism.

> As the self-proclaimed beneficiary of what could be called the public gift of Obomsawin's Indianness, the private and state-sponsored cultural press's non-Native audience was invited to participate in the corrective, post-Oka project of resettling one's home and salvaging Canada's "Indian thing" from the hands of what Sara Ahmed might call those "unfamiliar," "inassimilable," and "untouchable" Mohawks—most notably those associated with the spectacular media images of the belligerent Warriors.[35]

For Cornellier, the NFB, as an arm of the settler-colonial project, needs Obomsawin's Indianness. It needs to curate and deploy it to position itself as benevolent and postcolonial. The NFB needs Obomsawin as a vehicle to train new consumers of this curated Indianness.

While acknowledging Cornellier's critique, Isabelle St-Amand positions Obomsawin's intervention differently in her book about the literary works that emerged in the wake of Oka.[36] St-Amand locates in Obomsawin's work a rich example of what the Seneca scholar Michelle Raheja conceptualizes as "visual sovereignty":

> Visual sovereignty simultaneously addresses the settler population by creating self-representations that interact with older stereotypes but also, more importantly, connects film production to larger aesthetic practices that work toward strengthening treaty claims and more traditional (although by no means static) modes of cultural understanding.[37]

If Cornellier and St-Amand both recognize Obomsawin's undeniable contribution to Indigenous self-representation, they differ when it comes to their reading of what her cinematic oeuvre does to dismantle the settler-colonial gaze.

For my part, I am interested in how the images Obomsawin captures often exceed their bridging mission and recuperative potential and reveal instead the precarious and dangerous ontological status of the reserve in the edifice of settler colonialism. Reserves and their inhabitants stand as what Jodi A. Byrd calls "figures of transit." It is through and on Indigenous lands, bodies, and forms of knowledge that Canada and Québec have built themselves as settler states. Pushed to the margins of settler society and understood as standing outside of the present within liberal democracies, Indigenous peoples are, according to Byrd, forever deferred. Indeed, their inclusion in the present would point out the obvious: that Canada stands on someone else's land, and this someone else is still present. This is the challenge posed by the Mohawks' resolutely contemporary presence to white possessive logics that Obomsawin captures over and over again in her film.

Obomsawin's film establishes the reserve as a marginal space, a space of living death, with an evocative opening sequence: the camera captures, in an extreme long shot, a bucolic scene of leisure. From a distance, the viewer observes a group of golfers in bright polo shirts out on the green. The camera then slowly moves away from the golf players in the distance and toward the parking lot that stands between them and the ground occupied by the imagined viewer. The camera finishes its motion in a wide shot of the adjacent pine forest and the beautiful contested Kanien'kehà:ka burial ground, softly lit by the sun. Tombstones stand facing the parking lot, silent witnesses to what was once the vast expanse of Kanien'kehà:ka land. The image cuts to a close shot of a large wooden board where "Mohawk Territory No Trespassing!" is written in black paint. A small group of Kanien'kehà:ka men and women are sitting under the sign, guarding their land and their ancestors.

In its first thirty-three seconds, Obomsawin's documentary has already visually exceeded the director's narrative of intra-human conflict. Visually, the Kanien'kehà:ka are positioned outside of settler society, separated from the capitalist dream of well-earned leisure time by a parking lot full of the golfers' new cars. When the imagined viewer standing on Kanien'kehà:ka land is asked to map her position or territory, the camera, acting as the agent of her gaze, zooms in on lonely, eroded tombstones. Kanien'kehà:ka territory, in other words, is a space where even the buried are not at peace. The burial ground is silent and fragile-looking in the face of civil society's incessant encroachments (represented here by the golf course and parking lot). As the camera surveys the burial site, Obomsawin's narration describes the waves of expropriations of Mohawk land perpetrated first by the religious authorities in Nouvelle-France, then by the British colonial administration, and more recently by the town of Oka. "Even the burial ground," she says, "became the property of Oka," and its mayor now wants to use the land for a luxury expansion of the town's golf course.

With these images supported by her factual narration, Obomsawin delineates Kanien'kehà:ka territory as a repeatedly violated space, a zone open to invasion and gratuitous violence. No transgressions on the Kanien'kehà:ka's part can explain these successive waves of expropriation. The Kanien'kehà:ka were, and still are, simply standing in the way of settler society's expansion. These invasions belong to the systemic violence described by Žižek: they are the result of the smooth functioning (that is, the expansion) of settler communities. The camera's trajectory followed in this opening sequence creates a clear sense of the divide between Kanien'kehà:ka territory and settler society. In fact, as Obomsawin's images implacably put it, the players' peaceful enjoyment of their game is dependent on Indigenous people's retreat into silence and invisibility. By visually opposing tombstones to a golf course, and the violent zone of the reserve to the peaceful zone of settler society's leisure and recreation, Obomsawin offers a provoking reflection on how Indigenous people "continue to serve primarily as signposts and grave markers along the roads of empire"; they are acknowledged as past victims of colonization and genocide but are "simultaneously effaced and deferred" in the present.[38]

Obomsawin's extra-diegetic commentary serves as a bridging device. Her clear description of the Kanien'kehà:ka's claim to the pine forest and burial site documents at length the various tactics deployed by white settlers to forcefully expel the Kanien'kehà:ka from their land. Obomsawin appeals to the viewers' sense of justice and presents the Kanien'kehà:ka struggle as an effort to reclaim sovereign losses. Land claims are undoubtedly central to Kanien'kehà:ka sovereignty (and sovereignty is understood here in ways that exceed Western definitions), and they certainly constituted the precipitating factor in the Oka events. However, Obomsawin's visual narrative gestures, perhaps unconsciously, to a loss that cannot be redressed through land repatriation and that is not legible in the present. It gestures to a form of violence and loss that cannot be remedied without calling into question the smooth functioning of settler-colonial societies. Indeed, Obomsawin's opening sequence serves to expose the "unlivable, ungrievable conditions"[39] created by settler states. In these images, the small group of Kanien'kehà:ka sentries is positioned on the side of death, standing alongside tombstones, resolutely outside of civil society's borders. Obomsawin shows a space where there is no respite from white hegemony, even in death.

As Obomsawin films the pine forest and burial site, she introduces us to Kahentiiotsa, one of the film's central characters. Kahentiiotsa has come from a nearby reserve to support the Oka protest. Speaking directly to the camera, she explains her surprise when she arrived at the burial site: "This is the road youse [*sic*] been blocking for three months?" she exclaims. "It's a dirt road! I thought maybe it was a highway, you know? Geez!" Indeed, the Kanien'kehà:ka's dissent and their occupation of a seemingly insignificant dirt road and parcel of land can appear benign, yet they unleashed a deep-seated anxiety that spread from Oka to the highest governmental levels. Obomsawin utilizes Kahentiiosa's surprise to render legible for her viewers the disproportionate nature of the government's response. In 1990 Kanehsatà:ke had a population of approximately 1,800. At the height of the standoff, the Kanien'kehà:ka were more numerous: they did occupy more roads and blocked a main bridge between Montréal and the suburbs. Even then, the SQ officers, quickly followed by the soldiers deployed to contain the "Mohawk threat," seemed like a disproportionate response: "Suddenly the highest number of troops in the history of Indigenous-settler relations in North America was deployed to Kanehsatà:ke, as this was the most unambiguous form of exceptional relations, that of warfare. There were 2,650 soldiers deployed to handle fifty-five Warriors."[40] This intense repressive reaction indicates how vital the containment of First Nations' dissent and presence is to the existence of the settler-colonial project. This containment guarantees the illusion of a nonviolent zero level, of the settler societies' "normal state of things."

Obomsawin's desire to situate her argument at the level of shared humanity provides a way out—unwillingly, no doubt, given that her entire filmography critiques settler colonialism—for those who want to avoid the difficult ensemble of ethical questions that constitute the crux of the Oka standoff. The events in Oka brought to the fore the irreconcilable nature of Québec's identity discourse, which claims the status of an oppressed minority while actively repressing the Mohawks' assertion of sovereignty and affirmation of their distinct culture. Given its own struggle for recognition at the political and cultural levels, Québec would appear a natural ally for the Mohawks. However, as previously discussed, such an alliance would require the Québécois and Indigenous people to be structurally positioned as equals, and this is antithetical to the settler-colonial project, which rests on the removal, assimilation, and erasure of Indigenous peoples. The events in Oka revealed Kanehsatà:ke as such a space of removal, erasure, and repression and thus illuminated the artifice of Canada and Québec's self-congratulatory discourse as liberal and tolerant communities.

Indeed, Canada, the very nation that in 1982 recognized Aboriginal ancestral rights as constitutional rights (although in vague terms), subsequently rejected the Kanien'kehà:ka's assertion of sovereignty over their burial site and criminalized their dissent. This contradiction is exemplified in Obomsawin's movie when she shows excerpts of a press conference in which one Kanien'kehà:ka negotiator, an anguished motherly figure, reflects on the barricades' raison d'être and pleads to the public: "We are taking nothing that is not rightfully ours. Did you forget that?" Her comments are followed by those of then-prime minister Brian Mulroney, who affirms that "the Mohawks are terrorists and Canada does not negotiate with terrorists"—a position that powerfully reframes the debate away from Canada's violation of the very recognition of Indigenous peoples' rights that the nation recently enshrined in its own constitution.

The horizontal relationship of shared humanity that Obomsawin labors to present in her movie is in fact a vertical one, in which the settler-society rests on Indigenous spaces, cultures, and communities, slowly suffocating them, as Pierrot Ross-Tremblay laments in his intervention in *Québékoisie*. Contrary to settler communities, whose societal projects are driven by expansion and renewal, reserves were never devised with regeneration in mind and symbolize instead a transitory space between colonization and assimilation. The reserve is part and parcel of Žižek's understanding of "objective" violence; while the events in Oka were described by the press and felt by settlers as subjective, that is, "a perturbation of the 'normal,' peaceful state of things," I argue that it was but a continuation of the objective, systemic violence that organizes encounters between settlers and Indigenous peoples.[41] Indeed, despite what governmental representatives and settler media argued, the events in Oka were not a "crisis" and cannot be narrativized as solely belonging to the category of subjective violence. Instead, what the events in Oka rendered visible for a moment is the continuously operative force—the "objective violence"—that secures normalcy in Québec. Violent assimilation policies, police repression, and the criminalization of Indigenous dissent are all part of the objective violence that allows Québec to exist as a stable settler community.

The Mohawks' sovereignty and territorial claims indeed threatened Québec's ethical coherence and "white possessive logics" in such a powerful way that these demands needed to be repressed and contained at all costs in 1990. Moreton-Robinson writes:

> It takes a great deal of work to maintain Canada, the United States, Hawai'i, New Zealand, and Australia as white possessions. The regulatory mechanisms of these nation-states are extremely busy reaffirming and reproducing this possessiveness through a process of perpetual Indigenous dispossession ranging from the refusal of Indigenous sovereignty to overregulated piecemeal concessions.[42]

Violent repression is yet another aspect of the "work" needed to maintain white possession. The strength of this repression is visually articulated in one particularly poignant sequence of Obomsawin's documentary. She shows several long shots of Oka as it is invaded by the SQ: the camera captures aggressive searches performed on Kanien'kehà:ka by the SQ, and the seemingly endless rows of police cars and uniformed men. Obomsawin zooms in on a man who is prevented from crossing an SQ road blockade. He is distraught, on the verge of tears, and argues to no avail that his family is waiting for him on the other side. The Kanien'kehà:ka, Obomsawin tells us visually, have been contained and isolated by the SQ. These images of containment and repression are quickly replaced with disquieting footage of a riot in nearby Châteauguay, where a group of 7,000 white citizens rallies at a busy intersection to voice their anger about the Mercier Bridge closure. The camera captures a group of mostly French Québécois de souche (the majority in Châteauguay) performing a mock lynching, burning the effigy of a Mohawk Warrior as they chant and cheer in a febrile atmosphere. As the rioters scream "Sauvages!" and perform a type of Indian war hoot, they overturn a semitrailer truck delivering vegetables to the barricaded communities.[43] While the SQ officers witness and eventually manage the scene, their intervention seems benign in comparison to their muscled actions at the barricades.

From this rioting scene under the cover of night, Obomsawin transports us to a press conference led by the mayors of the seven municipalities adjacent to Oka. They have come to show their support for Mayor Jean Ouellette and explain their decision to the press in the following way: "We can't negotiate 75 percent of Québec's territory! Would you want us to negotiate your home, would you want us to negotiate 75 percent of the province [with Indigenous people]?" The citizens gathered at the town hall cheer and applaud. Obomsawin, for her part, adds no voice-over commentary to a scene that so openly depicts the current impossibility of Québec-Mohawk coexistence. Indeed, as this scene clearly demonstrates, Québec's existence, its cohesion as a linguistic and cultural community whose territorial base in part ensures its survival, depends on the continuous suppression of Indigenous people's land rights. Obomsawin does not explain what the 75 percent invoked in this press conference might refer to. Indigenous land claims were in the news at the time[44] and maps showing the province, if it were restituted to the Indigenous nations who claimed it as ancestral territory, proposed a radically different spatial repartition. As viewers, we are left to assume that this is the amount of land claimed by Indigenous populations across Québec. The number, coming from the mayor's mouth, recasts Kanien'kehà:ka demands as "unreasonable," while in fact this is about the percentage of land in Québec for which no treaties have ever been signed and on which Indigenous people retain ancestral rights that have been legally recognized by Canada's Supreme Court. Obomsawin's silence over Ouellette's comments illuminates the cognitive dissonance at work in Oka and elsewhere in Québec, which allows the settlers to criminalize Indigenous people's attempts to defend their ancestral land while recasting the French Québécois de souche—the occupiers—as victims.

Obomsawin later films an altercation between two citizens in Oka. An elderly man, interviewed by a journalist, voices his support for the golf-course project while a young man named Martin furiously shouts back at him: "Sacre ton camps chez vous, maudit chien sale de rat!" ("Go back home you dirty dog, you rat!"). Martin's friend attempts to calm him down as the journalists rush to interview the elderly golf supporter, who proceeds to invoke laws and due process. "Ils auraient pu prévenir ca" ("They could have prevented this"), the elderly man continues, speaking about the Mohawks. "Ils doivent respecter la loi" ("They need to respect the law"). In the background, the young man is becoming increasingly furious and finally screams to the uninterested elderly man and his media entourage: "C'est leur terre! C'est aux Indiens: c'est à eux autres, ok! Tabarnak de sans coeur!" ("It's their land! It's the Indians' land: it's theirs, ok! You heartless fuck!"). The passersby look at Martin with discomfort as the journalists continue to court the elderly representative of settler society's cognitive dissonance.

Martin, in his outburst, touches the crux of the Oka standoff: the burial site is Kanien'kehà:ka land and it was taken from them, and now this theft is obfuscated by a discourse about laws and due process. One of the townspeople recorded by Obomsawin remarks: "They [the Mohawks] know why they are fighting and it is worth more than nine holes in the ground." Another remarks: "I really wonder who is the most civilized here." Canada and Québec exist as a result of theft, occupation, and genocidal policies, making them in essence an unethical and oppressive project. This systemic violence, disseminated and normalized through the realm of symbolic violence, is what guarantees the settler status quo. It is a reality that Québec and Canada at large conveniently ignore and that the Mohawk uprising uncomfortably brought to the surface. Obomsawin quietly allows this discomfort to rise in this particular scene, letting Martin explain the nature of Québec's anxious reaction to Mohawk demands.

As the tension escalates during the 78-day standoff, Obomsawin's colleagues film the riots and racist demonstrations outside the barricades in the nearby cities of Oka and Châteauguay, documenting the violence that erupted in the public sphere during the crisis, which culminated in the stoning of a convoy of cars carrying frightened Mohawk elders and women away from Kahnawà:ke. The crisis brought international opprobrium to Québec and Canada, led to a backlash against Indigenous people in Québec, and spearheaded a new wave of Indigenous activism that Ladner and Simpson survey in their important book *This Is an Honour Song: Twenty Years since the Blockades*. During the crisis a number of international journalists mused, as this book does, over the apparent contradiction between the French Québécois de souche's discourse as an oppressed minority within Canada and its own colonial treatment of the Mohawks' plight. Québec had plenty of reasons to feel anxious, as Alain Gerbier wrote in the French newspaper *Libération*:

> The Québécois are in a delicate situation . . . How can they claim the right to independence for themselves and deny it to the First Nations of the land? In 1985, when he was in power, Rene Lévesque [an *independantiste*] had not hesitated to recognize the distinct character of the Aboriginal nations and the right for them to decide on the development of their own identity. But the present Québécois premier, Robert Bourassa (a federalist), allowed the July 11 attack at Oka, had to force himself to buy off the James Bay Cree to fulfill his dreams of harnessing hydro-electric power, and called in the army. For Bourassa the only good Indian . . . is an Indian who plays dead [fait le mort].[45]

While Gerbier's comments bluntly name the cognitive dissonance at work in Québec, he fails to acknowledge that even for Lévesque, this recognition of Indigenous people's distinct character would ultimately be subsumed under Québec's own sovereignty. Gerbier attributes the "delicate" nature of Québec's situation to its sovereignty discourse and seemingly asks, "If Québec can separate, why can't the Mohawks?" This question fails to address something more fundamental. Québec is in a delicate situation because a visible, audible, and legible Mohawk is an indisputable reminder of Québec's participation in and reliance on ongoing violence toward Indigenous people for its own ethical and cartographical integrity. The French Québécois de souche's mythscape as an oppressed and "colonized" minority at the hands of English Canada cannot coexist with the narrative of Québec as an oppressor that is consistently endangering Indigenous culture and sovereignty. The uncomfortable questions that Gerbier and others asked during the crisis, which revealed the dissonance at work in Québec's identity discourse, were quickly shut down in Québec's public sphere, where resentment toward the Kanien'kehà:ka is still palpable today.

Hamlet, Prince of Kinogamish: Something Is Rotten in the State of Québec

Obomsawin's unflinching film finds a powerful cinematic companion in *Mesnak* (2012) by the Huron-Wendat director and theater artist Yves Sioui Durand. The film begins with this tormented exchange between Hamlet and Horatio:

> Does it not, think'st thee, stand me now upon
> He that hath kill'd my king and whored my mother . . .
> Isn't not perfect conscience
> To quit him with this arm?[46]

In the film, this encounter takes place in a dark rehearsal room, where the young Innu actor Dave Brodeur (Victor Andrés Trelles-Turgeon) struggles to find the right emotional range for this famous scene. The camera closes in on Dave's concentrated face as he performs Shakespeare's text in French. His rendition is a cry for justice driven by rage. Dave/Hamlet urgently asks: isn't it a son's duty to avenge his parents and a prince's obligation to seek redress for his slain king? Dave's acting coach (Peter Batakliev) interrupts the young actor's speech and warns him against *l'écueil de la motivation unique* or "the trap of a single motivation." *Hamlet*, he argues, is a story that cannot be reduced to a violent outburst or an irrational quest for retribution. To play Hamlet, the director suggests, is to dive into deep, turbulent waters and struggle against violent undercurrents.

Mesnak delves lucidly into these waters. The film meditates specifically on the reserve and on the ontology of being Indigenous in a settler state, exploring the repercussions of existing against settler-state domination. *Mesnak* deploys Hamlet (both the character and the play's well-known plot) as a performative device through which settler states' subterranean violence (Žižek's objective systemic violence) can be performed in the open. The film illuminates these forces through a cinematic *mise-en-abyme* of Shakespeare's play in which Dave Brodeur is caught in a network of mirroring realities. Indeed, as he prepares to perform *Hamlet* onstage, Dave's personal life starts to echo Shakespeare's play in revealing ways. *Mesnak*'s opening scene sets up these two spheres' echoing central dilemma: what should Hamlet/Dave do when faced with the violence (both subjective and objective) and injustice that shape his family and his kingdom/reserve? The question is multivalent and animates Dave's work as an actor searching for his character's driving force. It also becomes Dave's central dilemma as his personal life begins to echo Hamlet's encounter with a broken world and his subsequent quest for truth and redress.

Dave Brodeur's life is the stuff of Shakespearean drama and thus begins with tragic events. In what seems to be the late 1970s, Dave's father Jean Ashini—a Red Power leader—dies in a suspicious hunting accident on reserve land; and Dave is subsequently taken from his grieving mother Gertrude (Kathia Rock), who has spiraled down into alcoholism and is deemed unfit to care for her son. Taken from the reserve of Kinogamish by the province's social services, Dave is raised by an adoptive family in Montréal, far from his community and culture. *Mesnak* does not show these tragic events but alludes to them throughout the film, which focuses on Dave's return to the reserve twenty years or so after the hunting tragedy. An anonymous letter sent to his Montréal apartment precipitates Dave's return to Kinogamish. It contains a photo of Gertrude accompanied by the message "Your mother needs you."

When Dave returns, the reserve is no longer fueled by the revolutionary energy of his father's Red Power days. It appears instead as a space away from time, resigned to its fate. Kinogamish's new chief, Claude St-Onge (Marco Collin), is about to grant a commercial license to a forestry corporation, opening reserve land to further settler-colonial encroachment despite his own community's opposition to the project. As the audience quickly understands, Claude St-Onge (the film's Claudius) played a central part in the suspicious hunting accident that killed Dave's father two decades before. St-Onge has since risen to power and replaced Dave's father as Kinogamish's leader and as Gertrude's lover. Now sober, Gertrude seems unaware of St-Onge's role in her previous husband's death, but Dave's reappearance on the reserve soon threatens her newfound balance. Instead of being a celebratory event, Dave's return is marked by violence and failed attempts to reconnect with his community. Gertrude rejects Dave. When he falls in love with Osalic (Eve Ringuette), a young, struggling Ophelia figure, their relationship ends tragically. Dave's voyage through the dark waters and potentially deadly undercurrents of his past parallels Hamlet's return to Elsinore and the fury it unleashes.

Mesnak transposes *Hamlet*'s existential interrogations and brutally expands to the reserve Shakespeare's vision of the family sphere as plagued by betrayal, incestuous desires, and violence. The film reveals the reserve—understood here as the space and its inhabitants—not as a protected realm of kinship but as one of containment, in which internalized colonialism threatens kinship and community and produces tortured filiation. The film dissects objective violence, making visible the repercussions of negotiating one's individual and communal identity under and against constant settler-colonial domination. *Mesnak*'s characters all struggle against the tentacles of a profoundly divisive body of laws—Canada's Indian Act—that defines and controls First Nations identity through an arithmetic of exclusion and extinction that actively projects the end of Indigenous nations as a distinct people (see chapter 4).

Mesnak relies on the explanatory power of violence and, in doing so, it rubs against liberal identity discourses in Québec, where friction and areas of tension have fallen out of favor and are too often ignored or undertheorized. Instead, many academics have turned to celebratory discourses of multiplicity and hybrid identities, focusing on what Simon Harel calls the "consensual nature of intercultural relations."[47] The relationship between the reserve and the settler majority is neither consensual nor intercultural in the cross-pollinating ways invoked by the discourses of *altérité* (otherness) and *écritures migrantes* (migrant literatures) that Harel describes here. These important discourses, which have widened the frames of investigation available to understand cultural identity in Québec, generally focus on intramural tensions if they address conflicts, and do not account for the violent undercurrents that sustain Québec's civil society and render these relations of "conflictual harmony"[48] possible in the first place. They do not, in other words, explain how Indigenous people continue to serve as "figures of transit" in liberal states, providing "the ontological and literal ground" on which these states can imagine themselves and debate *métissage* or multiculturalism.[49]

Byrd's reflection echoes Žižek's aforementioned understanding of the vertical structure of violence. Theatrical or cinematic performances often focus on subjective violence and on its tantalizing pyrotechnics without paying attention to the hidden objective violence that sustains such outbursts. Objective violence is normalized and hidden and thus difficult to apprehend, while subjective violence is spectacular and dramatic and offers the gratifying illusion of resolution. It is easy indeed to dismiss such explosive events as pure spectacle or as aberrations in an otherwise predictable environment, and thus prevent any real engagement of the audience with the subterranean violence that supports the edifice of civil society. In some rare cases, however, theater and cinema can render legible both subjective and objective violence. Diana Taylor and Ken Gonzales-Day, among others, convincingly demonstrate in their theoretical and artistic work how performances can reveal the objective violence that sustains political regimes and racial domination.[50] *Mesnak*'s Kinogamish (like Kanehsatà:ke) is thus not a space in crisis but a space of settler-colonial violence and as such, it serves as the ontological and literal ground on and against which Québec can articulate its sense of self as a community.

Director Sioui Durand labors to render this layered violence visible throughout *Mesnak*. A scene early in the movie provides a rich example of this revelatory work. The camera accompanies Dave Brodeur as he drives north toward Kinogamish. We see the changing northern landscape through the vehicle's windshield as if seated in the passenger seat. The view would be beautiful were it not for the cracked windshield that gives the landscape a scarred surface. The windshield, and by extension our gaze as we look through the fissured glass, is effectively stratified in what appears to be a vertical hierarchy. Everything above the glass's two horizontal wounds is sky, nature, and open vista: an open and undamaged space. Everything below the cracks bears the marks of containment and harnessing. Paved roads cut through the territory like scars and become smaller and smaller as they lead away from the cities. As the car moves north, these roads turn from asphalt to dirt and eventually funnel down to the small parcel of land that constitutes Kinogamish. The land that exists below the windshield's two visual scars is an eroded space marked by displacements and forced settlements. The camera follows Dave's journey to the reserve, a space that appears as the ultimate space of "otherness": Québec's brutal margins. The reserve itself is rundown, its prefabricated houses worn out. The only luxury homes belong to members of the band council, like Claude St-Onge, and they stand like obscene signs of the federal government's control over Kinogamish's self-governance.

Žižek's vertical structure of violence finds an apt visual representation in the car's split windshield. The lower part of the windshield forms the terrain of objective violence, a landscape now so normative that its scars appear banal. The upper part of our gaze is the terrain of subjective violence. This open vista is not totally free of conflicts in Québec. It has indeed been the stage of a tense and at times seemingly impossible relationship between the French Québécois de souche and the province's anglophone minority on the one hand, and between the French Québécois de souche and the rest of Canada on the other hand. Québec and Canada have often been described as "two solitudes" caught in a forced marriage.[51]

While this metaphor may give the impression of an irreconcilable divide between Québec and Canada, the two are, as previously stated, in a relation of conflictual harmony: that is, their union is vexed, but it is articulated within the realm of a common subjectivity and from a common structural position within civil society. The French Québécois de souche and Canadians articulate their national mythscapes and political aspirations within the same libidinal economy. Both are settler communities, even if the French Québécois de souche have the particularity of being both a colonizing force and a minority population later depossessed by the British Empire. Even so, when Québec speaks of sovereignty, it deploys the same rubrics of "nation," "governance," and "territory" as the federal government; thus, their conflict is articulated over a shared ontological terrain. This was rendered evident in the Oka events when Québec and Canada quickly joined forces to repress Mohawk dissent and criminalize their attempt to destabilize the shared terrain (obtained by and through the erasure of Indigenous sovereignty) on which Québec and Canada have historically quarreled.

If the upper part of the windshield is the terrain of subjective violence, the scarred landscape framed by the lower part of the cracked glass is the terrain of objective violence. Erased from this landscape is an entire population, namely the Indigenous peoples who occupied the territory long before

Québec and Canada came to be. It is their invisibility that provides the necessary condition for Canada and Québec to articulate their conflict. Their absence is the terrain, the "ossuary America" on which Québec and Canada can now perform their competing narratives.[52] In other words, while Québec and Canada live in conflictual harmony, their relationship with Indigenous people is one of antagonism.[53] In what Frank Wilderson calls the "genocidal modality of their grammar of suffering,"[54] Indigenous people constitute what the filmmaker Richard Desjardins calls *le peuple invisible*, "the invisible people." Their invisibility, actualized through genocide and maintained through pervasive and institutionalized forms of violence that target filiation in particular, is, as I argue, a necessary condition for Québec and Canada's sense of normalcy. In exploring Kinogamish's broken and tortured filiation, *Mesnak* labors to render visible genocidal violence rather than sovereign loss. Something is rotten in Kinogamish, Sioui Durand tells us in his film, but this is the very subterranean violence—Žižek's "objective violence"—that gave birth to Canada and Québec as settler states and that continues to sustain their national projects

Kinogamish as a Space of Abject Filiation

Mesnak was filmed mostly in and around the Innu reserve of Uashat Mak Mani-Utenam in the Côte-Nord region of Québec, and a large part of the film's dialogue is in French, Québec's official language. While Kinogamish is a fictive space, the movie makes no attempt to create an equally fictive settler state to surround it. Instead, *Mesnak* identifies Québec as the outside force that shapes and threatens the reserve of which Dave Brodeur becomes the uneasy ambassador. Indeed, throughout the movie, Brodeur comes to represent a threatening force from the outside for the people of Kinogamish. His return as the acculturated son brings the outside world into the reserve and threatens the community's fragile balance. While he is from Kinogamish, Brodeur belongs to both Québec and the reserve, defining himself now as being "from the city" and speaking French instead of Innu. Furthermore, his various interactions with the people of Kinogamish demonstrate his profound estrangement from Innu culture. His return to the reserve exposes the trauma inherent to and the violent nature of this space and, like Hamlet's return to Elsinore, unleashes both the violence of his environment and the people around him. Brodeur's body becomes the site on which competing ontological questions are violently articulated: his presence exposes how the very laws that have created the reserve have also violently targeted kinship and the possibility of community within that space, making the reserve a space of threatened filiation. *Mesnak* asks through his journey if one can truly love, forgive, or hope within a space written as part of the settler state's genocidal project.

More than a single character, Dave Brodeur comes to represent and stand in for central ontological questions pertaining to Indigenous identity. In French, *brodeur* is the term used to describe someone who embroiders and renders a fabric distinctive with thread. Brodeur—the embroiderer—is desperately trying to claim the connective tissue of his past, the missing thread that would allow him to draw a picture of his ancestry. For instance, his apartment shown at the beginning of *Mesnak* features walls covered with disparate Indigenous symbols—a painting of Gauguin's Tahitian women, a poster of Sitting Bull surrounded by a psychedelic halo, and an advertisement for a Mayan play. Stitched together, these symbols attest to his cultural and genealogical alienation and betray his desire to reconnect with his Indigenous identity. These symbols form a surrogate narrative for his unrecoverable past. Speaking with his adoptive father before making the decision to return to the reserve, Brodeur compares his three years in Kinogamish to "a hole in his head," echoing his biological father's fatal wound during the hunting accident as well as his own amnesia.

If *brodeur* activates the image of someone looking for a missing thread, it can also evoke a mispronunciation of the English word *brother*, a marker of filiation, community, and family lineage. This borrowing from English is not uncommon in Québec's parlance, wherein French is often peppered with Anglo-Saxon transplants. The surname Brodeur stems from the play *Hamlet le Malécite* (*Hamlet the Maliseet*), which served as a starting point for *Mesnak*. In the play, written by Yves Sioui Durand and Jean-Frédéric Messier, Dave is unaware of his family history and finds himself involved in an incestuous relationship with his half-sister Osalic. In *Mesnak*, Dave and Osalic are no longer related and it is Osalic and her brother Léo (Charles Buckell) who are devoured by an incestuous love, which Dave interrupts when he sets foot on the reserve. Despite this change between the play and the film, Dave continues to carry this patronymic sign of abject filiation (*brodeur*-brother) which he performs metonymically in *Mesnak* for the community's tortured kinship.

This tortured kinship results in large part from Canada's Indian Act, the body of laws though which the government enacts its power on Indigenous people. The Indian Act regulates nearly every aspect of Indigenous lives and determines, as I will examine at length in chapter 4, who is "Status Indian" (or First Nations), according to an ensemble of rules that have fluctuated over time to better serve the act's extinction project. Through these changes, however, the settler-colonial project has remained constant in one matter: its systematic attack on Indigenous women and children. The Indian Act contains provisions, for example, that until recently deprived Indigenous women of the right to pass on Indian status (that is, federal recognition) to their children. It also mandated the Residential School system. Outside of the Indian Act but following a similar mandate are the forced sterilization of Indigenous women in parts of Canada, and the social services' placement of Indigenous children in settler families en masse. These are all part of the Indian Act's targeted attacks on the matriarchal structures and the very fabric of Indigenous families.

The characters in *Mesnak* all bear the scars of the settler state's relentless targeting of Indigenous kinship and communities, and the film's first images of the reserve clearly show traces of this violence. The scene captures an Alcoholics Anonymous meeting in the Kinogamish community center, the camera lingering on the faces of the recovering alcoholics who share tales of ultimate isolation and otherness. One participant (Réal Junior Leblanc) speaks, his voice heavy with guilt, of a drunken episode during which he left his friend outside in the middle of a harsh winter night, only to find him frozen to death the following day. The other participants' reaction to this account of an involuntary fratricide is telling: they recognize the man's dispossession and his incapacity to form bonds and protect loved ones amid the violence of the reserve. Following the man's horrific testimonial of loss and shame, Claude St-Onge rises and proceeds to make a marriage proposal to David's mother Gertrude. The timing is incongruous, but as he makes his demand in marriage, St-Onge summons this AA community as witnesses and asks them to help and support Gertrude and him in their new life together. That Claude and Gertrude seal their engagement before a group of people so visibly hurting and scarred is telling of the entire community's tortured familial and communal ties. The Kinogamish community's capacity to form filial bonds has been violently interrupted, and children are left to fend for themselves while parents are either absent or broken: Osalic and Leo are siblings and possessive lovers; Claude St-Onge killed his bride-to-be's first husband; Dave's memories of his family are like "a hole in the head," while Gertrude is poisoned by self-hatred.

Mesnak's characters struggle to love and form bonds in the context of genocidal policies that have targeted the relational fabric of Indigenous communities. Devastating policies such as the Residential Schools were devised to break the transmission of memory, language, and culture. For more than 130 years, Indigenous children were violently taken from their communities and forced to attend these institutions. The stated goal of Canada's eighty Residential Schools was removal, isolation, and assimilation.[55] Violence and abuse were rampant, as demonstrated by the testimonials presented at Canada's Truth and Reconciliation Commission. There, former pupils have been and continue to speak of the schools' multigenerational ravages, which left many with a fundamental incapacity to form trusting bonds, a trauma that *Mesnak* labors to illuminate.

Mesnak channels this deep trauma and the multigenerational devastation that the Indian Act and its ramifications imposed on Indigenous communities. Dave's encounter with Osalic dramatizes the tremendous difficulty of forming loving bonds in a space devised as part of a genocidal project. Their first encounter takes place on the ceremonial territory near the riverbanks outside of Kinogamish, where Dave has set up camp next to an abandoned *shaputuan* (a large traditional tent). Osalic has come to the river to perform a cleansing ritual involving the burning of sacred herbs. As Dave and Osalic spend an idyllic day exploring the forest and rivers that surround Kinogamish, Sioui Durand's film captures the landscape's rugged beauty and its serenity. The stark contrast of these images with the dark, cramped feeling of the reserve shots that follow suggests that the unspoiled ceremonial and ancestral lands that surround the reserve might hold the promise of love and that healthy filiation may still exist. Indeed, Osalic and Dave's developing love story seems to locate a possibility for renewal and futurity in a reconnection with nature and ancestral practices. Osalic, showing Dave the river's flowing waters, describes how she longs to go to "the territories of the elders" where one "is still free to be an Innu." Later in the movie, Dave and Osalic devise a plan to leave together to find these ancestral territories and start anew.

Sioui Durand quickly dispels this promise of futurity with a particularly brutal scene between Osalic, Léo, and Dave. Osalic, hopeful and decided, has returned to the dilapidated house she shares with Léo to pack up for her journey to the ancestral territories. As she rummages for clothes, a hunting rifle, and ammunition to survive in the woods, Léo wakes up from his drunken stupor and realizes that he is about to lose the only person with whom he has a meaningful, if toxic, relationship. Léo, following Osalic from one room to the next, tries to convince her to stay, and, while Osalic initially refuses to hear him, she finally relents, demonstrating the extent of her incapacity to break free of this destructive filial bond. When Dave later comes by to pick Osalic up for their journey, he finds her in bed with Léo. Dave and Léo fight and, as they both reach for the rifle, Dave shoots it accidentally. No one is hurt, but the scene marks the end of Osalic and Dave's budding relationship and the promise of renewal it carried. This scene echoes the supposed hunting accident that claimed Dave's father's life and similarly ended the promise of community renewal that he had embodied through his affiliation with the Red Power movement.

As *Mesnak* suggests, renewal was foreclosed in many ways when Dave's father was killed. Dave's adoption outside of Kinogamish after his father's murder marked the loss of two generations. Dave's adoption is representative of what is now known as the "sixties scoop," a governmental assimilation policy that grew in the 1950s and continued for the next three decades at the same time that the Residential School system was slowing down. The federal government modified the Indian Act in 1951 to enable "provincial child welfare authorities to extend their operations to Indian reserves."[56] According to the statistics collected by the Department of Indian Affairs, an alarmingly high number of children—close to 5 percent of all Status Indians at the time—were placed in foster care between 1960 and 1990. Patrick Johnston coined the term "sixties scoop" to describe this phenomenon in his 1983 book *Native Children and the Child Welfare System*. Later, the final report of the Royal Commission on Aboriginal Peoples (1991–96) stated:

> Children who entered the [child welfare] system were generally lost to family and community—or were returned with there having been little input to change the situation from which they were taken in the first place. . . . An abysmal lack of sensitivity to children and families was revealed. Families approached agencies for help and found that what was described as being in the child's "best interest" resulted in their families being torn asunder and siblings separated. Social workers grappled with cultural patterns far different than their own with no preparation and no opportunities to gain understanding.[57]

This massive intervention reflects the same colonial attitudes that fueled the Residential School system and envisioned the end of Indigenous peoples as nations and cultures through the implementation of policies that systematically targeted clan and family structures.

Mesnak suggests that settler colonialism and the Indian Act's status system have, in many instances, transformed Indigenous bodies into instruments of violence, weapons turned against themselves. The Indian Act forces impossible decisions on Indigenous bodies: to be, or exist, as Indigenous peoples among (and despite) ongoing settler-state violence; or, as a result of the dismantling of the status system, not to be, and thus disappear into Canada's body politic. This fundamental question echoes Hamlet's famous meditation and is articulated by *Mesnak*'s characters throughout the movie. For Dave, Gertrude, Osalic, and the others, the response to this meditation lies between these two non-choices. They live in a state of obstinate and violent survival. It is this state of "living death," to borrow again from Cacho, that makes *Mesnak*'s characters truly contemporary Shakespearean figures.

Yves Sioui Durand channels this state of deadly life through the figure of Mesnak, the gigantic prehistoric-looking snapping turtle that dwells in Kinogamish's ponds and forests and that acts in this filmic adaptation as the ghost of Dave's father. Sioui Durand first introduces Mesnak in a flashback scene that recalls in impressionist images the hunting trip in which Dave's father was shot. The camera captures in blurry shades of grey a hunting scene gone wrong and shows us the young child who witnessed it all. The hunting scene marks the end of the father, the fall of a leader, and the eventual banishment of the son from Kinogamish. This flashback sequence is quickly followed by a closeup of Mesnak hissing at the viewers; her guttural warning, incongruous with her passive and slow demeanor, creating a chilling effect. Turtles are understood in many Indigenous communities as messengers between the world of the spirits and the material world, acting as constant reminders of the connection between humans and nature. By placing the shot of Mesnak's menacing stance right after the image of the hunting scene, Sioui Durand echoes the angry ghost of Hamlet's father.

The snapping turtle is indigenous to Québec, where it is known as the *tortue hargneuse* (hateful turtle) because of its tendency to inflict deep bite wounds when threatened. The snapping turtle's apparent aggression is partly explained by its vulnerability. Its long, snakelike neck prevents the turtle from fully retracting into its small inadequate shell, leaving it exposed to predators. Mesnak is not only the ghost of the slain father: it is also the symbol of Kinogamish, a community exposed to the settler state's eroding forces. Like the reserve's borders, which provide little protection against violence, Mesnak is exposed, in a permanent state of self-defense.

The Wapikoni Mobile: Narrating the Reserve

Viewers get a very different version of Uashat Mak Mani-Utenam in Réal Junior Leblanc's short film *L'Enfance déracinée* (*Uprooted Generation*, 2013). Leblanc, who plays a small part in *Mesnak*'s AA meeting scene, is a rising filmmaker who began his cinematic work with the Wapikoni Mobile project. Wapikoni Mobile was founded in 2003 by the filmmaker Manon Barbeau, in collaboration with the Council of Atikamekw nation and the First Nations Youth Council of Québec and Labrador, with financial support from the Assembly of First Nations and the National Film Board. The project consists of mobile recording studios that circulate in reserves, stopping for weeks at a time and serving as a creative hub. Any member of the visited communities can get logistical and creative support from Wapikoni's "mentors filmmakers" and to this day, the project has reached more than 4,000 participants in twenty Indigenous nations across Canada and the Americas.

With a digital archive (fully accessible online) of close to 900 short films and 600 musical recordings, the Wapikoni Mobile project offers a rich archive to counter Denise Bombardier's negative portrayal of the reserve life. Michelle Raheja argues that mainstream depictions of Indigenous peoples have long served "as pedagogy and knowledge-producing" devices.[58] Her work examines the complex relationships that Indigenous peoples have always had with these depictions and "retrieves and deciphers" how Indigenous filmmakers have scrutinized, harnessed, and sometimes reanimated these images.[59] Raheja is particularly interested in illuminating how Indigenous filmmakers have carved spaces of "visual sovereignty." For Raheja, visual sovereignty promotes the intellectual health of Indigenous communities by appealing to "a mass intergenerational, and transnational Indigenous audience," permitting the circulation and transmission of Indigenous knowledge. "Visual sovereignty, as expressed by Indigenous filmmakers, also involves the employment of editing technologies, that permit filmmakers to stage performances of oral narrative and Indigenous notions of time and space that are not possible through print alone."[60]

The Wapikoni Mobile is a prime example of visual sovereignty. Its filmmakers capture a wide array of narratives: quotidian stories of teenagers' woes, community healing anthems, and stories that honor elders, outline dreams, visualize hope, and name hurt. These films have now circulated in and have won awards in numerous film festivals around the world, offering this multiplicity of voices and perspectives in response to the flattening narratives perpetuated by Bombardier and the like. With its partnerships with Indigenous communities all over Canada and in Latin America, the Wapikoni Mobile has helped the transnational dissemination of Indigenous knowledge and Indigenous strategies to combat the effects of settler colonialism on specific languages and practices.

L'Enfance déracinée is a visual meditation on Leblanc's community's Residential School survivors and on their healing strategies. The film captures in particular the ritual burning of the last remaining building of the Residential School: the shoe-making workshop, where sexual assaults routinely took place. The main school building, which opened in 1951, was demolished shortly after its closure in 1971, and the land on which it stood has since been reclaimed in powerful ways. Standing on the periphery of the reserve, this open parcel of land now serves as a communal space and has hosted the widely popular Innu Nikamu (the Innu/Human sings) festival since 1985. Described as a reimagining of the traditional summer gatherings of the Innu people, the festival welcomes artists from Indigenous communities as well as non-Indigenous allies. It should be said that some of the most successful Indigenous singer-songwriters in Canada come from Mani-Utenam: Florent Vollant and Claude McKenzie (who were the duo Kashtin before Vollant's solo career took off) and Philippe McKenzie, for instance. It comes as no surprise that music has served as a healing process in that community.

Leblanc's film articulates visual sovereignty in provocative ways. It begins with a soundscape in which the rolling sounds of an old film-reel projector are juxtaposed to the sound of sweeping wind. Archival footage, split in two distinct narrative tracks on the screen, shows the young pupils of the school marching in neat ranks. The boys occupy the left side of the screen and the girls the right. As they march toward the middle of the screen, they disappear from the frame and seem to fall into a void. Captions on the screen explain that the schools were meant to "kill the Indian in the heart of the child." Following these images, the camera captures Leblanc standing on the land where the school once stood, his back to the camera. A gusty wind is moving snow across the open space.

Leblanc begins his poetic narration, which accompanies archival footage of the school's ribbon-cutting ceremony in 1951. As Leblanc asks, "Who were you to empty my village of its children?" viewers see images of Catholic priests and nuns, of the bishop blessing the new school. "I am the descendant of these uprooted children." Leblanc is proposing here a counter-narrative to this archival footage, which was meant to celebrate the civilizing mission of the school by highlighting its neat regimen of propriety and order. His own narrative serves as a counterpoint to the archival footage. Leblanc turns to Françoise Césarie Fontaine, an Innu woman from Mani-Utenam who offers a testimonial of her experience in the school. She was six when she was taken there and she speaks of it as a space where "she could not be herself." Leblanc's camera follows Fontaine as she paints and tells her story, alternating between French and Innu-Aimun, her mother-tongue, which allows her to visit the register of intimate trauma. It is in Innu-Aimun that she can name the abuse she suffered, and also describe the tactics she developed to protect herself and her best friend. "We were always together so no one could ever hurt us, deceive us . . . we were scared. I always lived in fear. Never again did I trust the priests and nuns."

Leblanc then visits the remaining school building, where a "spokesman of the Heavens" desecrated the flesh of the school's pupils. The place is quiet, peaceful even, under the winter sun. Fontaine continues to describe the impact of the school on the parents and the ways in which everyone carried their trauma with them: "It is as if everyone drank." Leblanc talks about "a dark memory" that no one spoke about and positions his film as a gesture of remembrance, a gesture of tender solidarity for his "sisters and brothers." Fontaine speaks of her paintings as reclaiming gestures, as a healing process, and after the camera captures her vivid pictures, Leblanc shifts his narration to the burning of the shoe-making unit, which the community of Mani-Utenam organized in collaboration with local firefighters as a way to heal. "The wounds are not yet healed, but my people's hope has been rekindled," Leblanc explains over archival footage juxtaposed with the recent images of the ritual burning. For a moment, the children from the past meet their older selves or relatives as they all stand in front of the burning building. "I know that today's youth will find a way to break free."

Leblanc's film offers a powerful meditation on intramural healing. Misery is not, contrary to what Bombardier argues, transmitted from one generation to the next in the reserves. Indigenous peoples have always resisted, and they continue to create new songs, new stories, and new rituals to respond to their ever-changing realities. Leblanc's film is a potent example of this: it provides an aural/oral/sensate history of the aftermath of the Residential Schools. As the fire consumes the building where so many horrible events took place, Leblanc speaks of the hope and pride he witnesses in the young generation of Innu people. He also positions himself as an active and responsible witness to his elders' trauma. This is an ode to renewal, a recording of history, and a sharing of strategies. It is, in Michelle Raheja's terms, an act of visual sovereignty which promotes the intellectual health of Mani-Utenam but also of Indigenous communities at large, who struggle with intergenerational trauma.

Tour de Char (*Car Ride*, 2009), by the cousins Jean-Baptiste Bacon-Riverin and Malcolm Riverin, takes the viewer for a philosophical car ride around the Innu community of Pessamit. The camera is positioned on the back seat of the car and captures images of the reserve as Bacon-Riverin drives around. The two young men communicate with the camera through the car's rearview and vanity mirrors. We thus mostly get to know them through their eyes, and these are hopeful eyes full of dreams. "We grew up here. It is a fun place to grow up in but, at our age, it becomes boring. . . . I have nothing to do aside from driving around with my friends," Riverin-Bacon explains. Riverin adds that "we spend our evenings talking about our dreams. Seriously, this village is too small for my dreams." The two describe their love of hip-hop music. "We want to story ourselves, to narrate ourselves," explains Bacon-Riverin. He speaks of his history books at school, which barely mentioned Indigenous peoples. "I will always remember this," he says. Riverin responds that he believes it is up to him, to his generation, to seek and excavate the culture that was not transmitted to them because of the interruption that the Residential Schools created. "It is our responsibility." They speak of longing to learn trapping and hunting. "If you left me in the woods right now, I would die. It is such a shame," explains Bacon-Riverin, somewhat humorously.

The two young men offer a stirring meditation on the effects of settler colonialism. They name the hurt, but they also articulate how the healing can take place and the steps they are taking in that direction. I read a powerful articulation of visual sovereignty in the two young men's staging of their message, which is clearly intended for other Indigenous youth across the globe: they anchor their reflection in a specific space, Pessamit, but insist on showing it to us as the soil that allows them to grow, spread their wings, be in motion. By choosing to capture Pessamit through a moving car, the two men position themselves as agents of change, always in movement, searching for new paths. Bacon-Riverin speak of going back to school after a hiatus, saying that he sees education as the only way forward. Riverin, for his part, speaks of traversing a difficult period. He is twenty and has three children in his charge; and he "is building [him]self a ladder to emerge from this hole." Both speak with tenderness about the reserve. They see it as a refuge, a home base, but they are aware of its current limited horizons. Their film documents the beginning of their journey and invites others to embark on similar quests.

Conclusion

The four films examined in this chapter articulate a portrait of the reserve that clashes with the reductive narratives offered by Bombardier and the mainstream media. Moving away from a narrative of the reserve-as-crisis, all four films examine the continuous violence, Žižek's objective violence, that underlies the reserve as a settler-colonial space of erasure. They do so in ways that illuminate how Indigenous peoples have been affected by and have themselves had an impact on this space of confinement. Obomsawin illuminates what happens when the settler state is confronted with the refusal of Indigenous people to quietly disappear. As the first full-length commercial fiction film made entirely in Québec by an Indigenous cast and crew, *Mesnak* performs an important intervention in defining how Indigenous people are represented on screen. By examining the reserve as a terrain of continuous and insidious structural domination—a space isolated from the settler state yet largely controlled by it—*Mesnak* challenges mainstream ahistorical depictions of the reserve as plagued by successive but unrelated crises and refuses to put the onus of bootstrapping, redemption, and healing solely on Indigenous individuals. Instead, it situates the reserve as a product of and the condition for settler-state projects. The two films from the Wapikoni Mobile project offer, for their part, portraits of the reserve that enact visual sovereignty, and imagine healing, resilience, and the futurity of reserves on Indigenous terms.

Chapter 4

✦

Endurance/Enduring Performance

Nadia Myre, La Marche Amun, and the Indian Act's Tumultuous Geographies

> Native women are going to raise the roof and decry the dirty house which patriarchy and racism have built on our backs.
>
> —Lee Maracle, *I Am Woman*

Between 1999 and 2002, the Anishinaabe visual artist Nadia Myre, with the help of her friend, the curator Rhonda Meier, enlisted the help of 250 friends and strangers to bead over the 56 pages of Canada's Indian Act, hiding the words of this wide-reaching body of colonial laws with more than 800,000 red and white glass beads. A veritable feat of endurance, Myre's monumental artwork denaturalizes the Indian Act and renders it illegible: a network of beaded lines erases the words of the text, giving each page the semblance of an aerial map of a disorienting visual landscape in which red dominates white. As a result, the piece calls attention to the terrain of objective violence; that is, to what has long lain under the law's text. It points and reorients the viewer's gaze to the very nations, bodies, and territories that have been and continue to be marginalized by the Indian Act's potent policies. (See figure 4.1.)

In 2010, as if surveying Myre's unsettling map, a group of Indigenous women completed La Marche Amun, a long-distance endurance protest march to demand an end to the gendered discrimination embedded in the Indian Act. Led by the well-known Innu activists and leaders Michèle Taïna Audette and Viviane Michel,[1] the women walked more than 300 miles (500 kilometers), departing from Wendake, a Huron-Wendat community enclave in the city of Québec, to arrive on Algonquian territory in Ottawa, Canada's capital, a month later. En route, the women used their moving bodies to articulate political meaning and perform a "conscious cultural act."[2] Borrowing from Dylan Robinson's evocative expression, I read the march as an act of "sensate sovereignty" in which the marchers patiently surveyed, crossed, and illuminated a landscape marked by an ensemble of gendered exclusionary

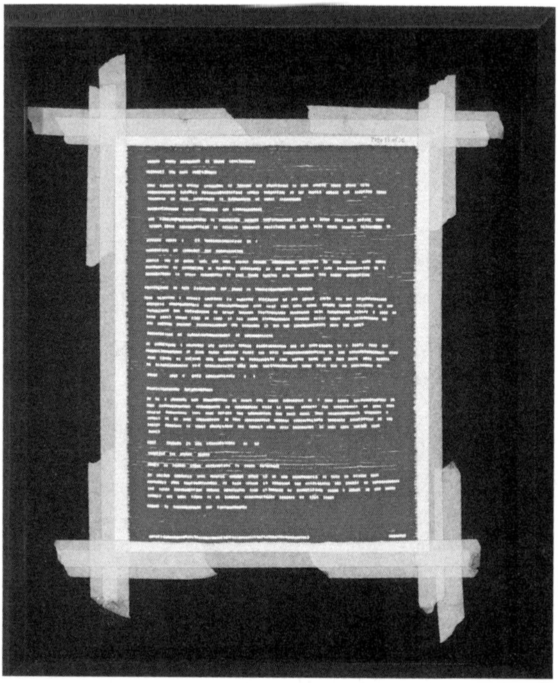

Figure 4.1. Nadia Myre, *Indian Act* (detail). (Art ©Nadia Myre; licensed by VAGA, New York)

lines created and naturalized by the Indian Act. Along the way, the marchers traversed Algonquian and Iroquoian ancestral territories in towns like Trois-Rivières, Donnacona,[3] Montréal, Gatineau, and Ottawa, where they attended informal and mediatized events organized by and for Indigenous and non-Indigenous groups. In other words, they traversed what the Seneca scholar Mishuana Goeman calls the "tumultuous geographies constructed around differing and constantly shifting power structures."[4]

In Canada, these tumultuous geographies (the terrain of objective violence) articulate the exclusion of Indigenous women along lines demarcating one province from another, reserves from settler communities, and rural from urban landscapes, as well as marking the discursive chasm that separates the French Québécois de souche's sense of sovereignty from that of the country at large and from that of specific Indigenous nations. Complex lines of exclusion shape Indigenous communities themselves: they separate those who have Indian status from those who do not, and urban Indigenous people from those who live on reserves. These tumultuous geographies, paired with the sexual violence that Sarah Deer, a Muscogee legal scholar and MacArthur fellow, describes as foundational to the settler-colonial project,[5] have historically rendered Indigenous women among the most vulnerable to dispossession. In traversing them, La Marche Amun called attention to settler colonialism's geography of exclusion, gendered and sexual violence, and erasure as enacted by the Indian Act.

It is not a coincidence that both Myre and the women of La Marche Amun's interventions targeted the Indian Act. As the Mi'kmaq scholar Bonita Lawrence argues, Canada's Indian Act "is a regulatory regime—a grammar—that has controlled every aspect of Indian life for more than a century . . . functioning discursively to naturalize colonial worldviews."[6] Despite some Canadian politicians who downplay the original genocidal intent of the law,[7] the Indian Act was created with the specific goal of bringing the "Indian problem" to an end by forcibly assimilating Indigenous peoples. Duncan Campbell Scott, superintendent of Indian affairs between 1913 and 1932, famously claimed: "I want to get rid of the Indian problem. Our objective is to continue until there is not a single Indian in Canada that has not been absorbed into the body politic . . . : that is the whole object of this bill."[8] To do so, the Indian Act radically remapped richly diverse Indigenous nations into a single category, the "Status Indian," which is "the only category of Native person to whom a historic nation-to-nation relationship with Canada" is recognized.[9] Since its creation in 1876, the Indian Act has been repeatedly amended in efforts to accelerate assimilation and extinguish this legal category. Indigenous people have responded to these incessant attacks on their land, bodies, cultures, and sovereignty with extraordinary resilience, and their endurance continues to defy the settler colonial project. This chapter focuses on Indigenous endurance—but before I begin, I must contextualize how the very notion of endurance is gendered and racialized under settler-colonial rule.

Settler Colonialism and Gendered Violence

As Lee Maracle decries it in this chapter's epigraph, Canada enacted its settler-colonial project on the backs of Indigenous women, targeting them with particularly damaging and violent policies. Following Maracle, Audra Simpson argues that Indigenous women's bodies "have *historically* been rendered less valuable because of what they are taken to represent: land, reproduction, Indigenous kinship and governance, an alternative to [settler-colonial] heteronormative and Victorian rules of descent."[10] Among the Haudenosaunee, for example, it was the women who owned land and transmitted status and clan affiliation, thus ensuring the renewal and stability of the community. In stripping Indigenous women of their Indian status if they married a non-status individual, the Indian Act "sought to divest Indian women from land by divesting them of their legal rights as Indians."[11]

Concretely, many matrilineal nations were profoundly altered by the imposition of these transmission rules as well as by the imposition of systems of governance that decentered clan mothers and the philosophical and political practices and understandings of sovereignty for which they acted as stewards. This institutionalized devaluation of Indigenous women, what Žižek would call objective violence, was further established at the symbolic level: the Canadian and French Québécois de souche mythscapes rely heavily, for instance, on tropes in which Indigenous women, standing in for territory and Indigeneity as a whole, fall in love with a settler and ultimately die to ensure the stability and futurity of settler existence on the continent.[12] As I argued in chapters 1 and 2, this mythscape is still sustained by a play like Alexis Martin's *Invention*, which echoes the early colonial play *Théâtre de Neptune*, and by *L'Empreinte*, which romanticizes a métis past in which "we," the French Québécois de souche, were birthed and nurtured by "our Native mothers." These cultural performances are all tributaries of this powerful trope of imagined consent bestowed by Indigenous women. As Simpson writes about Indigenous women: "Theirs are bodies that carry a symbolic load . . . so it is that they must be eradicated" or otherwise contained.[13] Saturated with such signifying power of reproduction, Indigenous women's bodies indeed threatened (and continue to threaten) Canada's self-proclaimed resolution of "the Indian problem" as well as the French Québécois de souche's current discourse of competing Nativeness.

The Indian Act attempted to control and eradicate the concrete and symbolic signifying power that accrued (and still accrues) on the bodies of Indigenous women. To do so it implemented rules regarding the transmission of status that conjugated assimilation through the exclusion of women. A staggering number of Indigenous women lost their Indian status for marrying non-Indigenous or non-status men (that is, non-Status Indians, Métis, Inuit, or members of a tribe located in the United States); and consequently, these women and their children were barred from residing on reserves or from taking part in the life of their communities.[14] This exclusion and devaluation has had dire consequences for Indigenous women. The disproportionate violence they face today—indicated, for instance, by the estimated 1,800 missing and murdered Aboriginal women whose disappearances remain under-investigated by federal and provincial authorities—is a direct repercussion of the Indian Act's gendered violence and of settler colonialism at large.[15] Sarah Deer contends that "rape in the lives of Native women is not an epidemic of recent mysterious origin. Instead, rape is a fundamental result of colonialism, a history of violence reaching back centuries."[16]

Deer's argument might explain in part why Canada and the United States are so slow to address the issue of violence against Indigenous women. Indeed, how does one address this gendered violence without confronting settler colonialism as its genesis and ever-renewable fuel? Deer, writing from a U.S. perspective, argues that to "define and adjudicate gendered crimes" is, for tribal nations, the "purest form of sovereignty"[17] specifically because it targets one of the very core mechanisms of settler colonial power. In Canada, Prime Minister Justin Trudeau has recently made good on his promise to create a National Inquiry on Missing and Murdered Indigenous Women (MMIW). However, the inquiry commissioners (who include the Marche Amun's Michèle Taïna Audette and other Indigenous leaders) started their investigation in September 2016 amid concerns about the inquiry's scope and criticism about its "lack of teeth to address the role police have played in MMIW investigations."[18] Since then, the inquiry has lost key commissioners and staff members and has repeatedly faced criticism from Indigenous leaders, the victims' families, and the press.[19] In August 2017, a group comprised of Indigenous leaders, activists, and victims' family members asked the government for a hard reset, insisting that the inquiry needed to be rebuilt from the ground up, with families of victims and communities at its center.[20]

In recent years, Canada's official discourse concerning its relationship with Indigenous communities has evolved from one of overt assimilation to one of recognition and accommodation. In other words, objective violence has not been eradicated but merely re-narrativized. This new discourse is no less problematic according to Glen Coulthard (Dene) and Elizabeth Povinelli, because it reproduces rather than fundamentally alter the asymmetrical relations of power that define settler colonialism. Consequently, recognition ultimately subsumes Indigenous sovereignty under that of settler nations.[21] Despite this change of tone, Canada's settler-colonial project requires land and resources and as such, it depends on the perpetual erosion of Indigenous communities and territories for its stability and expansion.[22] Thus, Canada's settler-colonial project, as delineated in the Indian Act, can imagine only two possible structural and ontological positions for Indigenous peoples (and Indigenous women in particular): within settler society's body politic, through assimilation, or outside of it, living—enduring—under a body of law that constantly erodes their rights to self-determination and their cultures and renders their bodies acutely vulnerable to sexual and other forms of violence.

Endurance/Enduring Performance

The notion of Indigenous peoples' enduring presence at the heart of this chapter is not static, nor has it ever been. As Coulthard argues in his work on reconciliation politics in Canada: "First Nations people have always resisted colonialism and fought back."[23] Canada exists in constant tension with the indomitable endurance of Indigenous communities, a resistant presence that is too often and conveniently rebranded, Chelsea Vowel writes, as "teetering on the edge of extinction" in settler-colonial discourse.

> Whether this belief is held by those who mourn our slow disappearance, or by those who wish we'd hurry up and vanish already, our continued presence must indeed be puzzling. Ours is the slowest

> apocalypse in human history it seems, because over 500 years later, millions of Indigenous peoples continue to exist all throughout the Americas.[24]

Vowel does not dispute here the tremendous difficulties faced by Indigenous peoples, but critiques how even their endurance is deployed to serve and confirm settler narratives of Indigenous disappearance instead of attesting to their futurity.

In this chapter, I examine Myre's *Indian Act* and La Marche Amun as performances that consciously embody and perform the structural position of endurance into which settler colonialism has forced Indigenous peoples, particularly Indigenous women. Together these two performance pieces meditate on what it means to endure against a settler-colonial project whose intended trajectory culminates with the end of Indigenous endurance. I employ *endurance* here to describe performances that stage or foreground the testing of a performer's physical, emotional, and/or spiritual resources, that insist on and render visible the performer's presence under trying circumstances. Here, endurance performance captures a different project from those embodied in the 1960s and 1970s by artists like Chris Burden or Tehching Hsieh, who voluntarily staged their bodies' struggle under self-imposed conditions like hunger, immobility, or isolation. I contend that, in deploying and staging Indigenous women's endurance as a performative language, La Marche Amun and Nadia Myre's beading project seize the settler-colonial state's grammar of extinction and erasure enacted by the Indian Act to perform its effects and mirror its mechanisms for a settler audience whose sense of self is articulated, as Taiaiake Alfred notes, on "a self-congratulatory version of Canadian history" in which Canada holds the part of a "benevolent peacemaker."[25] As I have argued thus far, the French Québécois de souche's wounded attachment to a narrative as a colonized, culturally endangered minority, and as fundamentally métis, further complicates the reception of these performances of endurance. Against these dominant mythscapes, Myre and the marchers from La Marche Amun challenge viewers to consider systemic and symbolic violence against Indigenous women not as a distant tragedy or a past event, but as the product of settler colonialism and as a condition for its continuation.

As performance pieces, La Marche Amun and Myre's *Indian Act* challenge the current theoretical vocabulary surrounding endurance performances, a genre often imbricated with notions of individual bravura and masculinity. Unlike the individual practices of endurance artists whose spectacularized bodies marked the genre in the 1960s and 1970s, *Indian Act* and La Marche Amun conjugate endurance through a communal participation and via seemingly less spectacular quotidian practices. In fact, these performances challenge us—viewers and scholars—to think of endurance not as a metaphor for an individual's malaise vis-à-vis society (as endurance performance art often is), but as a positioning within settler colonialism's structure of

Figure 4.2. Nadia Myre, *Indian Act.* (Photo by Denis Farley; art ©Nadia Myre; licensed by VAGA, New York)

power and assimilation rendered visible through a distillation to its simplest form. Through their performances, Myre and the women of La Marche Amun challenge participants and viewers to encounter the Indian Act's quotidian lines of gendered violence and exclusion. Their work asks us to react to this structural and ontological positioning and actively (re)map the Indian Act's cartography by imagining spaces of inclusion, dialogue, and coexistence within its tumultuous geographies.

(Re)Mapping the Indian Act's Tumultuous Geographies

The imposing scale of Nadia Myre's *Indian Act* strikes the viewer first: the piece comprises fifty-six white letter-sized white canvases striated with white and red. These colors visually render Canada's foundational racial history: white for the settler community, and red as a multivalent symbol for Indigenous bodies (red as racist epithet, but also red as one of the four directions of the Medicine Wheel, Red Power, etc.). Each beaded canvas is mounted on a black mat and, while some are clearly completed, others, roughly attached onto the mats with masking tape, appear to have been voluntarily left unfinished. (See figure 4.2.) The piece, which has traveled across Canada and the United States, demands space: when it was presented at the National

Gallery of Canada in Ottawa as part of the 2013 exhibit *Sakahàn*, *Indian Act* occupied an entire room, spreading over three walls. However, the piece only reveals its complex intervention when viewers zoom in on its unfinished frames and discover that each canvas, before being covered, consisted of the text of Canada's Indian Act. Using a traditional beading technique called *manidoominensikaan*, Myre, Meier, and their beading acolytes covered the text (partially or completely) with white beads and used equally minuscule red beads to cover the text's background, calling the viewer's attention to the document's topography, to its negative space. As a result, *Indian Act* reorients our gaze away from the words of the law and focuses our attention instead on the background, on the very material surfaces on which the law enacts its power; that is, on the canvas that stands here for Indigenous bodies, territories, and communities.

In rendering the text opaque and visually foregrounding Indigenous presence, the piece symbolically unravels the Indian Act's logic of erasure and assimilation. *Indian Act* performs "a (re)mapping gesture," in Mishuana Goeman's terms; that is, it labors "in the simultaneously metaphoric and material capacities of map making, to generate new possibilities."[26] In a symbolically potent gesture, Myre uses a traditionally feminine beading technique to perform this remapping: she saturates the landscape with red beads, where white beaded lines cut across like so many imposed borderlines, or like scars that simultaneously evoke injury and the possibility of healing. These borderlines/scars also suggest new configurations, new mappings of Indigenous sovereign territories (be they metaphoric or real). Myre's singular piece thus imagines and inscribes a radically reversed landscape, (re)mapping the structure of power enacted through the Indian Act.

The women of La Marche Amun performed a similar (re)mapping gesture in illuminating and protesting against the exclusion of more than 150,000 Indigenous women and their descendants from their communities as a result of the gendered discrimination contained in the Indian Act. As films such as *Mesnak* and *L'Enfance déracinée* clearly argue, the Indian Act violently remapped Indigenous territories, communities, and families over many generations: it broke ties and separated children from their parents (physically but also in terms of status exclusion). Walking through Algonquin (Abénaki and Anishinaabe) and Iroquois (Huron-Wendat and Mohawk) unceded territories, the bodies of the women who took part in La Marche Amun "broke through the abstraction"[27] of the Indian Act, in Rebecca Solnit's words, casting light on that which the act sought to contain, absorb, or erase. In 2010 Michèle Taïna Audette's oldest son, Amun, counted as one of the excluded; he only regained his status after Audette, Michel, and other Indigenous women successfully lobbied the government for change. This victory followed hard-won court battles by Indigenous women such as Sandra Lovelace (Maliseet), Jeannette Corbiere-Lavell (Anishinaabe), and Yvonne Bédard (Onondaga), whose decades-long lawsuits to reclaim their status led to the landmark Bill

C-31 in 1985, which amended the Indian Act to correct some of its most egregious discriminatory clauses.[28] Bill C-31 was followed by Bill C-3 in 2011, and together they allowed more than 100,000 excluded women and children to regain their Indian status. The Mi'kmaq lawyer Pam Palmater argues that Bill C-3, while addressing some of the discriminatory clauses of the Indian Act, perpetuates other forms of discrimination.[29] As the Mohawk scholar Taiaiake Alfred and others argue, the Indian Act cannot be part of a discourse of liberation because it cannot be amended enough to undo its racist, colonialist, and patriarchal roots.[30] Fundamentally, it serves the goal of extinction through assimilation and thus cannot coherently accommodate such concepts as Indigenous futurity, sovereignty, or self-governance. Palmater contends that getting rid of the Indian Act could lead to "more formal recognition of First Nations jurisdiction" only if the underlying objective of Canada's policies ceases to be assimilation. "Incremental legislative or policy changes are not enough."[31]

The Indian Act and the logic that underlies its laws are neither archaic nor remnants of a shameful past. On the contrary, the logic of gendered elimination and erasure of Indigenous peoples that organizes the act is still operative. This logic culminates when the settlers can present themselves as "native" to the Americas. Prime Minister Stephen Harper's aggressive rebranding of Canada during his two mandates reinforced this narrative on the international stage. At a G20 summit in 2009, only one year after his public apology to Indigenous peoples for the Residential School system, Harper obfuscated the country's genesis—the massive dispossession of Indigenous peoples—and positioned settler Canadians as indigenous to the land when he stated at a press conference that, contrary to other G20 countries, "Canada has no history of colonialism."[32]

Alexis Martin's plays and films like *L'Empreinte* participate in a similar enterprise of rewriting the genesis of the French Québécois de souche as métis who are the result of benevolent, harmonious encounters with Indigenous peoples. At the political level, the Democratic Institutions and Active Citizenship minister Bernard Drainville, under the leadership of Québec's premier Pauline Marois, echoed Harper's rebranding gesture in Québec in 2013. The now-defunct Charter of Québec Values[33] proposed secularizing the province following the French model, and established a set of "core-values" that would define Québec as a host society to newcomers. In doing so, the charter problematically naturalized a narrow definition of *Québécois*, subtly marking the French Québécois de souche as the new "natives" on the territory and once again erasing Indigenous presence and preexisting sovereignty. The charter banned any visible display of religious affiliation for employees of the state, and it operated in a highly gendered manner that particularly targeted Muslim women who wear the *hijab*. Without deploying the same register of structural violence as the Indian Act, the charter emulated its gendered discrimination in alarming ways, demonstrating that the settler state's mechanism of erasure and gendered discrimination is continuously operational, re-conjugated in forms that support the settler state's trajectory. I read La Marche Amun and *Indian Act* as performances that address the specific discrimination of the Indian Act as well as the structural violence and erasure that underlie settler societies.

La Marche Amun is part of a tradition of political work by Indigenous women that pits endurance and persistence against the government's apparently deliberate inertia when it comes to its political relationship with Indigenous peoples. In *Quel Canada pour les Autochtones?* (*Justice for Canada's Aboriginal Peoples?*) Renée Dupuis describes Canada's strategy as one of deliberate stalling. This apathy, she suggests, forces Indigenous communities to use the judicial system as a way to protect their rights, transforming what should be a political nation-to-nation relationship between Canada's polity and various Indigenous nations into a judicial one.[34] This lack of political will on the part of Canada, this deliberate strategy of letting things fester (the question of MMIW, land disputes such as the one in Oka, etc.), constitutes yet another test of Indigenous communities' endurance. For his part, Ghislain Picard, chief of the Assembly of First Nations of Québec and Labrador, argues that this strategy is a real deterrent to the development of Indigenous communities that cannot invest in their future if all their energy and resources are spent struggling.[35] In other words, the settler state benefits from maintaining Indigenous communities in a relationship of endurance against the eroding effects of its political inertia. In preventing, or at the very least slowing down, Indigenous self-governance and development, the settler state further solidifies its narrative, in which Indigenous communities are inherently incapable of governing themselves in sustainable ways and thus need the state's paternal oversight.

As a long-distance walk, La Marche Amun demanded stamina: the women walked more than 300 miles between Québec's and the nation's capitals, braving the elements and facing thirst, fatigue, blisters, stiff joints, and the waves of flies that appear around June in Québec, not to mention the indifference or hostility of some segments of the populations they tried to educate. (See figure 4.3.) The women of La Marche Amun walked without fanfare, followed by a van, and the number of marchers varied from day to day. They carried four walking sticks adorned with red, black, yellow, and white ribbons marking the directions of the Medicine Wheel. The march demanded a sustained engagement on the part of the women—a slow and reflective rhythm anchored in the land, its contours and landscapes; a rhythm that refused the catchphrases, quick fixes, or superficial readings often deployed by governments that may, in some cases, be willing to recognize past colonial wrongs, but which are reluctant to admit their present complicity in settler colonialism. Instead of a quotidian gesture, walking became a political project. Furthermore, to walk on a rural highway is not a benign gesture for Indigenous women in Canada: indeed, given the great number of Indigenous

Figure 4.3. La Marche Amun with Michèle Taïna Audette (*left*) and Viviane Michel (*right*) at the fore. (Photo by Stephane Lessard, *Le Nouvelliste*)

women (between ages 18 and 40) who were abducted and murdered along British Columbia's infamous Highway 16 between 1969 and 2011, or on the outskirts of Val d'Or, or in other communities across the country, walking on public roadways is a loaded political performance, a reclaiming of the road as a space for change. Currently, First Nations, Inuit, and Métis women are five to eight times more likely to die as a result of violence than other women in Canada.[36]

A monthlong walk can only begin to physically and politically reclaim a land marked by these exclusionary clauses, and survey the Indian Act's wide repercussions. Indigenous women have had to struggle not only against the settler state, but also against their own communities in their quest to regain Indian status. Much has been written about the negative reactions of some Indigenous leaders and communities to Bill C-31 and other judicial victories by Indigenous women against the Indian Act. This can be explained in part by the cultural and economic pressure that new members may put on communities that are already struggling financially and culturally. More importantly, though, First Nations women's victories illuminate what Frantz Fanon described as "internalized colonialism"; that is, how the gendered discrimination and patriarchal structures of exclusion imposed by colonial forces have become naturalized and read as "traditional" within some Indigenous communities.[37] Speaking about her experience during La Marche Amun,[38] Michèle Taïna Audette recalls meeting with men and women in the Indigenous communities she traversed for whom the Indian Act's regulation of status had come to be read as the extension of traditional customs that predated settler colonization.[39] Fostering discussion about the Indian Act's structure of exclusion, the march worked to illuminate and destabilize these forms of internalized colonialism in the communities it traversed. The marchers achieved this by holding gatherings in communities, giving interviews to non-Indigenous as well as Indigenous media, and having conversations with community members whom they met, before arriving in Ottawa for a final rally in front of Canada's Parliament.

As Taïna Audette's experience indicates, there are no easy and quick solutions for a body of law that has become an internalized grammar, and there are very few risk-free spaces in which to explore and dismantle this wide-reaching regulatory grammar. Undoing this regulatory regime requires time and vigilance. It demands a conscious blurring of the lines—whether the literal lines of the Indian Act or the geographical lines that have served to isolate individuals from communities—that an oppressive body of law has naturalized. Myre and the women of La Marche Amun perform this vigilant undoing. Indeed, each page of Myre's *Indian Act* necessitated over 70 hours of beading during 66 beading bees; if none of the participants reached the level of complete exhaustion often associated with endurance art, Myre describes the sustained communal beading as a form of endurance practice that was "very physical, moving into the realm of the spiritual. The physical rhythm of beading, the space and the sound of beading became a shared act of doing."[40] For Myre, this shared space and common doing, and its afferent sounds, helped to create a safer space than is generally available in the public sphere, in which to encounter the Indian Act and meditate on its effects. Tanya Lukin Linklater (Alutiiq) writes about the intimacy of practices such as beading, tanning hides, and sewing. In recording an oral history of the transmission of the art of making traditional James Bay mitts, she writes:

> I heard stories of relationships of daughters to mothers and nieces to aunties. I heard the physical labor of fixing the hides of caribou and moose. . . . I heard stories about processing grief while laboring on the hide of a moose through the seasons, and feeling their late relatives close to them while they sewed. I listened to stories about the meditative, repetitive qualities of sewing and beading, and the closeness to God they experienced in these practices handed down from their women relatives.[41]

In bringing together individuals from all origins through the common task of undoing the Indian Act, the beading bees reduced the distance, real and symbolic, between the beading volunteers. At a material level, participants performed this undoing by puncturing the Indian Act's text with needles, effectively lacerating it and erasing its words with beads. At a political level, this sustained encounter between beaders from Indigenous and settler communities performed an undoing of the silence that surrounds the Indian Act in the public sphere. Endurance is thus articulated in multiple ways in Myre's piece: it exists in the lengthy communal work required to cover each canvas, but also in the final product, which archives and asserts Indigenous peoples' resourceful endurance in the face of settler colonialism.

The Quechan playwright Preston Arrow-weed refers to the phenomenon described by Myre as a form "of praying located in doing." Speaking of his own experience organizing a walk from the Quechan community of Fort Yuma, California, to Washington, D.C., Arrow-weed locates transformative power in the reflection that arises from a sustained motion through or contact with a landscape, particularly a contested ancestral landscape.[42] Relationality is central to the work of many Indigenous artists: Lukin Linklater, Rosy Simas (Seneca), Jack Gray (Maori), and Emily Johnson (Yup'ik) all argue that relationships to land, ancestors, spaces, and objects are central to their practices. All explain that they carry their ancestors as they dance, walk, and exist, and that "past, present and future operate simultaneously" in Indigenous ways of being.[43] A similar reflection arose from La Marche Amun and finds echoes in a number of recent or recurrent long-distance walks by Indigenous peoples that have recently or are currently taking place. For instance, Josephine Mandamin (Anishinaabe) has walked "the equivalent of half of the Earth's circumference" as part of the Mother Earth Water Walk, a walking project she co-created in 2003 with another Anishinaabe grandmother to raise awareness about the environment and water conservation.[44] Their annual walks survey the periphery of the Great Lakes on both sides of the U.S. border with Canada.

In Québec, Stanley Vollant (Innu), who began walking in 2010, describes his 3,600-mile (6,000-kilometer) project, Innu Meshkenu, as a "journey of healing and reconnection" with the culture and the land.[45] In an effort to break isolation and inspire change, Vollant has walked intermittently for more than six years to meet the eleven First Nations whose ancestral territories currently form Québec and parts of Ontario and Labrador. Similarly, the 2013 Journey of the Nishiyuu, in which a group of young Cree men marched 900 miles (1,500 kilometers) in bitter subzero temperatures to go to Ottawa to meet Prime Minister Harper and ask him to honor his obligations, has been described as a performance "that votes with its feet."[46] Incidentally, in a potently symbolic gesture, Harper was nowhere to be seen on the day of the young Cree men's arrival in Ottawa. He had chosen instead to travel to Toronto to greet a panda on loan from China. "Pandagate" sparked criticism from Indigenous leaders who questioned Harper's sense of priority and the message it sent to their communities. Nevertheless, these walking projects are enacting a form of resilient sensate sovereignty. Occupying the land through walking contests settler-colonial lines of exclusion and affirms Indigenous peoples' ancestral rights that have never been extinguished. As performative acts, these walking projects "participate in weaving the textures of the land,"[47] marking with their moving bodies new connections between communities, Indigenous or not, and repatriating an embodied and experiential knowledge of the land that was central to Indigenous peoples but which has been interrupted by the creation of reserves and the imposition of a sedentary lifestyle.

Resentment and the Burden of Endurance

The (re)mapping performed by La Marche Amun and Myre's piece is hopeful—healing, even. But in leaving some of the pages of her *Indian Act* unfinished, Myre does not attempt to provide closure, nor does the work attempt to evacuate the notion of *ressentiment,* or "resentment," which is currently shunned as counterproductive in Canada's reconciliation discourse. Indeed, Canada's push for reconciliation with Indigenous peoples—through the Truth and Reconciliation Commission, among other structures—is aggressively built on the ideas of forgiving and closure. This is yet another form of Wolf's logic of elimination, operating here at a symbolic level: resentment must be erased as a last obstacle in the settler's trajectory toward legitimacy. In public discourse, following Friedrich Nietzsche, *ressentiment* has been pathologized as the reaction of the weak, as the incapacity to let go of the past and come to grips with the present. Indigenous resentment and perceived unwillingness to let go of the government's "errors of the past" is thus portrayed in the media, in the blogosphere, and by various politicians as yet another way that Indigenous cultures cannot survive in or adapt to present times.

To be clear, I am not arguing against reconciliation or the TRC, which many Indigenous communities desired and which has served as an invaluable healing space. I am, however, suspicious of how the Canadian government wants Indigenous peoples' pardon, yet continues to deny in more or less overt forms a colonial past that it constantly rearticulates in new eroding policies. In reaction to this ongoing colonialism, Glen Coulthard argues that "resentment is not only an entirely defendable position, but actually a sign of our critical consciousness, of our sense of justice and injustice, and of our awareness of, and unwillingness to reconcile ourselves with the structural and symbolic violence that is still very much part of our lives."[48] Coulthard and Dylan Robinson both argue that resentment can be a productive and ethical stance, a form of resistance that refuses to reconcile itself with colonial powers whose trajectory demands that Indigenous nations exist in a state of endurance.[49] In the same vein, Robinson adds that anger, as an affect, can

Figure 4.4. A beading bee in 2002 for the creation of *Indian Act*, with artist Nadia Myre (*right*). (Photo by Paul Litherland; art ©Nadia Myre; licensed by VAGA, New York)

also be productive, acting as a motor for modes of expression that "might themselves be far from angry."[50] Robinson cites as examples the round dances related to the Idle No More movement, explaining that though born of a rightful anger and resentment toward continuing injustice, the dances operated in a register of love, joy, and what he calls "enchantment."[51] In other words, reconciliation demands work, commitment, and endurance from all parties; it is not a form of facile intimacy.

The scope (in both time and effort) of Myre's project allows for the expression of this resentment and avoids the trap of this facile intimacy. Myre's beading sessions provide the time frame necessary for settler participants (who, as a group, tend to deflect Indigenous resentment) to "sit with" other participants' resentment and, perhaps, let its power affect and unsettle them. As Rhonda Meier recalls, "participants came for all sorts of reasons"; hers were "fueled by a sense of refusal, a desire to deface the legislation."[52] While no participant was ever asked to explain why she or he wanted to participate in the creation of *Indian Act*, some openly discussed their motivations in doing so. Nadia's father Robert Myre, who is non-Indigenous, beaded over a number of pages, while France Trépanier, a member of the Mi'kmaq nation, beaded "for deeply personal reasons, to connect with her ancestors."[53] Myre, who became a mother around the time of the creation of *Indian Act*, attributes her desire to create this monumental piece to her mother, a child of the "sixties scoop" who, removed from her community in Maniwaki, Québec, lost her Indian status because of Canada's forced adoption policy.[54] For his part, Barry Ace (Anishinaabe/Odawa) chose to bead over a page on taxation because he had been recently stuck in a byzantine situation about this particular clause of the Indian Act. In all of these cases, sitting for hours to labor over a text that imagines the end of Indigenous peoples is disorienting and unsettling. (See figure 4.4.)

Myre's beading sessions suggest that for once, this burden of endurance—the endurance required to resist the Indian Act, and the endurance required to let oneself be affected by resentment and contemplate one's complicity as a member of the settler-colonial community—could be more evenly distributed, and not rest solely on the shoulders of Indigenous subjects. In the same way that the rhythm of walking for a month allows for a sustained reflection, a beading volunteer who sits for hours beading over a text that imagines the end of Indigenous peoplehood can, if she chooses, feel disoriented and unsettled. Both Myre's and La Marche Amun's lengthy participatory processes invest time with affective power, investigating how endurance shapes one's perception of the organizing forces at play in the formation and understanding of one's own personal or communal identity.

Endurance Art, Social Contract

While endurance is central to both Nadia Myre's *Indian Act* and La Marche Amun, the two projects resist being categorized as endurance art alongside early endurance artists.[55] The position from which Myre and the women from La Marche Amun interrogate the state of enduring is radically different: their exploration stems from being in a structural state of endurance vis-à-vis an ensemble of assimilatory policies deployed by a settler state. Here, endurance is not performed as an individual self-imposed gesture of bravura, but as a communal seizing of the settler-colonial grammar, a gesture that forces this grammar's logic of extinction and violence into the open. Endurance is not a self-imposed challenge or a metaphor for something else. As such, these performances require an entirely different theoretical lens, one that decolonizes the assumptions that have heretofore underlain the analysis of endurance performance.

Patrick Anderson discusses the "masculinity deeply rooted in masochism" of the endurance performances of the 1960s and 1970s, noting their reliance on individual acts of prowess and the spectacularization of the body under duress.[56] Chris Burden and Tehching Hsieh, for example, voluntarily staged their bodies in a state of endurance, and their performances often reified notions of individualism and exceptionalism. Myre's work and La Marche Amun challenge endurance art's normative notions of exceptionalism and masculinity in their use of collective labor and seemingly unspectacular strategies. In both projects, the burden of endurance is shared by an ensemble of participants rather than by an "exceptional" individual. Unlike staging a hunger strike, putting oneself in danger, or vowing to remain immobile for days, there is nothing particularly spectacular about such quotidian gestures as walking or beading. However, when performed as a community gesture against settler colonialism's logic of elimination, these practices acquire a specific political resonance and a productive, spectacular quality. Walking and beading become affirmations of sovereignty and survivance. To walk or to bead—that is, to continue to invest territories and traditional practices as markers of Indigenous presence and as organizational structures—is indeed politically charged.

Early endurance performances explored and challenged the notion of contract implied between performer and audience as an organizing force in the public and artistic spheres. A performance like *Shoot* (1971) by Chris Burden, in which the performer willingly let himself be shot in the arm by a friend in front of an audience, challenged those who witnessed the shooting to reflect on the contract to which they had tacitly agreed upon entering a performance space. O'Dell writes, "Masochistic performance artists of the 1970s, such as Burden, sought to call attention to the structure of the contract to emphasize that the real power of the agreement lies there. . . . By pushing their actions to an extreme [the artists] could dramatize the importance of a transaction that is often overlooked or taken for granted."[57] Central to endurance artists' explorations was indeed the desire to illuminate the power at play in the tacit agreement—or contract—between artists and audience, between those who watch and those who are watched, between spectator and witness. Anderson argues that Burden's performances of self-starvation "summoned his audience to bear witness to their own spectatorial responsibilities in producing a scene of artistic encounter that would potentially endanger the life of the artist."[58] Burden and others called the spectators' attention to the often-overlooked transaction between audience and artists. They dared spectators to acknowledge the agreement they had tacitly accepted upon entering a performance space. Burden, for example, presented spectators with a dilemma: how far they would let him go in endangering himself through thirst or hunger? In the case of *Shoot*, despite the performance being dangerous, neither the shooter nor the audience chose to walk away from the agreement.

Most settler communities conveniently ignore the fundamental transaction that allowed (and continues to allow) settler-colonial communities to exist. The Idle No More grassroots movement reminded us in 2012 that "we are all treaty people." The Mohawk activist Ellen Gabriel describes Canada as founded on a "land grab" that was then naturalized by the Indian Act and the creation of reserves. To be clear, the Indian Act was never an agreement:

it was an imposition by settler-colonial forces that subsequently amended the law to better serve their expansionist agenda. The law and its categorization of Status Indians, ironically, became the only protection that Indigenous peoples had against total assimilation. In 1969, when the first prime minister Trudeau put forward his White Paper, an initiative to end the separate legal status for First Nations, abolish the Indian Act, and end the Department of Indian Affairs in the interest of so-called greater equality for Indigenous peoples, Indigenous leaders across Canada protested and insisted on keeping the Indian Act as the lesser of many evils. Harold Cardinal, a Cree lawyer, writer, and political activist, wrote about the Indigenous leaders' response to Trudeau's proposed changes:

> We do not want the Indian Act retained because it is a good piece of legislation. It isn't. It is discriminatory from start to finish. But it is a lever in our hands and an embarrassment to the government, as it should be. No just society and no society with even pretensions to being just can long tolerate such a piece of legislation, but we would rather continue to live in bondage under the inequitable Indian Act than surrender our sacred rights. Any time the government wants to honour its obligations to us we are more than happy to help devise new Indian legislation.[59]

The Indian Act, then, is not an agreement. It does, however, regulate the relationship between Indigenous people and the settler state. Members of the settler community tacitly agree to this profoundly asymmetrical ongoing societal contract, while often failing to grasp that colonialism is not over.

Myre and La Marche Amun similarly call attention to the conveniently hidden transactions (the erasure and exclusion of Indigenous peoples) that organize settler societies and allow them to exist. *Indian Act* does so by echoing the visual and performative language of wampum belts, which were central to traditional Iroquoian diplomacy of the northeast coast of North America. Wampum belts, as Sandra Dyck explains, enabled communication, exchange, and reciprocity and "served as invitations to enter into discussion, as documents of proposals tabled at or agreements made during meetings, and, particularly for the Iroquois, as records of laws, constitutions, and histories."[60] By beading *Indian Act* as a form of wampum belt—emulating the belt's two-color and horizontal beading motifs as well as its function as an archival device—Myre gives her piece a multivalent quality: it can be read as a proposed new societal contract, as a history of resilient endurance, or as an invitation to dialogue. Myre's piece is both the product and the archive of a form of diplomatic encounter in which beading volunteers from Indigenous and settler communities came together to (re)write, (re)imagine, and (re)map the set of rules that shape their relationship to each other. This encounter continues when the piece is presented in galleries and museums where a list of the names of the beading volunteers accompanies *Indian Act* like the signatories in a (re)imagined contract. A diplomatic encounter also takes place between the piece and the viewer, who pauses and perhaps allows him- or herself to be disoriented by this visual contract and, by extension, by the Indian Act as an ongoing body of laws. The piece's unfinished nature gestures to the living nature of the Indian Act and invites the viewer to participate in rethinking and decolonizing the relationship between Indigenous and settler communities.

Nation-to-Nation Diplomacy?

Both La Marche Amun and Myre's *Indian Act* were imagined and performed in large part on the territory of the province of Québec. As mentioned in chapter 3, Québec's territorial base is largely comprised of unceded land; that is, of land that was never surrendered by Indigenous nations, for which no treaties were ever signed, and on which ancestral rights are not extinguished. Québec, like the federal government, functioned for a long time under the assumption that all Indigenous territorial and ancestral rights recognized in Nouvelle-France had been extinguished in 1763 with the Paris Treaty.[61] Starting in the late 1980s, several important court cases recognizing Indigenous ancestral rights forced Québec to rethink its relationship with Indigenous people.

The relationship between Québec's national aspirations and Indigenous peoples' demands for self-determination and sovereignty is contentious yet deeply intertwined. In his book *De Kebec a Québec: Cinq siècles d'échanges entre nous* (*From Kebec to Quebec: Five Centuries of Exchanges between Us*), Eric Cardinal traces a contemporary parallel between the 1701 Grande Paix de Montréal (Great Peace of Montréal), which affirmed French and Indigenous sovereignty as coexisting, and the quest for sovereignty led by Indigenous peoples and French Québécois de souche in recent constitutional history. Since the late 1970s, Indigenous nations have engaged in tense campaigns to have their ancestral rights recognized within Canada's constitution and in federal and provincial policies. Cardinal argues that, for better or for worse, these campaigns—the repatriation of the constitution in 1982 and the failed Meech Lake (1987) and Charlottetown (1992) accords, which would have amended the constitution to meet some of Indigenous peoples' demands—were intimately linked to the French Québécois de souche's own quest for the recognition of their distinct status within Canada. As Eric Cardinal writes about the aftermath of the failed Charlottetown Accord:

> After seeing a new constitution for Canada rejected once again, First Nations leaders realized that their political leverage depended in large part on the climate surrounding the constitutional debate, and

> consequently, on the state of Québec's struggle. At the political level, First Nations have succeeded in accruing negotiating power in "fluid" political contexts created by Québec's demands and grievances.[62]

If Québec did make some significant gestures to change its relationship to Indigenous peoples, particularly under René Lévesque's leadership,[63] Cardinal argues that the province's "unilateral action during the 1980s can more readily be attributed to the province's autonomist politics and to its rejection of the repatriation of the Constitution in 1982 than to a real political will to create a 'nation-to-nation' relationship with Québec's First Nations."[64] Furthermore, even when Québec passed a motion in 1983 to recognize Indigenous nations as "distinct nations with rights to their cultures, languages, customs and traditions," the province specified that "these rights must be exercised within Québec society and consequently, should not imply sovereignty rights that might disrupt Québec's territorial integrity."[65] This understanding is far from the spirit of the Two-Row Wampum or the Grande Paix de Montréal. The Two-Row Wampum belt (1613) represents two canoes navigating side by side along two distinct and independent paths. It is the earliest mutual agreement between the Haudenosausnee people and European leaders. As with the Grande Paix de Montréal, the Two-Row Wampum imagined Indigenous sovereignty as equal to, not subsumed by, that of European settlers. Far from building on the spirit of these early agreements, the 1983 motion enforces a colonial understanding of Indigenous sovereignty and stands as a missed opportunity to lay down the base of a truly postcolonial political arrangement.

There is, as mentioned in chapter 2, a history of diplomacy and alliances between the French and the Indigenous nations in the northeastern regions of what is now Canada, which culminated with the Grande Paix de Montréal in 1701. Gilles Havard's in-depth analysis of this historic peace treaty does the important work of challenging a colonial history that presented Indigenous communities as passive recipients of European knowledge. Supported by a wealth of historical documents, Havard argues that the French were in fact greatly influenced by the sophisticated and complex diplomatic protocols that facilitated relationships between Indigenous nations at the time. The author discusses the gift economy, the wampum belts, and the envoys sent between Indigenous nations to prepare diplomatic conferences ahead of time, as well as the sophisticated oratory tradition that greatly impressed French colonial leaders. Havard notes of the structure of the Grande Paix de Montréal's negotiations that "the various elements that structured and adorned the protocol of the (peace) conferences were thus essentially of Amerindian origin."[66] Havard's work does not minimize France's self-interest in participating in diplomatic exchanges, or the ways it orchestrated conflicts among Indigenous nations in order to solidify its control of the territory. He provides an important counter-narrative to the one of primitive and warring cultures that is conveniently presented in colonial history as a way to justify colonization as a civilizing tool of advancement.

La Marche Amun and Nadia Myre's *Indian Act* participate in and help reshape this long tradition of First Nations diplomacy, as described by Havard and others like Georges Sioui (Huron-Wendat), whose research revisits his nation's diplomacy in Nouvelle-France.[67] Taiaiake Alfred employs the ritual of condolence of the Rotinohshonni people (a ceremony Havard describes as central to the Grande Paix) "as a metaphorical framework for [his] own thoughts on the state of Native America and the crucial role of indigenous traditions in alleviating the grief and discontent that permeate our existence" in his 1999 book *Peace, Power, Righteousness: An Indigenous Manifesto*.[68] Alfred employs the ritual of condolence to articulate a contemporary call for Indigenous nations' revitalization, demonstrating that their diplomatic traditions are capable of describing and responding to contemporary political challenges. The deployment by Myre and the women of La Marche Amun of performative strategies rooted in traditional practices and knowledge—beading, diplomatic envoys walking and marking an ancestral territory—should thus be read as diplomatic gestures meant to reopen dialogue and foster encounters, however uncomfortable they may be.

Myre's and La Marche Amun's diplomatic overtures challenge Québec's myths and narrative by enacting a form of sovereignty that is fundamentally at odds with Québec's nationalist project. La Marche Amun problematizes Québec's sense of territorial integrity, calling the onlookers' attention to the lines of exclusion that solidly delineate Québec's definition of itself (and specifically the French Québécois de souche narrative) and leave Indigenous nations at the margins. Walking from Wendake, a reserve in the heart of Québec's capital of Québec City, to Ottawa, the women drew a physical and political connection between the provincial and federal centers of power, aligning them as settler-colonial forces united in their common dependence on the erasure of Indigenous peoples. In drawing this connection, the women relocated the long-standing conflict between Canada and Québec's francophone majority as intracolonial: that is, as taking place within a shared structural position of power as colonial forces against Indigenous communities. The women thus foreclosed the tendency of the province's nationalist leaders and thinkers to align French Québécois de souche and Indigenous sovereignist aspirations as a common anticolonial struggle. As it stands, the liberal frame within which Québec defines itself cannot accommodate the rules of diplomatic engagement proposed by Myre and La Marche Amun. The province's investment in a minority discourse forecloses its full acknowledgment of its past and current role as a settler-colonial force. The gestures of recognition that various Québécois governments have performed in the last forty years can only imagine Indigenous sovereignty as subsumed under Québec's. Ghislain Picard, speaking for the Assembly of First Nations of Québec and Labrador in 1994, argued that Québec's sovereignty aspirations were "in direct conflict with that of First

Nations."[69] La Marche Amun, in particular, illuminated a lineage of power that intimately and uncomfortably links Canada and Québec. In doing so, the march illuminated a central contradiction in Québec's rhetoric: the difficulty of reconciling in one coherent narrative the province's history of resisting Canada's assimilatory policies toward the French Québécois de souche, *and* the province's settler-colonial role in eroding Indigenous rights and sovereignty.

Nadia Myre's *Indian Act*, which, as noted, resembles a wampum belt, borrows from the visual and performative language of Indigenous diplomacy. Wampum belts "variously served as invitations to enter into discussion, as documents of proposals tabled at or agreements made during meetings, and, particularly for the Iroquois, as records of laws, constitutions, and histories. Messages were 'spoken into' strings or belts of wampum, which were referred to as 'words' and thought to contain them, literally."[70] As Havard notes, "In reality, it was not the wampum belt as such that was important to the Native peoples; rather it was the use and process of exchanging gifts that resulted from it."[71] Wampum belts enabled performances of reciprocity; they recorded and facilitated the process of exchange and diplomacy, since each party had to offer something in return for the other party's proposal.

Myre created her piece through a process that similarly facilitated exchanges and encouraged reciprocity between the participants. Beading itself records a link with the past: the technique is traditional and is deployed to interrupt the continuation of a painful history shaped by the Indian Act. Myre's work is thus a recording of the past and an opening for the future that depends on the other parties—settlers, be they newcomers or newly arrived, French Québécois de souche or English-speaking—coming to the table with a real desire to negotiate. Myre stages a diplomatic encounter that requires reciprocity and both parties' commitment to a task whose revelatory powers only come in the repetitive "doing" that is the stringing of beads. By transforming the Indian Act into a document that resembles a wampum belt, Myre asks the viewers to reflect on their own participation in this societal contract. Myre's intervention aligns with other endurance art in the positioning demands it makes on its audience. However, while an audience member could choose to stop Burden's acolyte from shooting him and thus have agency in shaping the contract between artist and viewers, the viewer who negotiates with the demands of Myre's piece is left with questions that exceed the individual and reach a more societal scope. The viewer has to grapple with questions that cannot be answered on the spot and that defy easy answers.

Beading as performed by Indigenous communities in Canada has long been excluded from the world of high art and relegated instead to categories of craft or folk art, alongside other traditionally feminine practices. These classifications are, of course, never benign, as the Inuk curator and art historian Heather Igloliorte argues in her work on Cape Dorset painters and carvers of the early twentieth century.[72] So-called traditional beading and carving are often portrayed as rigidly static practices that are respectful of traditions to the point of foreclosing originality. Of course, this is not the case: these practices have always been and still are deeply engaged with the present, with political and communal life. Thus, to cast beading as a feminine craft rather than a potent artistic and political means of expression helps to downplay the real political role that this practice has served in recording agreements between nations. As the Mohawk activist Ellen Gabriel noted at the Truth and Reconciliation Commission, "it was the women in matrilineal cultures that were weaving the belts" and thus acted as the archivists of their nation's diplomatic relationships.[73]

Myre employs beading as a gesture of resistance, a political intervention that remaps spaces of Indigenous sovereignty, spaces in which self-determination is enacted. As Jolene Rickard argues, sovereignty can be articulated in the "doing" of traditions: "Tradition is also a strategic sovereignist resistance in the twenty-first century to ongoing coloniality and the flattening process of globalization. I've come to view sovereignty as an Indigenous tradition whose work is strategically never done."[74] Undoing the Indian Act is a decolonizing gesture that anchors and rearticulates the present and future by drawing from the ancestral knowledge and traditions that settler colonialism has long targeted.

If Nadia Myre anchors her work in the tradition of the wampum belts, the women of La Marche Amun participate in a long lineage of diplomatic envoys. Describing the preliminary exchanges that led to the Peace Conference of 1701 in Montréal, Havard writes, "talks were carried out by ambassadors who usually traveled by canoe on lakes and rivers to bring the 'word' of their nation."[75] Emissaries, who were mostly individuals who could converse in French and Indigenous languages, often traveled accompanied by war captives, who could be exchanged to establish favorable conditions for future negotiations. These mediators, called *trûchements* in French, acted as bridging agents between negotiating parties. Michèle Taïna Audette performed a similar role as a *trûchement* in her statement at the Aboriginal Affairs and Northern Development Committee on April 20, 2010, a few weeks before starting La Marche Amun. She addressed the members of the committee, preparing them with an oration whose cadence and structure—the repetition of the word *reinforce*, the sense of a message spreading from "all Quebekers" to Canadians—built a sense of urgency:

> On May 4, a symbolic event will begin. A group of women will be walking 500 kilometers from Wendake to Ottawa, to Parliament Hill, to deliver a message to Prime Minister Stephen Harper and his minister of Indian Affairs and Northern Development, Mr. Strahl. Each day we will be repeating the same message to everyone in Québec, to all Québeckers, and also to Canadians. We want to say that Canada is bringing in legislation to reinforce—and I mean reinforce—gender inequality, and we are demanding that Canada eliminate this kind of discrimination.[76]

As Havard notes in his account of the preparatory diplomatic work that preceded the 1701 Peace Conference in Montréal, "Large scale diplomatic meetings were preceded by invitations sent out several weeks, or even several months, in advance by interested party or parties."[77] The emissaries dispatched to allied and opposing nations were the best orators, chosen for their eloquence, theatricality, and abilities to convince, instead of hereditary chiefs. Centuries later, Audette's oration harked back to these emissaries' public-speaking skills. She addressed the committee members directly, telling them that they had the power to change history and achieve something meaningful. Her presentation was convincing and direct as she prepared these politicians for the event to come.

Audette's role as an emissary and a translator for Indigenous women recalls some of the most contested characters of colonization—Native American women such as La Malinche, Pocahontas, and Sacajawea who served as guides, partners, and translators for Europeans. These women's role as *trûchements*—imagined and real—have served to solidify colonial narratives and internalize sexism within First Nations communities. In *The Pocahontas Perplex*, written in 1975, Rayna Green (Cherokee) describes the complicated figure of Pocahontas in the colonial imagination as one whose virginal body stands in for America's rich lands, a woman whose sacrifice for her white lover rewrites conquest as willful submission. Colonial authorities have wielded the figures of Pocahontas, La Malinche, and Sacajawea (whose husband was French-Canadian) as a way to justify their presence, arguing that these women's supposedly promiscuous nature illustrated Native Americans' willingness to be colonized. After all, such colonial narratives argue, these women participated in colonial ventures that were, at their core, detrimental to the good of their nations.

Myre and the women of La Marche Amun imagine and enact spaces where Indigenous sovereignty and women's rights coexist. By employing traditional forms and vocabularies to address contemporary challenges in their communities, they articulate such spaces of Indigenous sovereignty and re-situate, as Jolene Rickard suggests, "traditional subjects from a frozen past" (and, I argue, from a frozen frame within the law) "to a dynamic present."[78] They create breaks, gaps in the unrelenting grammar of the Indian Act, moments where its logic of erasure comes undone, where specific Indigenous stories, stories of women and children, can be retold. Walking the territory across imposed borders, reimagining women's presence within communities, reclaiming lineages that have been interrupted by the Indian Act: these are all performances of Indigenous sovereignty anchored in non-Western understandings of the term.

The women of La Marche Amun, by physically traversing the lines of exclusion imposed by the Indian Act, performed a similar gesture of weaving and recording new alliances and new roadways. As they walked across Québec's vast expanse, crossing rural and urban landscapes, they invited those who witnessed their pilgrimage to position themselves vis-à-vis the Indian Act. Their walk does not signal that the premise of this contract is in itself acceptable or that enough amendments will one day make the Indian Act a just piece of legislation. Instead, La Marche Amun does complex and contradictory diplomatic work: it both resists colonial rules as a whole and strives to carve spaces of respite within the Indian Act's coercive legal framework. As Solnit argues, walking is a way to be "among people" without being "of" those people, a way to navigate an ecosystem and its various textures and inhabitants while maintaining one's individuality.[79] The very act of walking goes against the act's intent: walking refuses containment and embodies a resistant way for Indigenous people to be among settler communities without being of them.

In a collection of poems entitled *Tshissinuatshitakana-Bâtons à Message* (*Message Sticks*), the Innu poet Joséphine Bacon describes how the Innu people, who are a nomadic people, traditionally left wooden sticks in various positions on their territory to communicate visually with other nomads who might traverse it. These sticks served as warnings of dangers or illness ahead and acted as invitations to share and help one another. Bacon writes that words, thoughts, and intentions traveled through these sticks and that through them "speech was always in motion."[80] Bacon employs the image of the message stick to describe her work as a contemporary poet, but the metaphor captures equally well the work performed by La Marche Amun, whose crossing of the territory created and invited discussion between communities that normally do not cross paths. Every discussion in which the women engaged in the communities through which they passed acted as a message stick, marking the Indian Act's ravages and inviting help in healing them. Their work challenges nation-centric Western definitions and recenters the matrilineal structures of power and governance that the Indian Act specifically targeted.

These interventions challenge settler-colonial states, but they also challenge the fact that the fight for First Nations women's rights, and the very notion of Indigenous feminism, have at times been described as participating in a colonial agenda or as incompatible with a struggle for sovereignty. As Andrea Smith argues, many Indigenous activists have claimed that "if we successfully decolonize, then we will necessarily eliminate problems of sexism as well."[81] Smith argues that such a claim fails to address how it is "precisely through gender violence that we have lost our lands in the first place."[82] The fight for sovereignty, she argues (along with Sarah Deer and other Indigenous scholars and activists), must be articulated hand in hand with the improvement of Indigenous women's rights because "attacks on Native women's status are themselves attacks on Native sovereignty."[83]

In a radio interview two years after the march, Michèle Taïna Audette reflected on the success of La Marche Amun: "I see change as incremental . . . it happens through the stubborn steps of First Nations women."[84] The march, then, prepared the terrain, destabilized the current legal landscape, and performed a first step in laying the foundations for a new form of social contract between First Nations and settler communities and among First Nations communities themselves.

While endurance performances are not new or unique to First Nations artists and activists, they have been undertheorized as decolonizing performances. As this chapter argues, deploying endurance in the face of settler colonialism's logic of elimination is more than mere reaction: it is a performance that asserts sovereignty and seizes and unravels colonialism's grammar of extinction. Social media have served as a catalyzing force for Indigenous performances such as marches, round dances, and musical and visual pieces; navigating various websites and YouTube channels, one can see marches taking place around the world to protest global threats to Indigenous populations. In a sense, social media perform a remapping gesture, investing the virtual world of communications with decolonizing potential and claiming it as a space in which Indigenous sovereignty can be articulated.

These instances of endurance protests are certainly opening the settler public sphere, penetrating media that have historically been resistant to First Nations' voices. However, these gains are often precarious, as elder Tshaukuesh Elizabeth Penashue reminds us. After leading walks through her traditional territory in Labrador for the last thirty years, "as a symbol of Innu dedication to protecting the land, the children and the Innu way of life,"[85] Penashue was denied access to Muskrat Falls last spring by the provincial energy corporation Nalcor. The Innu have hunted at Muskrat Falls for generations; it is a place "full of stories," according to Penashue.[86] This restriction is a clear reminder of the inherently political nature of walking, of surveying contested territories and illuminating the stories, lineages, and tumultuous geographies that settler-colonial states and their laws have tried to erase.

Chapter 5

✦

Theater in Contested Lands

Repatriating Ancestors amid Violence

One cannot live carrying the dead on one's back.
—Yves Sioui Durand, director and cofounder of Ondinnok (2010)

For these old souls, I say, "Dear God, forgive us. We're in a different society."
—Carmen Lucas, Kwaayii elder and monitor for archaeological excavations in San Diego County (2008)

Prologue

This last chapter zooms out of Québec and Canada (somewhat abruptly) but remains resolutely anchored there. It adopts what Chadwick Allen calls a "trans-Indigenous methodology,"[1] inviting disparate case studies (in their modes of performance and their geography, for instance) into a productive conversation in order to illuminate complex, echoing Indigenous practices related to the repatriation of ancestors and ancestral forms of knowledge. I do not read these case studies under the rubric of sameness: doing so would ignore the specific trajectories of the distinct Indigenous and settler-colonial nations involved. Instead, I juxtapose Indigenous performances of repatriation—the transnational adaptation of an ancient Mayan play devised by Ondinnok, an Indigenous theater company based in Montréal, and a legal repatriation case opposing the Kumeyaay nation to the University of California, San Diego in southern California—and I read them, following Allen, "across genre and media, aesthetic systems and worldviews, technologies and practices, tribes and nations, the Indigenous-settler binary, and historical periods and geographical regions."[2] In tracing these echoing practices and the epistemologies they reclaim and re-center, this last chapter examines trans-Indigenous performative strategies that illuminate and defy the objective violence that underlies settler colonialism in its multiple forms. In the cases I examine, this violence targets memory and the long dead, the ancestors whose presence in the earth beneath our feet continues to contest the archives of power.

In reading a theatrical performance and a legal case together, I also resist the siloing of Indigenous theater and cultural practices as purely aesthetic, and focus as well on the political, historical, and diplomatic work that they do (and have always done). As Dylan Robinson writes, many Indigenous traditions have "functional ontologies":[3] they assert relationships to the land, the living and the dead, they record the rules of living together, and they archive ways of understanding the world. In this sense, the Kumeyaay's request for repatriation and the performance of *Xajoj Tun Rabinal Achi* activate and perform a web of ancient and contemporary diplomatic, political, and relational ties to the land, the ancestors, and other nations. They participate in interventions that are eminently political and healing.

Finally, these last case studies emerged organically from my situated practice as a French Québécoise de souche scholar relocated on Kumeyaay territory at the University of California, San Diego (UCSD). They stem from the engagement I have taken in conversation with the communities I now call home. They also follow Ondinnok's own transnational work, its explicit work toward creating a transnational Indigenous theater around concepts of recovery, renewal, and futurity.

Mise-en-Scène

A young Indigenous woman walks slowly onstage and heads toward a bench adorned with a series of masks that form a detachable bas-relief. She stops in front of the mask of a weathered Mayan face as if the elder had silently hailed her. The performer slowly lifts the mask, places it on her abdomen, and turns to face the audience. Her pose evokes for a moment the ubiquitous displays of Indigenous life found in natural-history museums worldwide. Here, however, the young woman interrogatively returns the audience's gaze and disrupts the usual one-sidedness of museum encounters with Indigenous bodies. The image is striking: the past, its ancient mask nestled on the young woman's womb, seems alive, rooted in the present. Moving slowly, the performer places the mask over her face; her body progressively becomes a surrogate of ancient gestures. A temporally blurred image breaks through: the old Mayan figure seems to materialize and speak through the body of a living person. The image is fleeting, but at that moment in the 2010 production of *Xajoj Tun Rabinal Achi* by the Montréal-based company Ondinnok, the masked woman exists suspended across time and geographical boundaries. She is past and present, herself and other, and her body bridges the divisive borders imposed on Indigenous communities by colonial powers.[4]

Staged in 2010 at Montréal's Présence Autochtone/First Peoples' Festival, Ondinnok's adaptation of the Mayan dance drama *Xajoj Tun Rabinal*

Achi, translated into French by Alain Breton, was an unsettling experience: a moment of cartographical and temporal collisions that revealed oft-buried narratives. The encounter between a pre-Spanish conquest text and contemporary Indigenous performers stands as one of these collisions. Indeed, the play dramatizes a moment when Mayan nations were sovereign and as yet untouched by the Europeans. The same cannot be said for the unique cast of Indigenous performers from across the Americas that was assembled by director Yves Sioui Durand and choreographer Patricia Iraola for this adaptation of the Mayan play. These performers and the communities from which they stem belong to a moment of what Ngũgĩ wa Thiong'o might call "postcolonial colonialism."[5] Ngũgĩ destabilizes the term *postcolonial* as a settled marker and writes: "Is the colonial period that follows the act of colonialism also postcolonial? Can you then have postcolonial colonialism?"[6] This unresolved term aptly describes the situation of many Indigenous populations of the Americas, Australia, and New Zealand who, after colonization, "never went through an independence stage"[7] and struggle with ongoing internal colonialism in countries that generally portray themselves as postcolonial. Coming from Canada, Guatemala, and Chile, the artists in Ondinnok's production articulate their identities against settler-state borders, policies, and institutions that remain colonialist at their core.

The text of *Xajoj Tun Rabinal Achi* and the complicated ways in which it was transmitted permeated Ondinnok's production, creating a second collision, occurring this time between the text and its context. While the script is unmarked by the horrors of the Spanish conquest, its transmission history is marked by colonial censorship and the devaluation of Mayan culture. The play has gone through a complex performance cycle since the conquest, lying dormant as a result of Spanish Catholic colonial authorities' repression and, more recently, during Guatemala's civil war (1960–96), which greatly affected the region of Rabinal, and reemerging during periods of relative political stability.[8]

Ondinnok's adaptation echoed the play's cyclical history in the overarching corrective gesture it sought to perform: throughout the performance, and at times independently of the play's storyline, there are interludes of what Sioui Durand calls "divinatory theater." (See figure 5.1.) During these interludes, performers halted the performance of the Mayan play and, as one performer read excerpts of Mayan divinatory texts—the *Popol Vuh* and the *Chilam Balam* from the region of Chumayel—performers aided by ritual objects imbued with the spirits of ancestors, such as bones and rocks, symbolically unearthed ancestral figures, celebrated and mourned them, and finally laid them to rest. Together, the performers enacted a form of repatriation, an embodied response to the Europeans' material and cultural pillaging and a redrawing of borderlines that have scarred Indigenous landscapes since the conquest. *Xajoj Tun Rabinal Achi* became a ritualized performance of "surrogation": the actors stood in for ancestors and became vehicles through

Figure 5.1. Three masked performers commune with ritual objects during an interlude of divinatory theater. *From left*: Lara Kramer, Leticia Vera, and Patricia Iraola in Ondinnok's *Xajoj Tun Rabinal Achi*. (Photo by Martine Doyon)

which the victims of the genocide against Indigenous populations of the Americas could be repatriated, remembered, and mourned.[9] The performers achieved these regenerative gestures when they channeled and rendered visible the characters of the Mayan play and, more broadly, when they brought forth unnamed ancestral figures for which they acted as mediators and stewards onstage. This happened through the performers' transformative mask work and through their intimate communion with ritual objects. Attesting to the production's potent affective power, Alexandre Cadieux, a theater critic for Montréal's *Le Devoir*, wrote that it "establishes a living contact between the present and the vestiges of a civilization massacred by mankind." To encounter this loss, even momentarily, left the critic with "an indescribable sensation of vertigo."[10]

Ondinnok's dramaturgical repatriation project and the moments of what I call "vertiginous consciousness" that it created find a striking echo at the University of California, San Diego (UCSD), where I currently do research in the fields of theater and dance studies. Here, bones—the very real material remains of two Indigenous bodies exhumed from the site of the chancellor's residence at UCSD in 1976—are at the center of an ongoing and bitter repatriation dispute between the Kumeyaay nation and a group of researchers from UCSD and other University of California (UC) campuses.[11] The Kumeyaay, also known as the Tipai-Ipai or Diegueños, comprise thirteen federally recognized culturally and linguistically related bands that have historically occupied parts of Baja California and the San Diego area.[12] Today the Kumeyaay are part of California's large Native American community.[13] San Diego County itself has more reservations than any other county in the United States.[14] Despite the size of the Native American population and the fact that UCSD stands on Kumeyaay ancestral land, Native Americans remain largely absent from the public sphere in San Diego and at UCSD (the university attracts and retains a dismally low number of Native American students). The dispute between UCSD and the Kumeyaay, which received local and national print and television coverage, stands as an exception to this state of affairs.

Since 2006, the Kumeyaay have pressed the University of California at San Diego for the repatriation of the remains of those they regard as ancestors. They want to put the remains to rest and give them a proper burial—to perform a literal, as opposed to a dramaturgical, repatriation. Unlike Ondinnok's work, which garnered generally favorable reviews, the Kumeyaay's repatriation project has been consistently resisted by a small but very vocal group of scientists from the UC system whose publicized performance of opposition replays deep-seated colonial scenarios and betrays a profound resistance to Indigenous epistemologies. In 2012, after rounds of failed negotiations, the Kumeyaay Cultural Repatriation Committee (KCRC) intensified its efforts, taking UCSD to federal court.[15] The KCRC argued then that by keeping the contested remains, UCSD violates the 2010 amendments to the Native American Grave Protection and Repatriation Act (NAGPRA), a federal law designed to correct a long history of insensitive and unethical handling of Indigenous bones and funerary objects.[16]

The disinterment of the chancellor's-house remains, as they are known, brings to the surface polarizing questions over whose explanatory power is privileged to name and understand the past. As the Kwaayii elder Carmen Lucas laments in the epigraph for this chapter, the two bodies unearthed at UCSD have surfaced in a vastly "different society" from the one in which they first existed, and they now occupy a contested position. The anthropologist Ann Kakaliouras proposes the notion of "repatriatability" to define remains that have the potential to be returned to a Native American tribe under NAGPRA. These "repatriatables," Kakaliouras argues, form an ontological and epistemological category of their own: they are in flux, forming "an uneasy bridge"[17]—temporally, spatially, and affectively—and illuminating seemingly irreconcilable understandings of the world. As repatriatables, the chancellor's-house remains reveal such irreconcilable differences: on the one hand, the group of UC scientists cast the remains as commodities, but also as sources of knowledge for humanity—a category from which Indigenous knowledge and Indigenous individuals as complex beings have so often been excluded historically. On the other hand, the Kumeyaay position these remains as subjects and ancestors who deserve to be put to rest.

Leveraging Kakaliouras's anthropological concept to discuss theater and performance, I argue that, as a nexus of competing narratives and worldviews, the repatriatable remains found at UCSD gain a wider performative potential. I expand the category of repatriatables to include remains and living bodies that do not fall under NAGPRA jurisdiction and can be repatriated in a more symbolic realm. These bodies or remains are what I call "performative repatriatables," and they embody what Joseph Roach calls "memory and counter-memory":[18] that is, they render visible Indigenous presence and epistemologies where they have been and continue to be violently erased.

Circum-Atlantic societies like the United States and Canada have invented themselves through the performance of "incomplete forgetting."[19] Until 1990, when NAGPRA was implemented, anthropologists and archaeologists concerned with the Americas labored largely unquestioned within this economy of incomplete forgetting. These researchers unearthed Indigenous remains only to erase them once again by denying them the dignity of a burial and by unilaterally imposing on them a Western reading that constitutes a further act of silencing.[20] The remains found at UCSD act as uncomfortable reminders of these practices and of the genocidal project that sustained what Roach calls the "invention of a New World."[21] These remains simultaneously act as incriminating witnesses, as evidence of the "destruction, dispossession, and scientific objectification of [Indigenous] cultures and heritages,"[22] and perform as surrogates for departed Kumeyaay and other Native American ancestors, holding open a place in memory—a mourning space, however imperfect it may be. The chancellor's-house remains may predate the conquest, but in the dispute with UCSD they have come to stand in for the victims of subsequent genocidal campaigns against Native Americans leading to the creation of the United States.

Similarly, *Xajoj Tun Rabinal Achi* dramatizes a precolonial Mayan society—but the play, as the living remains of an ancient practice many times buried and carefully unearthed, narrates the violent cultural erasure that sustained colonial projects. In both Ondinnok and the Kumeyaay's repatriation projects, performative repatriatables stand in for a past that they can never fully replace. The two bodies found at UCSD and Ondinnok's adaptation of *Xajoj Tun Rabinal Achi* act as reminders of what existed, and they illuminate by comparison the devastating losses suffered by Indigenous communities.

Indigenous repatriation projects inevitably trigger anxiety in settler populations. Repatriation (or the attempt to repatriate) constitutes a disruption of the dominant culture's explanatory power: it names and reclaims Indigenous bodies as meaning-makers and pushes them from a position of absence into the public sphere. In both Ondinnok's production and the Kumeyaay repatriation case, the material remains of Indigenous presence bring to the surface—and at times provoke a symbolic reenactment of—the originary violence that created the so-called New World. While theater affords Ondinnok's founding questions a more permissive explorative arena, one in which radical reimaginings are perhaps still possible because they are read as merely existing in the aesthetic realm, similar investigations and repatriation performances are often met outside of the artistic sphere with the powerful response of a civil society that is concerned with preserving the status quo. In other words, Indigenous performative repatriatables can be productively wielded in the theater space to illuminate loss and actively imagine redress in ways that currently seem impossible in the "real" world.

The Multiple Exhumations of the Chancellor's-House Remains

In 1976, an archaeological team unearthed the remains of a man and a woman on UCSD's cliff-top property in La Jolla, near San Diego. The team found the well-preserved and heretofore undisturbed remains lying together in what appeared to be a double burial. Through radiocarbon dating, scientists estimated the remains to be 8,977 to 9,603 years old, making them among the oldest human remains found in the Americas.[23] The site from which the remains were removed houses the university chancellor's official residence, a rambling 1950s adobe home called University House. It is well known that the residence and parts of neighboring La Jolla sit atop a Native American burial site known to the Kumeyaay as Skeleton Hill.[24]

After their excavation in 1976, the remains were stored in various institutions until 2006, when the Kumeyaay demanded their repatriation. Apparently, these successive custodianships took place without UCSD's full approval or knowledge, and the remains left no paper trail after 1976.[25] Furthermore, "the remains ha[d] never been studied by UC San Diego faculty other than in connection with this repatriation process."[26] It was only when the KCRC petitioned for the repatriation and reinterment of the remains on reservation land that UCSD was forced to recognize its responsibility toward the remains in a process that unleashed passionate debate.

Why did bones that UCSD had apparently forgotten suddenly trigger such heated opposition? The dispute is a complex affair that pits three parties against one another: the Kumeyaay (KCRC); UCSD, which has oscillated since 2006 between favoring and denying repatriation; and a group of UC researchers who oppose both the Kumeyaay and the university (when it has favored repatriation), demanding that the remains be kept at UCSD for scientific purposes. All three parties have taken legal actions to resolve this standoff: the Kumeyaay filed the aforementioned complaint against UCSD in April 2012, and the researchers soon followed in an attempt to block repatriation.[27]

Of all three parties, the university's performance has been the most ambivalent. In 2008, for example, the administration supported repatriation as "the wisest, most appropriate, and most respectful action to take at this point."[28] Despite this initial positive response, the university dragged its feet between

2008 and 2012, failing to return the remains. These delays were largely due to disagreements among members of an internal committee formed to advise the university regarding this NAGPRA case and to strained communication between the university and the KCRC. Some facts complicate the university's apparent goodwill and help explain its oscillating behavior vis-à-vis repatriation. University House is in dire need of renovation, and any retrofitting work could unearth more remains and trigger further NAGPRA disputes. Kumeyaay tribal leaders have suggested that the university, weary of the ethical and public relations challenges attached to the cliff-top property and its buried residents, tried to "bargain repatriation of the skeletons for the Indians' blessing on the University House project."[29] In other words, the university may have recast the chancellor's-house remains as bridging commodities that could be exchanged to guarantee the viability of a future expansion project.

Meanwhile, the university faced internal pressure from a small group of its own researchers who oppose repatriation. These researchers—UCSD's Margaret Schoeninger (who served on the internal advisory committee), UC Berkeley's Timothy White, and UC Davis's Robert Bettinger—have steadfastly rejected the Kumeyaay's claim of affiliation to the remains. The professors expressed their opposition on various stages such as high-profile scientific journals and academic committees. These stages are far from neutral and have been and remain, in many cases, largely inaccessible to Native Americans.[30] Although the three researchers have claimed to speak in the name of the entire UC community, a dissenting group within the university—with Professor Ross Frank[31] as one of its leaders—has questioned the researchers' interpretation of the data. The three researchers have repeatedly stated: "There is insufficient evidence to support the conclusion that the Kumeyaay are descended from the people who were buried at the site."[32] In fact, the researchers assert that the remains fail to even "meet the legal definition of 'Native American' under NAGPRA."[33] Deploying a narrow reading of NAGPRA, the researchers maintain that the remains are in fact not Native American at all, and that as a result, the remains should not be returned to the Kumeyaay since they were not subject to the act in the first place.[34] In their lawsuit, the researchers recast the contested remains as "early humans" or "New World remains."[35] In a press interview, James McMannis, the researchers' lawyer, added dismissively: "the idea that we're going to turn this incredible treasure over to some local tribe because they think it's grandma's bones is crazy."[36]

Unearthing the Dead, Burying the Past?

In their campaign to prevent repatriation, the UC researchers are performing a well-rehearsed colonial scenario that has served to (re)write and (re)name an entire continent. Having "discovered" the remains, the UC researchers position themselves as experts on Indigenous matter and authenticity.[37] They argue that they alone can legitimately claim knowledge of and assign meaning to these unearthed bodies. Michel de Certeau writes: "The Conqueror will write the body of the other and trace their own history . . . *This is writing that conquers*. It will use the New World as if it were a blank 'savage' space on which Western desire will be written."[38] De Certeau describes here the pervasive nature of colonial rewriting, a process that renames land, dismantles community structures, and imposes borders; the reservations stand as violent examples of the ongoing nature of this remapping. The same colonial rewriting flattens richly diverse sovereign nations into one people, the "Indians." The "body of the other" on which history is forcefully written includes not only the living but, as the Kumeyaay repatriation dispute clearly demonstrates, the dead, the long buried, the distant ancestors whose presence and history constitute a perpetual and often more ancient and ancestral counter-narrative to the conqueror's rewriting.

In his oft-cited *Cities of the Dead*, Joseph Roach discusses the evocative and frequently threatening nature of bodies—bodies that come to stand for an entire community and its history, and bodies that contradict hegemonic narratives. Roach describes "surrogation" as the process through which a community regenerates and reimagines itself by investing symbolic and associative power in performed effigies. These effigies, he writes, are "fabricated by human bodies and the associations they invoke," and while living bodies can stand in as performed effigies, "so can corpses."[39] For colonial projects that depend for their coherence on portraying the land as a blank, "savage" space ready for the taking, the dead others act as haunting effigies, uncomfortable reminders of the fragility of the colonial discursive enterprise. These effigies interrupt the conqueror's performance of continuity and legitimacy and thus must be reburied (symbolically or literally) or their evocative power otherwise deflected.

The chancellor's-house remains illuminate implicit and disturbing links between genocide and current settler states' discourses of legitimacy. Again, the remains predate the conquest: the man and woman at the heart of this dispute did not die in the violent campaigns led by the United States against Native Americans. However, their excavation and the possibility of their return to a community bring to the surface questions surrounding ownership and restoration. As effigies or stand-ins for the following generations of Native Americans who did live and die under colonial regimes, the remains unearth violence and genocide; they are a bridge through which the dead who came after them can also be brought home. The remains have the power to trigger intolerable yet invaluable moments of vertiginous consciousness in the settler community.

In *Red, White & Black*, Frank Wilderson helps us understand the nature of these moments of vertiginous consciousness. He argues that sovereignty constitutes one of the modalities of Native Americans' grammar of suffering, one that can be articulated in terms of repair and redress, ideas that are comprehensible to today's civil society. Indeed, the tremendous territorial and sovereignty losses suffered by Native Americans can be marked on maps, and restitution, although improbable, is within the realm of the imaginable. However, for Wilderson, civil society cannot imagine, much less accommodate, a form of redress for genocide, the second modality of Native Americans' grammar of suffering. More importantly, he argues that civil society cannot tolerate the effigies of genocidal victims. These effigies' evocative power poses too great a threat to civil society's ethical coherence. The erasure of memory, understood as a living repository of cultures, languages, lineages, and filiations, constitutes a loss so great, so impossible to fathom, that it becomes impossible to grieve or redress. It constitutes a loss of temporality itself, and such a loss is ungrievable. How, indeed, does one mourn the millions of Native Americans dead as a result of colonization? How does one mourn those who could have been? What does it mean to be ungrieved and ungrievable? These are the questions that surfaced alongside the chancellor's-house remains when the Kumeyaay brought them to public attention.

The UC researchers' response to the Kumeyaay exemplifies what Wilderson describes as civil society's incapacity to tolerate reminders of the genocide of Native Americans. This incapacity is widespread. Ward Churchill notes that discourses which deny the genocidal campaigns against Native Americans are found "in more-or-less equal parts at all points on the ideological compass of the dominant society."[40] That dominant society, if it is to retain its ethical coherence, cannot recognize the spatial and temporal obliteration of Native Americans. To admit the foundational role of genocide in the settling of North America is to admit that all non-native North Americans—excepting the enslaved people who were brought here against their will—are part of an unethical societal and national project. The genocide of Indigenous populations haunts the American national narrative. Any affirmation of Indigenous sovereignty, kinship, and freedom in settler states is therefore necessarily "inhabited by the forgetting of [their] condition of possibility" and haunted by their "burial, by the violence of forgetting."[41]

These authors help us understand the UC researchers' apparently visceral reaction toward the Kumeyaay. If settler states maintain their coherence through careful performances of forgetting, then burial sites and archaeological digs offer a rich symbolic ground for these performances to be reenacted. Settlers unearth the past and cast remains as bridges with a past that they alone can "identify," that is, name. The Kumeyaay's repatriation demand interrupts this economy of forgetting and challenges this performance of legitimacy. It complicates the assumption that excavation necessarily leads to visibility and a better understanding of a past people. In other words, the Kumeyaay interrupt the narrative of a benevolent scientific understanding that often surrounds the excavation of human remains. They demand that everyone look at archaeological digs as performances that reinscribe a violent colonial activity.

Symbolically, the KCRC repatriation project performed a second unearthing of the chancellor's-house skeletons, one that allowed objectified remains to reintegrate a human lineage and to stand in for subsequent generations of Native Americans. When they brought the remains from hidden museum storage spaces into the public eye, the Kumeyaay asked that the signifying power of the remains finally be acknowledged. The KCRC's intervention effectively recast the remains as performative repatriatables, and forced discussions that uncomfortably illuminated past and present violence toward Indigenous bodies. Their insistence on presenting the remains as ancestors, as links between today's tribes and their ancestral land, revealed an ontological gap between a large segment of the Western academic world and the Kumeyaay's ways of understanding the world.

The Kumeyaay's claim of affiliation constitutes an interruption of colonial remappings at more than one level. Indeed, if space and bodies were remapped by colonial powers, time was similarly reimagined through the detemporalization of Indigenous populations. Discursively placed in what Kevin Bruyneel calls "colonial time," Indigenous people were remapped by settler-colonial powers as out of time, and their presence was closely linked with untenable demands of authenticity that deny Native Americans a contemporary presence and the possibility to traverse temporal boundaries and articulate an identity in the "now."[42] This remapping of Native American temporality performs a radical gesture of closure: it positions Native Americans as barren, incapable of renewal, imagining them without credible successors, and—as is the case for the chancellor's-house remains—without links to a distant past. When the Kumeyaay speak of the remains as their ancestors and position the tribe as the steward of the remains, they are actively performing a counter-mapping of time and space. They perform continuity and argue that they are a community with links to the past, a community that can renew itself through surrogation.

With the remains suddenly charged with such evocative power, the battle over repatriation became loaded, especially for the small group of UC researchers who were opposed to the KCRC's claim. The stakes were suddenly higher than repatriation: they had to do with ownership of the truth. The UC researchers' multifaceted performance—in open letters to high-impact scientific journals such as *Science* and *Nature*,[43] testimonies before the UC-wide Advisory Group on Cultural Repatriation of Human Remains and Cultural Items, legal briefs, and press interviews—merits attention. Ironically, the researchers were aided in their opposition campaign by NAGPRA, the very law that was supposed to facilitate repatriation.

When the KCRC first contacted UCSD in 2006, NAGPRA stipulated that tribes, to repatriate, had to demonstrate a cultural affiliation with the remains or objects.[44] Many Native American tribes, having been displaced or otherwise uprooted by settler-state policies, found it difficult to provide the robust evidence demanded by NAGPRA. Oral history, the main historical archive for many Native American communities, often did not persuade NAGPRA committees. The law was amended in 2010 so that the tribes historically closest to the territories in which remains were found could be recognized as culturally affiliated. More importantly, the repatriation process often illuminated seemingly irreconcilable views of the world. The very understanding of bones, for example, of what they mean as a category of "things"—the mere "biological husks of a once living but now dead being"[45] for the West, versus the embodiment of ancestors for the Kumeyaay—revealed profoundly divergent epistemes. Unsurprisingly, tribes found that anthropologists, who had authoritatively and often unilaterally told the story of Native North Americans, did not grant these epistemes equal status.

This kind of devaluation is clearly at work in the UC researchers' various performances. The researchers cast the Kumeyaay as antiscience, ignoring their collaboration with San Diego State University's Dr. Arion Mayes, who performed investigative analysis on the remains in noninvasive ways that did not desecrate the bones.[46] The UC researchers conveniently ignored the KCRC's attempts to render scientific testing more respectful of the Kumeyaay's role as custodians of the dead. Instead, they portrayed the tribe as "ideology driven."[47] Ironically, they never questioned the very bias driving their own campaign against repatriation, namely their conviction that science itself is nonideological and that academic work somehow exists outside of structures of power that reinforce hegemonic narratives.

In a letter published in *Science* in May 2011, Bettinger, White, and Schoeninger, along with two other colleagues, wrote: "The University of California favors the ideology of a local American Indian group over the legitimacy of science . . . The potential loss of the La Jolla skeletons would have a profoundly negative impact on our knowledge of the peopling of the Americas."[48] Here the researchers perform an interesting pas de deux that simultaneously recognizes and denies the power of the chancellor's-house remains: they cast the remains as universal patrimony, their DNA as a source of knowledge that could benefit all. To prevent research, they argue, would deny humanity a source of precious knowledge. The researchers, interestingly, fold the Kumeyaay into the "we" of a universal humanity while simultaneously denying the tribe any relation to—and therefore power over—the remains. The researchers also conveniently ignore the fact that humanity's patrimony, understood in the letter to *Science* as Western scientific knowledge, cannot be separated from the violence perpetrated against Native American and other racialized bodies. The very creation of NAGPRA is testimony to this abuse. The collected bodies of Native Americans—silenced and dehumanized—still crowd museums and research institutes. Museological "collections" of human remains, as Rebecca Tillett argues, cannot be uncoupled from "notions of ownership inherent within the concept of slavery."[49] Similarly, there are "implicit and disturbing links between the collection of human remains and the 'souvenirs' taken during actual acts of genocide against Native peoples in the United States."[50]

In August 2014, the Northern District of California's Ninth Circuit Court of Appeals dismissed the challenge brought forth by White, Schoeninger, and Bettinger as to whether or not the remains qualified as Native Americans, and the remains were finally repatriated in spring 2016. The university transferred the remains without much media attention and issued no statement about what it planned to do to rebuild its strained relations with Kumeyaay communities.

Repatriation projects are met differently in the artistic realm, an area of exploration where destabilizing narratives and symbolic forms of repatriation have the potential to provoke productive encounters between spectators and Indigenous performers.

The *Xajoj Tun Rabinal Achi* Text and Context

Ondinnok could not have chosen a more evocative play to explore repatriation than *Xajoj Tun Rabinal Achi*, a fifteenth-century Mayan court drama.[51] Indeed, the play's performance history is a fascinating account of what Gerald Vizenor calls "survivance." This active, obstinate presence is woven into *Xajoj Tun Rabinal Achi* both in the epistemological framework of the play's text and in its production history. *Xajoj Tun Rabinal Achi* is relatively unknown outside of Guatemala, where the dance drama ritual—its 3,000 verses and its choreography, which deploy established geometrical patterns that symbolically establish the characters as belonging to the same world[52]—is carefully preserved in San Pablo Rabinal by the ensemble El Grupo Danza Drama Rabinal Achi, led by José Léon Coloch Garniga, the current holder of the ritual.[53] The preconquest play has defied centuries of colonial censorship and appropriation as well as Guatemala's more recent bloody armed conflicts. At times it has been performed and transmitted clandestinely.[54]

The play's text merits careful attention because it uniquely dramatizes a time when Mayan civilization existed untrampled by Europeans. *Xajoj Tun Rabinal Achi*'s text and highly stylized performance technique are difficult, even impenetrable, for contemporary audiences, regardless of their cultural backgrounds. Indeed, the dance drama's performance features masks and costumes that render Cawek and his opponent almost identical, and there are nonrealist movements such as counterclockwise promenades in the performance space that mark the 260 days of the Mayan divinatory theater.[55] The text itself is infused with references to Mayan cosmology and collapses several centuries of historical events into episodes that are neither organized chronologically nor contextualized in the play. Historically spoken and danced to the sound of trumpets (*tun*), the play dramatizes the trial of Cawek, a warrior from a neighboring nation accused of treason by the people of Rabinal. In this trial, Cawek and his judge, the Man of Rabinal, are positioned not as ontologically opposed but as two continuous forces whose tension is necessary to the world's equilibrium—Mayan epistemology was unmarked by Christianity's notions of absolute good and evil.[56] *Xajoj Tun Rabinal Achi* distills many generations of Mayan stories, practices, and beliefs and functions as a repository of a precolonial epoch of Mayan sovereignty.

The play brings to life a trial and, as Dennis Tedlock, who translated the text into English, argues, "the representation of Cawek's death at the hands of his captors requires a major revision of received notions about the role of human sacrifice in ancient Mesoamerica."[57] Indeed, the Spanish colonizers, in their campaign to denigrate Mayan religion, culture, and sovereignty, labored to reframe Mayan sacrifices as a barbaric custom, conveniently forgetting their own use of capital punishment and the violence of the Inquisition. *Xajoj Tun Rabinal Achi* contradicts this reductive assertion by presenting the sacrifice of Cawek as the legitimate execution of a prisoner who is tried and found guilty by his peers of dreadful offenses.

It comes as no surprise that a play which portrays a sovereign nation applying justice within its own coherent cosmological and epistemological frameworks provoked the ire of Spanish colonial and religious authorities. After the conquest, these forces regularly banned the play, arguing that it would incite human sacrifices, rebellion, and chaos.[58] The parallel between this colonial tactic and the campaign of epistemological devaluation currently led by UC researchers is disturbing. In a rhetorical move that echoes colonial and religious authorities, the researchers present science as the only valid way to understand the remains unearthed on the UCSD campus and frame the Kumeyaay's position as "antiscience." The researchers invoke the menace that repatriation poses to "our" knowledge and the loss of "our" scientific patrimony.

The Mayans, like the Kumeyaay, responded to this colonial devaluation after the conquest in ingenious ways. For one thing, they removed from *Xajoj Tun Rabinal Achi* "all but the outlines of the original religious content from public view," assigning it instead to the Road Guide (K'amol B'e), "a native priest-shaman who does most of his work behind the walls of houses and on mountaintops."[59] Importantly, it was the performance strategies, not the text itself, or the preconquest world it encapsulates, that the Mayans altered to ensure the play's survivance. Many Mayan texts were markedly altered by the conquest; that is, their content has been updated to include the episode of contact, often as a way to establish a genealogy of Indigenous presence in a given territory that could then be deployed as a legitimizing tool to assert territorial rights before colonial rule.[60]

For its part, the text of *Rabinal Achi* does not attempt to draw an organized genealogy of the Quiche and Rabinaleb, the respective nations of

Cawek and his opponent; instead, as previously noted, the play collapses historical events and anecdotes from many centuries into a single time frame. Breton writes that "even though it was transcribed into Latin characters during the colonial period, [the play] suffers from no European influence. Not one word, not one phrase, not the slightest allusion betrays the presence of an intervention on the path of Hispanization or conversion."[61] Breton notes that, for reasons that are not fully understood, *Rabinal Achi* bears no trace of updating; "the substance of the tale goes back to the pre-Hispanic period."[62] It appears that Mayan dramatists acted as stewards of the play and chose to bury its meaning and render it opaque to the uninitiated rather than alter it. The performance tactics—the deployment of the Road Guide character, for example—and the structure of the play thus contain layers of resistance and ingenious survivance tactics that were aimed at protecting and preserving Indigenous knowledge and worldviews. Ondinnok adopted similar tactics in its adaptation of the play.

Xajoj Tun Rabinal Achi, the text and its performance tradition,[63] constitutes a performative repatriatable. The text, like the chancellor's-house remains, transmits cultural, historical, and cosmological knowledge that is at odds with Western cosmologies. The play, like the bones found in La Jolla, is understood by the Mayans not as an archival remnant of the past, the shell of a world that once was, but as a living repertoire, as Diana Taylor's work argues, connecting the past to the present.[64] It constitutes knowledge that Dwight Conquergood describes as "embodied, tacit, intoned, gestured, improvised, coexperienced, covert—and all the more meaningful because of its refusal to be spelled out."[65]

Xajoj Tun Rabinal Achi is, at its core, a play-ritual that protects the region of Rabinal from an ancient curse laid on it by Cawek. When the play is performed now, it is preceded by preparatory rituals during which the Road Guide invites the spirits of both Cawek and his captors to become visible for a day. On the day of the performance, as they enact Cawek's trial, the actors are visited by the spirits of these ancestors. In his account of a 1998 performance of the play in San Pablo Rabinal, Tedlock describes how the performers, aided by the sound of the trumpets, bring "*Rabinal Achi* into the present world from another one—a prior world, yes, but also a parallel one, in the sense that it is always there."[66]

This coupling of theatrical ritual and regeneration is central to Ondinnok's work. Ondinnok, an Indigenous theater company founded in 1985 and based in Montréal, defines its theater as an attempt to "re-conquer [Indigenous] imaginary" and "to repatriate a memory in order to unleash a future."[67] Like the Kumeyaay, Ondinnok understands itself as a steward of Indigenous cultural capital and, as such, is invested in repatriating, honoring, and reimagining First Nations heritage. The company, whose Huron-Wendat name means "a healing ritual that reveals the secret longing of the soul,"[68] performs what Roach calls a "dramaturgy of cultural renewal."[69]

Unlike some of Ondinnok's past productions in which Indigenous loss was explored explicitly, colonial trauma remained unnamed onstage in *Xajoj Tun Rabinal Achi*.[70] While the text does not refer to colonial violence and trauma onstage, Ondinnok's production was fundamentally a repatriation project. The production explored traumatic loss in complex shades of longing and mourning, but these embodied meditations often took place outside of the text itself, in the performance strategies devised by director Yves Sioui Durand and in the interludes of "divinatory theater" that he added to the Mayan play, in which performers interrupted the course of the Mayan play and performed transformative mask work and other communing gestures onstage, aided by excerpts of Mayan divinatory texts. The Indigenous performers never spoke directly of loss, violence, or dispossession. Instead, they performed gestures of communion with distant ancestors by retelling their story and becoming vessels of remembrance.

Ondinnok's *Xajoj Tun Rabinal Achi*

Spectators slowly find their seats at Montréal's Excentris, a sleek (and now defunct) performance space located downtown. On the proscenium stage, a trickster figure (Yves Sioui Durand) sleeps on one of the three benches upstage. His face and the back of his head are covered with devilish red masks, and a colorful headdress is perched on his head. The sleeping Trickster's long velvet robe decorated with gold is reminiscent of the garbs worn by Spanish conquistadors, and the long blond tresses that emerge from his headdress mark this devil figure as European. (See figure 5.2.) The central bench, on which he sleeps peacefully, is carved with Mayan iconography. The other benches, simpler in design, are each adorned with three masks whose timeless visages face the audience. Eight fist-sized rocks create a central path leading downstage from the central bench.

The masked Trickster slowly emerges from sleep, faces the audience, and announces in a resounding and omnipotent voice: "Lumières!" ("Lights!"). As the stage becomes illuminated, the Trickster breaks into an incongruous jig while the other performers join him onstage accompanied by the thunderous sounds of Tibetan horns. José Léon Coloch Garniga and his son José Manuel Coloch Xolop, the official holders of the *Rabinal Achi* ritual in Guatemala, enter first. The two men are dressed in the traditional costumes and masks in which they perform the play-ritual in San Pablo Rabinal, and each holds a cymbal and a large animal bone. The two men sit on the central bench next to two women wearing long dresses (Catherine Joncas and Leticia Vera).

As the Trickster crosses the stage from stage right to stage left, dragging a heavy burden consisting of a deer's skull and antlers, the eight other performers crawl onstage, each toward one of the rocks that form the central pathway. Once there, each performer delicately lifts the rock to his or her

Figure 5.2. The Trickster sets the stage for the performance: Yves Sioui Durand in Ondinnok's *Xajoj Tun Rabinal Achi.* (Photo by Martine Doyon)

abdomen and then to the sky. Rocks play a central role in a number of Indigenous rituals, and in many sweat lodges they are referred to as "grandfathers." Here, the rocks play a similar role, symbolizing ancestors and a connection to the past. This gesture of communion between performers and ancestors, coupled with the Trickster's dragging of material remains, anchors the evening's performance in a larger temporal frame of remembrance and announces Ondinnok's repatriation gesture.

Once all the performers have connected with their respective rock or ancestor, they come down off the front of the stage and form a semicircle in front of the audience. Each performer kneels and places his or her rock back on the stage to mark the periphery of this ritual performance space. A moment of silent suspension and marked expectation follows this opening sequence. Before long, one of the performers hoists him- or herself onstage, rock in hand. This single performer walks the perimeter of the stage and then, as if responding to an impulse, heads toward one of the masks, placing his or her rock at the foot of the bench, in front of the mask. Only then does the performer lift the mask, hold it up to his or her abdomen and, finally,

Figure 5.3. A performer observes a mask before performing the transformative work that will allow him to become Cawek for the night. *From left*: Rodrigo Ramis, Catherine Joncas, José Léon Coloch Garniga, José Manuel Coloch Xolop, and Leticia Vera in Ondinnok's *Xajoj Tun Rabinal Achi*. (Photo by Martine Doyon)

put it on. This evocative transfer between the rock or ancestor and the mask that renders this ancestor visible establishes a bridge between past and present, a way to communicate with and be visited by ancestors. Sioui Durand's rehearsal techniques work specifically on developing the actors' capacity to recognize and attune to these impulses or summonings and to respond to them onstage.

This temporal connection is further established by the prologue that follows in which the Trickster introduces the characters and sets the stage for *Xajoj Tun Rabinal Achi*. As the Trickster speaks, the masked performer embodies the characters of the play one by one, bringing them to life onstage. (See figures 5.3 and 5.4.) That Sioui Durand chose to have the prologue spoken by the Trickster rather than by one of the other performers (as it would be in Guatemala) is important. Deploying symbols and religious markers of the European conquerors, the Trickster plays God, demands light, gives life to characters, and creates the world of the play. He then turns these symbols around by bringing to life a play that clearly contests the worldview of the conquest and by participating in a ritual that commemorates and celebrates Indigenous communities. With the Trickster, Sioui Durand inscribes the play,

Figure 5.4. A masked performer embodies all the characters of *Xajoj Tun Rabinal Achi* during the Trickster's prologue. *From left*: Catherine Joncas, José Léon Coloch Garniga, José Manuel Coloch Xolop, Leticia Vera, and Rodrigo Ramis. (Photo by Martine Doyon)

the story it tells, and its adaptation in Montréal within the larger context of the conquest and colonization, rendering visible for the audience the forces against which both this Mayan play and, importantly, all of its performers have had to position themselves since the conquest.

At the end of the prologue, the performer removes the mask, his or her entire body and facial expression now charged with Cawek's energy, and launches into the captive's first monologue, marking the beginning of Cawek's trial. This is a pivotal moment in Ondinnok's adaptation: contrary to how the play is performed in Guatemala, the Ondinnok performer who climbs onstage and becomes Cawek is different every night. As Sioui Durand explains: "Every night, one performer is summoned by the ancestors to embody Cawek. In turn, when the story has been told, one of the performers is chosen to play the sacrifice victim."[71] Cawek, then, is portrayed by at least two actors each night, a man or a woman. Charles Bender and Nicoletta Dolce played Cawek on the night I saw the play, but archival footage shows that Hélène Ducharme, Patricia Iraola, and Rodrigo Ramis were Cawek on other nights. The only characters played by the same actors every night are the Man of Rabinal and Lord Five Thunders, both performed in the Quiche language by Garniga and Xolop, and the Man of Rabinal's wife, played by Joncas. These are Cawek's main interlocutors. The play consists mostly of alternating monologues between Cawek and his captors in which Cawek's crime is recalled, his motivation questioned, and his fate slowly sealed. The rest of the performers rearrange themselves around the chosen Cawek every night with great fluidity, becoming the Ixoq Mun (servant) or the silent Eagle and Jaguar warriors, or acting as a chorus echoing Cawek's hallucinations when he drinks the potions his captors give him as part of his trial.

For his adaptation, Sioui Durand cut significant portions of the original text and focused on key moments in Cawek's trial when the warrior journeyed from anger and defiance to a quiet yet mournful contemplation of his imminent death. In one instance, Cawek meditates at length on the link between his identity and his impending beheading. He talks about his own head and face in relation to his forebears, appealing to a deeper sense of community that he fears will be lost after his execution. Moments before his beheading, Cawek contemplates a round drinking vessel and asks: "'Could this be the skull of my grandfather? Could this be the skull of my father?' He then imagines that his own head will become a work of some kind, an artifact."[72] As Tedlock notes, "Heads, and especially faces, have played a central role in Mayan notions of identity and personhood throughout history."[73] The head and the face are closely linked to notions of kinship; in fact, the Mayan word for *face* belongs to a semantic field related to species, filiation, and relationality. In other words, to show one's face is to reveal one's lineage, to divulge one's affiliation to a community and a place.

Divinatory Theater: Repatriation in the Theater Space

This relationship between face and filiation is revisited by the actors who, like the young woman described in this chapter's opening sequence, work with masks onstage during the interludes of divinatory theater that Sioui Durand added to the original Mayan play. In these moments, the performers step away from the play and read passages from the *Popol Vuh* (1000–1697 AD) and the *Chilam Balam* (from the region of Chumayel in the seventeenth and eighteenth centuries), two foundational texts of the Mayan cosmology that contain creation myths, genealogies, and predictions based on the Mayan calendar. These interludes, seemingly unrelated to Cawek's storyline, allow a performative repatriation to take place onstage. Accompanied by textual excerpts from these two genealogical and mythological texts, the actors, summoned by ancestors, rise and perform their communion with the masks that have called upon them, as Sioui Durand explains. For instance, by putting on the ancestor's mask—his face—the young woman in the opening sequence claims a complex lineage across time and space. At the end of the interlude, her slow removal of the mask constitutes a form of becoming, the embodied

Figure 5.5. A performer brandishes a bone while another carries a fellow performer on his back during an interlude of divinatory theater. *From left*: Lara Kramer, Charles Bender, Patricia Iraola, and José Manuel Coloch Xolop (*back*) in Ondinnok's *Xajoj Tun Rabinal Achi*. (Photo by Martine Doyon)

articulation of what an Indigenous presence both informed by the past and alive in the "now" might be. (See figure 5.5.)

Perhaps because he was keenly aware of the possible pitfalls of representation, Sioui Durand moved away from explicitness—that is, from transparent or mimetic representations—and toward a strategic use of opacity in *Xajoj Tun Rabinal Achi*. Ondinnok's production powerfully acknowledged and mourned the trauma of broken communities, of ancestors lost in genocidal campaigns that accompanied the conquest and colonialism. It did not, however, offer trauma as the only lens through which the audience could apprehend Indigenous bodies onstage. In refusing to perform or locate loss in an explicit way, Ondinnok strategically displaced the burden of representing trauma away from the Indigenous performers—avoiding the reinscription of their bodies as sites of devastation.

In Ondinnok's production, trauma and repatriation were performed in the interstices between the various elements of the event. The production carved a time apart during the prologue and the interludes of divinatory theater, a temporal gap in which mourning and repatriation could take place. More specifically, moments of "vertiginous consciousness" occurred in the gap between actors and audience, the play and its historical context, and the story and the loss it elucidated. While the story of Cawek and the Man of Rabinal does not directly dramatize postcolonial loss, it relentlessly points to this trauma by showing what *was*, what existed *before* the advent of the colonial forces. This juxtaposition, I argue, elicits moments (even if only fleeting) of visceral clarity among audience members, a vertiginous and uncomfortable contemplation of the immensity of Indigenous losses and the difficulty of mourning them. The play illuminates contemporary demands for sovereignty and self-governance based on Indigenous models by dramatizing a moment when Mayan epistemologies were the foundations of sovereign nations. The current state of affairs for Indigenous communities acts as a point of comparison for the audience, brought to mind by the events onstage. Cawek's trial, in which he is judged and sentenced by his peers and within his own value system, stands in sharp contrast to the justice systems that many Indigenous people face worldwide. The ancestors commemorated during the prologue and the interludes of divinatory theater illuminate the ungrieved and ungrievable nature of colonial genocide. Ondinnok's production created a confronting encounter between a play that dramatizes what *was*, and the spectators' awareness of what has taken place in Indigenous communities since the fifteenth century and what now *is* for many Indigenous communities.

Opacity as Repatriation

Though added by Sioui Durand, the interludes of divinatory theater in Ondinnok's production echo a practice that surrounds the performance of *Xajoj Tun Rabinal Achi* in Guatemala. When the play is performed there, it is understood that the ghosts of the characters visit the performers, allowing them to retell their stories, and a single actor performs each ghost-character. Actors perform one role for the entirety of the play. Yves Sioui Durand disrupted this performance mode, destabilizing the symbiotic relationship between performers and their roles that not only shapes the performance in Guatemala but also usually rules Western realist theater. By breaking Cawek's part in two, he denied the audience a certain kind of narrative or even empathic identification, the emotional reward of following a character's journey from beginning to end.

Throughout the performance, the cast of Ondinnok oscillated between acting as translators for their audience—providing a point of entry into the text—and leaving spectators in the uncomfortable position of outsiders. The unfixed production values certainly played a part in this estrangement: no musical or lighting effects were repeated, and no narration or gesture rendered transparent how or why actors were "summoned" to play particular characters. Similarly, the actors performed in Mayan, French, English, and Spanish (with no translation); and the divinatory theater interludes, while often symbolically rich, were at times impenetrable. In sum, the production's demanding theatrical and ritualistic vocabulary often left the audience on the outside, viewing a performance they could not fully access. This opacity, however, was often deployed as a gesture of resistance, reappropriation, and healing, in much the same way that opacity can be deployed as a form of resistance, a way to reclaim and preserve a sense of self, as Saidiya Hartman points out about the hidden subtexts of the songs and dances of enslaved people. Hartman argues that, given the slave's lack of agency, opacity had no performative or transformative power.[74] In the case of Indigenous bodies, however, opacity can allow performers to redefine themselves outside of the colonial or victimizing gaze. Indeed, the production's opacity denied the audience the possibility of folding Indigenous trauma into their own sense of guilt or discomfort. It contested any reductive marking of Indigenous bodies as sites of devastation, reclaiming instead the sense of being unmarked, whole, and complex.

The Kumeyaay's repatriation project deploys opacity in similar ways. The KCRC opposes any form of scientific testing that breaks the surface of the bone, claiming that this would desecrate the soul of the remains. Their claim is that these bones should remain whole and illegible to us, that there is something sacred in being opaque. Returning the remains to the ground is the only way to restore illegibility and opacity to these humans from the past. In the case of Ondinnok's production, keeping the performers' bodies and certain aspects of the productions opaque, illegible, and unattainable was a way to deny the audience catharsis, the momentary purging that would enable them to return to the status quo once the play was over. The largely non-Indigenous audience was certainly reminded at various times that this ritual was not intended for them, not meant to assuage their guilt toward the Indigenous population that constitutes for many—in Montréal as well as La Jolla—the "unknown other."

Whether or not the production succeeded is up for debate. While a critic like Cadieux welcomed the production's opacity, others lamented it. The production frustrated the critic Mélanie Grondin, who called it "fascinating but hermetic";[75] she wondered why Ondinnok did not try to render the meaning of the play-ritual more accessible. Grondin's critique illuminates the assumption that visibility and legibility go hand in hand, that Indigenous bodies should be transparently understandable to the settler majority. Such assumptions are not surprising given the settler state's history of presenting itself as the "expert" on "Indians." Laws like Canada's Indian Act (which continues to regulate who is and isn't "Indian") are articulated around demands of complete transparency for Indigenous subjects. These standards of authenticity give the white majority the say over whose bodies count as "Indian." When Ondinnok deploys opacity and illegibility onstage, it challenges this construction. Ondinnok recasts non-Indigenous audience members as *non*experts, bringing them face-to-face with Indigenous bodies that refuse reductive markings. But what if the audience refuses to be recast this way?

Repatriation and "Colonial Agnosia"

Ondinnok's repatriation project raises challenging questions about the limits of empathy when seemingly irreconcilable narratives shape a sense of self for audience members and performers. The Kumeyaay's repatriation project stages a similar encounter. How does one (or *can* one) witness a presence, a remapping, or a demand for repatriation that, in the reality it illuminates, threatens to disarticulate one's own self-definition? The UCSD case demonstrates the difficulty of this encounter, where the settler state has yet to end structural discrimination against Indigenous populations or make redress an integral part of its political and societal project. Settler states depend on the ongoing trauma of Indigenous communities for their economic development, cartographic integrity, and stable sense of identity. Excentris stands on land that was appropriated at great human cost. UCSD as an institution and, more broadly, research in the Americas as a field of inquiry, have benefited and continue to benefit from the dispossession of Native Americans. To expose that loss through performative repatriatables and think of redress and healing in this context are challenging acts for the performers and for those who witness repatriation projects. They induce moments of vertiginous consciousness, a sensation of sudden clarity—a sinking of the solar plexus, if you will—about the violence that continues to hold one's settler-colonial privilege in place.

Such moments of vertiginous consciousness constitute a menace so great that they are quickly diverted, dismissed, or folded and neatly renarrativized. This renarrativization takes multiple forms, ranging from violent repression to an insidious type of misreading or misrecognition of Indigenous material remains, presence, and demands. When it comes to how gestures of Indigenous reappropriation or repatriation might be received, Audra Simpson notes: "The very notion of Indigenous nationhood which demarcates identity and seizes tradition in ways that may be antagonistic to the encompassing frame of the state, may be simply unintelligible to the Western and/or imperial ear."[76] Simpson echoes Jodi A. Byrd's notion of "colonial agnosia,"[77] or the incapacity of non-Indigenous interlocutors or spectators to read Indigenous presence and demands outside of reductive colonial narratives.

In the case of Grondin's critique, colonial agnosia is the refusal to encounter the illegible body onstage. It is also the demand that Indigenous bodies make themselves legible to "us" rather than "us" having to face bodies that elude our grasp. For the UC researchers, colonial agnosia is a refusal to see the remains as anything other than inert objects that are available for study. The Kumeyaay's repatriation project and Ondinnok's theater of repatriation complicate and at times decouple visibility and legibility, burying and forgetting. They propose instead that to unearth in the name of science does not necessarily lead to a better understanding of the remains that have surfaced. As the Kumeyaay case suggests, excavating remains can instead trigger a reenactment of colonial violence and a further misreading of Indigenous bodies.

Conversely, as Ondinnok illuminates in its theater-ritual, unearthing remains in the symbolic realm can be a way to mourn and reclaim a common lineage across the borders imposed on Indigenous communities by colonial and settler states. In the cases of Ondinnok and of the Kumeyaay, it is the gesture of burying that allows memory and lineage to be performed and reclaimed. To bury is to restore complexity, to undo the reductive markings of the colonial gaze. The Kumeyaay's and Ondinnok's understanding of burying stands in sharp contrast with Western notions of burying where burial is coupled with loss, finality, and/or the removal of the repressed. Both repatriation projects use opacity as a way to confront settler audiences/interlocutors with what "we" can't (normally) see. More importantly, these two performances illuminate how stages—from the theatrical stage to the performance platforms afforded to scientists and representatives of settler states—are still far from being level. The Indigenous groups who perform and demand repatriation continue to face structures and audiences threatened by the claim for presence, filiation, and ultimately, futurity.

CONCLUSION

This book begins with a photo taken in 1990, during the events that shook the border between Kanehsatà:ke and Oka and radically reshaped Indigenous activism in Québec and in Canada. It seems fitting to end with a reflection on Idle No More, an Indigenous grassroots movement that started in December 2012 and remains active today. The waves of activism and political protests that organized around Oka and, more recently, around Idle No More feature condensed and highly visible public spectacles of Indigeneity, moments when Indigenous performances of presence, community, and sovereignty burst into the public sphere to disrupt Canada and the French Québécois de souche's status quo. These two political movements, born in reaction to similar unilateral moves by settler-colonial governments, illuminate settler colonialism as an ongoing structure rather than a discrete moment from the distant past. The strategies deployed in Oka and those that Idle No More employs in its nationwide protests are vastly different. Read together, however, these two moments of colliding encounters between Indigenous and settler communities encapsulate this book's investigation.

Idle No More began in late 2012, when four women used the catalyzing power of social media to organize nationwide protests against Canada's proposed Omnibus Bill C-45. This sweeping bill, which was ultimately adopted, unilaterally changed legislation contained in sixty-four acts and regulations, among them the Indian Act, the Navigation Protection Act, and the Environmental Assessment Act. These changes dramatically affect Indigenous communities (which were not consulted), their eroding territory, and their infringed-upon sovereignty.[1] Canada's unilateral revisiting of the laws that organize its relationship with Indigenous peoples is not surprising and echoes the gesture of the mayor of Oka in 1990, when he decided to expand a golf course on contested Mohawk land. Little has changed in a quarter of a century. Despite the adoption of Bill C-45—or, more likely, because of it—Idle No More is still active, protesting against oil and mining development projects that affect Indigenous communities, for example, and campaigning for a (now operative) public inquiry on the thousands of missing and murdered Aboriginal women.

The early days of the movement were marked by high-profile hunger strikes by Chief Teresa Spence and Grand Elder Raymond Robinson, as well as by flash mobs and other seemingly spontaneous gatherings that reinvested public spaces with political power. More recent interventions have taken the shape of peaceful demonstrations, long-distance marches, artistic projects, and teach-ins springing up across the country. With no official leader, the movement relies on many spokespeople and on provincial coalitions to deliver its decolonizing message. The movement is, in many ways, indebted to the Mohawk protesters who occupied the border between Kanehsatà:ke and Oka in 1990. But while the Oka Crisis energized a new wave of Indigenous resistance in Canada, the Mohawks' stance—which many settlers perceived as threatening and violent, as seen in Alanis Obomsawin's film—failed to rally a significant number of settler allies. The issues around which Idle No More rallies today are, in essence, not that different from those which united the Mohawks in 1990. Both decry Canada's ongoing settler-colonial encroachment on Indigenous rights, lands, and resources. Despite this common critique, however, Idle No More has attracted many more settler allies, who join protests and post messages of solidarity and support on Facebook and other social media.

For many journalists and activists, these talks of solidarity and alliances between settlers and Indigenous peoples are encouraging, signaling a change since 1990 and indicating that reconciliation between Indigenous peoples and settler Canadians is now possible. For their part, many weary Indigenous activists have raised concerns about the very concept of settler allies and the role they might play in coopting, settling, and domesticating the movement. As these self-proclaimed allies start to employ the language of analogy—or deploy "decolonization as a metaphor," to borrow from Eve Tuck and Wayne Yang's work—it becomes clear that decolonization movements like Idle No More can be penetrated by settler colonialism's logic of elimination, erasure, and replacement. Tuck and Yang write:

> When metaphor invades decolonization, it kills the very possibility of decolonization; it recenters whiteness, it resettles theory, it extends innocence to the settler, it entertains a settler future. *Decolonize* (a verb) and *decolonization* (a noun) cannot easily be grafted onto pre-existing discourses/frameworks, even if they are critical, even if they are anti-racist, even if they are justice frameworks. . . . When we write about decolonization, we are not offering it as a metaphor; it is not an approximation of other experiences of oppression. Decolonization is not a swappable term for other things we want to do to improve our societies and schools. Decolonization doesn't have a synonym.[2]

They contend that an "easy absorption, adoption, and transposing of decolonization is yet another form of settler appropriation,"[3] another way for settler-colonial subjects to avoid facing the difficult questions that decolonization practices, if embraced, bring to the fore. Decolonization, these two authors argue, should be unsettling, for it requires what Frantz Fanon called "a program of complete disorder."[4] To decolonize is to radically rethink and undo the current structures of power. It begins by rendering visible what settler colonialism continually attempts to erase or naturalize, and, crucially, it involves the repatriation of "Indigenous land and life."[5] Given decolonization's exigencies, settler solidarity should be demanding and confronting; it should translate into real listening, followed by meaningful actions. Solidarity, these critiques argue, cannot be limited to "liking" a post on Facebook. It involves, as Dylan Robinson suggests, "listening to anger and being Idle No More."[6]

The Indigenous performances that this book examines strive for decolonization and, in doing so, collide with settler interlocutors. The repatriation work that I document in chapter 5 performs the demands on settlers that Tuck and Yang articulate so urgently in their work. The repatriation that Ondinnok performs onstage and the Kumeyaay demand from UCSD renders visible the threatening nature of solidarity, especially when such a stance demands that settlers let go of privileges long unquestioned. Ondinnok's deployment of opacity, its tactic of illegibility onstage, and its refusal of facile empathy when it comes to Indigenous bodies and performances, all aim to unsettle settler audiences. Ondinnok challenges audience members who may be used to the privilege that underpins settler colonialism and that positions settlers as experts on naming and reading Indigenous bodies. The theater company makes demands of its audiences and holds them accountable. Similarly, the Kumeyaay's repatriation request challenges UC scientists' so-called neutral scientific expertise. In doing so, the Kumeyaay articulate a difficult concept: namely, that decolonization demands a greater respect for differences and that Western worldviews may, in some instances, be irreconcilable with Indigenous epistemologies. The Kumeyaay people, then, refuse to see decolonization as a metaphor and place repatriation as decolonization's central and nonnegotiable starting point. The scientists' reactions, their attempt to rewrite the remains as non-Native American, betray the profound threat that decolonization poses to the edifice of settler-colonial privilege.

For many well-meaning settler allies, joining Idle No More's struggle for decolonization makes possible what Tuck and Yang call "a set of evasions, or settler moves to innocence, that problematically attempt to reconcile settler guilt and complicity, and rescue settler futurity."[7] These moves to innocence give settlers respite and allow them to fantasize about reconciliation without having to do the uncomfortable and destabilizing work of decolonization. These moves to innocence can take on many forms, but they always perform the foundational parasitic scenario of settler colonialism wherein settlers arrive, appropriate Indigenous space (be it material or epistemological), eliminate or erase Indigeneity (but not entirely, since this Indigeneity serves to demarcate the settler from others), and stay. In attempting to find respite and claim innocence, settlers often invoke settler colonialism as an event of the past, asking why they should pay for the crimes of distant ancestors and thus refusing to recognize settler colonialism as a structure that organizes and permeates entire societies.

Alexis Martin's play *Invention du chauffage central en Nouvelle-France*, and by extension the Québec it historicizes, resorts to such "moves to innocence." In his play, Martin takes refuge in an idyllic, prelapsarian Nouvelle-France, which he dramatizes as a moment of alliances and friendly encounters with Indigenous peoples. By removing Indigenous characters from the later chapters of his historical play, Martin avoids the difficult reality that Québec quickly betrayed all the alliances made during the early moments his play celebrates. The narrative of Nouvelle-France having been a less violent colonial force, or at least a more benevolent one, constitutes an important move to innocence in the French Québécois de souche's mythscape. Added to this is a narrative that defines these very settlers and their descendants as colonized by the British. While the British did attempt to assimilate French Canadians and deployed oppressive political and economic policies, the intracolonial conflict between francophone and anglophone settlers too often serves to absolve Québec of its past and present complicity in oppressing Indigenous peoples.

This self-absolving move is present in *Invention* when Takraliq, the play's only contemporary Indigenous character, appears onstage. Her testimonial of Residential School abuse serves as what Tuck and Yang call "a fantasy of reconciliation."[8] After telling her harrowing story, Takraliq makes no demand on her French Québécois de souche interlocutor, and offers a form of absolution by sharing with her a piece of seal blubber. The blubber, which warms Mireille's body, creates a connection between the two women. This reconciliation, performed onstage in the absence of a substantial Indigenous audience, performs a settler move to innocence that is, in essence, a foreclosing of decolonization. It is no less violent than the outbursts of settler intolerance that Obomsawin films in the street of Châteauguay. Like the protesters, Martin forecloses dialogue and refuses to be unsettled. In fact, *Invention* illuminates Takraliq's pain as a way to solidify its narrative of Québec; it thus operates within a settler-colonial logic of elimination. It settles Takraliq's pain, pushes her aside, and replaces her with a settler body. Her pain serves to assuage Mireille's guilt while making very few demands on her.

The performances by Indigenous artists and activists examined in the chapters of this book all struggle in some ways with the strategies of avoidance and moves to innocence that their settler interlocutors deploy. Performances like Nadia Myre's *Indian Act* and La Marche Amun employ endurance as decolonizing gestures. They perform their critique of the Indian Act through endurance work that both embodies and questions settler colonialism's logic of elimination and the genocidal policies that maintain Indigenous peoples in a constant state of endurance. Myre, Viviane Michel, and Michèle Taïna Audette perform endurance to mirror and denaturalize the gendered process through which Canada's Indian Act projected the end of Indigenous peoples' endurance, discriminating against Indigenous women. The endurance that Myre, Michel, and Audette embody and render visible is not an act of bravura but a foregrounding of the structural position and ontology of Indigenous peoples.

The demands that the endurance/enduring performances of Myre, Michel, and Audette make on audiences are perhaps less confrontational than those articulated by the Mohawks' barricades and roadblocks or the Kumeyaay's legal battle with UCSD, but they are nevertheless deeply challenging. The women ask settler audiences to contemplate their tacit agreement with the Indian Act as a genocidal social contract unilaterally devised by the settler state to organize its relationship with Indigenous nations. As settler audiences, we are asked to position ourselves vis-à-vis this pervasive social contract, its objective violence, and hold ourselves accountable for the privileges that we derive from this positioning. This is the unsettling work that decolonization demands. Given the format of Myre's piece, it may be possible for viewers to evade answering the challenging questions posed by her visual artwork. But, for those willing to be unsettled by her work's political intervention, *Indian Act* denaturalizes settler colonialism's gendered violence and imagines its end. That La Marche Amun, along with other forms of lobbying, succeeded in having the Indian Act amended in 2011 (Bill C-3) attests to the power of its intervention. Some might criticize the amendment of the Indian Act as merely participating in the futurity of settler colonialism rather than demanding its end. Indeed, as many Indigenous scholars have argued, the Indian Act is, in fact, profoundly incompatible with decolonization. For their part, Michel and Audette, both of whom lead major Indigenous women coalitions in Québec and Canada, respectively, position their performances as belonging to a decolonizing continuum built through multiple unsettling gestures, small and large.

In showing the violence that organizes the reserve, both Obomsawin and Sioui Durand perform courageous work. Sioui Durand's portrait of the reserve offers little respite to viewers, mirroring the continuous settler-colonial violence that shapes and erodes the reserve. Similarly, Obomsawin documents a moment of Indigenous dissent that triggered a response in Québec's society which bypassed its usual move to innocence. As Obomsawin's film reveals, the threat that Mohawk sovereignty posed to Québec's national discourse in 1990 was met with anxiety and violence rather than evasion. Québec's call for a military response revealed how two seemingly opposed settler-colonial communities, namely Canada and Québec, suddenly align when it comes to protecting settler colonialism's ethical coherence and cartographical integrity.

Taken together, these performances illuminate the profoundly challenging nature of decolonization and reveal how settler colonialism infiltrates even the most progressive and reparative projects. More than diagnostic tools, they also interrupt, mirror, challenge, and unsettle settler colonialism. They do so at times by mirroring and denaturalizing its logic of elimination. In other cases, they collapse time through performance to illuminate a repetitive scenario of erasure and displacement, rendering visible for a moment the

Indigenous presence and genealogies that settler colonialism constantly tries to erase.

In response to the French Québécois de souche's national discourse, these Indigenous performances collectively refuse the province's move to innocence and remind the province of its ongoing role as a settler-colonial force. These performances echo and support the repeated stance of Indigenous communities in Québec, affirming that Québec cannot dream of a nation without first talking to the original occupants of the territory. During the last election campaign in Québec, which culminated with the Parti Québécois's defeat, Melissa Mollen-Dupuis (Innu), a spokesperson for the Québec chapter of Idle No More, posted a detailed analysis of each political party's political platform regarding Indigenous peoples on her Facebook page.[9] While the Green Party, the Option Nationale party, and the Québec Solidaire party outlined policies and affirmed their commitment to ameliorating the strained relationship between Québec and Indigenous peoples, the two main parties—the Parti Libéral du Québec and the Parti Québécois—barely mentioned Indigenous peoples in their respective agendas. Chief Ghislain Picard later posted a comment on his own Facebook page voicing his frustration with what he perceived as yet another failed encounter between Indigenous and Québécois leaders. He wrote: "Québec politics leaves me with a bad taste." Then, borrowing from the lyrics of the 1987 song "Beds Are Burning" written by the group Midnight Oil in support of Australia's Pintupi nation, Picard wrote: "My 1st letter to the head of the new government will say this: 'the lease is up and there is rent to pay.' "[10]

Picard's comments are more than a *boutade* (quip); they translate a real sense of impatience and frustration among Indigenous peoples when it comes to Québec's political discourse. Idle No More was born in part out of this feeling of political impasse. This book, which offers a critique of the Québécois de souche's national project, might be criticized for offering little in terms of solution. As a performance-studies scholar, I remain cautious when it comes to celebrating performances as liberatory acts or as prescriptions for change. As this book argues, performances act as powerful diagnostic tools and can render visible what national discourses consistently aim to erase. They can challenge, they can unsettle, they can participate in decolonization, but they can also be (as Tuck and Yang argue) infiltrated by the very discourses and practices they seek to undo. The performances analyzed in this book do all this and demand critical attention for it. In meditating on these performances' proposed "program of complete disorder" or in tracing the ways in which they fail to meet their inclusive mission, I offer a self-critical and vigilant attempt to stand in solidarity with decolonization.

NOTES

Introduction

1. Oka is located some 30 miles (50 kilometers) west of Montréal, next to Kahnesatà:ke.

2. The Royal Twenty-Second Regiment, the most famous francophone regiment of the Canadian armed forces, is commonly known as "Vandoo," an Anglicized mispronunciation of the French word *vingt-deux* (twenty-two). Québec City is the regiment's headquarters, and its battalions serve as a local infantry for the province.

3. Audra Simpson, *Mohawk Interruptus: Political Life across the Borders of Settler States* (Durham, N.C.: Duke University Press, 2014), 2.

4. Kiera Ladner and Leanne Simpson, *This Is an Honour Song: Twenty Years since the Blockades* (Winnipeg, MB: Arbeiter Ring, 2010), 1.

5. See Jennifer Wells, "A Warrior, a Soldier and a Photographer—Remembering the Oka Crisis," *The Star*, August 22, 2015, https://www.thestar.com/news/insight/2015/08/22/a-warrior-a-soldier-and-a-photographer-remembering-the-oka-crisis.html.

6. Simpson, *Mohawk Interruptus*, 149.

7. See Patrick Wolfe, "Settler Colonialism and the Elimination of the Native," *Journal of Genocide Research* 8, no. 4 (2006): 388.

8. Slavoj Žižek, *Violence: Six Sideways Reflections* (London: Profile Books, 2008), 1.

9. Ibid., 2.

10. Ibid.

11. Ibid.

12. I draw my working definition of settler colonialism from Patrick Wolfe, who writes that "settler colonialism erects a new colonial society on the expropriated land base of indigenous populations" (Wolfe, "Settler Colonialism," 388). This new society is then stratified following an "organizing grammar of race" which positions settlers as superior to natives (388). Settler colonialism is not a discrete event but an ongoing formation, which has elimination as an organizing principle. Wolfe offers the following important distinction: "settler colonialism is inherently eliminatory but not invariably genocidal" (ibid.). Elimination, however, is never complete; rather, this "process of replacement maintains the refractory imprint of the native counter-claim," and settler colonial societies depend on this "replaced other" to maintain their sense of self as communities (389).

13. Wolfe, "Settler Colonialism," 388.

14. Ibid., 387.

15. Idle No More is an ongoing, grassroots, activist movement founded in 1992 through social media (#idlenomore), as a response to then Prime Minister

Stephen Harper's Omnibus Bill C-45, which unilaterally revised the laws affecting Indigenous peoples and lifted protection on their lands.

16. Aileen Moreton-Robinson, *The White Possessive: Property, Power, and Indigenous Sovereignty* (Minneapolis: University of Minnesota Press, 2015), xix.

17. See Alanis Obomsawin, *Kanehsatake: 270 Years of Resistance*, video, dir. Alanis Obomsawin (Montréal: National Film Board of Canada, 1993).

18. Wendy Brown, "Wounded Attachments," *Political Theory* 21, no. 3 (1993): 390–410.

19. Jocelyn Létourneau, *A History for the Future: Rewriting Memory and Identity in Quebec* (Montréal, QC: McGill-Queen's University Press, 2004), 8.

20. On the night of November 4, 1981, in what is known as La Nuit des Longs Couteaux (The Night of the Long Knives) in Québec and as the "Kitchen Meeting" in English Canada, Prime Minister Pierre Elliott Trudeau convened the premiers of all the provinces in a negotiation round in the kitchens of Ottawa's Chateau Laurier, the hotel where the premiers resided. Québec Premier René Lévesque, having decided to stay in a hotel in nearby Hull, Québec, was not alerted to this round of negotiation and thus did not sign the agreement which was devised that night. The following failed Meech Lake Accord (1987) and Charlottetown Accord (1992) were series of amendments designed to bring Québec to ratify the 1982 Constitution.

21. See Department of Justice of Canada, *The Constitution Acts 1867 to 1982* (Ottawa, ON, 2013), 63, http://laws.justice.gc.ca/PDF/CONST_E.pdf.

22. These changes were the recognition of Québec as a distinct society, increased power with respect to immigration in the province, financial compensation for provinces that opted out of federal programs in areas of exclusive provincial jurisdiction, and input in Senate and Supreme Court appointments.

23. Glen S. Coulthard, "#Idlenomore in Historical Context," in *The Winter We Danced: Voices from the Past, the Future and the Idle No More Movement*, ed. Kino-nda miimi Collective (Winnipeg, MB: ARP Books, 2014), 35.

24. See Shiri Pasternak, *Grounded Authority: The Algonquins of Barriere Lake against the State* (Minneapolis: University of Minnesota Press, 2017).

25. Coulthard, "#Idlenomore," 35.

26. Châteauguay is a town bordering the Mohawk reserve of Kahnà:wake.

27. Brown, "Wounded Attachments," 391.

28. Diana Taylor, *Disappearing Acts: Spectacles of Gender and Nationalism in Argentina's "Dirty War"* (Durham, N.C.: Duke University Press, 1997), ix. Taylor draws here from Benedict Anderson's concept of nations as imagined communities. See Benedict Anderson, *Imagined Communities* (London: Verso, 2006).

29. Taylor, *Disappearing Acts*, ix.

30. Wolfe, "Settler Colonialism," 389.

31. Jodi A. Byrd, *The Transit of Empire* (Minneapolis: University of Minnesota Press, 2011), xviii.

32. Anderson, *Imagined Communities*.

33. Joseph Roach, *Cities of the Dead: Circum-Atlantic Performance* (New York: Columbia University Press, 1996), 7.

34. See "Terminology," Indigenous and Northern Affairs Canada, http://www.aadnc-aandc.gc.ca/eng/1100100014642/1100100014643. While the term *reservation* is commonly used in the United States to describe lands allocated to Native

Americans, in Canada, the term *reserve* is more common. The Indian Act defines an "Indian reserve" as "the tract of land, the legal title of which is vested in Her Majesty, that has been set apart by Her Majesty for the use and benefit of a band."

35. Lorenzo Veracini, "Introducing Settler Colonial Studies," *Settler Colonial Studies* 1, no. 1 (2011): 3.

36. Bruno Cornellier, "Interculturalism, Settler Colonialism, and the Contest Over 'Nativeness,'" in *Biopolitics and Memory in Postcolonial Literature and Culture*, ed. Michael R. Griffiths (Surrey, Eng.: Ashgate, 2016), 78.

37. See, for instance, Andrew Potter's infamous editorial "How a Snowstorm Exposed Quebec's Real Problem: Social Malaise," in the March 20, 2017 issue of *McLean's*. Potter, the director of the McGill Institute for the Study of Canada, claimed that "compared to the rest of the country, Quebec is an almost pathologically alienated and low-trust society," arguing that the province is a corrupt place, incapable of solidarity. The author was widely criticized for his unsupported claims and lost his directorship at McGill. Potter's article, an example of exaggerated criticism of Québec, is, however, counterbalanced by an affirmed tendency in Québec to read all critiques from the rest of Canada as pure Québec-bashing, Québecophobia, or Francophobia. The expression Québec bashing has its own Wikipedia entry and is the object of frequent editorials in newspapers like *Le Devoir* or *La Presse*.

38. See Corrie Scott, "How French Canadians Became White Folks, or Doing Things with Race in Québec," *Ethnic and Racial Studies* 39, no. 7 (2016): 1280–97.

39. Ibid., 1280.

40. Ibid.

41. Ibid., 1281.

42. Ibid., 1289–90.

43. See Corrie Scott, *De Groulx à Laferrière: Un Parcours de la race dans la littérature québécoise* (Montréal, QC: XYZ, 2014).

44. Following my colleague Bruno Cornellier, to whom I am indebted in so many ways, I choose not to reproduce the racially loaded word deployed here by Vallières. I do this as a recognition of the historical violence that this term carries.

45. See also the famous poem "Speak White" written in 1968 by Michele Lalonde, which blackens the French Québécois de souche by harnessing the expression "speak white," which is often deployed against the French Québécois de souche to signify their lower status within Anglo Canada. (See the poem at http://neobeatniks.livejournal.com/55613.html.) In 1989, the Italo-Québécois playwright Marco Micone penned a polemic response poem entitled "Speak What?" that redirects the critique toward the French Québécois de souche and famously invites them to be more inclusive of new immigrants coming from the countries of "Montale and Neruda." Micone argues that the French Québécois de souche have become the elite they once decried, and he writes in a mix of French and English: "Vous souvenez-vous du vacarme des usines / and of the voice des contremaîtres / you sound like them more and more" ("Do you remember the factory's noise / and the foremen's voices / you sound like them more and more"). See the full poem in *Cahiers de Théâtre Jeu* 50 (1989): 83–85.

46. See Adam Gaudry and Darryl Leroux, "White Settler Revisionism and Making Métis Everywhere: The Evocation of Métissage in Quebec and Nova

Scotia," *Critical Ethnic Studies* 3, no. 1 (spring 2017): 116–42; and Scott, *De Groulx à Laferrière*, among others.

47. See Gaudry and Leroux, "White Settler Revisionism," 116–42; and Scott, *De Groulx à Laferrière*, among others.

48. Sean Mills, *The Empire Within: Postcolonial Thought and Political Activism in Sixties Montreal* (Montréal, QB: McGill-Queen's University Press, 2010), Kindle edition.

49. Ibid., 4–5.

50. Ibid., 3.

51. Elder Lyle Longclaws's words serve as an epigraph for Tomson Highway's play *Dry Lips Oughta Move to Kapuskasing* (Markham, ON: Fifth House, 1989).

52. "The Royal Proclamation and Reconciliation," panel, Truth and Reconciliation Commission of Canada, Québec National Event, Montréal, QC, April 26, 2013.

53. I use the term *arrivant* following Jodi A. Byrd, who herself draws it from the African-Caribbean poet Kamau Brathwaite, "to signify those people forced into the Americas through the violence of European and Anglo-American colonialism and imperialism around the globe." Byrd, *The Transit of Empire*, xix.

54. Dylan Robinson, "Enchantment's Irreconcilable Connection: Listening to Anger, Being Idle No More," in *Performance Studies in Canada*, ed. Laura Levin and Marlis Schweitzer (Montréal: McGill-Queen's University Press, 2017), 211–12.

55. Scott, "How French Canadians," 1284.

56. Darryl Leroux, "The Spectacle of Champlain: Commemorating Québec," *Borderlands* 9, no. 1 (2010): 2.

57. Daniel Salée, "Les Peuples autochtones et la naissance du Québec: Pour une réécriture de l'histoire?" *Recherches Sociographiques* 51, no. 1–2 (2010): 156, cited in Gaudry and Leroux, "White Settler Revisionism."

58. Diana Taylor, *The Archive and the Repertoire: Performing Cultural Memory in the Americas* (Durham, N.C.: Duke University Press, 2003), 28.

59. "Sensate Sovereignty" was the title of a working group convened by Robinson at the American Comparative Literature Association annual conference held in Seattle, Washington, March 27–29, 2015.

60. Kevin Bruyneel, *The Third Space of Sovereignty: The Postcolonial Politics of U.S.-Indigenous Relations* (Minneapolis: University of Minnesota Press, 2007), xvii.

61. Duncan Bell, "Mythscapes: Memory, Mythology, and National Identity," *British Journal of Sociology* 54, no. 1 (March 2003): 66.

62. Nawel Hamidi and Pierrot Ross-Tremblay, "Gamau: Confluence des personnes, des idées et des actions," in *Perspectives d'avenir pour le Québec: Le Regard de jeunes chercheurs*, ed. Simon Thibault and Magali Brodeur (Québec, QC: Presses de L'Université du Québec, 2013), 229–46.

63. Chadwick Allen, *Trans-Indigenous Methodologies for Global Native Literary Studies* (Minneapolis: University of Minnesota Press, 2012), xiv.

64. Ann M. Kakaliouras, "An Anthropology of Repatriation: Contemporary Physical Anthropological and Native American Ontologies of Practice," *Current Anthropology* 53, no. 5 (2012): 210–21.

65. Roach, *Cities of the Dead*, 26.

Chapter 1

1. Alexis Martin, *Histoire révélée du Canada français 1608–1998* (*The Revealed History of French Canada 1608–1998*) (Montréal, QC: Dramaturges Éditeurs, 2016). Unless noted, all translations from French to English are mine.

2. Elsa Pépin, "Au pays des mots gelés," *Voir* 2, February, 2, 2012, https://voir.ca/scene/2012/02/02/alexis-martin-et-daniel-briere-au-pays-des-mots-geles.

3. Alexis Martin, "Bibliographie géographique et commentée de la pièce 'Invention du chauffage central en Nouvelle-France,'" *Blog du NTE*, January, 16, 2012, http://www.nte.qc.ca/category/blog/invention-du-chauffage-central-en-nouvelle-france/

4. Michel Bélair, "L'Hiver: Mode d'emploi," *Le Devoir*, February 4, 2012, http://www.ledevoir.com/culture/theatre/341779/theatre-l-hiver-mode-d-emploi. "Le froid a vraiment forgé notre identité. Et c'est encore et toujours vrai. Il nous a, par exemple, fait tisser dès les départ des alliances avec les Amérindiens, ne serait-ce que pour réussir à 'passer l'hiver.'"

5. Alexis Martin, "Une structure dramatique en forme de flocon de neige," *Blog du NTE*, June 23, 2011, http://www.nte.qc.ca/2011/06/23/une-structure-dramatique-en-forme-de-flocon-de-neige. "Le premier volet de la trilogie sur l'histoire du Canada français comporte six branches qui constituent chacune un séquencier dont la temporalité est réversible. Cette structure dramatique, de type 'hexagonale diachronique,' évoque la forme d'un cristal de neige. Ainsi, six séquences d'évènements qui représentent les scènes, convergent toutes vers un centre qui constitue le géométral, c'est-à-dire l'espace-temps ordonnant la structure générale de la trilogie. Ce géométral, toujours situé en 1998, est le lieu neutre qui permet les passages d'une époque à l'autre et d'un thème à l'autre."

6. Alan Filewod, *Performing Canada: The Nation Enacted in the Imagined Theatre* (Kamloops, BC: University College of the Cariboo, 2002), xvii.

7. Ibid., 1.

8. See Anderson, *Imagined Communities*, 6. "Or l'essence d'une nation est que tous les individus aient beaucoup de choses en commun et aussi que tous aient oublié bien des choses . . . Tout citoyen français doit avoir oublié la Saint-Barthélémy, les massacres du Midi au XIIIe siècle."

9. Byrd, *The Transit of Empire*, xvii.

10. To my knowledge, no critic commented on *Invention*'s use of redface or questioned why First Nations actors had not been cast in the play.

11. I am aware of the ways that the term "cultural amnesia" problematically appropriates the language of disability as metaphor.

12. In cinema, for example, see *Séraphin*: *Un homme et son péché* (2002), *Nouvelle France* (2004), *Le Survenant* (2005), *Aurore* (2005), *Histoire de famille* (2006), *Le Déserteur* (2008), *Esimésac* (2012), and *Louis Cyr* (2013), among other films historicizing Québec's rural past.

13. Also see *Quand je serai parti vous vivrez encore* by Michel Brault (1999), *Octobre* (1994), or *15 février 1839* (2001) by Pierre Falardeau.

14. Bruno Cornellier, "Je me souviens (maintenant): Altérité, Indianité et mémoire collective," *Canadian Journal of Film Studies* 19, no. 2 (Fall 2010): 99.

15. See Hugo Pilon-Larose, "Diversité culturelle à l'écran: Constat d'échec pour l'UDA," *La Presse*, January 26, 2015, http://www.lapresse.ca/arts/nouvelles/201501/24/01-4838103-diversite-culturelle-a-lecran-constat-dechec-pour-luda.php.

16. See, for instance, the debate around the use of blackface in Québec, and Nydia Dauphin's "Why the Hell Are Quebec Comedians Wearing Blackface?" published on the online publication Huffington Post Canada in 2013 (http://www.huffingtonpost.ca/nydia-dauphin/blackface-in-quebec_b_3276801.html). Other articles include Dan Delmar's "Blackface Controversy Highlights Quebec's Media Diversity Problem," published in the *Montréal Gazette* in 2016 (http://montrealgazette.com/opinion/columnists/dan-delmar-blackface-controversy-highlights-quebecs-media-diversity-problem). For the lack of representation of Indigenous peoples and so-called minorities in the 375th anniversary of the city of Montréal in 2017, see CBC News's "'That Won't Happen Again': City of Montréal apologizes for ad criticized for lack of diversity," published online in 2017 (http://www.cbc.ca/news/canada/montreal/montreal-video-ad-diversity-1.4089759).

17. Cornellier, "Je me souviens," 99.

18. Mark Rifkin, "Settler Common Sense," *Settler Colonial Studies* 3, no. 3-4 (2013): 323.

19. Bell, "Mythscapes," 66.

20. Anderson, *Imagined Communities*.

21. Bruno Cornellier, "The Struggle of Others: Pierre Vallières, Québécois Settler Nationalism, and the N-Word Today," *Discourse* 39, no. 1 (2017): 34.

22. Ibid., 36.

23. Ibid.

24. See, for example, Claude Jasmin, "Je suis fier de ma race," *Le Devoir*, May 30, 2013, http://www.ledevoir.com/societe/actualites-en-societe/379397/je-suis-fier-de-ma-race. Jasmin argues for the "race francaise en Amerique du Nord" ("French race in North America"). See also the website for the Fédération des Québécois de Souche (http://quebecoisdesouche.info/a-propos/).

25. Characters in the play incorrectly refer to Membertou as the Etchemin (Maliseet) chief. Membertou was the chief or Sagamo of the Mi'kmaqs, not the Maliseet. Whether or not this is an error by the author or a dramatization of the early settlers' mislabeling of the First Nations they encountered remains unclear in the play.

26. The cast for the first production and tour included Émilie Bibeau, Benoît Drouin-Germain, Luc Guérin, Pierre-Antoine Lasnier, Alexis Martin, Carl Poliquin, and Danielle Proulx (Dominique Pétin on tour). The cast for the remount in 2014 included Gary Boudreault, Benoît Drouin-Germain, Steve Laplante, Pierre-Antoine Lasnier, Alexis Martin, François Papineau, Dominique Pétin, Carl Poliquin, Danielle Proulx, and Marie-Eve Trudel.

27. Alexis Martin, *Invention du chauffage central en Nouvelle France* (Montréal, QC: Dramaturges Éditeurs, 2016), 7. "Les anciens Amérindiens disent qu'il y a, au nord de Tadoussac, un pays où le froid est si grand, l'air si dense, que les MOTS y gisent gelés. Tous les MOTS prononcés par toutes les bouches au mitan de l'hiver et qui s'échappent malgré nous, malgré tout: ces paroles gelées vont rejoindre le pays mystérieux de Pipmuacan, à des centaines de pouces de notre bouche et de notre conscience."

28. Pierre Pelleprat, *La Relation des missions jésuites dans les îles et la Terre Ferm* (Québec, QC: Presses de l'Université Laval, 2009), 31.

29. See the work of the Cree scholar Val Napoleon, and Hadley Friedland among others at the Indigenous Law Research Unit at the University of Victoria, Canada, https://www.uvic.ca/law/about/indigenous/indigenouslawresearchunit/index.php.

30. Martin, *Invention*, 97.

31. Ibid., 21.

> Neige Neige dans ton cortège bleuissant
> Sourires d'enfants qui tombent dru
> Parmi les ménagères de la mort
> Neige Neige sels vaginaux des naissances obscures
> Tabarnac tu vas geler avec tes bottes mouillées
> Neige Neige précipité des oublis primordiaux
> Feuille d'absolu dans la grande déchiqueteuse
> Ah comme la neige a neigé!
> Ah comme elle a neigé la neige!
> Ah comme elle a neigé la neige

32. Émile Nelligan, *Poésies Complètes 1896–1899* (Montréal, QC: Fides, 1952), 82–83.

33. Gilles Vigneault, *Mon Pays*, Columbia Records, 1966. The song was written in 1964 for a 1965 film entitled *La Neige a fondu sur Manicouagan* by Arthur Lamothe (National Film Board of Canada), but it was first recorded in 1965.

34. Gaston Miron, *L'Homme Rapaillé* (Paris: Gallimard, 1999).

35. Robert Charlebois, *Demain l'hiver*, Gamma Records, 1967.

36. Taylor, *Disappearing Acts*, 77–78.

37. Lori Saint-Martin, "Mise à mort de la femme et 'libération' de l'homme: Godbout, Aquin, Beaulieu," *Voix et Images* 10, no. 1 (1984): 107.

38. Martin, *Invention*, 18.

39. Rifkin, "Settler Common Sense," 322.

40. Darryl Leroux, "Now I Am Métis: How White People Become Indigenous," presentation, Native Speakers Series, University of Saskatchewan, Saskatoon, 2015.

41. Even recently, Québec signed La Paix des Braves with the Cree nation after years of judicial battles due to Québec failing to meet the terms of the first agreement it signed with the Cree in 1975 (the Convention de la Baie James et du Nord Québécois). While Québec's gesture is positive (the province negotiated on its own without Canada at the table), it was also a strategic gesture that the sovereignist party marked by claiming that the accord was a historic nation-to-nation agreement between the Québec and Cree nations. Furthermore, this amendment does not erase the fundamental problems of treaties, which are, in many ways, an extension of the settler-colonial project (see Taiaiake Alfred, *Peace, Power, Righteousness: An Indigenous Manifesto* (Toronto: Oxford University Press, 2009).

42. Martin, *Invention*, 33. "United States of America! Calice, ce monde là ont mis un homme sur la lune! Mais icitte, on est fixé sur des vieilles affaires, on est perdu dans nos souvenirs, fuck! Y faut en finir avec les vieilles affaires, la France, la bière d'épinette pis la pêche à l'anguille, tabarnac!"

43. This line was cut from the published version of the play.

44. Byrd, *The Transit of Empire*, 221.

45. Anderson, *Imagined Communities*, 7.

46. See Erin Hurley's excellent chapter on Montréal's Expo 67 in her book *National Performance: Representing Québec from Expo 67 to Celine Dion* (Toronto, ON: University of Toronto Press, 2011) on the topic of Québec's rebranding through this international event.

47. Albert Memmi, whose book *Portrait du colonisé* had been circulating clandestinely in Québec since its publication in 1957, added an extra chapter when his book was finally published in Québec in 1972. In this chapter entitled "Les Canadiens français sont-ils colonisés?" or "Are French Canadians Colonized?" Memmi concluded that despite their relative affluence, the French Canadians presented multiple characteristics of the colonized: internalized shame and sense of inferiority, cultural forgetting, economic and linguistic oppression, and so on. Albert Memmi, *Portrait du colonisé: Précédé du Portrait du colonisateur* (Montréal, QC: L'Étincelle, 1972).

48. Martin, *Invention*, 69–70.

> MIRON: Faut que tu passes du français colonial, aliéné, au français tout court; puis là, faut que tu sautes encore jusqu'à la littérature! Ça fait deux sauts. Es-tu bon sauteur Pierre? . . .
>
> LEBEAU: Je sais pas.
>
> MIRON: On a perdu l'instinct du mot français, tu comprends? Y faudrait regagner la bonne berge, mais on a la bouche pleine de miel, du miel anglais mal assimilé, et les entrailles pleines d'amertume; on est pauvre de mots, les métaphores se filent mal.

49. Ibid., 70.

50. Ibid.

51. Ibid., 81. "Les images veulent pas que les mots les disent! Ok! . . . disent la peine de . . . des gens . . . les images veulent pas que les mots parlent esti!!! Y me semblent (sic) que je suis assez clair, calice!"

52. Between 1957 and 1959, Radio-Canada aired *Radisson*, a historical drama featuring Jacques Godin as Radisson, René Caron as Desgroseillers, and a host of other prominent actors.

53. In 1970, the Front de Libération du Québec (Québec Liberation Front) abducted two government officials and killed one in what is referred to as the 1970 October Crisis. At the demand of Montréal's mayor and the Québec government, Canada's Prime Minister Trudeau deployed the War Measures Act in Québec to address terrorism threats in the province. The widespread arrests and suspension of habeas corpus sparked controversy in Québec.

54. Martin, *Invention*, 10.

55. This line was cut in the published version of the play.

56. Hamidi and Ross-Tremblay, "Gamau," 234.

57. See "Report on the Affairs of British North America / From Earl of Durham," Early Canadiana Online, http://eco.canadiana.ca/view/oocihm.32374/6?r=0&s=1. Durham famously wrote that the conflict between Upper and Lower Canada was essentially ethnic and that he had found "two nations warring within the bosom of a single state."

58. Durham, cited in Scott, "How French Canadians," 1284.

59. Hamidi and Ross-Tremblay, "Gamau," 234.

60. Martin, *Invention*, 75–76.
61. Ibid., 75.
62. Ibid., 75. The Etchemin are now known as the Maliseet or Wolastoqiyik.
63. Hamdi and Ross-Tremblay, "Gamau," 234.
64. Filewod, *Performing Canada*, xii.
65. Jerry Wasserman, *Spectacles of Empire: Marc Lescarbot's Theatre of Neptune in New France* (Vancouver, BC: Talonbooks, 2006), 79.
66. Ibid., 24.
67. Filewod, *Performing Canada*, xiv.
68. Ibid., xiv.
69. Martin, *Invention*, 17.
70. On the subject of First Nations' great oratory traditions and skills, see Gilles Havard, *The Great Peace of Montreal of 1701: French-Native Diplomacy in the Seventeenth Century* (Montréal: McGill University Press, 2001); Georges Sioui, *Huron Wendat: The Heritage of the Circle* (Vancouver: University of British Columbia Press, 1999); and Robert Warrior, *The People and the Word: Reading Native Nonfiction* (Minneapolis: University of Minnesota Press, 2005).
71. *Qallunaat* is the Inuktitut word for people who are not Inuit, typically a white person.
72. Martin, *Invention*, 61.
73. Ibid., 59.
74. Ibid., 59–60. The white man came the same day it was the same snow as today / The white man said that my parents would not receive the government's family allowance if their children did not go to the school of the white. / The school of the white. / 800 miles from my home. 800 mailinik anarraniivanga / At the beginning I was alone, for days alone / Empty beds around me and the silence / Heavy / Falling snow.
75. Ibid., 60.
76. Ibid., 62.
77. Ibid., 63.
78. Saidiya Hartman, *Scenes of Subjection: Terror, Slavery, and Self-Making in Nineteenth-Century America* (New York: Oxford University Press, 1997), 18.
79. Ibid., 18.
80. Martin, *Invention*, 97.
81. Catherine Cole, *Performing South Africa's Truth Commission* (Bloomington: Indiana University Press, 2010), 91–92.
82. Philip Auslander, *Liveness: Performance as Mediatized Culture* (New York: Routledge, 1999), 128–29.

Chapter 2

With the expression "ruse of the métis turn," I am gratefully borrowing from Frank Wilderson's chapter "The Ruse of Analogy" in *Red, White & Black: Cinema and the Structure of U.S. Antagonisms* (Durham, N.C.: Duke University Press, 2010). The first epigraph is from Jean Désy, *Amériquoisie* (Montréal, QC: Mémoire d'Encrier, 2016), 6 ("L'autochtonie, c'est la communauté des gens qui sont nés ou qui sont arrivés dans un pays, sur un territoire, dans un espace géographique afin de l'habiter, mais surtout d'aimer y habiter"). The second epigraph is from Wolfe, "Settler Colonialism," 388.

1. Carole Poliquin, *L'Empreinte*, DVD, dir. Yvan Dubuc and Carole Poliquin (Montréal, QC: Les Productions ISCA; 2015). See the film poster and promotional material.

2. This notion of the Québécois de souche predates the film. Lionel Groulx (1878–1967) described the French-Canadian "race" as wanted and created by God in a sort of cultural vacuum. Groulx denied any *métissage* but was attached to this notion of "de souche."

3. *Tout le monde en parle* (Montréal: Avanti Ciné Vidéo, Le gars de la TV, Jacques K. Primeau Télé Inc., Radio Canada, 2015), February 22, 2015.

4. See Gaudry and Leroux, "White Settler Revisionism," 116–42.

5. Dupuis is loosely drawing from Georges Sioui, *Huron Wendat: The Heritage of the Circle* (Vancouver, BC: University of British Columbia Press, 1999).

6. *Enquête*, a television show airing on Radio-Canada, recently reported on the widespread abuse of First Nations women perpetrated with impunity by agents of the Sûreté du Québec in Val d'Or, Québec. See http://ici.radio-canada.ca/nouvelles/special/2015/10/femmes-autochtones-val-dor/index.html.

7. Deni Ellis Béchard and Natasha Kanapé-Fontaine, *Kuei, je te salue: Conversation sur le racisme* (Montréal, QC: Les Éditions Écosociété, 2016); Béchard, *Kuei My Friend: Conversations on Race and Reconciliation* (Vancouver, BC: Talon Books, 2018).

8. Bruno Cornellier, *La "Chose Indienne": Cinéma et politiques de la représentation autochtone au Québec et au Canada* (Montréal: Nota Bene, 2015), 14.

9. See Thomas King, *The Inconvenient Indian: A Curious Account of Native People in North America* (Minneapolis: University of Minnesota Press, 2013).

10. Serge Bouchard has written a host of articles on the Indigenous peoples of Canada, and since 2001 he has hosted *De remarquables oubliés*, a radio show airing on Radio-Canada in which he documents the lives of important yet forgotten historical figures of the Americas. Many of these figures are Indigenous people.

11. Eve Tuck and Wayne K. Yang, "Decolonization Is Not a Metaphor," *Decolonization: Indigeneity, Education, Society* 1, no. 1 (2012): 3.

12. *R. v. Powley*, [2003] 2 S.C.R. 28533 at para. 207, 2003 SCC 43, https://scc-csc.lexum.com/scc-csc/scc-csc/en/item/2076/index.do.

13. *Daniels v. Canada* (Indian Affairs and Northern Development), [2016] 1 S.C.R. 35945 at para. 99, 2016 SCC 12, https://scc-csc.lexum.com/scc-csc/scc-csc/en/item/15858/index.do.

14. See Chelsea Vowel and Darryl Leroux, "White Settler Antipathy and the *Daniels* Decision," *TOPIA: Canadian Journal of Cultural Studies* 36 (Fall 2016): 30–42.

15. John Ralston Saul, *A Fair Country Telling Truths about Canada* (Toronto, ON: Penguin Canada Books, 2008).

16. Olive P. Dickason, "From 'One Nation' in the Northeast to 'New Nation' in the Northwest: A Look at the Emergence of the Métis," in *New Peoples: Being and Becoming Métis in North America* (Lincoln: University of Nebraska Press, 1985), 18.

17. Adam Gaudry, "Commentary, Métis Issues on @IndigenousXca," *Aboriginal Policies Studies* 5, no. 1 (2015): 94. More broadly, see Adam Gaudry, "The Métis-ization of Canada: The Process of Claiming Louis Riel, Métissage, and the

Métis People as Canada's Mythical Origin," *Aboriginal Policy Studies* 2, no. 2 (2013): 64–87.

18. Gaudry, "Commentary,"95.

19. Chelsea Vowel, "The Mythology of Métissage: Settler Moves to Innocence," âpihtawikosisân, March 11, 2015, http://apihtawikosisan.com/2015/03/the-mythology-of-metissage-settler-moves-to-innocence/.

20. Dickason, "From 'One Nation,' " 29. Parenthesis not in the original.

21. Tuck and Yang, "Decolonization," 9.

22. See Gaudry and Leroux, "White Settler Revisionism," 116–42.

23. "Communauté," Nation Métisse Autochtone de la Gaspésie, Bas-Saint-Laurent et Îles-de-la-Madeleine, http://metisgaspesie.com/.

24. Graeme Hamilton, "Mikinaks Call Themselves Quebec's Newest Aboriginal Community, Others Are Calling Them a Fraud," *National Post*, July 7, 2016, http://news.nationalpost.com/news/canada/the-mikinaks-call-themselves-quebecs-newest-aboriginal-community-others-are-calling-them-a-fraud.

25. Chris Andersen, *"Métis" Race, Recognition, and the Stuggle for Indigenous Peoplehood* (Vancouver, BC: University of British Columbia Press, 2014), 8.

26. Ibid., 9.

27. Philip J. Deloria, *Playing Indian* (New Haven, Conn.: Yale University Press, 1998), 8.

28. Kim Tallbear, *Native American DNA: Tribal Belonging and the False Promise of Genetic Science* (Minneapolis: University of Minnesota Press, 2013), 1.

29. See Gaudry and Leroux, "White Settler Revisionism," 116–42.

30. Tuck and Yang, "Decolonization," 9.

31. La Grande Alliance of 1603 was concluded at La Pointe Saint-Mathieu between Samuel de Champlain and François Gravé du Pont as representatives of France and leaders of the Maliseet, Innu, and Algonquian nations.

32. Maureen G. Elgersman, *Unyielding Spirits: Black Women and Slavery in Early Canada and Jamaica* (New York: Routledge, 2013), 4.

33. See Les Productions ISCA, "L'Empreinte: Un voyage au coeur de notre identité," http://lempreinte.quebec/.

34. Alain Beaulieu et al., introduction to *Les Autochtones et le Québec: Des premiers contacts au Plan Nord*, ed. Alain Beaulieu, Stéphan Gervais, and Martin Papillon (Montréal, QC: Les Presses de l'Université de Montréal, 2013), 17.

35. Peter Cook, "Les Premiers Contacts vus à travers les sources documentaires européennes," in *Les Autochtones et le Québec: Des premiers contacts au Plan Nord*, ed. Alain Beaulieu, Stéphan Gervais, and Martin Papillon (Montréal, QC: Les Presses de l'Université de Montréal, 2013), 68.

36. Maxime Gohier, "Les Politiques coloniales françaises et anglaises à l'égard des Autochtones," in *Les Autochtones et le Québec: Des premiers contacts au Plan Nord*, ed. Alain Beaulieu, Stéphan Gervais, and Martin Papillon (Montréal, QC: Les Presses de l'Université de Montréal, 2013), 117.

37. Nawel Hamidi and Pierrot Ross-Tremblay, "Les Écueils de l'extinction: Les Premiers Peuples, les négociations territoriales et l'esquisse d'une ère postcoloniale," *Recherches Amérindiennes du Québec* 43, no. 1 (2013): 52.

38. Ibid., 53.

39. Ibid.

40. See the collection Récits et Médias Autochtones at the Presses de l'Université de Montréal, and the Americana collection at the Presses de l'Université Laval. Both are headed by non-Indigenous scholars and both publish works written mostly by non-Indigenous authors.

41. Dickason, "From 'One Nation,' " 20.

42. Ibid.

43. *L'Empreinte*: "Comme les autochtones exigent qu'il y ait des mariages, il faut qu'il y ait des mariages entre les Français et les Indiens. C'est la façon de faire amérindienne. Champlain va souhaiter que nos fils les Français marrient [*sic*] des Amérindiennes et que nous fassions un seul peuple. C'est unique dans le projet colonial. Une proximité que l'on ne voit pas ailleurs. C'est un trait distinct de notre histoire coloniale, un trait dont on aurait raison d'être fier plutôt que de l'occulter."

44. Gilles Havard, " 'Protection' and 'Unequal Alliance': The French Conception of Sovereignty over Indians in New France," in *French and Indians in the Heart of North America*, ed. Robert Englebert and Guillaume Teasdale (East Lansing: University of Michigan Press, 2013), 115.

45. Ibid., 117.

46. Leroux, "Now I Am Métis." Leroux draws here from Yves Beauregard, "Mythe ou réalité: Les Origines amérindiennes des Québécois: Entrevue avec Hubert Charbonneau," *Cap-aux-Diamants: La Revue d'Histoire du Québec*, no. 34 (summer 1993): 38–42.

47. Leroux, "Now I Am Métis." Leroux draws here from the research of Bertrand Desjardins in "La Contribution différentielle des immigrants français à la souche canadienne-française," *Annales de Normandie* 58, nos. 3-4 (2008): 72.

48. In Cook, "Les Premiers Contacts," 67.

49. See Delice Mugabo, "On Rocks and Hard Places: A Reflection on Antiblackness in Organizing against Islamophobia," *Critical Ethnic Studies* 2, no. 2 (Fall 2016): 159–83; Bruno Cornellier, "The Struggle for Others: Pierre Vallières, Québécois Settler Nationalism and the N-Word Today," *Discourse: Theoretical Studies in Media and Culture* 39, no. 1 (2017): 31–66; and Charmaine Nelson, *Slavery, Geography and Empire in Nineteenth-Century Marine Landscapes of Montreal and Jamaica* (New York: Routledge, 2016). See also Bruno Cornellier and Rachel Zellars, "L'Histoire des noirs, le racisme et la toponymie des lieux au Québec," Le Huffington Post Québec, October 14, 2015, http://quebec.huffingtonpost.ca/bruno-cornellier/histoire-noirs-quebec-quebecois-commission-toponymie_b_8285402.html.

50. *L'Empreinte*: "Une part de moi-même m'échappe. Quand j'ai débarqué en Amérique, j'étais Français et bientôt, je ne vivais ni ne pensais plus comme un Français. J'étais devenu Canadien, du mot Iroquois Kanata. Ma tribu s'est donnée d'autres noms depuis—Canadiens Français, Québécois—mais dans l'idée que nous nous faisons de nous mêmes, quelque chose s'est dérobé, un fil s'est rompu en chemin. Ce n'est peut-être pas un hasard si la question d'identité resurgit constamment dans notre histoire, comme si aucune réponse ne nous avait encore pleinement satisfaits."

51. Cornellier, "Je me souviens," 117.

52. Bouchard in *L'Empreinte*.

53. Marcel Beaulieu and Francis Leclerc, *Mémoires affectives*, dir. Francis Leclerc, DVD (Montréal: Palomar Productions, 2004).

54. Cornellier, "Je me souviens," 110. "Ainsi, l'Indien, lorsque libéré, désincarné de sa réalité politique et historique et soumis au régime discursif et pédagogique qui l'inscrit/l'écrit dans la mythologie nationaliste dominante, devient ici l'un des principaux symboles de la différence culturelle et de la territorialité québécoise en terre d'Amérique."

55. Cook, "Les Premiers Contacts," 55.

56. See Ismael Houdassine, "'The Revenant,' un film anti-canadien-français selon Roy Dupuis," Le Huffington Post Québec, October 22, 2016, http://quebec.huffingtonpost.ca/2016/01/22/the-revenant-reaction-de-roy-dupuis_n_9057998.html.

57. See Shari Huhndorf, *Going Native: Indians in the American Cultural Imagination* (Ithaca, N.Y.: Cornell University Press, 2001). Also see Deloria, *Playing Indian*.

58. Chelsea Vowel, "Settlers Claiming Métis Heritage Because They Just Feel More Indigenous," *rabble.ca*, March 11, 2015, http://rabble.ca/blogs/bloggers/apihtawikosisan/2015/03/settlers-claiming-m%C3%A9tis-heritage-because-they-just-feel-more-.

59. Delâge, *L'Empreinte*.

60. Hamidi and Ross-Tremblay, "Gamau," 234.

61. Jessica Kolopenuk, "Windigo Incarnate: Consuming 'Native American DNA,'" *GeneWatch* 27, no. 2 (2014), http://www.councilforresponsiblegenetics.org/genewatch/GeneWatchPage.aspx?pageId=531.

62. Cited in Kolopenuk, "Windigo Incarnate."

63. Leanne Simpson, *Islands of Decolonial Love* (Winnipeg, MN: ARP Books, 2013), 105.

64. *L'Empreinte*: "Nous avons eu des mères indiennes. Quelques pères aussi, mais surtout des mères. Leurs voix nous ont bercés. Comme les trois-quarts des Québécois d'origines canadiennes françaises, j'ai moi aussi des ancêtres autochtones. Je découvre dans ma généalogie une famille qui s'est plusieurs fois liée avec les Premières Nations. J'ai donc 92 liens de parentés. Je reconnais également les noms d'interprètes et d'explorateurs fameux qui ont vécu avec les Amérindiens, qui ont été adoptés par eux. Les Couture, Marcellet, Perreault, Pelletier, Lefebvre, sans compter tous ces colons qui le temps d'un voyage de traite, ont cédé à la 'magie des bois.'"

65. Leroux, "Now I Am Métis."

66. Gérard Bouchard, "Le faux 'sang indien' des Québécois," *La Presse*, March 7, 2016, http://www.lapresse.ca/debats/nos-collaborateurs/gerard-bouchard/201502/06/01–4841971-le-faux-sang-indien-des-quebecois.php. Bouchard incorrectly states Rousseau's first name as Jean-Jacques.

67. The BALSAC database is a partnership between several universities in Québec and the Université du Québec à Chicoutimi. This digitized database comprises marriage records and other documents that allow the automatic re-creation of more than four centuries of genealogical relations and kinship structures in the province. See http://balsac.uqac.ca/english/.

68. Bouchard, "Le faux 'sang indien.' "

69. Melissa Meyer, *Thicker Than Water: The Origins of Blood as Symbol and Ritual* (New York: Routledge, 2005), 1.

70. Tallbear, *Native American DNA*, 46.

71. Meyer, *Thicker Than Water*, 208.

72. Amy Bombay, Kimberly Matheson, and Hymie Anisman, "The Intergenerational Effects of Indian Residential Schools: Implications for the Concept of Historical Trauma," *Transcultural Psychiatry* 51, no. 3 (2014): 321.

73. Tuck and Yang, "Decolonization," 9.

74. Mary Louise Fellows and Sherene Razack, "The Race to Innocence: Confronting Hierarchical Relations among Women," *Journal of Gender, Race, and Justice* 1 (1998): 335.

75. Tallbear, *Native American DNA*, 37.

76. Ibid., 9.

77. Hélène Vézina, Michèle Jomphe, Ève-Marie Lavoie, Claudia Moreau, and Damian Labuda, "L'Apport des données génétiques à la mesure généalogique des origines amérindiennes des Canadiens français," *Cahiers Québécois de Démographie* 41, no. 1 (2012): 88.

78. Tallbear, *Native American DNA*, 41.

Chapter 3

The first epigraph is from Denise Bombardier, "Jusqu'à quand des reserves au Canada?" *La Presse*, April 18, 2016, http://www.journaldemontreal.com/2016/04/18/jusqua-quand-des-reserves-au-canada. "Ces territoires où vivent exclusivement des autochtones sont une honte pour le Canada. Ces ghettos, financés à coups de milliards depuis des décennies, sont pour la plupart des lieux inhumains. Isolés, à l'écart de toute civilisation, ils maintiennent la misère qui se transmet de génération en génération et ses habitants sont parmi les damnés de la terre." The second epigraph is from Chelsea Vowel, *Indigenous Writes: A Guide to First Nations, Métis, and Inuit Issues in Canada* (Winnipeg, MB: Highwater, 2016), 266.

1. Denise Bombardier, "La Culture Autochtone que tue," *Le Journal de Montréal*, January 21, 2015, http://www.journaldemontreal.com/2015/01/21/la-culture-autochtone-qui-tue.

2. See the archive of her editorials at *Le Journal de Montréal*: "Denise Bombardier," *Le Journal de Montréal*, http://www.journaldemontreal.com/opinions/denise-bombardier.

3. Christianne Hacault, "41% des Canadiens veulent la fin des avantages accordés aux Autochtones," Radio-Canada.ca, November 4, 2016, http://ici.radio-canada.ca/regions/manitoba/2016/10/04/001-sondage-autochtones-abolir-statut-angus-reid.shtml.

4. Jody Porter, "First Nations Students Get 30 Per Cent Less Funding Than Other Children," *CBC News*, March 14, 2016, http://www.cbc.ca/news/canada/thunder-bay/first-nations-education-funding-gap-1.3487822. Also see Daniel Schartz, "How Does Native Funding Work?" *CBC News*, February 6, 2013, http://www.cbc.ca/news/canada/how-does-native-funding-work-1.1301120.

5. I use the term *First Nations* here because the reserve falls under the Indian Act, which recognizes its inhabitants as *First Nations* people or *Status Indians*.

6. Jill Carter, "Discarding Sympathy, Disrupting Catharsis: The Mortification of Indigenous Flesh as Survivance-Intervention," *Theatre Journal*, 67, no. 3 (2015): 431.

7. While the Canadian government argues that the importation of cigarettes from the United States to Canada via Mohawk territory is illegal, the Mohawks maintain that as a sovereign people, it is within their right to move merchandise across their land. They do not recognize the U.S.-Canada border.

8. Caroline Alphonso and Tu Thanh Ha, "Expecting Flu Assistance, Reserves Get Body Bags from Ottawa," *The Globe and Mail*, September 16, 2009, http://www.theglobeandmail.com/news/politics/expecting-flu-assistance-reserves-get-body-bags-from-ottawa/article1202910/.

9. I thank Karyn Recollet for her reminder: Indigenous people have never ceased to "surge," and thus to call their many modes of political agency "resurgent" is a misnomer.

10. Gerald Vizenor, *Fugitive Poses: Native American Indian Scenes of Absence and Presence* (Lincoln: University of Nebraska Press, 2000), 15.

11. Aileen Moreton-Robinson, *The White Possessive: Property, Power, and Indigenous Sovereignty* (Minneapolis: University of Minnesota Press, 2015).

12. Lisa Marie Cacho, *Social Death, Racialized Rightlessness, and the Criminalization of the Unprotected* (New York: New York University Press, 2012), 7.

13. The Mohawks use alternatively "Mohawks" and "Kanienkehakas" (People of the Flint) to refer to themselves. I will use both in this chapter to reflect the film's participants' usage of both terms.

14. For legal reasons, Kanehsatà:ke was not technically a reserve in 1990, even though the Mohawks had repeatedly petitioned the Canadian government to officially grant the community the land in the Oka region on which Mohawk occupation is historically documented. Though not a reserve and thus not benefiting from the few protections this title grants a community, Kanehsatà:ke was perceived as a reserve by many in the media.

15. Longclaws's comment was made famous by the Cree playwright Tomson Highway in his play *Dry Lips Oughta Move to Kapuskasing* (1989).

16. See Karyn Recollet, "Glyphing Decolonial Love through Urban Flash Mobbing and *Walking with Our Sisters*," *Curriculum Inquiry* 45, no. 1 (2015): 129–45; Eve Tuck and C. Ree, "A Glossary of Haunting," in *Handbook of Autoethnography*, ed. Stacey Holman Jones, Tony E. Adams, and Carolyn Ellis (New York: Routledge, 2013), 639–58; Angie Morrill, Eve Tuck, and the Super Futures Haunt Qollective, "Before Dispossession, or Surviving It," *Liminalities: A Journal of Performance Studies* 12, no. 1 (2016): 1–20; Bonita Lawrence, *"Real" Indians and Others: Mixed-Blood Urban Native Peoples and Indigenous Nationhood* (Vancouver, BC: University of British Columbia Press, 2012).

17. Simpson, *Mohawk Interruptus*, 152.

18. "Indian Act," Justice Laws Website, http://laws-lois.justice.gc.ca/eng/acts/i-5/page-4.html#h-13. The Indian Act is current as of March 5, 2018.

19. "Constitution Acts 1867 to 1982," Justice Laws Website, http://laws-lois.justice.gc.ca/eng/Const/section-91.html.

20. Anthony Hall, "Indigenous Peoples: Treaties," *Historica Canada*, last modified July 23, 2015, http://www.thecanadianencyclopedia.ca/en/article/aboriginal-treaties/.

21. Vowel, *Indigenous Writes*, 243–51.

22. Hall, "Indigenous Peoples."

23. Ibid.

24. See Yamri Taddese, "Feds Pouring Big Money into Aboriginal Litigation," *Law Times*, November 11, 2013, http://www.lawtimesnews.com/201311113587/headline-news/feds-pouring-big-money-into-aboriginal-litigation. It is estimated that Aboriginal Affairs and Northern Development Canada, the government agency in charge of the administration of First Nations peoples, paid around $110,000,000 in legal fees for court battles against Aboriginal people in 2012–2013. This is more than any other agency.

25. Cacho, *Social Death*, 7.

26. Wolfe, "Settler Colonialism," 388.

27. See "Drinking Water Advisories: First Nations South of 60," Government of Canada, http://www.hc-sc.gc.ca/fniah-spnia/promotion/public-publique/water-dwa-eau-aqep-eng.php.

28. Interestingly, Mani-Utenam was transformed to become Kinogamish. The roads were covered with sand and the reserve was made to look more rural and isolated.

29. The Sûrete du Québec (SQ) is the provincial police force that was first called in by the mayor of Oka to break the barricades. When they failed, the Canadian army was called in.

30. See John Ciaccia, *The Oka Crisis: A Mirror of the Soul* (Dorval, QC: Maren Publications), 47–49, 80–81. The SQ's infamously repressive approach to law enforcement in Québec's First Nations communities was documented by Alanis Obomsawin in *Un Incident a Restigouche* (1984), a documentary about a violent SQ attack on the Restigouche reserve.

31. While theories abounded suggesting that Lemay died in an instance of friendly fire, the coroner's report later demonstrated that Lemay died from a bullet coming from the Mohawk side.

32. See, for instance, http://www.lapresse.ca/cinema/nouvelles/201207/17/01-4553715-la-grande-dame-de-lonf.php or https://www.gazettedesfemmes.ca/2561/la-grande-dame-du-cinema-autochtone/.

33. Randolph Lewis, *Alanis Obomsawin: The Vision of a Native Filmmaker* (Lincoln: University of Nebraska Press, 2006), 117.

34. Ibid., 102.

35. Bruno Cornellier, "The Things about Alanis' Indianness: Indigenous Reality and the Burden of Education at the National Film Board of Canada," *Canadian Journal of Film Studies* 21, no. 2 (2012): 10.

36. Isabelle St-Amand, *La Crise d'Oka en récits* (Québec, QC: Les Presses de l'Université Laval, 2015).

37. Michelle Raheja, *Reservation Reelism, Red-Facing, Visual Sovereignty, and Representations of Native Americans in Film* (Lincoln: University of Nebraska Press, 2010), 19.

38. Byrd, *The Transit of Empire*, 6.

39. Ibid., 38.

40. Simpson, *Mohawk Interruptus*, 152.

41. Žižek, *Violence*, 2.

42. Moreton-Robinson, *The White Possessive*, xi.

43. These were not the only examples of explosive racism. Simon Bédard, a radio host who later ran for elected office, famously said on air, during the events in Oka in 1990: "Tu rentres là avec l'armée pis tu nettoies tout ça. Cinquante morts, 100 morts, 125 morts, ça vient de s'éteindre. On enterre ça pis on continue à vivre!" (You go in there with the army and you clean this all up. Fifty dead, 100 dead, 125 dead, that's the end of it. We bury that and we go on living!)

44. This article, published after the events in Oka, attests to the growing importance of land claims in the public sphere. Jules Dufour, "Les Revendications territoriales des peuples autochtones au Québec," *Cahiers de Géographie du Québec* 37, no. 101 (September 1993): 263–90.

45. Ciaccia, *The Oka Crisis*, 115.

46. Yves Sioux Durand and Jean-Frédéric Messier, *Hamlet le Malécite* (unpublished script).

> Ne te semble t'il pas qu'un devoir m'incombe?
> Celui qui a tué mon roi et prostitué ma mère.
> Ne dois-je pas en toute conscience le châtier avec ce bras?

47. Simon Harel, "Les Loyautés conflictuelles de la literature québécoise," *Quebec Studies* 44 (2007–08): 41.

48. Wilderson, *Red, White & Black*, 48.

49. Byrd, *The Transit of Empire*, 221.

50. See Diana Taylor's *Disappearing Acts*, or Ken Gonzales-Day's photo project, *Erased Lynching Series* (2002–11), among other excellent works on the topic of objective violence performed.

51. See Hugh MacLennan, *Two Solitudes* (Toronto, ON: McClelland and Stewart, 2008).

52. Simon Harel, *Braconnages identitaires: Un Québec palimpseste* (Montréal, QC: VLB, 2008), 59.

53. See Wilderson, *Red, White & Black*. Wilderson draws an important distinction between conflict and antagonism when it comes to the structural relationship of Native Americans with settler states. Wilderson argues that there are two modalities to the Native American grammar of suffering—sovereignty and genocide. In their capacity to name and reclaim sovereignty and a land (which Wilderson understands to be possible though improbable), Native Americans stand closer to settler communities than to what Wilderson calls the black "Slave," the socially dead for whom repatriation and sovereignty are unimaginable. In other words, land and sovereignty claims are articulated as conflicts on a shared terrain. It is in the genocidal modality of their grammar of suffering that Native Americans align with the "Slave" and occupy an antagonistic position vis-à-vis white settler society.

54. Wilderson, *Red, White & Black*, 49.

55. The Anishinaabe filmmaker Kevin Papatie traces the dramatic effect of Residential Schools in his 2007 movie *L'Amendement* (*Abinodjic Madjinakini*). Over the span of four generations, Papatie demonstrates the loss of Anishinaabe language and culture.

56. Lawrence, *"Real" Indians and Others*, 112.

57. Royal Commission on Aboriginal Peoples, *Final Report*, vol. 1 (Toronto, ON: Indian and Northern Affairs Canada, 1996), 26.

58. Raheja, *Reservation Reelism*, x.
59. Ibid., xi.
60. Ibid., 196.

Chapter 4

The epigraph is from Lee Maracle, *I Am Woman: A Native Perspective on Sociology and Feminism* (Vancouver, BC: Raincoast Books, 2002), 22.

1. Michele Taïna Audette served as the president of Québec Native Women from 1998 to 2004 and again in 2010 and 2012. Viviane Michel has been the president since 2012. Taïna Audette also served as president of the Native Women's Association of Canada from 2012 to 2015 and ran and lost as a Liberal Party candidate for the federal elections to represent the region of Manicouagan, Québec.

2. Rebecca Solnit, *Wanderlust: A History of Walking* (New York: Penguin Books, 2000), 14.

3. Donnacona, located near Québec City, is named after the Iroquoian chief Donnacona, who lived in Stadaconé (now Québec City) and was taken to France by force by Jacques Cartier in 1536. He died in France in 1539.

4. Mishuana Goeman, *Mark My Words: Native Women Mapping Our Nations* (Minneapolis: University of Minnesota Press, 2013), 1.

5. Sarah Deer, *The Beginning and End of Rape: Confronting Sexual Violence in Native America* (Minneapolis: University of Minnesota Press, 2015).

6. Bonita Lawrence, "Gender, Race, and the Regulation of Native Identity in Canada and the United States: An Overview," *Hypatia* 18, no. 2 (2003): 3.

7. See the controversy surrounding the use of the word *genocide* at the new Canadian Museum for Human Rights in Winnipeg, Manitoba, to describe the "past injustices" perpetrated by the Canadian government on First Nations communities. "Human Rights Museum Sparks Debate over Term 'Genocide,'" *CBC News*, July 26, 2013, http://www.cbc.ca/news/canada/manitoba/human-rights-museum-sparks-debate-over-term-genocide-1.1400154. Also see Pamela Palmater, "Human Rights Museum or Harper Propaganda? Genocide in Canada Denied," July 29, 2013, http://rabble.ca/blogs/bloggers/pamela-palmater/2013/07/human-rights-museum-or-harper-propaganda-genocide-canada-deni. Similarly, the former prime minister Paul Martin created a commotion at the Truth and Reconciliation Commission on Indian Residential Schools in Montréal in April 2013 when he referred to the Residential School policy as one of "cultural genocide." See "Paul Martin Accuses Residential Schools of 'Cultural Genocide,'" April 26, 2013, http://www.cbc.ca/news/politics/paul-martin-accuses-residential-schools-of-cultural-genocide-1.1335199.

8. John Leslie, ed., *The Historical Development of the Indian Act* (Ottawa, ON: Department of Indian and Northern Development, Treaties and Historical Research Branch, 1978), 114.

9. Lawrence, "Gender, Race, and the Regulation of Native Identity," 6.

10. Simpson, *Mohawk Interruptus*, 156.

11. Ibid., 149.

12. For more on this, see Rayna Green, "The Pocahontas Perplex: The Image of Indian Women in American Culture," *Massachusetts Review* 16, no. 4 (1975): 698–714; Janice Acoose, *Iskwewak: Neither Indian Princesses nor Easy Squaws*

(Toronto, ON: Women's, 1995); and Monique Mojica, *Princess Pocahontas and the Blue Spots* (Toronto, ON: Three O'Clock, 1991).

13. Simpson, *Mohawk Interruptus*, 149.

14. Lawrence writes: "Taking into account that for every woman who lost status and had to leave her community, all of her descendants also lost status and for the most part were permanently alienated from Native culture, the scale of cultural genocide caused by gender discrimination becomes massive. Indeed, when Bill C-31 was passed in 1985, there were only 350,000 Status Indians left in Canada." Approximately 100,000 individuals regained status with Bill C-31 by 1995 (Lawrence, "Gender, Race, and the Regulation of Native Identity," 9).

15. Aside from the aforementioned Simpson, Deer, and Palmater, see the issue of *English Journal* on "Native Feminism" edited by Eve Tuck and Karyn Recollet (106, no. 1 [2016]); or see *Critically Sovereign: Indigenous Gender, Sexuality, and Feminist Studies*, ed. Joanne Barker (Durham, N.C.: Duke University Press, 2017).

16. Deer, *Beginning and End of Rape*, x.

17. Ibid., xvi.

18. Marie Annette Pember, "Canada's National Inquiry into Missing and Murdered Indigenous Women Begins," Indian Country Today, September 1, 2016, http://indiancountrytodaymedianetwork.com/2016/09/01/canadas-national-inquiry-missing-and-murdered-indigenous-women-begins-165645.

19. See Nawel Hamidi and Pierrot Ross-Tremblay, "Le Mandat doit être revisé," *La Presse*, July 18, 2017, http://plus.lapresse.ca/screens/37c5dc68–6aba-4d81–9763-fa451d06b972%7C_0.html.

20. Gloria Galloway, "Inquiry's Remaining Commissioners Must Resign, Indigenous Families Say," *The Globe and Mail*, August 8, 2017, https://beta.theglobeandmail.com/news/politics/inquirys-remaining-commissioners-must-resign-indigenous-families-say/article35900193/.

21. See Glen S. Coulthard, "Subjects of Empire: Indigenous Peoples and the Politics of Recognition in Canada," *Contemporary Political Theory* 6 (2007): 437–60; and Elizabeth Povinelli, *The Cunning of Recognition: Indigenous Alterities and the Making of Australian Multiculturalism* (Durham, N.C.: Duke University Press, 2002).

22. In 2012, Prime Minister Harper's Conservative government voted a series of laws that exemplified this erosion. The Omnibus Bill C-45, which sparked the Idle No More Movement, unilaterally amended the Indian Act and the Navigation Protection Act, among other laws. These amendments effectively opened protected Indigenous territories to commercial development and lifted environmental assessment requirements on a series of waterways that are vital to Indigenous communities.

23. Glen Coulthard, "Recognition, Reconciliation and Resentment in Indigenous Politics," lecture presented at Simon Fraser University, Vancouver, British Columbia, November 16, 2011.

24. Chelsea Vowel, "Indigenous Languages Crucial to Cultural Flourishing," Rabble.ca, December 4, 2013, http://rabble.ca/blogs/bloggers/apihtawikosisan/2013/12/indigenous-languages-crucial-to-cultural-flourishing.

25. Paulette Regan, *Unsettling the Settler Within: Indian Residential Schools, Truth Telling, and Reconciliation in Canada* (Vancouver, BC: University of British Columbia Press, 2010), ix.

26. Goeman, *Mark My Words*, 3.

27. Solnit, *Wanderlust*, 244.

28. Bill C-31 (1985), "An Act to Amend the Indian Act," allowed women who married Status Indians from other bands to retain their own band membership. It allowed for the limited reinstatement of Indians who had lost or been denied status because of the gender discrimination contained in the Indian Act. In 2011, Bill C-3 corrected the gendered discrimination contained in Bill C-31's "limited reinstatement" clause, allowing the grandchildren of women who had lost their Indian status through marriage to regain it.

29. Pamela Palmater, "Bill C-3: Senate Considerations More about Blood 'Purity' and 'Benefits' than Equality," PamPalmater.com, December 7, 2010 (http://www.pampalmater.com/?s=Bill+C-3).

30. Gerald Taiaiake Alfred, "Restitution Is the Real Pathway to Justice for Indigenous Peoples," in *Response, Responsibility, and Renewal: Canada's Truth and Reconciliation Journey*, ed. Gregory Younging (Ottawa, ON: Aboriginal Healing Foundation Research Series, 2009), 184.

31. Pamela Palmater, "Stretched beyond Human Limits: Death by Poverty in First Nations," *Canadian Review of Social Policy* 65-66 (2011): 120.

32. David Ljunggren, "Every G20 Nation Wants to Be Canada, Insists PM," *Reuters,* September 25, 2009, http://www.reuters.com/article/columns-us-g20-canada-advantages-idUSTRE58P05Z20090926.

33. See "Projet de Loi No 60: Charte affirmant les valeurs de laïcité et de neutralité religieuse de l'état ainsi que d'égalité entre les femmes et les hommes et encadrant les demandes d'accommodement," Commission des droits de la personne et des droits de la jeunesse, December 2013, http://www.cdpdj.qc.ca/Publications/memoire_PL_60_charte_valeurs.pdf.

34. Renée Dupuis, *Quel Canada pour les autochtones? La Fin de l'exclusion* (Montréal, QC: Boréal, 2001), 37.

35. Denis Bouchard, Eric Cardinal, and Ghislain Picard, *De Kébec à Québec; Cinq siècles d'échanges entre nous* (Montréal, QC: Les Intouchables, 2008), 87.

36. The Royal Canadian Mounted Police identified 1,750 missing and murdered Aboriginal women and girls. See Royal Canadian Mounted Police, *Missing and Murdered Aboriginal Women: 2015 Update to the National Operatonal Overview* (Ottawa, ON, 2015).

37. Lawrence, "Gender, Race, and the Regulation of Native Identity," 18.

38. Michel Lacombe, "Michèle Audette: La Militante Nomade," *Radio-Canada.ca,* April 16, 2012, http://ici.radio-canada.ca/emissions/le_21e/2015-2016/chronique.asp?idChronique=213811.

39. Lacombe, "Michèle Audette: La Militante Nomade."

40. Dana Claxton, "Red Woman White Cube: First Nations Art and Racialized Space" (master's thesis, Simon Fraser University, 2007), 44.

41. Tanya Lukin Linklater, "Artist Statement," *Dance Research Journal* 48, no. 1 (2016): 25.

42. Preston Arrow-weed (playwright) in discussion with the author, November 22, 2013.

43. Lukin Linklater, "Artist Statement," 27.

44. For more information on Mandamin's work and advocacy, see "Josephine Mandamin, First Nations Elder and Water Walker," Center for Humans and Nature, http://www.humansandnature.org/josephine-mandamin.

45. See Stanley Vollant, "Puamun Meshkenu," http://www.innu-meshkenu.com/.

46. Gloria Galloway, "Nishiyuu: A Movement of Cree Youth Who Voted with Their Feet," *Globe and Mail*, March 25, 2013, https://www.theglobeandmail.com/news/politics/nishiyuu-a-movement-of-cree-youth-who-voted-with-their-feet/article10327993/.

47. Tim Ingold, "Bringing Things to Life: Creative Entanglements in a World of Materials," paper presented at ESRC National Centre for Research Methods, University of Manchester, Oxford, Manchester, July 2010, p. 11.

48. Coulthard, "Recognition, Reconciliation and Resentment in Indigenous Politics."

49. Dylan Robinson, "Embracing Resentment and Reconciliation," paper presented at "In the Balance: Indigeneity, Performance, Globalization," London, October 25, 2013.

50. Robinson, "Enchantment's Irreconcilable Connection," 220.

51. Ibid.

52. Rhonda L. Meier (artist) in discussion with the author, October 14, 2014.

53. Ibid.

54. Nadia Myre (artist) in discussion with the author, January 7, 2014.

55. Endurance performances of the 1960s and 1970s are not an entirely new phenomenon: similar impulses have long been recorded in rituals and religious practices around the world. In *So Much Wasted*, Patrick Anderson discusses the self-starving spectacles of Henry Tanner and Molly Fancher in the 1880s as echoing precursors to the works of Chris Burden and his contemporaries. See Patrick Anderson, *So Much Wasted: Hunger, Performance, and the Morbidity of Resistance* (Durham, N.C.: Duke University Press, 2010).

56. Anderson, *So Much Wasted*, 25.

57. Kathy O'Dell, *Contract with the Skin: Masochism, Performance Art, and the 1970s* (Minneapolis: University of Minnesota Press, 1998), 2.

58. Anderson, *So Much Wasted*, 25.

59. Harold Cardinal, *The Unjust Society* (Vancouver, BC: Douglas and MacIntyre, 1999), 140.

60. Sandra Dyck, "Making Contact," in *Nadia Myre En[counter]s* (Montréal, QC: Editions Art Mûr, 2011), 49.

61. See Bouchard, Cardinal, and Trudel, *De Kébec à Québec*, 66–67. Also see Dupuis, *Quel Canada*, 93–94.

62. Bouchard, Cardinal, and Trudel, *De Kébec à Québec*, 92. "Après ce rejet d'une nouvelle constitution pour le Canada, les Premières Nations réalisent que leur poids politique dépend largement de la conjecture du débat constitutionnel et, conséquemment, de la bataille du Québec. Il s'avère que sur le plan politique, les Premières Nations ont réussi à accroitre leur pouvoir de négociation dans des contextes politiques 'fluides' créés par les demandes et griefs du Québec."

63. While Ghislain Picard recalls Québec's sovereignist Premier René Lévesque (1976–80 and 1981–85) as sympathetic to Indigenous peoples, many of

Lévesque's successors engaged in negotiations for more practical reasons, among them the creation of Québec's large-scale hydroelectric projects on Cree, Inuit, and Naskapi territories. Aside from the territories covered by the modern agreements signed between Québec and these nations in 1975 and again in 2002, most of the province of Québec exists quite literally on unceded, contested land where Indigenous sovereignty and self-determination are under constant threat. Recent development projects—Le Plan Nord, proposed mining laws, and unauthorized forestry projects on Anishnabe territory near Lac Barrière—all show that the provincial government's understanding of Indigenous sovereignty is, more often than not, merely symbolic.

64. Bouchard, Cardinal, and Trudel, *De Kébec à Québec*, 81. "Son action unilatérale, pendant les années 1980, peut être attribuée davantage à sa politique autonomiste et au rejet du rapatriement de la Constitution canadienne qu'à une réelle volonté de créer une relation 'nation à nation' avec les peuples autochtones du Québec."

65. Bouchard, Cardinal, and Trudel, *De Kébec à Québec*, 79. "Ces droits doivent s'exercer au sein de la société québécoise, et ne sauraient par conséquent impliquer des droits de souveraineté qui puissent porter atteinte à l'intégrité territorial du Québec."

66. Gilles Havard, *The Great Peace of Montreal of 1701: French-Native Diplomacy in the Seventeenth Century* (Montréal, QC: McGill University Press, 2001), 25.

67. See Georges Sioui, *Huron-Wendat: The Heritage of the Circle*, in which he retraces the rich tradition of diplomacy of the Huron-Wendat people.

68. Gerald Taiaiake Alfred, *Peace, Power, Righteousness: An Indigenous Manifesto* (Toronto, ON: Oxford University Press, 2009), 8.

69. Bouchard, Cardinal, and Trudel, *De Kébec à Québec*, 93.

70. Dyck, "Making Contact," 49.

71. Havard, *The Great Peace of Montreal of 1701*, 23.

72. Heather Igloliorte, "Inuit Art—Modern Meets Contemporary," paper presented at McCord Museum, Montréal, June 2010.

73. John Cree, Ellen Gabriel, and Skawmennati Fragnito, "Two Row Wampum and Reconciliation," round-table, Truth and Reconciliation Commission, Québec National Event, Montréal, April 26, 2013.

74. Jolene Rickard, "Visualizing Sovereignty in the Time of Biometric Sensors," *South Atlantic Quarterly* 11, no. 2 (2011): 478.

75. Havard, *The Great Peace of Montreal of 1701*, 18.

76. Michèle Audette, Standing Committee on Aboriginal Affairs and Northern Development, Number 010, 3rd session, 40th Parliament, April 20, 2010.

77. Havard, *The Great Peace of Montreal of 1701*, 20.

78. Rickard, "Visualizing Sovereignty," 472.

79. Solnit, *Wanderlust*, 532.

80. Joséphine Bacon, *Bâtons à message—Tshissinuatshitakana* (Montréal, QC: Mémoire d'Encrier, 2009), 7.

81. Andrea Smith, "Native American Feminism, Sovereignty, and Social Change," *Feminist Studies* 31, no. 1 (2005): 121.

82. Ibid.

83. Ibid., 123.

84. Lacombe, "Michèle Audette."

85. Justin Brake, "Elizabeth Penashue Prepares for Final Walk, Denied Visit to Muskrat Falls," *Newfoundland & Labrador: The Independent*, December 2, 2014, http://theindependent.ca/2014/02/12/elizabeth-penashue-prepares-for-final-walk-denied-visit-to-muskrat-falls/.

86. Ibid.

Chapter 5

1. Allen, *Trans-Indigenous Methodologies*, xiv.

2. Ibid., xviii.

3. Robinson, "Enchantment's Irreconcilable Connection," 212.

4. *Xajoj Tun Rabinal Achi*, coproduction of Les Productions Ondinnok and Festival Présence Autochtone, directed by Yves Sioui Durand, choreographed by Patricia Iraola; cast: Charles Bender, Marco Collin, Nicoletta Dolce, Yves Sioui Durand, Hélène Ducharme, Patricia Iraola, Catherine Joncas, Lara Kramer, Mireya Bayancela Ordonez, Rodrigo Ramis, Leticia Vera, José Léon Coloch Garniga, and José Manuel Coloch Xolop.

5. Ngũgĩ wa Thiong'o, *Globalectics: Theory and the Politics of Knowing* (New York: Columbia University Press, 2012), 49.

6. Ibid., 50.

7. Ibid.

8. Ondinnok's adaptation marked a new transnational cycle in the play's long history: it constituted the first adaptation of the play and the second time the play traveled outside of Guatemala. Excerpts of Tedlock's translation received a public reading in 1996 at the Miami Museum of Science. A version of the entire play was later codirected by Leandro Sotto and Sally Goers Fox at the University of Buffalo.

9. Roach, *Cities of the Dead*, 36.

10. Alexandre Cadieux, "Acte de mémoire et de dialogue," *Le Devoir*, June 22, 2010, http://www.ledevoir.com/culture/theatre/291362/theatre-acte-de-memoire-et-de-dialogue.

11. Out of respect for the ancestors found under the chancellor's residence, no photos of the remains are featured in this chapter.

12. These federally recognized bands or tribes are the Barona, Inaja-Cosmit, La Posta, Manzanita, Mesa Grande, San Pasqual Band, Campo, Ewiiaapaayp, Sycuan, Viejas, Capitan Grande, Jamul, and the Iipay Nation of Santa Ysabel.

13. According to the U.S. Census Bureau, in 2010 California and Oklahoma had the largest populations of self-identifying American Indians or Native Alaskans (723,225 and 482,760, respectively).

14. San Diego County counts 18 federally recognized reservations separated along the following tribal groupings: Kumeyaay, Payoomkawichum, Kuupiaxchem, and Cahuilla. Riverside County (California) and Sandoval County (New Mexico) each count 12 federally recognized reservations, the second-highest concentration in the country.

15. The KCRC is a designated tribal entity representing twelve Kumeyaay tribes on repatriation issues. These tribes are the Barona, Campo, Ewiiaapaayp, Inaja-Cosmit, Jamul, La Posta, Manzanita, Mesa Grande, San Pasqual, Iipay Nation of Santa Ysabel, Sycuan, and Viejas. Repatriation takes place on the tribal

land closest to the site(s) where the remains or cultural objects were found. In the UCSD case, it would be the La Posta band, whose land is located in eastern San Diego County.

16. NAGPRA was amended in 2010 so that remains which were deemed "culturally unidentifiable," that is, for which cultural affiliation proved difficult to establish, should be returned to the "Indian tribe or Native Hawaiian organization from whose tribal land, at the time of the excavation or removal, the human remains were removed." Native American Graves Protection and Repatriation Regulations, *Code of Federal Regulations*, Public Lands: Interior, section 10.11.c.1 (2010), 212, https://www.gpo.gov/fdsys/pkg/CFR-2010-title43-vol1/pdf/CFR-2010-title43-vol1.pdf.

17. Ann Kakaliouras, "An Anthropology of Repatriation: Contemporary Physical Anthropological and Native American Ontologies of Practice," *Current Anthropology* 53, no. 5 (2012): 214.

18. Roach, *Cities of the Dead*, 20.

19. Ibid., 6.

20. See Thomas W. Killion, ed., *Opening Archaeology: Repatriation's Impact on Contemporary Research and Practice* (Santa Fe, N.M.: School for Advanced Research Press, 2008).

21. Roach, *Cities of the Dead*, 36.

22. Kakaliouras, "Anthropology of Repatriation," 214.

23. Donald Tuzin, "Report on Current Issues Surrounding Human Remains," internal report, University of California, San Diego, 2007, p. 1.

24. Thomas Larson, "UCSD and the Land of the Dead," *San Diego Reader*, April 30, 2008, 6. "Archaeologist Malcolm Rogers found 11 burials in 1929 and 1936; 6 burials were discovered in 1947 and 1948; 2 in 1949 by a Scripps ichthyologist; another in 1950 from under the patio area; and 6 more in 1956."

25. Tuzin, "Report on Current Issues," 2.

26. Gary Matthews, "Repatriation Request to UC San Diego," letter to Rory Hume, May 23, 2008, p. 3.

27. In May 2012, UCSD replied by asking the Southern District of California Court to dismiss both cases.

28. Matthews, "Repatriation Request to UC San Diego," 3.

29. Larson, "UCSD and the Land of the Dead," 6.

30. There was, for example, no Native American member on the ad hoc academic committee assembled by the UCSD to respond to the Kumeyaay's repatriation demand.

31. Ross Frank, a professor in the Ethnic Studies Department at UCSD whose research focuses on the First Peoples of the Southwest, has served on the UCSD advisory committee on the chancellor's house repatriation case and has consistently advocated for repatriation of the remains to the Kumeyaay.

32. Memorandum of Points and Authorities in Opposition to Motions to Dismiss First Amended Complaint under Fed. R. Civ. .P. 12(B)(7), 12(B)(1), and 12(B)(6), *White v. University of California*, 765 F.3d 1010 (9th Cir. 2014), 3–4, http://pages.ucsd.edu/~rfrank/class_web/UnivHouse/white-opposition.pdf.

33. Ibid., 5.

34. *White, Bettinger, Schoeninger v. UCSD, UC Regents, Yudof, Fox, & Matthews* No.12–17489, 2.

35. Ibid., 2.

36. Pat Flynn, "Dispute Erupts over Ancient Remains Found at UCSD," *San Diego Union Tribune*, April 24, 2012, http://www.sandiegouniontribune.com/news/education/sdut-dispute-erupts-over-ancient-human-remains-found-2012apr24-story.html.

37. See Vine Deloria, Jr., *Custer Died for Your Sins: An Indian Manifesto* (Norman: University of Oklahoma Press, 1969); Bruyneel, *The Third Space of Sovereignty*; and Simpson, *Mohawk Interruptus*.

38. Michel de Certeau, *The Writing of History*, trans. Tom Conley (New York: Columbia University Press, 1998), xxv.

39. Roach, *Cities of the Dead*, 36.

40. Ward Churchill, *A Little Matter of Genocide: Holocaust and Denial in the Americas 1492 to the Present* (San Francisco: City Lights, 2001), 4.

41. Lisa Lowe, "The Intimacies of Four Continents," in *Haunted by Empire: Geographies of Intimacy in North American History*, ed. Ann Laura Stoler (Durham, N.C.: Duke University Press, 2006), 206.

42. Bruyneel, *The Third Space of Sovereignty*.

43. See, for example, Rex Dalton, "No Burial for 10,000-Year Bones," *Nature* 45 (2008): 1156–57, http://www.nature.com/news/2008/081029/full/4551156a.html; or Margaret Schoeninger, Jeffery L. Bada, Patricia M. Masters, Robert L. Bettinger, and Tim D. White, "Unexamined Bodies of Evidence," *Science* 332 (May 20, 2011): 916.

44. Under NAGPRA, cultural affiliation is "established when the preponderance of the evidence—based on geographical, kinship, biological, archeological, linguistic, folklore, oral tradition, historical evidence, or other information or expert opinion—reasonably leads to such a conclusion." Native American Graves Protection and Repatriation Regulations, *Code of Federal Regulations*, Public Lands: Interior, section 10 (1996), 193, https://www.law.cornell.edu/cfr/text/43/part-10.

45. Kakaliouras, "Anthropology of Repatriation," 213.

46. Larson, "UCSD and the Land of the Dead," 5.

47. Schoeninger et al., "Unexamined Bodies of Evidence," 916.

48. Ibid.

49. Rebecca Tillett, "'Resting in Peace, Not in Pieces': The Concerns of the Living Dead in Anna Lee Walters's Ghost Singer," *Studies in American Indian Literatures* 17, no. 3 (2005): 86.

50. Ibid.

51. Little is known about *Xajoj Tun Rabinal Achi*'s author or authors, or its date of composition. It belongs to a genre described as "warrior dances whose pre-Hispanic origins are undeniable," and which "still held an important place in the Indigenous ceremonies at the beginning of the colonial period" (Michel Breton, *Rabinal Achi: A Fifteenth-Century Maya Dynastic Drama* [Boulder: University of Colorado Press, 2007], 3). While other warrior dances have been lost, *Rabinal* survived almost intact for reasons that have not yet been fully established.

52. Dennis Tedlock, *Rabinal Achi: A Mayan Dance Drama of War and Sacrifice* (New York: Oxford University Press, 2005), 14.

53. In 1940, the family acquired a copy of the "Pérez Manuscript," a transcription of the play in the Quiche language dating from 1913. Breton argues that

this copy of the *Pérez Manuscript* is most likely a copy of an earlier manuscript by Bartolo Sis, which is "itself a part of an uninterrupted series of transcriptions going back to the sixteenth century" (*Rabinal Achi*, 16). The Xolop family has used the manuscript along with oral transmission to pass on the play from one generation to the next. Garniga's son, José Manuel Coloch Xolop, now performs alongside his father. Since 2005, when *Rabinal Achi* was listed by UNESCO as part of the list of masterpieces of the oral and intangible heritage of humanity, the family has been pressured by various levels of government to relinquish their stewardship of the manuscript.

54. Breton, *Rabinal Achi*, 3.

55. Phillip B. Zarrilli, Bruce McConachie, Gary Jay Williams, and Carol Fisher Sorgenfrei, *Theatre Histories: An Introduction* (New York: Routledge, 2006), 70.

56. Tedlock, *Rabinal Achi*, 250.

57. Ibid., 4.

58. Ibid., 5.

59. Ibid.

60. See, for example, Dennis Tedlock, *Popol Vuh: The Definitive Edition of the Mayan Book of the Dawn of Life and the Glories of Gods and Kings* (New York: Touchstone Book, 1996); and Francisco Hernandez Arana Xajila, *The Annals of Cakchiquels and Titles of the Lords of Totonicapan,* trans. Dionisio José Chonay and Delia Goetz (Norman: University of Oklahoma Press, 1967).

61. Breton, *Rabinal Achi*, 4–5.

62. Ibid., 4.

63. Documented in Breton, *Rabinal Achi*; Tedlock, *Rabinal Achi*; and others.

64. Diana Taylor, *The Archive and the Repertoire: Performing Cultural Memories in the Americas* (Durham, N.C.: Duke University Press, 2003), xvii.

65. Dwight Conquergood, "Performance Studies: Interventions and Radical Research," *TDR: The Drama Review* 46, no. 2 (2002): 146.

66. Tedlock, *Rabinal Achi*, 14.

67. Ondinnok, ondinnok.org, 2016, http://www.ondinnok.org/en.

68. Ibid.

69. Roach, *Cities of the Dead*, 136.

70. See, for example, Ondinnok's *Le Porteur des peines du monde* (1985–95), *Hamlet le Malécite* (2004), and *Contes d'un Indien urbain* (2006).

71. Yves Sioux Durand (director), in discussion with the author, June 25, 2010.

72. Tedlock, *Rabinal Achi*, 151.

73. Ibid., 146.

74. Saidiya Hartman, *Scenes of Subjection: Terror, Slavery, and Self-Making in Nineteenth-Century America* (New York: Oxford University Press, 1997), 35–36.

75. Mélanie Grondin, "Fascinant mais hermétique," *Rover Culture and Conversation*, June 24, 2010, http://roverarts.com/2010/06/fascinant-mais-hermetique/.

76. Audra Simpson, "Paths Toward a Mohawk Nation: Narratives of Citizenship and Nationhood in Kahnawake," in *Political Theory and the Rights of Indigenous Peoples*, ed. Duncan Ivision, Paul Patton, and Will Sanders (Cambridge: Cambridge University Press, 2000), 114.

77. Jodi A. Byrd, "Fracturing Futurity: Colonial Agnosia and the Untimely Indigenous Present," presentation at the University of California, San Diego, February 3, 2012.

Conclusion

1. For instance, changes to the Indian Act reduce the protection afforded to treaty lands, and open those lands to development without a majority approval from the community. The changes to the Navigation and Environmental Assessment acts effectively remove most of the environmental assessment requirements previously asked of natural resources developers.

2. Tuck and Yang, "Decolonization Is Not a Metaphor," 3.

3. Ibid.

4. Frantz Fanon, *The Wretched of the Earth*, trans. Richard Philcox (New York: Grove, 1963), 36.

5. Tuck and Yang, "Decolonization Is Not a Metaphor," 1.

6. Robinson, "Enchantment's Irreconcilable Connection," 211.

7. Tuck and Yang, "Decolonization Is Not a Metaphor," 1.

8. Ibid.

9. Mélissa Mollen-Dupuis, "Plateformes électorale 2014—Autochtones et Premières Nations" (Facebook post), April 3, 2014, https://www.facebook.com/notes/melissa-mollen-dupuis/plateforme-%C3%A9lectorale-2014-autochtones-et-premi%C3%A8res-nations/10152171578801743.

10. Ghislain Picard, "La Politique Québécoise" (Facebook post), March 21, 2014, https://www.facebook.com/ghislain.picard.7/posts/676227025756968.

INDEX

Page numbers in **boldface** refer to illustrations.